BY BRANDON SANDERSON®

THE STORMLIGHT ARCHIVE®

The Way of Kings
Words of Radiance
Oathbringer
Rhythm of War

THE MISTBORN® SAGA

THE ORIGINAL TRILOGY

Mistborn
The Well of Ascension
The Hero of Ages

THE WAX AND WAYNE SERIES

The Alloy of Law
Shadows of Self
The Bands of Mourning

Elantris
Warbreaker
Arcanum Unbounded: The Cosmere® Collection
Legion: The Many Lives of Stephen Leeds

ALCATRAZ VS. THE EVIL LIBRARIANS

Alcatraz vs. the Evil Librarians
The Scrivener's Bones
The Knights of Crystallia
The Shattered Lens
The Dark Talent

THE RECKONERS

Steelheart
Firefight
Calamity

SKYWARD

Skyward
Starsight

The Rithmatist

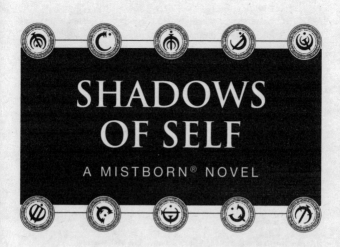

SHADOWS
OF SELF

A MISTBORN® NOVEL

BRANDON SANDERSON®

TOR®
fantasy

Tor Publishing Group
New York

This is a work of fiction. All of the characters, organizations, and events portrayed in this novel are either products of the author's imagination or are used fictitiously.

SHADOWS OF SELF: A MISTBORN NOVEL

Copyright © 2015 by Dragonsteel Entertainment, LLC

Mistborn®, The Stormlight Archive®, Reckoners®, Cosmere®, and Brandon Sanderson® are registered trademarks of Dragonsteel Entertainment, LLC.

Interior illustrations by Isaac Stewart and Ben McSweeney

Edited by Moshe Feder

A Tor Book
Published by Tom Doherty Associates/Tor Publishing Group
120 Broadway
New York, NY 10271

www.tor-forge.com

Tor® is a registered trademark of Macmillan Publishing Group, LLC.

ISBN 978-0-7653-7856-9

Our books may be purchased in bulk for promotional, educational, or business use. Please contact your local bookseller or the Macmillan Corporate and Premium Sales Department at 1-800-221-7945, ext. 5442, or by email at MacmillanSpecialMarkets@macmillan.com.

First Edition: October 2015
First Mass Market Edition: October 2016

Printed in the United States of America

20   18   18   17   16   15   14   13   12   11

FOR MOSHE FEDER

Who took a chance on me

CONTENTS

ACKNOWLEDGMENTS

This book has a somewhat storied past, as I wrote a third of it during the process of writing another book. (I was waiting for editorial notes to come back; I believe it was the final Wheel of Time book.) I had to drop work on this and dive into the other book.

By the time I came back, my vision for a new trilogy about Wax, Wayne, and Marasi had transformed—so the first third took some serious work to whip into shape and make match the last two thirds, as I wrote them. I relied a lot on the excellent editorial vision of my editor, Moshe Feder, my agent, Joshua Bilmes, and my editorial assistant, the Instant Peter Ahlstrom. Special thanks as well to my editor in the UK, Simon Spanton.

In addition, my writing group was—as always—invaluable. They include Emily Sanderson, Karen and Peter Ahlstrom, Darci and Eric James Stone, Alan Layton, Ben "please get my name right this time" Olsen, Danielle Olsen, Kathleen Dorsey Sanderson, Kaylynn ZoBell, Ethan and Isaac Skarstedt, and Kara and Īsaac Stewart.

We did a blitz of a beta read, and some vigilant people jumped in with excellent commentary. They were: Jory Phillips, Joel Phillips, Bob Kluttz, Alice Arneson, Trae Cooper, Gary Singer, Lyndsey Luther, Brian T. Hill, Jakob Remick, Eric James Stone, Bao Pham, Aubree Pham, Steve Godecke, Kristina Kugler, Ben Olsen, Samuel Lund, Megan Kanne, Nate Hatfield, Layne Garrett,

Kim Garrett, Eric Lake, Karen Ahlstrom, Isaac Skarstedt, Darci Stone, Īsaac Stewart, Kalyani Poluri, Josh Walker, Donald Mustard III, Cory Aitchison, and Christi Jacobsen.

Over the years, it's been incredibly satisfying to see the artwork for my novels develop. I've always had this wild vision for including way more art than usual—basically all I can get away with. Three wonderful artists made this possible on this volume. Chris McGrath did the cover, and I *love* his depictions of the characters. My good friend and now full-time art director Īsaac Stewart did the maps and symbols, as well as the heavy design lifting on the broadsheet. Art on the broadsheet was done by the ever-excellent Ben McSweeney.

At JABberwocky, my agency, thanks go to Eddie Schneider, Sam Morgan, Krystyna Lopez, and Christa Atkinson. In the UK, John Berlyne of the Zeno Agency deserves your applause.

From Tor Books, many thanks to Tom Doherty, Linda Quinton, Marco Palmieri, Karl Gold, Diana Pho, Nathan Weaver, Edward Allen, and Rafal Gibek. Ingrid Powell was the proofreader. Copyediting was done by Terry McGarry, and the audiobook is by my personal favorite reader, Michael Kramer. Other audiobook pros who deserve thanks are Robert Allen, Samantha Edelson, and Mitali Dave. Adam Horne, my new executive assistant, gets his name in a book for the first time in this one. Well done, Adam!

Finally, big thanks to my family, as always. A wonderful wife and three little boys who still get confused as to why the books Daddy writes have so few pictures.

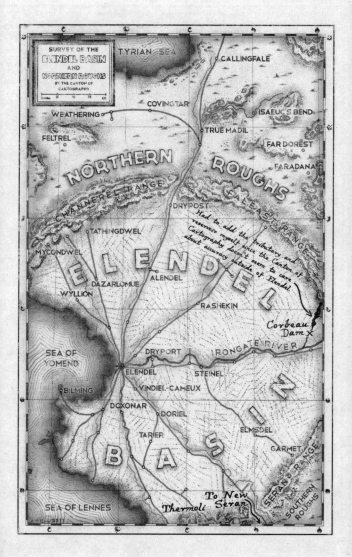

SURVEY OF THE
ELENDEL BASIN
AND
NORTHERN ROUGHS
BY THE CANTON OF
CARTOGRAPHY

0 miles   25   50   75   100

TYRIAN SEA

CALLINGFALE

COVINGTAR

WEATHERING

ISAEUC'S BEND

FELTREL

TRUE MADIL

FAR DOREST

FARADANA

NORTHERN   ROUGHS

CHANNEREL RANGE

DRYPOST

FAR EAST RANGE

TATHINGDWEL

Had to add the tributary and
reservoir myself since the Canton of
Cartography doesn't seem to care
about accuracy outside of Elendel.

MYCONDWEL

ELENDEL

DAZARLOMUE   ALENDEL

WYLLION

RASHEKIN

Corbeau
Dam ✕

SEA OF
YOMEND

DRYPORT

IRONGATE RIVER

ELENDEL

STEINEL

BILMING

VINDIEL-CAMEUX

DOXONAR   DORIEL

BASIN

ELMSDEL

TARIER

GARMET

SERAN RANGE

SEA OF LENNES

Thermoli

To New
Seran

SOUTHERN
ROUGHS

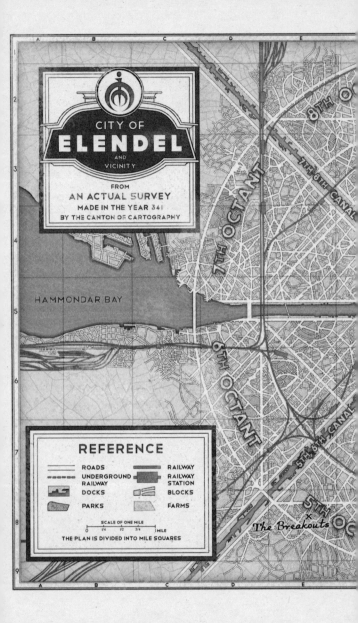

CITY OF
ELENDEL
AND
VICINITY

FROM
AN ACTUAL SURVEY
MADE IN THE YEAR 341
BY THE CANTON OF CARTOGRAPHY

HAMMONDAR BAY

REFERENCE

ROADS		RAILWAY	
UNDERGROUND RAILWAY		RAILWAY STATION	
DOCKS		BLOCKS	
PARKS		FARMS	

SCALE OF ONE MILE
1/4   1/2   3/4   1 MILE
THE PLAN IS DIVIDED INTO MILE SQUARES

8TH O
7TH & 8TH CANAL
8TH OCTANT
7TH OCTANT
6TH OCTANT
5TH OCTANT
5TH OC
The Breakouts

1ST OCTANT

2ND OCTANT

6TH-1ST CANAL

1ST-2ND-CANAL

×Madion Ways

×The University

×Lestib Square
×Governor's Mansion

Hammond
Promenade×

Field of Rebirth

IRONGATE RIVER

3RD OCTANT

×Winsting's "Cottage"

4th Octant Church of the Survivor

×Bournton District

4TH CANAL

The
Village

4TH-5TH CANAL

Ladrian
Mansion×

Tindwyl
Promenade
×

ZoBell Tower
×

4th Octant
Constabulary
Precinct Office×

4TH OCTANT

My friend, annotated
with locations as per
your instructions...
again.   —Nazh

SHADOWS OF SELF

PROLOGUE

Waxillium Ladrian, lawman for hire, swung off his horse and turned to face the saloon.

"Aw," the kid said, hopping down from his own horse. "You didn't catch your spur on the stirrup and trip."

"That happened *once*," Waxillium said.

"Yeah, but it was *super* funny."

"Stay with the horses," Waxillium said, tossing the kid his reins. "Don't tie up Destroyer. I might need her."

"Sure."

"And *don't* steal anything."

The kid—round-faced and seventeen, with barely a hint of stubble on his face despite weeks of trying—nodded with a solemn expression. "I promise I won't swipe nothin' of yours, Wax."

Waxillium sighed. "That's not what I said."

"But . . ."

"Just stay with the horses. And try not to talk to anyone." Waxillium shook his head, pushing into the saloon, feeling a spring in his step. He was filling his metalmind a smidge, decreasing his weight by about ten percent. Common practice for him these days, ever since he'd run out of stored weight during one of his first bounty hunts a few months back.

The saloon, of course, was dirty. Practically everything out here in the Roughs was dusty, worn, or broken. Five years out here, and he still wasn't used to that. True, he'd spent most of those five years trying to make a living as a clerk, moving farther and farther from population centers in an effort to avoid getting recognized. But in the Roughs, even the larger population centers were dirtier than those back in Elendel.

And here, on the fringes of populated lands, dirty didn't even *begin* to describe life. The men he passed in the saloon sat slumped low to their tables, hardly looking up. That was another thing about the Roughs. Both plants and people were more prickly, and they grew lower to the ground. Even the fanlike acacias, which did stretch high at times, had this fortified, hardy sense about them.

He scanned the room, hands on hips, hoping he'd draw attention. He didn't, which nagged at him. Why wear a fine city suit, with a lavender cravat, if nobody was going to notice? At least they weren't snickering, like those in the last saloon.

Hand on his gun, Waxillium sauntered up to the bar. The barkeep was a tall man who looked to have some Terris blood in him, from that willowy build, though his refined cousins in the Basin would be horrified to see him chewing on a greasy chicken leg with one hand while serving a mug with the other. Waxillium tried not to be nauseated; the local notion of hygiene was another thing he wasn't yet accustomed to. Out here, the fastidious ones were those who remembered to wipe their hands on their trousers between picking their nose and shaking your hand.

Waxillium waited. Then waited some more. Then cleared his throat. Finally, the barkeep lumbered over to him.

"Yeah?"

"I'm looking for a man," Waxillium said under his breath. "Goes by the name of Granite Joe."

"Don't know him," the barkeep said.

"Don't— He's only the *single* most notorious outlaw in these parts."

"Don't know him."

"But—"

"It's safer to not know men like Joe," the barkeep said, then took a bite of his chicken leg. "But I have a friend."

"That's surprising."

The barkeep glared at him.

"Ahem," Waxillium said. "Sorry. Continue."

"My friend might be willing to know people that others won't. It will take a little time to get him. You'll pay?"

"I'm a lawman," Waxillium said. "I do what I do in the name of justice."

The barkeep blinked. Slowly, deliberately, as if it required conscious effort. "So . . . you'll pay?"

"Yes, I'll pay," Waxillium said with a sigh, mentally counting what he'd already spent hunting Granite Joe. He couldn't afford to go in the hole again. Destroyer needed a new saddle, and Waxillium went through suits frightfully quick out here.

"Good," the barkeep said, gesturing for Waxillium to follow. They wove through the room, around tables and past the pianoforte, which sat beside one of the pillars, between two tables. It didn't look like it had been played in ages, and someone had set a row of dirty mugs on it. Next to the stairs, they entered a small room. It smelled dusty.

"Wait," the barkeep said, then shut the door and left.

Waxillium folded his arms, eyeing the room's lone chair. The white paint was flaking and peeling; he didn't doubt that if he sat down, he'd end up with half of it stuck to his trousers.

He was growing more comfortable with the people of the Roughs, if not their particular habits. These few months chasing bounties had shown him that there *were* good men and women out here, mixed among the rest. Yet they all had this stubborn *fatalism* about them. They didn't trust authority, and often shunned lawmen, even if it meant letting a man like Granite Joe continue to ravage and plunder. Without the bounties set by the railroad and mining companies, nothing would ever—

The window shook. Waxillium stopped, then grabbed the gun at his side and burned steel. The metal created a sharp warmth within him, like the feeling after drinking something too hot. Blue lines sprang up pointing from his chest toward nearby sources of metal, several of which were just outside the shuttered window. Others pointed downward. This saloon had a basement, which was unusual out in the Roughs.

He could Push on those lines if he needed to, shoving on the metal they connected to. For now, he just watched as a small rod slipped between the window casements, then lifted, raising the latch that held them closed. The window rattled, then swung open.

A young woman in dark trousers hopped in, rifle in one hand. Lean, with a squarish face, she carried an unlit cigar in her teeth and looked vaguely familiar to Waxillium. She stood up, apparently satisfied, then turned to close the window. As she did, she saw him for the first time.

"Hell!" she said, scrambling backward, dropping her cigar, raising her rifle.

Waxillium raised his own gun and prepared his Allomancy, wishing he'd found a way to protect himself from bullets. He could Push on metal, yes, but he wasn't fast enough to stop gunfire, unless he Pushed on the gun before the trigger was pulled.

"Hey," the woman said, looking through the rifle sights. "Aren't you that guy? The one who killed Peret the Black?"

"Waxillium Ladrian," he said. "Lawman for hire."

"You're kidding. That's how you introduce yourself?"

"Sure. Why not?"

She didn't answer, instead looking away from her rifle, studying him for a few moments. Finally she said, "A cravat? Really?"

"It's kind of my thing," Waxillium said. "The gentleman bounty hunter."

"Why would a bounty hunter need a 'thing' in the first place?"

"It's important to have a reputation," Waxillium said, raising his chin. "The outlaws all have them; people have heard of men like Granite Joe from one side of the Roughs to the other. Why shouldn't I do the same?"

"Because it paints a target on your head."

"Worth the danger," Waxillium said. "But speaking of targets . . ." He waved his gun, then nodded toward hers.

"You're after the bounty on Joe," she said.

"Sure am. You too?"

She nodded.

"Split it?" Waxillium said.

She sighed, but lowered her rifle. "Fine. The one who shoots him gets a double portion though."

"I was planning to bring him in alive. . . ."

"Good. Gives me a better chance of killing him first." She grinned at him, slipping over to the door. "The name's Lessie. Granite *is* in here somewhere, then? Have you seen him?"

"No, I haven't," Waxillium said, joining her at the door. "I asked the barkeep, and he sent me in here."

She turned on him. "You asked the barkeep."

"Sure," Waxillium said. "I've read the stories. Barkeeps know everything, and . . . You're shaking your head."

"*Everyone* in this saloon belongs to Joe, Mister Cravat," Lessie said. "Hell, half the people in this town belong to him. You *asked the barkeep?*"

"I believe we've established that."

"Rust!" She cracked the door and looked out. "How in Ruin's name did *you* take down Peret the Black?"

"Surely it's not that bad. *Everyone* in the bar can't . . ."

He trailed off as he peeked out the door. The tall barkeep hadn't run off to fetch anyone. No, he was out in the taproom of the saloon, gesturing toward the side room's door and urging the assembled thugs and miscreants to stand up and arm themselves. They looked hesitant, and some were gesturing angrily, but more than a few had guns out.

"Damn," Lessie whispered.

"Back out the way you came in?" Waxillium asked.

Her response was to slip the door closed with the utmost care, then shove him aside and scramble toward the window. She grabbed the windowsill to step out, but gunfire cracked nearby and wood chips exploded off the sill.

Lessie cursed and dropped to the floor. Waxillium dove down beside her.

"Sharpshooter!" he hissed.

"Are you always this observant, Mister Cravat?"

"No, only when I'm being shot at." He peeked up over the lip of the windowsill, but there were a dozen places nearby where the shooter could be hiding. "This is a problem."

"There's that razor-sharp power of observation again." Lessie crawled across the floor toward the door.

"I meant in more ways than one," Waxillium said, crossing the floor in a crouch. "How did they have time to get a sharpshooter into position? They must have *known* that I was going to show up today. This whole place could be a trap."

Lessie cursed softly as he reached the door and cracked it open again. The thugs were arguing quietly and gesturing toward the door.

"They're taking me seriously," Waxillium said. "Ha! The reputation is working. You see that? They're frightened!"

"Congratulations," she said. "Do you think they'll give me a reward if I shoot you?"

"We need to get upstairs," Waxillium said, eyeing a stairwell just outside their door.

"What good will that do?"

"Well, for one thing, all the armed people who want to kill us are down here. I'd rather be somewhere else, and those stairs will be easier to defend than this room. Besides, we might find a window on the other side of the building and escape."

"Yeah, if you want to jump two stories."

Jumping wasn't a problem for a Coinshot; Waxillium could Push off a dropped piece of metal as they fell, slowing himself and landing safely. He was also a Feruchemist, and could use his metalminds to reduce his weight far more than he was doing now, shaving it down until he practically floated.

However, Waxillium's abilities weren't widely known, and he wanted to keep it that way. He'd heard the stories of his miraculous survivals, and liked the air of mystery around them. There was speculation that he was Metalborn, sure, but so long as people didn't know exactly what he could do, he'd have an edge.

"Look, I'm going to run for the steps," he said to the woman. "If you want to stay down here and fight your way out, great. You'll provide an ideal distraction for me."

She glanced at him, then grinned. "Fine. We'll do it your way. But if we get shot, you owe me a drink."

There is *something familiar about her,* Waxillium thought. He nodded, counted softly to three, then burst out of the door and leveled his gun at the nearest thug. The man jumped back as Waxillium shot three times— and missed. His bullets hit the pianoforte instead, sounding a discordant note with each impact.

Lessie scrambled out behind him and went for the stairs. The motley collection of thugs leveled weapons with cries of surprise. Waxillium swung his gun back— out of the way of his Allomancy—and shoved lightly on the blue lines pointing from him toward the men in the room. They opened fire, but his Push had nudged their guns enough to spoil their aim.

Waxillium followed Lessie up the steps, fleeing the storm of gunfire.

"Holy hell," Lessie said as they reached the first landing. "We're alive." She looked back at him, cheeks flushed.

Something clicked like a lock in Waxillium's mind. "I *have* met you before," he said.

"No you haven't," she said, looking away. "Let's keep—"

"The Weeping Bull!" Waxillium said. "The dancing girl!"

"Oh, God Beyond," she said, leading the way up the stairs. "You remember."

"I *knew* you were faking. Even Rusko wouldn't hire someone that uncoordinated, no matter how pretty her legs are."

"Can we go jump out a window now, please?" she said, checking the top floor for signs of thugs.

"Why were you there? Chasing a bounty?"

"Yeah, kind of."

"And you really didn't know they were going to make you—"

"This conversation is done."

They stepped out onto the top floor, and Waxillium waited a moment until a shadow on the wall announced someone following them upstairs. He fired once at the thug who appeared there, missing again, but driving the man back. He heard cursing and arguing below. Granite Joe might own the men in this saloon, but they weren't overly loyal. The first few up the steps would almost certainly get shot, and none would be eager to take the risk.

That would buy Waxillium some time. Lessie pushed into a room, passing an empty bed with a pair of boots beside it. She threw open the window, which was on the opposite side of the building from the sharpshooter.

The town of Weathering spread before them, a lonely collection of shops and homes, hunkered down as if waiting—in vain—for the day when the railroad would stretch its fingers this far. In the middle distance, beyond the humble buildings, a few giraffes browsed lazily, the only sign of animal life in the vast plain.

The drop out the window was straight down, no roof to climb onto. Lessie regarded the ground warily. Waxillium shoved his fingers in his mouth and whistled sharply.

Nothing happened.

He whistled again.

"What the hell are you doing?" Lessie demanded.

"Calling my horse," Waxillium said, then whistled again. "We can hop down into the saddle and ride away."

She stared at him. "You're serious."

"Sure I am. We've been practicing."

A lone figure walked out onto the street below, the kid who had been following Waxillium. "Uh, Wax?" the kid called up. "Destroyer's just standing there, drinking."

"Hell," Waxillium said.

Lessie looked at him. "You named your horse—"

"She's a little too placid, all right?" Waxillium snapped, climbing up onto the windowsill. "I thought the name might inspire her." He cupped his hand, calling to the boy below. "Wayne! Bring her out here. We're going to jump!"

"Like hell we are," Lessie said. "You think there's something magical about a saddle that will keep us from breaking the horse's back when we drop into it?"

Waxillium hesitated. "Well, I've read about people doing this. . . ."

"Yeah, I've got an idea," Lessie said. "Next, why

don't you call out Granite Joe, and go stand out in the road and have a good old-fashioned showdown at noon."

"You think that would work? I—"

"No, it won't work," she snapped. "Nobody does that. It's stupid. Ruin! How *did* you kill Peret the Black?"

They stared at each other a moment.

"Well . . ." Waxillium started.

"Oh hell. You caught him on the crapper, didn't you?"

Waxillium grinned at her. "Yeah."

"Did you shoot him in the back too?"

"As bravely as any man ever shot another in the back."

"Huh. There might be hope for you yet."

He nodded toward the window. "Jump?"

"Sure. Why not break both my legs before getting shot? Might as well go all in, Mister Cravat."

"I think we'll be fine, Miss Pink Garter."

She raised an eyebrow.

"If you're going to identify me by my clothing choices," he said, "then I figure I can do the same."

"It shall never be mentioned again," she said, then took a deep breath. "So?"

He nodded, flaring his metals, preparing to hold on to her and slow them as they fell—just enough to make it seem like they'd miraculously survived the jump. As he did, however, he noticed one of his blue lines moving—a faint but thick one, pointing across the street.

The window in the mill. Sunlight glinted off something inside.

Waxillium immediately grabbed Lessie and pulled her down. A fraction of a second later, a bullet streaked over their heads and hit the door on the other side of the room.

"Another sharpshooter," she hissed.

"Your power of observation is—"

"Shut it," she said. "Now what?"

Waxillium frowned, considering the question. He glanced at the bullet hole, gauging the trajectory. The sharpshooter had aimed too high; even if Waxillium hadn't ducked, he'd likely have been all right.

Why aim high? The moving blue line to the gun had indicated the sharpshooter running to get into position before shooting. Was it just rushed targeting? Or was there a more sinister reason? *To knock me out of the sky? When I flew out the window?*

He heard footsteps on the stairs, but saw no blue lines. He cursed, scrambling over and peeking out. A group of men were creeping up the steps, and not the normal thugs from below. These men wore tight white shirts, had pencil mustaches, and were armed with crossbows. Not a speck of metal on them.

Rusts! They knew he was a Coinshot, and Granite Joe had a kill squad ready for him.

He ducked back into the room and grabbed Lessie by the arm. "Your informant said Granite Joe was in this building?"

"Yeah," she said. "He most certainly is. He likes to be close when a gang is being gathered; he likes to keep an eye on his men."

"This building has a basement."

". . . So?"

"So hang on."

He grabbed her in both hands and rolled onto the ground, causing her to yelp, then curse. Holding her over him, he increased his weight.

He had a great deal of it stored in his metalmind by now, after weeks of siphoning it off. Now he drew it all out, magnifying his weight manyfold in an instant. The wooden floor cracked, then *burst* open beneath them.

Waxillium fell through, his fine clothing getting ripped, and dropped through the air, towing Lessie after him. Eyes squeezed closed, he Pushed the hundreds of blue lines behind him, those leading to the nails in the floor below. He blasted them downward to shatter the ground level's floor and open the way into the basement.

They crashed through the ground floor in a shower of dust and splinters. Waxillium managed to slow their descent with a Steelpush, but they still came down hard, smashing into a table in a basement chamber.

Waxillium let out a puffing groan, but forced himself to twist around, shaking free of the broken wood. The basement, surprisingly, was paneled in fine hardwoods and lit by lamps shaped like curvaceous women. The table they had hit bore a rich white tablecloth, though it was now wadded in a bunch, the table legs shattered and the table itself at an angle.

A man sat at the table's head. Waxillium managed to stand up in the wreckage and level a gun at the fellow, who had a blocky face and dark blue-grey skin—the mark of a man with koloss heritage. Granite Joe. Waxillium appeared to have interrupted his dinner, judging by the napkin tucked into his collar and the spilled soup on the broken table in front of him.

Lessie groaned, rolling over and brushing splinters off her clothing. Her rifle had apparently been left upstairs. Waxillium held his gun in a firm grip as he eyed the two duster-wearing bodyguards behind Granite

Joe, a man and a woman—siblings, he'd heard, and crack shots. They'd been surprised by his fall, obviously, for though they'd rested hands on their weapons, they hadn't drawn.

Waxillium had the upper hand, with the gun on Joe—but if he *did* shoot, the siblings would kill him in a heartbeat. Perhaps he hadn't thought through this line of attack quite as well as he should have.

Joe scraped at the remnants of his broken bowl, framed by splatters of red soup on the tablecloth. He managed to get some onto his spoon and lifted it to his lips. "You," he said after sipping the soup, "should be dead."

"You might want to look at hiring a new group of thugs," Waxillium said. "The ones upstairs aren't worth much."

"I wasn't referring to them," Joe said. "How long have you been up here, in the Roughs, making trouble? Two years?"

"One," Waxillium said. He'd been up here longer, but he had only recently started "making trouble," as Joe put it.

Granite Joe clicked his tongue. "You think your type is new up here, son? Wide-eyed, with a low-slung gunbelt and bright new spurs? Come to reform us of our uncivilized ways. We see dozens like you every year. The others have the decency to either learn to be bribed, or to get dead before they ruin too much. But not you."

He's stalling, Waxillium thought. Waiting for the men upstairs to run down.

"Drop your weapons!" Waxillium said, holding his gun on Joe. "Drop them or I shoot!"

The two guards didn't move. *No metal lines on the guard on the right,* Waxillium thought. *Or on Joe him-*

self. The one on the left had a handgun, perhaps trusting the speed of his draw against a Coinshot. The other two had fancy hand-crossbows in their holsters, he bet. Single-shot, made of wood and ceramic. Built for killing Coinshots.

Even with Allomancy, Waxillium would never be able to kill all three of them without getting shot himself. Sweat trickled down his temple. He was tempted to just pull his trigger and shoot, but he'd be killed if he did that. And they knew it. It was a standoff, but *they* had reinforcements coming.

"You don't belong here," Joe said, leaning forward, elbows on his broken table. "We came here to escape folks like you. Your rules. Your assumptions. We don't want you."

"If that were true," Waxillium said, surprised at how level his voice was, "then people wouldn't come to me crying because you killed their sons. You might not need Elendel's laws up here, but that doesn't mean you don't need any laws at all. And it doesn't mean men like you should be able to do whatever you want."

Granite Joe shook his head, standing up, hand to his holster. "This isn't your habitat, son. Everyone has a price up here. If they don't, they don't fit in. You'll die, slow and painful, just like a lion would die in that city of yours. What I'm doing today, this is a mercy."

Joe drew.

Waxillium reacted quickly, Pushing himself off the wall lamps to his right. They were firmly anchored, so his Allomantic shove Pushed him to the left. He twisted his gun and fired.

Joe got his crossbow out and loosed a bolt, but the shot missed, zipping through the air where Waxillium had been. Waxillium's own bullet flew true for once, hitting the female guard, who had pulled out her crossbow. She dropped, and as Waxillium crashed into the wall, he Pushed—knocking the gun out of the other guard's hand as the man fired.

Waxillium's Push, unfortunately, also flung his own gun out of his hand—but sent it spinning toward the second bodyguard. His gun smacked the man right in the face, dropping him.

Waxillium steadied himself, looking across the room at Joe, who seemed baffled that both his guards were down. No time to think. Waxillium scrambled toward the large, koloss-blooded man. If he could reach some metal to use as a weapon, maybe—

A weapon clicked behind him. Waxillium stopped and looked over his shoulder at Lessie, who was pointing a small hand-crossbow right at him.

"Everyone up here has a price," Granite Joe said.

Waxillium stared at the crossbow bolt, tipped with obsidian. Where had she been carrying that? He swallowed slowly.

She put herself in danger, scrambling up the stairs with me! he thought. *How could she have been . . .*

But Joe had known about his Allomancy. So had she. Lessie *knew* he could spoil the thugs' aim, when she'd joined him in running up the steps.

"Finally," Joe said, "do you have an explanation of why you didn't just *shoot* him in the saloon room, where the barkeep put him?"

She didn't respond, instead studying Waxillium. "I did warn you that everyone in the saloon was in Joe's employ," she noted.

"I . . ." Waxillium swallowed. "I still think your legs are pretty."

She met his eyes. Then she sighed, turned the crossbow, and shot Granite Joe in the neck.

Waxillium blinked as the enormous man dropped to the floor, gurgling as he bled.

"That?" Lessie said, glaring at Waxillium. "That's all you could come up with to win me over? 'You have nice legs'? Seriously? You are *so* doomed up here, Cravat."

Waxillium breathed out in relief. "Oh, *Harmony*. I thought you were going to shoot me for sure."

"Should have," she grumbled. "I can't believe—"

She cut off as the stairs clattered, the troop of miscreants from above having finally gathered the nerve to rush down the stairwell. A good half dozen of them burst into the room with weapons drawn.

Lessie dove for the fallen bodyguard's gun.

Waxillium thought quickly, then did what came most naturally. He struck a dramatic pose in the rubble, one foot up, Granite Joe dead beside him, both bodyguards felled. Dust from the broken ceiling still sprinkled down, illuminated in sunlight pouring through a window above.

The thugs pulled to a stop. They looked down at the fallen corpse of their boss, then gaped toward Waxillium.

Finally, looking like children who had been caught in the pantry trying to get at the cookies, they lowered their weapons. The ones at the front tried to push through the ones at the back to get away, and the whole clamorous mess of them swarmed back up the steps, leaving the forlorn barkeep, who fled last of all.

Waxillium turned and offered his hand to Lessie, who let him pull her to her feet. She looked after the retreating group of bandits, whose boots thumped on wood in their haste to escape. In moments the building was silent.

"Huh," she said. "You're as surprising as a donkey who can dance, Mister Cravat."

"It helps to have a thing," Waxillium noted.

"Yeah. You think I should get a thing?"

"Getting a thing has been one of the most important choices I made in coming up to the Roughs."

Lessie nodded slowly. "I have no idea what we're talking about, but it sounds kinda dirty." She glanced past him toward Granite Joe's corpse, which stared lifelessly, lying in a pool of his own blood.

"Thanks," Waxillium said. "For not murdering me."

"Eh. I was gonna kill him eventually anyway and turn him in for the bounty."

"Yes, well, I doubt you were planning to do it in front of his entire gang, while trapped in a basement with no escape."

"True. Right stupid of me, that was."

"So why do it?"

She kept looking at the body. "I've done plenty of things in Joe's name I wish I hadn't, but as far as I know, I never shot a man who didn't deserve it. Killing you . . . well, seems like it would have been killing what you stood for too. Ya know?"

"I think I can grasp the concept."

She rubbed at a bleeding scratch on her neck, where she'd brushed broken wood during their fall. "Next time, though, I hope it won't involve making quite so big a mess. I *liked* this saloon."

"I'll do my best," Waxillium said. "I intend to change things out here. If not the whole Roughs, then at least this town."

"Well," Lessie said, walking over to Granite Joe's corpse, "I'm sure that if any evil pianos were thinking of attacking the city, they'll have second thoughts now, considering your prowess with that pistol."

Waxillium winced. "You . . . saw that, did you?"

"Rarely seen such a feat," she said, kneeling and going through Joe's pockets. "Three shots, three different notes, not a single bandit down. That takes skill. Maybe you should spend a little less time with your thing and more with your gun."

"Now *that* sounded dirty."

"Good. I hate being crass by accident." She came out with Joe's pocketbook and smiled, tossing it up and catching it. Above, in the hole Waxillium had made, an equine head poked out, followed by a smaller, teenage one in an oversized bowler hat. Where had he gotten that?

Destroyer blustered in greeting.

"Sure, *now* you come," Waxillium said. "Stupid horse."

"Actually," Lessie said, "seems to me like staying away from you during a gunfight makes her a pretty damn *smart* horse."

Waxillium smiled and held out his hand to Lessie. She took it, and he pulled her close. Then he lifted them out of the wreckage on a line of blue light.

PART ONE

1

SEVENTEEN YEARS LATER

Winsting smiled to himself as he watched the setting sun. It was an ideal evening to auction himself off.

"We have my saferoom ready?" Winsting asked, lightly gripping the balcony banister. "Just in case?"

"Yes, my lord." Flog wore his silly Roughs hat along with a duster, though he'd never been outside of the Elendel Basin. The man was an excellent bodyguard, despite his terrible fashion sense, but Winsting made certain to Pull on the man's emotions anyway, subtly enhancing Flog's sense of loyalty. One could never be too careful.

"My lord?" Flog asked, glancing toward the chamber behind them. "They're all here, my lord. Are you ready?"

Not turning away from the setting sun, Winsting raised a finger to hush the bodyguard. The balcony, in the Fourth Octant of Elendel, overlooked the canal and the Hub of the city—so he had a nice view of the Field of Rebirth. Long shadows stretched from the statues of the Ascendant Warrior and the Last Emperor in the green park where, according to fanciful legend, their

corpses had been discovered following the Great Catacendre and the Final Ascension.

The air was muggy, slightly tempered by a cool
breeze off Hammondar Bay a couple of miles to the
west. Winsting tapped his fingers on the balcony railing, patiently sending out pulses of Allomantic power
to shape the emotions of those in the room behind him.
Or at least any foolish enough not to be wearing their
aluminum-lined hats.

Any moment now . . .

Initially appearing as pinprick spots in the air, mist
grew before him, spreading like frost across a window.
Tendrils stretched and spun about one another, becoming streams—then rivers of motion, currents shifting
and blanketing the city. Engulfing it. Consuming it.

"A misty night," Flog said. "That's bad luck, it is."

"Don't be a fool," Winsting said, adjusting his cravat.

"He's watching us," Flog said. "The mists are His
eyes, my lord. Sure as Ruin, that is."

"Superstitious nonsense." Winsting turned and strode
into the room. Behind him, Flog shut the doors before
the mists could seep into the party.

The two dozen people—along with the inevitable
bodyguards—who mingled and chatted there were a
select group. Not just important, but also very much at
odds with one another, despite their deliberate smiles
and meaningless small talk. He preferred to have rivals
at events like this. Let them all see each other, and let
each know the cost of losing the contest for his favor.

Winsting stepped among them. Unfortunately many
did wear hats, whose aluminum linings would protect
them from emotional Allomancy—though he had personally assured each attendee that none of the others
would have Soothers or Rioters with them. He'd said

nothing of his own abilities, of course. So far as any of them knew, he wasn't an Allomancer.

He glanced across the room to where Blome tended bar. The man shook his head. Nobody else in the room was burning any metals. Excellent.

Winsting stepped up to the bar, then turned and raised his hands to draw everyone's attention. The gesture exposed the twinkling diamond cuff links he wore on his stiff white shirt. The settings were wooden, of course.

"Ladies and gentlemen," he said, "welcome to our little auction. The bidding begins now, and it ends when I hear the offer I like most."

He said nothing more; too much talk would kill the drama. Winsting took the drink one of his servers offered and stepped out to mingle, then hesitated as he looked over the crowd. "Edwarn Ladrian is not here," he said softly. He refused to call the man by his silly moniker, Mister Suit.

"No," Flog said.

"I thought you said everyone had arrived!"

"Everyone who said they were coming," Flog said. He shuffled, uncomfortable.

Winsting pursed his lips, but otherwise hid his disappointment. He'd been *certain* his offer had intrigued Edwarn. Perhaps the man had bought out one of the other crime lords in the room. Something to consider.

Winsting made his way to the central table, which held the nominal centerpiece of the evening. It was a painting of a reclining woman; Winsting had painted it himself, and he was getting better.

The painting was worthless, but the men and woman in this room would still offer him huge sums for it.

The first one to approach him was Dowser, who ran

most of the smuggling operations into the Fifth Octant. The three days of scrub on his cheeks was shadowed by a bowler that, conspicuously, he had not left in the cloakroom. A pretty woman on his arm and a sharp suit did little to clean up a man like Dowser. Winsting wrinkled his nose. Most everyone in the room was a despicable piece of trash, but the others had the decency not to *look* like it.

"It's ugly as sin," Dowser said, looking over the painting. "I can't believe this is what you're having us 'bid' on. A little cheeky, isn't it?"

"And you'd rather I was completely forthright, Mister Dowser?" Winsting said. "You'd have me proclaim it far and wide? 'Pay me, and in exchange you get my vote in the Senate for the next year'?"

Dowser glanced to the sides, as if expecting the constables to burst into the room at any moment.

Winsting smiled. "You'll notice the shades of grey on her cheeks. A representation of the ashen nature of life in a pre-Catacendric world, hmmm? My finest work yet. Do you have an offer? To get the bidding started?"

Dowser said nothing. He would eventually make a bid. Each person in this room had spent weeks posturing before agreeing to this meeting. Half were crime lords like Dowser. The others were Winsting's own counterparts, high lords and ladies from prominent noble houses, though no less corrupt than the crime lords.

"Aren't you frightened, Winsting?" asked the woman on Dowser's arm.

Winsting frowned. He didn't recognize her. Slender, with short golden hair and a doe-eyed expression, she was uncommonly tall.

"Frightened, my dear?" Winsting asked. "Of the people in this room?"

"No," she said. "That your brother will find out . . . what you do."

"I assure you," Winsting said. "Replar knows exactly what I am."

"The governor's own brother," the woman said. "Asking for bribes."

"If that truly surprises you, my dear," Winsting said, "then you have lived too sheltered a life. Far bigger fish than I have been sold on this market. When the next catch arrives, perhaps you will see."

That comment caught Dowser's attention. Winsting smiled as he saw the gears clicking behind Dowser's eyes. *Yes,* Winsting thought, *I did just imply that my brother himself might be open to your bribery.* Perhaps that would up the man's offer.

Winsting moved over to select some shrimp and quiche from a server's tray. "The woman with Dowser is a spy," Winsting said softly to Flog, who was always at his elbow. "Perhaps in constabulary employ."

Flog started. "My lord! We checked and double-checked each person attending."

"Well you missed one," Winsting whispered. "I'd bet my fortune on it. Follow her after the meeting. If she splits from Dowser for any reason, see that she meets with an accident."

"Yes, my lord."

"And Flog," Winsting said, "do be straightforward about it. I won't have you trying to find a place where the mists won't be watching. Understand?"

"Yes, my lord."

"Excellent," Winsting said, smiling broadly as he

strolled over to Lord Hughes Entrone, cousin and confidant to the head of House Entrone.

Winsting spent an hour mingling, and slowly the bids started to come in. Some of the attendees were reluctant. They would rather have met him one-on-one, making their covert offers, then slipping back into Elendel's underbelly. Crime lords and nobles alike, these all preferred to dance around a topic, not discuss it openly. But they did bid, and bid well. By the end of his first circuit of the room, Winsting had to forcibly contain his excitement. No longer would he have to limit his spending. If his brother could—

The gunshot was so unexpected, he at first assumed that one of the servers had broken something. But no. That crack was so sharp, so earsplitting. He'd never heard a gun fired indoors before; he hadn't known just how stunning it could be.

He gaped, the drink tumbling from his fingers as he tried to find the source of the shot. Another followed, then another. It became a storm, various sides firing at one another in a cacophony of death.

Before he could cry for help, Flog had him by the arm, towing him toward the stairs down to the saferoom. One of his other bodyguards stumbled against the doorway, looking with wide eyes at the blood on his shirt. Winsting stared for too long at the dying man before Flog was able to tear him away and shove him into the stairwell.

"What's happening?" Winsting finally demanded as a guard slammed the door behind them and locked it. The bodyguards hurried him down the dim stairway, which was weakly lit by periodic electric lights. "Who fired? What *happened*?"

"No way of knowing," Flog said. Gunfire still sounded above. "Happened too fast."

"Someone just started firing," another guard said. "Might have been Dowser."

"No, it was Darm," another said. "I heard the first shot from his group."

Either way, it was a disaster. Winsting saw his fortune dying a bloody death on the floor above them, and he felt sick as they finally reached the bottom of the stairs and a vaultlike door, which Flog pushed him through.

"I'm going to go back up," Flog said, "see what I can salvage. Find out who caused this."

Winsting nodded and shut the door, locking it from the inside. He settled into a chair to wait, fretting. The small bunker of a room had wine and other amenities, but he couldn't be bothered. He wrung his hands. What would his brother say? Rusts! What would the papers say? He'd have to keep this quiet somehow.

Eventually a knock came at the door, and Winsting glanced through the peephole to see Flog. Behind him, a small force of bodyguards watched the stairwell. It seemed the gunfire had stopped, though from down here it had sounded only like faint popping.

Winsting opened the door. "Well?"

"They're all dead."

"*All* of them?"

"Every last one," Flog said, walking into the room.

Winsting sat heavily in his chair. "Maybe that's good," he said, searching for some glimmer of light in this dark disaster. "Nobody can implicate us. Maybe we can just slip away. Cover our tracks somehow?"

A daunting task. He owned this building. He'd be

connected to these deaths. He'd need an alibi. Hell, he was going to *have* to go to his brother. This could cost him his seat, even if the general public never discovered what had happened. He slumped in his chair, frustrated. "Well?" he demanded. "What do you think?"

In response, a pair of hands grabbed Winsting by the hair, pulled his head back, and efficiently slit his exposed throat.

2

I figure I should write one of these things, the small book read. *To tell my side. Not the side the historians will tell for me. I doubt they'll get it right. I don't know that I'd like them to anyhow.*

Wax tapped the book with the end of his pencil, then scribbled down a note to himself on a loose sheet.

"I'm thinking of inviting the Boris brothers to the wedding," Steris said from the couch opposite the one Wax sat upon.

He grunted, still reading.

I know Saze doesn't approve of what I've done, the book continued. *But what did he expect me to do? Knowing what I know . . .*

"The Boris brothers," Steris continued. "They're acquaintances of yours, aren't they?"

"I shot their father," Wax said, not looking up. "Twice."

I couldn't let it die, the book read. *It's not right. Hemalurgy is good now, I figure. Saze is both sides now, right? Ruin isn't around anymore.*

"Are they likely to try to kill you?" Steris asked.

"Boris Junior swore to drink my blood," Wax said.

"Boris the Third—and yes, he's the brother of Boris Junior; don't ask—swore to . . . what was it? Eat my toes? He's not a clever man."

We can use it. We should. Shouldn't we?

"I'll just put them on the list, then," Steris said.

Wax sighed, looking up from the book. "You're going to invite my mortal enemies," he said dryly, "to our wedding."

"We have to invite *someone*," Steris said. She sat with her blonde hair up in a bun, her stacks of papers for the wedding arrangements settled around her like subjects at court. Her blue flowered dress was fashionable without being the least bit daring, and her prim hat clung to her hair so tightly it might as well have been nailed in place.

"I'm certain there are better choices for invitations than people who want me dead," Wax said. "I hear family members are traditional."

"As a point of fact," Steris said, "I believe your remaining family members actually do want you dead."

She had him there. "Well, yours don't. Not that I've heard anyway. If you need to fill out the wedding party, invite more of them."

"I've invited all of my family as would be proper," Steris said. "And all of my acquaintances that merit the regard." She reached to the side, taking out a sheet of paper. "You, however, have given me only *two* names of people to invite. Wayne and a woman named Ranette—who, you noted, *probably* wouldn't try to shoot you at your own wedding."

"Very unlikely," Wax agreed. "She hasn't tried to kill me in years. Not seriously, at least."

Steris sighed, setting down the sheet.

"Steris . . ." Wax said. "I'm sorry, I didn't mean to be

flippant. Ranette will be fine. We joke about her, but she's a good friend. She won't ruin the wedding. I promise."

"Then who will?"

"Excuse me?"

"I have known you for an entire year now, Lord Waxillium," Steris said. "I can accept you for who you are, but I am under no illusions. *Something* will happen at our wedding. A villain will burst in, guns firing. Or we'll discover explosives in the altar. Or Father Bin will inexplicably turn out to be an old enemy and attempt to murder you instead of performing the ceremony. It *will* happen. I'm merely trying to prepare for it."

"You're serious, aren't you?" Wax asked, smiling. "You're actually thinking of inviting one of my enemies so you can *plan* for a disruption."

"I've sorted them by threat level and ease of access," Steris said, shuffling through her papers.

"Wait," Wax said, rising and walking over. He leaned down next to her, looking over her shoulder at her papers. Each sheet contained a detailed biography. "Ape Manton . . . The Dashir boys . . . Rusts! Rick Stranger. I'd forgotten about him. Where did you get these?"

"Your exploits are a matter of public record," Steris said. "One that is of increasing interest to society."

"How long did you spend on this?" Wax asked, flipping through the pages in the stack.

"I wanted to be thorough. This sort of thing helps me think. Besides, I wanted to know what you had spent your life doing."

That was actually kind of sweet. In a bizarre, Steris sort of way.

"Invite Douglas Venture," he said. "He's kind of a

friend, but he can't hold his liquor. You can count on him making a disturbance at the after-party."

"Excellent," Steris said. "And the other thirty-seven seats in your section?"

"Invite leaders among the seamstresses and forge-workers of my house," Wax said. "And the constables-general of the various octants. It will be a nice gesture."

"Very well."

"If you want me to help more with the wedding planning—"

"No, the formal request to perform the ceremony that you sent to Father Bin was the only task required of you by protocol. Otherwise I can handle it; this is the perfect sort of thing to occupy me. That said, some-day I *would* like to know what is in that little book you peruse so often."

"I—"

The front door to the mansion slammed open down below, and booted feet thumped up the steps. A moment later, the door to the study burst open and Wayne all but tumbled in. Darriance—the house butler—stood apologetically just behind him.

Wiry and of medium height, Wayne had a round clean-shaven face and—as usual—wore his old Roughs clothing, though Steris had pointedly supplied him with new clothing on at least three occasions.

"Wayne, you could try the doorbell sometime," Wax said.

"Nah, that warns the butler," Wayne said.

"Which *is* kind of the point."

"Beady little buggers," Wayne said, shutting the door on Darriance. "Can't trust them. Look, Wax. We've got to go! The Marksman has made his move!"

Finally! Wax thought. "Let me grab my coat."

Wayne glanced toward Steris. "'Ello, Crazy," he said, nodding to her.

"Hello, Idiot," she said, nodding back.

Wax buckled on his gunbelt over his fine city suit, with vest and cravat, then threw on his mistcoat duster. "Let's go," he said, checking his ammunition.

Wayne pushed his way out the door and barreled down the stairs. Wax paused by Steris's couch. "I . . ."

"A man must have his hobbies," she said, raising another sheet of paper and inspecting it. "I accept yours, Lord Waxillium—but *do* try to avoid being shot in the face, as we have wedding portraits to sit for this evening."

"I'll remember that."

"Keep an eye on my sister out there," Steris said.

"This is a dangerous chase," Wax said, hastening to the door. "I doubt Marasi will be involved."

"If you think that, then your professional faculties are suspect. It's a dangerous chase, so she'll *find* a way to be involved."

Wax hesitated by the door. He glanced back at her, and she looked up, meeting his eyes. It felt as if there should be something more to their parting. A send-off of some sort. Fondness.

Steris seemed to sense it too, but neither said anything.

Wax tipped his head back, taking a shot of whiskey and metal flakes, then charged through the doorway and threw himself over the balcony railing. He slowed himself with a Push on the silver inlays in the marble floor of the entrance hall, hitting with a thump of boots on stone. Darriance opened the front door ahead of him as he raced out to join Wayne at the coach, for the ride to . . .

He froze on the steps down to the street. "What the hell is that?"

"Motorcar!" Wayne said from the back seat of the vehicle.

Wax groaned, hastening down the steps and approaching the machine. Marasi sat behind the steering mechanism, wearing a fashionable dress of lavender and lace. She looked much younger than her half sister, Steris, though only five years separated them.

She was a constable now, technically. An aide to the constable-general of this octant. She'd never fully explained to him why she would leave behind her career as a solicitor to join the constables, but at least she'd been hired on not as a beat constable, but as an analyst and executive assistant. She shouldn't be subjected to danger in that role.

Yet here she was. A glint of eagerness shone in her eyes as she turned to him. "Are you going to get in?"

"What are you doing here?" Wax asked, opening the door with some reluctance.

"Driving. You'd rather Wayne do it?"

"I'd rather have a coach and a good team of horses." Wax settled into one of the seats.

"Stop being so old-fashioned," Marasi said, moving her foot and making the devilish contraption lurch forward. "Marksman robbed the First Union, as you guessed."

Wax held on tightly. He'd guessed that Marksman would hit the bank three days ago. When it hadn't happened, he'd thought the man had fled to the Roughs.

"Captain Reddi thinks that Marksman will run for his hideout in the Seventh Octant," Marasi noted, steering around a horse carriage.

"Reddi is wrong," Wax said. "Head for the Break-outs."

She didn't argue. The motorcar thumped and shook until they hit the new section of paving stones, where the street smoothed out and the vehicle picked up speed. This was one of the latest motorcars, the type the broadsheets had been spouting about, with rubber wheels and a gasoline engine.

The entire city was transforming to accommodate them. *A lot of trouble just so people can drive these contraptions,* Wax thought sourly. Horses didn't need ground this smooth—though he did have to admit that the motorcar turned remarkably well, as Marasi took a corner at speed.

It was still a horrible lifeless heap of destruction.

"You shouldn't be here," Wax said as Marasi took another corner.

She kept her eyes forward. Behind them, Wayne leaned halfway out one of the windows, holding his hat to his head and grinning.

"You trained as an attorney," Wax said. "You belong in a courtroom, not chasing a killer."

"I've done well caring for myself in the past. You never complained then."

"Each time, it felt like an exception. Yet here you are again."

Marasi did something with the stick to her right, changing the motor's gears. Wax never had been able to get the hang of that. She darted around several horses, causing one of the riders to shout after them. The swerving motion pushed Wax against the side of the motorcar, and he grunted.

"What's wrong with you lately?" Marasi demanded.

"You complain about the motorcar, about me being here, about your tea being too hot in the morning. One would almost think you'd made some horrible life decision that you regret deep down. Wonder what it could be."

Wax kept his eyes forward. In the mirror, he saw Wayne lean back in and raise his eyebrows. "She might have a point, mate."

"You're not helping."

"Wasn't intending to," Wayne said. "Fortunately, I know which horrible life decision she's talkin' about. You really should have bought that hat we looked at last week. It was lucky. I've got a fifth sense for these things."

"Fifth?" Marasi asked.

"Yeah, can't smell worth a heap of beans. I—"

"There," Wax said, leaning forward and looking through the windscreen. A figure bounded out of a side street soaring through the air, landed in the street, then launched himself down the thoroughfare ahead of them.

"You were right," Marasi said. "How did you know?"

"Marks likes to be seen," Wax said, slipping Vindication from her holster at his side. "Fancies himself a gentleman rogue. Keep this contraption moving steadily, if you can."

Marasi's reply was cut off as Wax threw open the door and leaped out. He fired down and Pushed on the bullet, launching himself upward. A Push on a passing carriage sent it rocking and nudged Wax to the side, so that when he came down, he landed on the wooden roof of Marasi's motorcar.

He grabbed the roof's front lip in one hand, gun up beside his head, wind blowing his mistcoat out behind him. Ahead, Marks bounded down the thoroughfare in a series of Steelpushes. Deep within, Wax felt the comforting burn of his own metal.

He propelled himself off the motorcar and out over the roadway. Marks always performed his robberies in daylight, always escaped along the busiest roadways he could find. He liked the notoriety. He probably felt invincible. Being an Allomancer could do that to a man.

Wax sent himself into a series of leaps over motorcars and carriages, passing the tenements on either side. The rushing wind, the height and perspective, cleared his mind and calmed his emotions as surely as a Soother's touch. His worries dissolved, and for the moment there was only the chase.

The Marksman wore red, an old busker's mask covering his face—black with white tusks, like a demon of the Deepness from old stories. And he was connected to the Set, according to the appointment book Wax had stolen from his uncle. After so many months the usefulness of that book was waning, but there were still a few gems to exploit.

Marks Pushed toward the industrial district. Wax followed, bounding from motorcar to motorcar. Amazing how much more secure he felt while hurtling through the afternoon air, as opposed to being trapped in one of those horrible motorized boxes.

Marks spun in midair and released a handful of something. Wax Pushed himself off a lamppost and jerked to the side, then shoved Marks's coins as they passed, sending them out of the way of a random motorcar below. The motor swerved anyway, running toward the canal, the driver losing control.

Rust and Ruin, Wax thought with annoyance, Pushing himself back toward the motorcar. He tapped his metalmind, increasing his weight twentyfold, and came down on the hood of the motorcar.

Hard.

The smash crushed the front of the motorcar into the ground, grinding it against the stones, slowing and then stopping its momentum before it could topple into the canal. He caught a glimpse of stunned people inside, then released his metalmind and launched himself in a Push after Marks. He almost lost the man, but fortunately the red clothing was distinctive. Wax spotted him as he bounded up off a low building, then Pushed himself high along the side of one of the city's shorter skyscrapers. Wax followed, watching as the man Pushed himself in through a window on the top floor, some twelve or fourteen stories up.

Wax shot up into the sky, windows passing him in a blur. The city of Elendel stretched out all around, smoke rising from coal plants, factories, and homes in countless spouts. He neared the top floor one window to the left of where Marks had entered, and as he landed lightly on the stonework ledge, he tossed a coin toward the window Marks had used.

The coin bounced against the glass. Gunfire sprayed out of the window. At the same time, Wax increased his weight and smashed through his own window by leaning against it, entering the building. He skidded on glass, raising Vindication toward the plaster wall separating him from Marks.

Translucent blue lines spread around him, pointing in a thousand different directions, highlighting bits of metal. The nails in a desk behind him, where a frightened man in a suit cowered. The metal wires in the walls, leading to electric lamps. Most importantly, a few lines pointed *through* the wall into the next room.

These were faint; obstructions weakened his Allomantic sense.

One of those lines quivered as someone in there turned and raised a gun. Wax rolled Vindication's cylinder and locked it into place.

Hazekiller round.

He fired, then *Pushed,* flaring his metal and drilling that bullet forward with as much force as he could. It tore through the wall as if it were paper.

The metal in the next room dropped to the floor. Wax threw himself against the wall, increasing his weight, cracking the plaster. Another slam with his shoulder smashed through, and he broke into the next room, weapon raised, looking for his target.

He found only a pool of blood soaking into the carpet and a discarded submachine gun. This room was some kind of clerk's office. Several men and women pressed against the floor, trembling. One woman raised a finger, pointing out a door. Wax gave her a nod and crouched against the wall next to the doorway, then cautiously glanced out.

With a painful grating sound, a filing cabinet slid down the hallway toward him. Wax ducked back out of the way as it passed, then leaped out and aimed.

His gun immediately lurched backward. Wax grabbed it with both hands, holding tight, but a second Push launched his other pistol out of its holster. His feet started to skid, his gun hauling him backward, and he growled, but finally dropped Vindication. She tumbled all the way down the hall to fetch up beside the ruins of the filing cabinet, which had crashed into the wall there. He would have to come back for her once this was over.

Marks stood at the other end of the hallway, lit by

soft electric lights. He bled from a shoulder wound, his face hidden by the black-and-white mask.

"There are a thousand criminals in this city far worse than I am," a muffled voice said from behind the mask, "and yet you hunt *me,* lawman. Why? I'm a hero of the people."

"You stopped being a hero weeks ago," Wax said, striding forward, mistcoat rustling. "When you killed a child."

"That wasn't my fault."

"You fired the gun, Marks. You might not have been aiming for the girl, but *you fired the gun.*"

The thief stepped back. The sack slung on his shoulder had been torn, either by Wax's bullet or some shrapnel. It leaked banknotes.

Marks glared at him through the mask, eyes barely visible in the electric light. Then he dashed to the side, holding his shoulder as he ran into another room. Wax Pushed off the filing cabinet and threw himself in a rush down the hallway. He skidded to a stop before the door Marks had gone in, then Pushed off the light behind, bending it against the wall and entering the room.

Open window. Wax grabbed a handful of pens from a desk before throwing himself out the window, a dozen stories up. Banknotes fluttered in the air, trailing behind Marks as he plummeted. Wax increased his weight, trying to fall faster, but he had nothing to Push against and the increased weight helped only slightly against air resistance. Marks still hit the ground before him, then Pushed away the coin he'd used to slow himself.

A pair of dropped pens—with metal nibs—Pushed ahead of himself into the ground was enough, barely, to slow Wax.

Marks leaped away, bounding out over some streetlamps. He bore no metal on his body that Wax could spot, but he moved a lot more slowly than he had earlier, and he trailed blood.

Wax followed him. Marks would be making for the Breakouts, a slum where the people still covered for him. They didn't care that his robberies had turned violent; they celebrated that he stole from those who deserved it.

Can't let him reach that safety, Wax thought, Pushing himself up over a lamppost, then shoving on it behind him to gain speed. He closed on his prey, who checked on Wax with a frantic glance over his shoulder. Wax raised one of the pens, gauging how risky it would be to try to hit Marks in the leg. He didn't want a killing blow. This man knew something.

The slums were just ahead.

Next bound, Wax thought, gripping the pen. Bystanders stared up from the sidewalks, watching the Allomantic chase. He couldn't risk hitting one of them. He had to—

One of those faces was familiar.

Wax lost control of his Push. Stunned by what he'd seen, he barely kept himself from breaking bones as he hit the street, rolling across cobbles. He came to a rest, mistcoat tassels twisted around his body.

He drew himself up on hands and knees.

No. Impossible. NO.

He scrambled across the street, ignoring a stomping black destrier and its cursing rider. That face. That *face*.

The last time he had seen that face, he had shot it in the forehead. Bloody Tan.

The man who had killed Lessie.

"A man was here!" Wax shouted, shoving through

the crowd. "Long-fingered, thinning hair. A face almost like a bare skull. Did you see him? Did anyone see him?"

People stared at him as if he were daft. Perhaps he was. Wax raised his hand to the side of his head.

"Lord Waxillium?"

He spun. Marasi had stopped her motorcar nearby, and both she and Wayne were climbing out. Had she actually been able to tail him during his chase? No . . . no, he'd told her where he thought Marks would go.

"Wax, mate?" Wayne asked. "You all right? What did he do, knock you from the air?"

"Something like that," Wax mumbled, glancing about one last time.

Rusts, he thought. *The stress is digging into my mind.*

"So he got away," Marasi said, folding her arms, looking displeased.

"Not yet he didn't," Wax said. "He's bleeding and dropping money. He'll leave a trail. Come on."

3

I need you to stay behind as we go into those slums," Wayne said, determined to impress solemnity into his voice. "It's not that I don't want your help. I do. It's just going to be too dangerous for you. You need to stay where I know you're safe. No arguments. I'm sorry."

"Wayne," Wax said, walking past. "Stop talking to your hat and get over here."

Wayne sighed, patting his hat and then forcing himself to put it down and leave it in the motorcar. Wax was a right good fellow, but there were a lot of things he didn't understand. Women for one. Hats for another.

Wayne jogged over to where Wax and Marasi peered into the Breakouts. It seemed a different world in there. The sky inside was strung with clotheslines, derelict bits of clothing dangling like hanged men. Wind blew out of the place, happy to escape, carrying with it uncertain scents. Food half cooked. Bodies half washed. Streets half cleaned.

The tall, compact tenements cast deep shadows even in the afternoon. As if this were the place dusk came for a drink and a chat before sauntering out for its evening duty.

"The Lord Mistborn didn't want there to be slums in the city, you know," Marasi said as the three of them entered. "He tried hard to prevent them from growing up. Built nice buildings for the poor, tried to make them last . . ."

Wax nodded, absently moving a coin across his knuckles as he walked. He seemed to have lost his guns somewhere. Had he bummed some coins off Marasi? It never was fair. When Wayne borrowed coins off folks, he got yelled at. He did forget to ask sometimes, but he always offered a good trade.

As they penetrated deeper into the Breakouts, Wayne lagged behind the other two. *Need a good hat . . .* he thought. The hat was important.

So he listened for some coughing.

Ah . . .

He found the chap nestled up beside a doorway, a ratty blanket draped over his knees. You could always find his type in a slum. Old, clinging to life like a man on a ledge, his lungs half full with various unsavory fluids. The old man hacked into a glove-wrapped hand as Wayne settled down on the steps beside him.

"What, now," the man said. "Who are you?"

"What, now," Wayne repeated. "Who are you?"

"I'm nobody," the man said, then spat to the side. "Dirty outer. I ain't done nothing."

"I'm nobody," Wayne repeated, taking his flask from the pocket of his duster. "Dirty outer. I ain't done nothing."

Good accent, that was. Real mumbly, a classic vintage, wrapped in a blanket of history. Closing his eyes and listening, Wayne thought he could imagine what people sounded like years ago. He held out the flask of whiskey.

"You trying to poison me?" the man asked. He clipped off words, left out half the sounds.

"You trying to poison me?" Wayne repeated, working his jaw as if his mouth were full of bits of rock he kept trying to chew. Some northern fields mix in this one, for sure. He opened his eyes and tipped the whiskey at the man, who smelled it, then took a sip. Then a swig. Then a gulp.

"So," the man asked, "you an idiot? I've a son that's an idiot. The real kind, that was born that way. Well, you seem all right anyway."

"Well, you seem all right anyway," Wayne said, standing up. He reached over to take the man's old cotton cap off his head, then gestured toward the whiskey flask.

"In trade?" the man asked. "Boy, you *are* an idiot."

Wayne pulled on the cap. "Could you say another word that starts with 'h' for me?"

"Huh?"

"Rusting wonderful," Wayne said. He hopped back down the steps onto the street and ditched his duster in a cranny—and along with it his dueling canes, unfortunately. He kept his wooden knucklebones though.

The clothing underneath his duster was Roughs stock, not so different from what they wore in these slums. Buttoned shirt, trousers, suspenders. He rolled up the sleeves as he walked. The clothing was worn, patched in a few places. He wouldn't trade it for the world. Took years to get clothing that looked right. Used, lived-in.

Be slow to trust a man with clothing that was too new. You didn't get to wear new, clean clothing by doing honest work.

Wax and Marasi had paused up ahead, speaking to

some old women with scarves on their heads and bundles in their arms. Wayne could almost hear what they were saying.

We don't know nothing.

He came running past here mere moments ago, Wax would say. *Surely you—*

We don't know nothing. We didn't see nothing.

Wayne wandered over to where a group of men sat under a dirty cloth awning while eating bruised fruit. "Who're those outers?" Wayne asked as he sat down, using the accent he'd just picked up from the old man.

They didn't even question him. A slum like this had a lot of people—too many to know everyone—but you could easily tell if someone belonged or not. And Wayne belonged.

"Conners for sure," one of the men said. He had a head like an overturned bowl, hairless and too flat.

"They want someone," another man said. Rust and Ruin, the chap's face was so pointy, you could have used it to plow a field. "Conners only come here if they want to arrest someone. They've never cared about us, and never will."

"If they did care," bowl-head said, "they'd do something about all those factories and power plants, dumping ash on us. We ain't supposed to live in ash anymore. Harmony said it, he did."

Wayne nodded. Good point, that. These building walls, they *were* ashen. Did people care about that, on the outside? No. Not as long as *they* didn't have to live in here. He didn't miss the glares Wax and Marasi drew, pointed at them by people who passed behind, or who pulled windows closed up above.

This is worse, Wayne thought. *Worse than normal.*

He'd have to talk to Wax about it. But for now there was a job to do. "They *are* looking for something."

"Stay out of it," bowl-head said.

Wayne grunted. "Maybe there's money in it."

"You'd turn in one of our own?" bowl-head said with a scowl. "I recognize you. Edip's son, aren't you?"

Wayne glanced away, noncommittal.

"You listen here, son," bowl-head said, wagging his finger. "Don't trust a conner, and *don't* be a rat."

"I ain't a rat," Wayne said, testily. He *wasn't*. But sometimes, a man just needed cash. "They're after Marks. I overheard them. There's a thousand notes on his head, there is."

"He grew up here," plow-face said. "He's one of us."

"He killed that girl," Wayne said.

"That's a lie," bowl-head said. "Don't you go talking to conners, son. I mean it."

"Fine, fine," Wayne said, moving to rise. "I'll just go—"

"You'll sit back down," bowl-head said. "Or I'll rap you something good on your head, I will."

Wayne sighed, sitting back down. "You olders always talk about us, and don't know how it is these days. Working in one of the factories."

"We know more than you think," bowl-head said, handing Wayne a bruised apple. "Eat this, stay out of trouble, and don't go where I can't see you."

Wayne grumbled, but sat back and bit into the apple. It didn't taste half bad. He ate the whole thing, then helped himself to a couple more.

It happened soon enough. The men of the fruit-eating group broke apart, leaving Wayne with a basket full of cores. They split with a few amicable gibes at one another, each of the four men claiming he had some important task to be about.

Wayne stuffed another apple in each pocket, then stood up and sauntered off after bowl-head. He tailed the fellow fairly easily, nodding occasionally at people, who nodded back as if they knew him. It was the hat. Put on a man's hat, surround your mind with his way of thinking, and it changed you. A man in dockworker's clothing passed by, shoulders slumped, whistling a sad tune. Wayne picked up the melody. Rough life that was, working the docks. You had to commute each day on the canal boats—either that or find a bed out near the waterfront of the bay, where you were about as likely to get stabbed as have breakfast.

He'd lived that life as a youth. Had the scars to prove it, he did. But as a chap grew, he wanted more to his days than a fight on every corner and women who couldn't remember his name one day to the next.

Bowl-head ducked into an alley. Well, every rusting street in here felt like an alley. Bowl-head entered an alley's alley. Wayne stepped up to the side of the tiny roadway, then burned bendalloy. Allomancy was a useful trick, that it was. Burning the metal set up a nice little bubble of sped-up time around him. He strolled around the corner, staying inside the bubble—it didn't move when he did, but he could move within it.

Yup. There he was, bowl-head himself, crouching beside a rubbish pile, waiting to see if anyone followed him. Wayne had *almost* made the bubble too big and caught the man in it.

Sloppy, sloppy, Wayne thought. A mistake like that on the docks could cost a man his life. He fished a ratty blanket out of the part of the rubbish pile that was inside his bubble, then wandered back around the corner and dropped the bubble.

Inside the speed bubble, he'd have been moving so quickly bowl-head wouldn't have seen more than a blur—if that. He wouldn't think anything of it, Wayne was certain. If he were wrong, he'd eat his hat. Well, one of Wax's hats at least.

Wayne found a set of steps and settled down. He pulled his cap down half over his eyes, sidled up to the wall in a comfortable position, and spread the blanket around himself. Just another homeless drunk.

Bowl-head was a careful one. He waited inside the alley a whole five minutes before creeping out, looking back and forth, then hastening to a building across the street. He knocked, whispered something, and was let in.

Wayne yawned, stretched, and tossed aside the blanket. He crossed the street to the building that bowl-head had entered, then started checking the shuttered windows. The ancient shutters were so old, a good sneeze might have knocked them off. He had to be careful to avoid getting splinters in his cheeks as he listened at each window in turn.

The men of the slums had an odd sense of morality to them. They wouldn't turn in one of their own to the constables. Not even for a reward. But then again, a chap needed to eat. Wouldn't a man like Marks want to hear just how loyal his friends were?

". . . was a pair of conners for sure," Wayne heard at a window. "A thousand notes is a lot, Marks. A whole lot. Now, I'm not saying you can't trust the lads; there's not a bad alloy in the bunch. I *can* say that a little encouragement will help them feel better about their loyalty."

Ratting out a friend: completely off-limits.

Extorting a friend: well, that was just good business sense.

And if Marks didn't act grateful, then maybe he hadn't been a friend after all. Wayne grinned, slipping his sets of wooden knucklebones over his fingers. He stepped back, then charged the building.

He hit the shutters with one shoulder, crashing through, then tossed up a speed bubble the moment he hit the floor. He rolled and came up on his feet in front of Marks—who was inside the speed bubble. The man still wore his red trousers, though he'd removed his mask, and was bandaging his shoulder. He snapped his head up, displaying a surprised face with bushy eyebrows and large lips.

Rusts. No wonder the fellow normally wore a mask.

Wayne swung at his chin, laying him out with one punch. Then he spun, fists up, but the other half-dozen occupants of the room, including bowl-head, stood frozen just outside the edge of his speed bubble. Now that was right lucky.

Wayne grinned, heaving Marks up onto his shoulder. He took his knuckles off, slipping them into his pocket, and got out an apple. He took a juicy bite, waved farewell to bowl-head—who looked forward with glassy eyes, frozen—then tossed Marks out the window and followed after.

Once he passed beyond the edge of his speed bubble, it automatically collapsed.

"What the hell was that!" bowl-head yelled inside.

Wayne heaved the unconscious Marks up onto his shoulder again, then wandered back down the road, chewing on his apple.

"Let me talk to the next ones," Marasi said. "Maybe I can get them to say something."

She felt Waxillium's eyes on her. He thought she was trying to prove herself to him. Once he'd have been right. Now she was a constable—fully credentialed and in the city's employ. This was her *job*. Waxillium didn't agree with her decision, but her actions were not subject to his approval.

Together they walked up to a group of young outcasts sitting on the steps of the slums. The three boys watched them with suspicion, their skin dirty, their too-big clothing tied at the waists and ankles. That was the style, apparently, for youths of the streets. They smelled of the incense they'd been smoking in their pipes.

Marasi stepped up to them. "We're looking for a man."

"If you need a man," one of the boys said, looking her up and down, "I'm right here."

"Oh please," Marasi said. "You're . . . what, nine?"

"Hey, she knows how long it is!" the boy said, laughing and grabbing his crotch. "Have you been peeking at me, lady?"

Well, that's a blush, Marasi thought. *Not terribly professional.*

Fortunately, she'd spent time around Wayne and his occasional colorful metaphors. Blushes would happen. She pressed onward. "He came shooting through here less than an hour ago. Wounded, trailing blood, wearing red. I'm sure you know who I'm speaking of."

"Yeah, the man of hours!" one of the boys said, laughing and referencing a figure from old nursemaid tales. "I know him!"

Treat them like a belligerent witness, she thought. *At a trial. Keep them talking.* She needed to learn how to deal with people like these boys in the real world, not just in sterile practice rooms.

"Yes, the man of hours," Marasi said. "Where did he go?"

"To the edge of dusk," the boy said. "Haven't you heard the stories?"

"I'm fond of stories," Marasi said, slipping a few coins from her pocketbook. She held them up. Bribery felt like cheating, but . . . well, she *wasn't* in court.

The three boys eyed the coins, a sudden hunger flashing in their eyes. They covered it quickly, but perhaps showing off money in this place wasn't terribly wise.

"Let's hear a story," Marasi said. "About where this . . . man of hours might be staying. The location of dusk, if you will. Here in these tenements."

"We might know that," one of the boys said. "Though, you know, stories cost a lot. More than that."

Behind her, something clinked. Waxillium had gotten out a few coins too. The boys glanced at those, eager, until Waxillium flipped one up into the air and Pushed until it was lost.

The boys grew quiet immediately.

"Talk to the lady," Waxillium said softly, with an edge to his voice. "Stop wasting our time."

Marasi turned to him, and behind her the boys made their decision. They scattered, obviously not wanting to deal with an Allomancer.

"That was very helpful," Marasi said, folding her arms. "Thank you so much."

"They were going to lie to you," Waxillium said, glancing over his shoulder. "And we were drawing the wrong kind of attention."

"I realize they were going to lie," Marasi said. "I was going to catch them in it. Attacking someone's false story is often one of the best methods of interrogation."

"Actually," Waxillium said, "the best method of interrogation involves a drawer and someone's fingers."

"Actually," Marasi said, "it does *not*. Studies show that forced interrogation results in bad information almost all the time. Anyway, what is wrong with you today, Waxillium? I realize you've been flaunting your 'tough Roughs lawman' persona lately—"

"I have not."

"You *have*," she said. "And I can see why. Out in the Roughs, you acted the gentleman lawman. You yourself told me you clung to civilization, to bring it with you. Well, here you're around lords all the time. You're practically *drowning* in civilization. So instead, you lean on being the Roughs lawman—to bring a little old-fashioned justice to the city."

"You've thought about this a lot," he said, turned away from her, scanning the street.

Rust and Ruin. He thought she was infatuated with him. *Arrogant, brutish . . . idiot!* She puffed out and stalked away.

She was *not* infatuated. He had made it clear there would be nothing between them, and he was engaged to her sister. That was that. Couldn't the two of them have a professional relationship now?

Wayne lounged on the steps leading up to a nearby building, watching them and sloppily taking bites out of an apple.

"And where have you been?" Marasi asked, walking up to him.

"Apple?" Wayne said, handing another one toward her. " 's not too bruised."

"No thank you. Some of us have been trying to find a killer, not a meal."

"Oh, that." Wayne kicked at something beside him on the ground, hidden in the shadow of the steps. "Yeah, took care of that for you."

"You took . . . Wayne, that's a person at your feet! Rusts! He's bleeding!"

"Sure is," Wayne said. "Not my fault at all, that. I did knock 'im upside the head though."

Marasi raised a hand to her mouth. It was *him*. "Wayne, where . . . How . . ."

Waxillium gently pushed her aside; she hadn't seen him approach. He knelt down, checking Marks's wound. Waxillium then looked up at Wayne and nodded, the two sharing an expression they often exchanged. The closest Marasi had been able to figure, it meant something between "Nice work" and "You're a total git; *I* wanted to do that."

"Let's get him to the constabulary offices," Waxillium said, lifting the unconscious Marks.

"Yes, fine," Marasi said. "But aren't you going to ask *how* he did this? Where he's been?"

"Wayne has his methods," Waxillium said. "In a place like this, they're far better than my own."

"You knew," she said, leveling a finger at Waxillium. "You knew we weren't going to get anywhere asking questions!"

"I suspected," Waxillium said. "But Wayne needs space to try his methods—"

"—onnacount of my being so incredible," Wayne added.

"—so I did my best to find Marks on my own—"

"—onnacount of *him* being unable to accept that I'm better at this sorta thing than he is—"

"—in case Wayne failed."

"Which never happens." Wayne grinned and took a bite of his apple, hopping off his steps to walk beside Waxillium. "Except that one time. And that other one time. But those don't matter, onnaccount of my getting hit to the head enough times that I can't remember them."

Marasi sighed inwardly, falling into step with the two. They had so much history that they moved in concert subconsciously, like two dancers who had performed together countless times. That made life particularly difficult for the newcomer who tried to perform with them.

"Well," Marasi said to Wayne, "you could at least tell *me* what you did. Perhaps I could learn from your methods."

"Nah," Wayne said. "Won't work for you. You're too pretty. In an unpretty sort of way to me, mind you. Let's not go around that tree again."

"Wayne, sometimes you completely baffle me."

"Only sometimes?" Waxillium asked.

"I can't give her all I got, mate," Wayne said, thumbs behind his suspenders. "Gotta save some for everyone else. I dole it out with no respect for privilege, class, sex, or mental capacity. I'm a rusting saint, I am."

"But *how*," Marasi said. "How did you find him? Did you make some of these people talk?"

"Nah," Wayne said. "I made them not talk. They're better at that. Comes from practice, I suspect."

"You should take lessons," Waxillium added.

Marasi sighed as they approached the entrance to the Breakouts. The human flotsam who earlier had cluttered the stairwells and alleyways in here had melted away, perhaps finding the attention of several lawmen too discomforting. It—

Waxillium stiffened. Wayne did as well.

"What—?" Marasi began, right as Waxillium dropped Marks and reached for his mistcoat pocket. Wayne shoved his shoulder into Marasi, pushing her away as something zipped down out of the air and clacked against the paving stones where they'd been standing. More projectiles followed, though she wasn't really looking. She instead let Wayne tow her to relative cover beside a building, then both of them began craning to search the skyline for the sniper. Waxillium took to the air with a dropped coin, a dark rush of twisting mistcoat tassels. At times like this he looked more primal, like one of the ancient Mistborn from the legends. Not a creature of law, but a sliver of the night itself come to collect its due.

"Aw, hell," Wayne said, nodding toward Marks. The body slumped in the middle of the road, and now had a prominent wooden shaft sticking out of it.

"Arrow?" Marasi asked.

"Crossbow bolt," Wayne said. "Haven't seen one of those in years. You really only want them for fighting Allomancers." He looked up. Above, Waxillium gave chase, soaring toward the top of one of the buildings.

"Stay here," Wayne said, then dashed off down an alleyway.

"Wait—" Marasi said, raising a hand.

But he was gone.

Those two, she thought in annoyance. Well, obviously someone didn't want Marks to be captured and spill what he knew. Perhaps she could learn something from the crossbow bolt or the corpse itself.

She knelt down beside the body, checking first to make certain he was dead—hoping perhaps that the crossbow bolt had not finished the job. He *was* dead, unfortunately. The bolt was firmly lodged in the head. Who knew that a crossbow could penetrate a skull like that? Marasi shook her head, reaching into her handbag to get her notepad and do a write-up of the position the body had fallen in.

You know, she thought. *The assassin is lucky. They were gone so fast, they couldn't have known that they dealt a killing blow. If I were looking to make sure Marks was finished off, I'd certainly . . .*

She heard something click behind her.

. . . double back and check.

Marasi turned slowly to find a ragged-looking man leaving an alleyway, holding a crossbow. He inspected her with dark eyes.

The next part happened quickly. Before Marasi had time to take a step, the man rushed her. He fired the crossbow over his shoulder—causing a Wayne-like yelp to come out of the alleyway—then grabbed Marasi by the shoulder as she tried to run.

He whipped her about, raising something cold to her neck. A glass dagger. Waxillium dropped to the ground in front of them, mistcoat unfurling around him.

The two stared at one another, a coin in Waxillium's right hand. He rubbed it with his thumb.

Remember your hostage training, woman! Marasi thought. *Most men take a hostage out of desperation.* Could she use her Allomancy? She could slow time around her, speeding it up for everyone outside her speed bubble. The opposite of what Wayne could do.

But she hadn't swallowed any cadmium. Stupid! A mistake the other two would never make. She needed to stop being embarrassed with her powers, weak though they were. She'd used them effectively on more than one occasion.

The man breathed in and out raggedly, his head right next to hers. She could feel the stubble of his chin and cheek against her skin.

Men who take hostages don't want to kill, she thought. *This isn't part of the plan. You can talk him down, speak comforting words, seek common ground and build upon it.*

She didn't do any of that. Instead, she whipped her hand out of her handbag, gripping the small, single-shot pistol she kept inside. Before even considering what she was doing, she pressed the barrel against the man's chin, pulled the trigger . . .

And blew the bottom of his head up out of the top.

4

Wax lowered his hand, looking at the new corpse beside Marasi. Her shot had taken off a big chunk of the face. Identifying the man would be near impossible.

It would have been anyway. Suit's minions were notoriously difficult to trace.

Don't worry about that right now, he thought, taking out a handkerchief. He walked over and held it up to Marasi, who stood with wide eyes, blood and bits of flesh sprayed across her face. She stared straight ahead and did not look down. She'd dropped the pistol.

"That was . . ." she said, eyes ahead. "That was . . ." She took a deep breath. "That was unexpected of me, wasn't it?"

"You did well," Wax said. "People assume a captive to be in their power. Often the best way to escape is by fighting back."

"What?" Marasi said, finally taking the handkerchief.

"You discharged a pistol right beside your head," Wax said. "You are going to have trouble hearing. Rusts . . . you've probably done some permanent damage to your ear. Hopefully it won't be too bad."

"What?"

Wax gestured toward her face, and she looked at the handkerchief, as if seeing it for the first time. She blinked, then glanced down. She looked away from the corpse immediately and began wiping at her face.

Wayne, grumbling, staggered out of the alleyway, a new hole in his clothing at the shoulder and a crossbow bolt in his hand.

"So much for interrogating him," Marasi said with a grimace.

"It's all right," Wax said. "Living was more important."

". . . What?"

He smiled at her reassuringly as Wayne waved to some other constables, who had finally arrived on the scene and were making their way into the slums.

"Why does this keep happening to me?" Marasi asked. "Yes, I know I won't be able to hear your reply. But this is . . . what, the third time someone has tried to use me as a hostage? Do I *exude* indefensibility or something?"

Yes, you do, Wax thought, though he didn't say it. *That's a good thing. It makes them underestimate you.* Marasi was a strong person. She thought clearly in times of stress; she did what needed to be done, even if it was unpleasant. However, she was also very keen on dressing nicely and making herself up.

Lessie would have had none of that. The only times Wax had seen her in a dress were when they'd made the occasional trip to Covingtar to visit the Pathian gardens there. He smiled, remembering a time she'd actually worn trousers *under* the dress.

"Lord Ladrian!" Constable Reddi trotted over, wearing the uniform of a captain in the constabulary. The lean man had a neatly clipped, drooping mustache.

"Reddi," Wax said, nodding to him. "Is Aradel here?"

"The constable-general is engaged in another investigation, my lord," Reddi said with a crisp tone. Why did Wax always want to smack this man after talking to him? He was never insulting, always impeccably proper. Maybe that was reason enough.

Wax pointed toward the buildings. "Well, if you'd kindly have your men secure the area; we should probably question those nearby and see if, by some miracle, we can discover the identity of the man Lady Colms just killed."

Reddi saluted, though it wasn't technically necessary. Wax had a special deputized forbearance in the constabulary, allowing him to do things like . . . well, jump through the city armed and firing. But he wasn't in their command structure.

The other constables moved to do as he requested anyway. As he glanced at the Marksman, Wax forcibly kept his anger in check. At this rate, he would *never* track down his uncle Edwarn. Wax had only the slightest hint of what the man was trying to accomplish.

It can make anyone into an Allomancer, you see. . . . If we don't use it, someone else will.

Words from the book Ironeyes had given him.

"Excellent work, my lord," Reddi said in a calm voice, nodding to the fallen Marksman. The clothing was distinctive. "Another miscreant dealt with, and with your customary efficiency."

Wax said nothing. Today's "excellent work" was just another dead end.

"Hey, look!" Wayne said nearby. "I think I found one of that fellow's teeth! That's good luck, ain't it?"

Marasi looked woozy, settling down on a nearby set of steps. Wax was tempted to go comfort her, but would she interpret it the wrong way? He didn't want to lead her on.

"My lord, could we talk?" Reddi said as more constables flooded the area. "I mentioned the constable-general and another case. I was actually already on my way to find you when we heard of your chase here."

Wax turned to him, immediately alert. "What has happened?"

Reddi grimaced, showing uncharacteristic emotion. "It's bad, my lord," he said more softly. "*Politics* is involved."

Then Suit might be involved as well. "Tell me more."

"It, well, it's connected to the governor, my lord. His brother, you see, was hosting an auction last night. And, well, you should see for yourself. . . ."

Marasi didn't miss Waxillium grabbing Wayne by the shoulder and pointing toward a waiting constabulary carriage. He didn't come for her. How long would it be before that damnable man was willing to accept her as, if not an equal, a colleague?

Frustrated, she made toward the carriage. Unfortunately, she ran into Captain Reddi on the way. He spoke, and she had to strain her ringing ears—and guess a little—to figure out what he was saying.

"Constable Colms. You are out of uniform."

"Yes, sir," she said. "It is my day off, sir."

"Yet here you are," he said, hands clasped behind his back. "How is it that you find your way, consistently, into situations like this, despite *explicitly* being told that it is not your assignment, as you are not a field constable?"

"Pure happenstance I'm sure, sir," Marasi said.

He gave her a sneer at that. Funny. He usually saved those for Waxillium, when the man wasn't looking. He said something she couldn't make out, then nodded toward the motorcar she'd brought—which was technically constabulary property; she'd been told to become proficient in driving motorcars and report on their effectiveness to the constable-general. He wanted to test them as replacements for horse-drawn carriages.

"Sir?" she said.

"You've obviously been through a great deal this day, constable," Reddi said, more loudly. "Don't argue with me on this. Head home, clean up, and report for duty tomorrow."

"Sir," Marasi said. "I'd like to brief Captain Aradel on my pursuit of the Marksman, and his subsequent demise, before the details become fuzzy. He will be interested, as he's followed this case personally."

She stared Reddi in the eyes. He outranked her, yes, but he wasn't her boss. Aradel was that to both of them.

"The constable-general," Reddi said with some obvious reluctance, "is away from the offices at the moment."

"Well then, I'll report to him and let him dismiss me, sir," Marasi said. "If that is his wish."

Reddi ground his teeth and started to say something, but a call from one of the other constables diverted him. He waved toward the motorcar, and Marasi took it as dismissal to do as she'd said. So, when the carriage with Waxillium pulled away, she followed in the motor.

By the time the trip had ended, at a fashionable mansion overlooking the city's Hub, she had started to recover. She was still feeling shaken, though she hoped she didn't show it, and she could hear with her left ear, if not on the other side, where she'd fired the gun.

As she climbed out of the motorcar, she found herself wiping her cheek again with her handkerchief, though she had long since cleaned off the blood. Her dress had been thoroughly ruined. She grabbed her constable's coat from the back of the motorcar and threw it over the top to hide the stains, then rushed over to join Waxillium and the others as they descended from the carriage.

Only one other constabulary carriage, she noted, inspecting the drive. Whatever had happened here, Aradel didn't want to make a big show of it. As Waxillium walked up toward the front, he glanced about and found her, then waved her over to him.

"Do you know what this might be about?" he asked her quietly as Reddi and several other constables conferred near the carriage.

"No," Marasi said. "They didn't brief you?"

Waxillium shook his head. He glanced down at her bloodied dress, which peeked out underneath the sturdy brown jacket. He made no comment however, instead striding up the steps, tailed by Wayne.

Two constables, a man and a woman, guarded the door into the mansion. They saluted as Reddi caught up to Waxillium—pointedly ignoring Marasi—and led the way in through the doors. "We've tried to keep this very tightly controlled," Reddi said. "But word will get out, with Lord Winsting involved. Rusts, this is going to be a nightmare."

"The *governor's brother*?" Marasi asked. "What happened here?"

Reddi pointed up a set of steps. "We should find Constable-General Aradel in the grand ballroom. I warn you, this is not a sight for delicate stomachs." He glanced at Marasi.

She raised an eyebrow. "Not an hour ago, I had a man's head *literally* explode all over me, Captain. I believe I will be fine."

Reddi said nothing further, leading the way up the steps. She noticed Wayne pocketing a small, decorative cigar box they passed—Citizen Magistrates brand—replacing it with a bruised apple. She'd have to see that he swapped the cigar box back at some point.

The ballroom upstairs was littered with bodies. Marasi and Waxillium stopped in the doorway, looking in at the chaos. The dead men and women wore fine clothes, sleek ball gowns or tight black suits. Hats lay tumbled from heads, the fine tan carpet stained red in wide patches around the fallen. It was as if someone had tossed a basket of eggs into the air and let them fall, their insides seeping out all over the floor.

Claude Aradel, constable-general of the Fourth Octant, picked through the scene. In many ways, he didn't look like a constable should. His rectangular face had a few days' worth of red stubble on it; he shaved when the mood struck him. His leathery skin, furrowed with wrinkles, attested to days spent in the field, not behind a desk. He was probably pushing sixty at this point, though he wouldn't divulge his true age, and even the octant records had a question mark next to his birth date. What was certain was that Aradel didn't have a drop of noble blood in him.

He'd left the constabulary about ten years ago, giving no official reason for his departure. Rumor was he'd hit the silent ceiling on promotions a man could get without being noble. A lot could change in ten years though, and when Brettin had retired—soon after the execution of Miles Hundredlives almost a year ago—the hunt for a new constable-general had landed on Aradel. He'd come out of retirement to accept the position.

"Ladrian," he said, looking up from a corpse. "Good. You're here." He crossed the room and gave a glance to Marasi, who saluted. He didn't dismiss her.

"Aw," Wayne said, peeking in, "the fun is already over."

Waxillium stepped into the room, taking Aradel's proffered hand. "That's Chip Erikell, isn't it?" Waxillium asked, nodding to the nearest corpse. "Thought to run smuggling in the Third Octant?"

"Yes," Aradel said.

"And Isabaline Frellia," Marasi said. "Rusts! We have a file on her as tall as Wayne, but the prosecutors have never been able to charge her."

"Seven of these bodies belong to people of equivalent notoriety," Aradel said, pointing to several corpses among the fallen. "Most from crime syndicates, though a few were members of noble houses with . . . dubious reputations. The rest were high-ranking representatives from other important factions. We have near thirty notable stiffs, along with a handful of guards each."

"That's half of the city's criminal elite," Waxillium said softly, crouching down beside a body. "At least."

"All people we've never been able to touch," Aradel said. "Not for lack of trying, mind you."

"So why is everyone so grim?" Wayne asked. "We

should be throwing a bloomin' party, shouldn't we? Someone went and did our work for us! We can take the month off."

Marasi shook her head. "A violent change in power in the underworld can be dangerous, Wayne. This was a hit of huge ambition, someone eliminating rivals wholesale."

Aradel glanced at her, then nodded in agreement. She felt a surge of satisfaction. The constable-general was the one who had hired her, picking her application out of a dozen others. Every other person in the pile had had years of constable experience. Instead, he'd chosen a recently graduated law student. He saw something promising in her, obviously, and she intended to prove him right.

"I can't fathom someone doing this," Waxillium said. "Toppling so many of the city's underworld powers at once won't favor the perpetrators; that's a myth from penny novels. Murders on this scale will just draw attention and unify opposition from every other surviving gang and faction as soon as word gets out."

"Unless it was done by an outsider," Marasi said. "An uncertain element from the start, someone who stands to gain if the entire system crumbles."

Aradel grunted, and Waxillium nodded in agreement.

"But how," Waxillium whispered. "How did someone achieve this? Surely their security must have rivaled any in the city." He began moving about, pacing off distances, looking at certain bodies, then at others, whispering to himself as he periodically knelt down.

"Reddi said that the governor's brother was involved, sir?" Marasi asked Aradel.

"Lord Winsting Innate."

Lord Winsting, head of House Innate. He had a vote in the Elendel Senate, a position he gained once his brother was elevated to governor. He had been corrupt. Marasi and the rest of the constables knew it. In retrospect, she wasn't surprised to find him in the middle of something like this. The thing was, Winsting had always seemed a small catch to Marasi.

The governor, however . . . well, perhaps that hidden file on her desk—full of hints, guesses, and clues—would finally be relevant.

"Winsting," she asked Aradel. "Is he . . . ?"

"Dead?" Aradel asked. "Yes, Constable Colms. From the invitations we found, he initiated this meeting, under the guise of an auction. We located his corpse in a saferoom in the basement."

This drew Waxillium's attention. He stood up, looking directly at them, then muttered something to himself and paced off another body. What was he searching for?

Wayne wandered over to Marasi and Aradel. He took a swig from a silver flask engraved with someone else's initials. Marasi pointedly did not ask him which of the dead he'd taken it from. "So," he said, "our little house leader was friendly with criminals, was he?"

"We've long suspected he was crooked," Aradel said. "The people love his family though, and his brother went to great lengths to keep Winsting's previous lapses out of the limelight."

"You're right, Aradel," Waxillium said from across the room. "This will be bad."

"I dunno," Wayne said. "Maybe he didn't know these folks were all trouble."

"Doubtful," Marasi said. "And even if it were true, it wouldn't matter. Once the broadsheets get ahold of this . . . The governor's sibling, dead in a house full of known criminals under very suspicious circumstances?"

"What I'm hearing," Wayne said, taking another swig, "is that I was wrong. The fun *isn't* over."

"Many of these people shot one another," Waxillium said.

They all turned to him. He knelt beside another body, inspecting the way it had fallen, then looked up toward some bullet holes in the wall.

Being a lawman, particularly out in the Roughs, had required Waxillium to teach himself a wide variety of skills. He was part detective, part enforcer, part leader, part scientist. Marasi had read a dozen different profiles of him by various scholars, all investigating the mindset of a man who was becoming a living legend.

"What do you mean, Lord Ladrian?" Aradel asked.

"The fight here involved multiple parties," Waxillium said, pointing. "If this was an unexpected hit by someone external—and Lady Colms is right, that would have made the most sense—one would expect the victims to have died from a barrage fired by the enemy who burst in. The corpses don't tell that story. This was a melee. Chaos. Random people firing one at another. I think it began when someone started shooting from the *middle* of the group outward."

"So it *was* one of the attendees who began it," Aradel said.

"Maybe," Waxillium said. "One can only tell so much from the fall of the bodies, the sprays of blood. But something is odd here, very odd. . . . Were they all shot?"

"No, strangely. A few of the attendees were killed by a knife in the back."

"Have you identified everyone in the room?" Waxillium asked.

"Most of them," Aradel said. "We wanted to avoid moving them too much."

"Let me see Lord Winsting," Waxillium said, standing, his mistcoat rustling.

Aradel nodded to a young constable, and she led them out of the ballroom, through a doorway. Some kind of secret passage? The musty stairwell beyond was narrow enough to force them to walk single file, the constable at the front carrying a lamp.

"Miss Colms," Waxillium said softly, "what do your statistics tell you about this kind of violence?"

Oh, so we're using last names now, are we? "Very little. I can count on the fingers of one hand the number of times something like this has happened. The first place I'd look is for connections between the people killed. Were they all in smuggling, Captain Aradel?"

"No," he said from behind. "Some smugglers, some extortionists, some gambling tycoons."

"So it's not a specific attempt to consolidate power in a certain type of criminal activity," Marasi said, her voice echoing in the damp stone stairwell. "We need to find the connection, what made these specific people targets. The one most likely behind it is dead."

"Lord Winsting," Waxillium said. "You're saying he lured them here, planned an execution, and it went wrong?"

"It's one theory."

"He ain't that kind of slime," Wayne said from near the end of the line.

"You know of Winsting?" Marasi asked, looking over her shoulder.

"Not specifically, no," Wayne said. "But he was a

politician. Politician slime is different from regular slime."

"I find myself agreeing," Captain Aradel said. "Though I wouldn't put it so colorfully. We knew that Winsting was crooked, but in the past he kept mostly to small-time schemes. Selling cargo space to smugglers when it suited him, some shady real-estate deals here and there. Cash in exchange for political favors, mostly.

"Recently, rumors started that he was going to put his Senate vote up for sale. We were investigating, with no evidence so far. Either way, killing those willing to pay him would be like blasting your silver mine with dynamite to try finding gold."

They reached the bottom of the stairwell, where they found four more corpses. The guards, apparently, all killed with bullets to the head.

Waxillium knelt. "Shot from behind, from the direction of the saferoom," he whispered. "All four, in rapid succession."

"Executed?" Marasi asked. "How did the killer get them to stand there and take it?"

"He didn't," Waxillium said. "He moved too quickly for them to respond."

"Feruchemist," Wayne said softly. "Damn."

They were called Steelrunners, Feruchemists who could store up speed. They'd have to move slowly for a time, then could draw upon that reserve later. Waxillium looked up. Marasi saw something in his eyes, a hunger. He thought his uncle was involved. That was what he thought *every* time a Metalborn committed crimes. Waxillium saw Suit's shadow over his shoulder each way he turned, the specter of a man whom Waxillium hadn't been able to stop.

Suit still had Waxillium's sister, best as they could

tell. Marasi didn't know much of it. Waxillium wouldn't talk about the details.

He stood up, expression grim, and strode to the door behind the fallen men. He threw it open and entered, Marasi and Wayne close behind, to find a single corpse slumped in an easy chair at the center of the room. His throat had been slit; the blood on the front of his clothing was thick, dried like paint.

"Killed with some sort of long knife or small sword," Aradel said. "Even more strange, his *tongue* was cut out. We've sent for a surgeon to try to tell us more of the wound. Don't know why the killer didn't use a gun."

"Because the guards were still alive then," Waxillium said softly.

"What?"

"They let the killer pass," Waxillium said, looking at the door. "It was someone they trusted, perhaps one of their number. They let the murderer into the saferoom."

"Maybe he was just moving very quickly to get past them," Marasi said.

"Maybe," Waxillium agreed. "But that door has to be unlocked from the inside, and it hasn't been forced. There's a peephole. Winsting let the murderer in, and he wouldn't have done that if the guards had been killed. He's sitting calmly in that chair—no struggle, just a quick slice from behind. Either he didn't know someone else was in here, or he trusted them. Judging by the way the guards fell outside, they were still focused on the steps, waiting for danger to come. They were still guarding this place. My gut says it was one of their own, someone they let pass, who killed Winsting."

"Rusts," Aradel said softly. "But . . . a Feruchemist? Are you sure?"

"Yeah," Wayne said, from the doorway. "This wasn't

a speed bubble. Can't shoot out of one of those, mate. These fellows were killed before *one* could turn about. Wax is right. Either this is a Feruchemist, or somebody figured out how to fire out of speed bubbles—which is somethin' we'd *really* like to know how to do."

"Someone moving with Feruchemical speed explains the knife deaths up above," Waxillium said, standing. "A few swift executions in the chaos, while everyone else was shooting. Quick and surgical, but the killer would be safe despite the firefight. Captain Aradel, I suggest you gather the names of Winsting's companions and staff. See if any corpses that should be here, aren't. I'll look into the Metalborn side—Steelrunners aren't common, even as Feruchemists go."

"And the press?" Marasi asked.

Waxillium looked to Aradel, who shrugged. "I can't keep a lid on this, Lord Ladrian," Aradel said. "Not with so many people involved. It's going to get out."

"Let it," Waxillium said with a sigh. "But I can't help feeling that's the point of all this."

"Excuse me?" Wayne said. "I thought the point was killing folks."

"Lots of folks, Wayne," Waxillium said. "A shift in power in the city. Were those upstairs the main target? Or was this an attack on the governor himself, a sideways strike upon his house, a message of some sort? Sent to tell Governor Innate that even he is not beyond their reach. . . ." He tipped Winsting's head back, looking at the gouged-out mouth. Marasi looked away.

"They removed the tongue," Waxillium whispered. "Why? What are you up to, Uncle?"

"Excuse me?" Aradel asked.

"Nothing," Waxillium said, dropping the head back to its slumped position. "I have to go sit for a portrait.

I assume you'll be willing to send me a report once you've detailed all of this?"

"I can do that," Aradel said.

"Good," Waxillium said, walking toward the door. "Oh, and Captain?"

"Yes, Lord Ladrian?"

"Prepare for a storm. This wasn't done quietly; it was done to be noticed. This was a challenge. Whoever did this isn't likely to stop here."

PART TWO

5

Wayne tugged on his lucky hat. It was a coach-man's hat—something like a wide-brimmed bowler, only one that didn't have three ounces of fancy shoved up its backside. He nodded to himself in his mirror, then wiped his nose. Sniffles. He'd started storing up health the day before, just after finding all those corpses.

He already had a nice cushion of healing he could draw upon, tucked away in his metalmind bracers. He hadn't needed much lately, and always spent days when he had a hangover as sickly as he could manage, since he was going to have an awful time of it anyway. But the way things smelled, with all those important folk dead, warned him. He'd soon need some healing. Best to expand that cushion as he could.

He went light at it today, though. Because it was today, a day when he was going to need some luck. He was tempted to call it the worst day of his life, but that would certainly be an exaggeration. The worst day of his life would be the one when he died.

Might die today though, he thought, looping on his belt and slipping his dueling canes into their straps, then wiping his nose again. *Can't be certain yet.* Every man had to die. He'd always found it odd that so many died when they were old, as logic said that was the point in their lives when they'd had the most practice not dying.

He wandered out of his room in Wax's mansion, idly noticing the scent of morning bread coming from the kitchens. He appreciated the room, though he really only stayed because of the free food. Well, that and because of Wax. The man needed company to keep him from going more strange.

Wayne wandered down a carpeted corridor that smelled of polished wood and servants who had too much time. The mansion was nice, but really, a man shouldn't live in a place that was so big; it just reminded him how small he was. Give Wayne nice, cramped quarters, and he'd be happier. That way he'd feel like a king, with so much *stuff* it crowded him.

He hesitated outside the door to Wax's study. What was that sitting on the stand beside the doorway? A new candelabra, pure gold, with a white lace doily underneath. *Exactly* what Wayne needed.

He fished in his pocket. Rich people didn't make sense at all. That candelabra was probably worth a fortune, and Wax just left it lying around. Wayne fished in his other pocket, looking for something good to trade, and came out with a pocket watch.

Ah, that, he thought, shaking it and hearing the pieces rattle inside. *How long since this thing actually told time?* He picked up the candelabra, pocketed the doily underneath, then put the candelabra back in place with the pocket watch hanging from it. Seemed like a fair trade.

Been needing a new handkerchief, he thought, blowing his nose into it, then pushed open the door and wandered in.

Wax stood before an easel, looking at the large artist's sketch pad he had filled with intricate plans. "Up all night, were you?" Wayne asked with a yawn. "Rusts, man, you make it hard to loaf about properly."

"I don't see what my insomnia has to do with your laziness, Wayne."

"Makes me look bad, 'sall," Wayne said, looking over Wax's shoulder. "Proper loafing requires company. One man lying about is being idle; two men lying about is a *lunch break*."

Wax shook his head, walking over to look at some broadsheets. Wayne leaned in, inspecting Wax's paper. It held long lists of ideas, some connected by arrows, with a sketch of the way the bodies had fallen in both the ballroom and the saferoom.

"What's all this, then?" Wayne asked, picking up a pencil and drawing a little stick figure with a gun shooting at all the dead bodies. His hand trembled as he drew the stick gun, but otherwise it was a right good stick figure.

"Proof to me that a Steelrunner is involved," Wax said. "Look at the pattern of deaths in the ballroom. Four of the most powerful people in the room were killed with the same gun, and they were the only ones up there killed by that weapon—but it's the same one that killed the guards outside the saferoom. I'd bet those four above were shot first, dead in an eyeblink, so fast that it sounded like a single long shot. Thing is, judging by the wounds, each shot came from a different location."

Wayne didn't know a lot about guns, seeing as how he couldn't try to use one without his arm doing an impersonation of a carriage on a bumpy road, but Wax was probably right. Wayne moved down to start sketching some stick figures of topless women in the center of the picture, but Wax stepped over and plucked the pencil from his fingers.

"What's that?" Wayne asked, tapping the center of the sketch pad, where Wax had drawn a bunch of straight lines.

"The pattern the killer used baffles me," Wax said. "The four people in the party he shot, they all fell while in random conversations—look how they were lying. Everyone else who died was part of the larger shoot-out, but these four, they died while the party was still going on. But why did he shoot them from different directions? See, best I can guess, he fired first here, killing Lady Lentin. Her dropped drink was stomped on many times over the next few minutes. But then the killer used his speed to move quickly over here and fire in another direction. Then he moved again, and again. Why four shots from different places?"

"Who was standing where he shot?"

"The people he killed, obviously."

"No, I mean, who was standing near him when he fired his gun. Not who did he shoot, but who was he near when he shot?"

"Ahh . . ." Wax said.

"Yep. Looks to me like he was trying to set them all off," Wayne said, sniffling. "Get everyone in the room shootin' at each other. See? It's like how, to start a bar fight, you throw a bottle at some fellow and then turn to the person next to you and cry out, 'Hey, why'd you throw that bottle at that nice fellow? Rusts, he looks big. And now he's comin' for you, and—' "

"I understand the concept," Wax said dryly. He tapped the drawing pad. "You might have something."

"It's not catching."

Wax smiled, writing some notes on the side of the pad. "So the killer wanted to sow chaos. . . . He started a firefight by bouncing around the room, making it look like various parties were attacking one another. They would already have been tense, suspicious of one another. . . ."

"Yup. I'm a genius."

"You just recognized this because the killer was making others do his work for him, which is an expertise of yours."

"As I said. Genius. So how are you going to find him?"

"Well, I was thinking of sending you to the Village to—"

"Not today," Wayne said.

Wax turned to him, raising his eyebrows.

"It's the first of the month," Wayne said.

"Ah. I had forgotten. You don't need to go *every* month."

"I do."

Wax studied him, as if waiting for a further comment or wisecrack. Wayne said nothing. This was actually serious. Slowly, Wax nodded. "I see. Then why haven't you left yet?"

"Well, you know," Wayne said. "It's like I often say . . ."

"Greet every morning with a smile. That way it won't know what you're planning to do to it?"

"No, not that one."

"Until you know it ain't true, treat every woman like

she has an older brother what is stronger than you are?"

"No, not . . . Wait, I said that?"

"Yes," Wax said, turning back to his notes. "It was a very chivalrous moment for you."

"Rusts. I should really write these things down."

"I believe that is another thing you often say." Wax made a notation. "Unfortunately, you'd first have to learn how to write."

"Now, that's unfair," Wayne said, walking over to Wax's desk and poking around in its drawers. "I can write—I know four whole letters, and one's not even in my name!"

Wax smiled. "Are you going to tell me what you always say?"

Wayne found a bottle in the bottom drawer and lifted it up, dropping in the lace he'd taken from outside as a replacement. "If you're going to have to do something awful, stop by Wax's room and trade for some of his rum first."

"I don't believe you've ever said that."

"I just did." Wayne took a gulp of the rum.

"I . . ." Wax frowned. "I have no response to that." He sighed, setting down his pencil. "However, since you're going to be indisposed, then I suppose *I* will have to go visit the Village."

"Sorry. I know you hate that place."

"I will survive," Wax said, grimacing.

"Wanna piece of advice?"

"From you? Probably not. But please feel free."

"You should stop by Wax's room before you go," Wayne said, trailing out toward the door, "and pinch some of his rum."

"The rum you just pocketed?"

Wayne hesitated, then took the rum out of his pocket. "Ah, mate. Sorry. Tough for you." He shook his head. Poor fellow. He pulled the door closed behind him, took a pull on the rum, and continued on his way down the stairs and out of the mansion.

Marasi tugged at the collar of her jacket, glad for the seaborne wind that blew across her. It could get warm in her uniform—a proper one today, with a buttoned white blouse and brown skirt to match the brown coat.

Next to her, the newsman wasn't so thankful for the wind. He cursed, throwing a heavy chunk of iron—it looked like a piece of an old axle—onto his stack of broadsheets. On the street, the traffic slowed in a moment of congestion. Motorcar drivers and coachmen yelled at one another.

"Ruin break that Tim Vashin," the newsman grumbled, looking at the traffic. "And his machines."

"It's hardly his fault," Marasi said, digging in her pocketbook.

"It is," the newsman said. "Motors were fine, nothing wrong with them for driving in the country or on a summer afternoon. But they're cheap enough now, everyone has to have one of the rusting things! A man can't take his horse two blocks without being run down half a dozen times."

Marasi exchanged coins for a broadsheet. The yelling subsided as the traffic clot loosened, horses and machines once again flowing across the cobbles. She raised the broadsheet, scanning above the fold for stories.

"Say," the newsman said. "Weren't you just here?"

"I needed the afternoon edition," Marasi said absently, walking away.

"Cry of Outrage in the Streets!" the headline read.

A cry like that of twisting metal sounds through Elendel as people take to the streets, outraged by government corruption. One week after the governor's veto of bill 775, the so-called workers'-rights manifesto, his brother Winsting Innate has been found dead after an apparent dealing with known criminals.

Winsting was killed in his mansion, perhaps a casualty of constable action against these criminal elements. Among the fallen is the notorious Dowser Maline, long suspected of running ore-smuggling operations into the city, undercutting the work of honest men. The constables admit no culpability for the deaths, but suspicions about the mysterious circumstances have led to a general outcry.

Marasi reached into her handbag and took out the morning edition of the same paper. "Mystery at Lord Winsting's Mansion!" the headline read.

Constables have disclosed that Lord Winsting, brother of the governor, was found dead in his mansion home last night. Little is known of the mysterious circumstances of the death, though several members of high society are rumored to have been present.

Every other story in the paper was the same in both editions, save for one report on the floods in the east, which had an extra line updating casualty estimates.

The Winsting story had nudged two others off the page, in part because of the size of its headline. The *Elendel Daily* was hardly the most reputable news source in the Basin, but it did know its market. News stories that people agreed with, or were scared by, sold the most copies.

Marasi hesitated on the steps of the Fourth Octant Precinct of the Constabulary. People flowed on the sidewalks, bustling, anxious, heads down. Others loitered nearby, men in the dark jackets of teamsters, hands shoved in pockets, eyes shaded by peaked hats.

Out of work, Marasi thought. *Too many idle men out of work.* Motorcars and electric lights were changing life in Elendel so quickly it seemed that the common man had no hope of keeping up. Men whose families had worked for three generations in the same job suddenly found themselves unemployed. And with the labor disputes at the steel mills . . .

The governor had recently given political speeches to these men, making promises. More coach lines to compete with rail lines, going places the railroad could not. Higher tariffs on imports from Bilming. Empty promises, mostly, but men losing hope clung to such promises. Winsting's death could dash those promises. How would people react if they began to wonder if the governor, Replar Innate, was as corrupt as his brother?

A fire is kindling in the city, Marasi thought. She could almost feel the heat coming off the page of the broadsheet in her hands.

She turned and entered the constabulary offices, worrying that Lord Winsting might actually do more harm to Elendel dead than he had alive—which was saying something.

Wax climbed out of the carriage, nodding to his coachman and indicating that the man should continue on
home rather than wait for his master.

Wax pulled on his aluminum-lined hat—broad-
brimmed, Roughs style, matching his duster, though he
wore a fine shirt and cravat underneath. The hat and
mistcoat made him stand out like a man who had
brought a shotgun to a knife fight. Workers passed in
suspenders and caps, bankers in vests and monocles,
constables in helms or bowlers and militaristic coats.

No Roughs hats. Maybe Wayne was right about
that; he never would shut up about the importance of
a hat. Wax took a deep breath, then stepped into the
Village.

It had probably once been just an ordinary city street.
A wide one, but still just a street. That was before the
trees. They sprouted here, pushing cobblestones aside,
creating a dense canopy that ran the length of the thoroughfare.

It was a place that felt like it shouldn't be. No mere
park—this was a forest, uncultivated and unmanicured,
fresh and primal. You couldn't bring a carriage or motor into the Village; even without the trees, the ground
would be too rough now, rolling and uneven. The
buildings along the street had been engulfed and become the property of the Village. He couldn't help
wondering if this was what all of Elendel would be like
without the hand of men. Harmony had made the Basin ferociously fecund; men didn't farm here so much
as fight to harvest quickly enough.

Wax strode forward, arrayed as if for battle. Vindication and his Sterrion at his hips, short-barreled shot-

gun in its holster on his thigh, metal burning inside of him. He pulled the brim of his hat low, and entered another world.

Children wearing simple white smocks played among the trees. Older youths wore the tinningdar, the Terris robe marked with a V pattern running down the front. These looked up from the steps of buildings to watch him pass. The air smelled *soft* here. Soft air. A stupid metaphor, and yet there it was. That smell reminded him of his mother.

Whispers rose around Wax like spring shoots. He kept his eyes forward, trudging across the too-springy ground. There were no gates into or out of the Village, yet you couldn't enter or leave without being identified. Indeed, moments after his entry, a young woman with streaming golden hair was sent running ahead of him to bear news of his arrival.

They've found peace for themselves here, Wax thought. *They've made peace for themselves. You shouldn't resent them so.*

After a short walk, he emerged from a stand of trees to find three Terrismen waiting for him, arms folded, all wearing the robes of Brutes, Feruchemists who could increase their strength. Their features were varied enough that one wouldn't have pegged them as relatives. Two had the height that was often the Terris heritage, and one had skin that was darker—some of the Originators from ancient Terris had been dark of skin; Wax's own tan probably came from that lineage. None of the men here had the elongated features seen in the ancient paintings. That was a thing of mythology.

"What is it you need, outsider?" one of the men said.

"I want to speak with the Synod," Wax said.

"Are you a constable?" the man said, looking Wax up and down. Children peeked out from behind nearby trees, watching him.

"Of a sort," Wax said.

"The Terris police themselves," another of the men said. "We have an arrangement."

"I'm aware of the compact," Wax said. "I just need to speak to the Synod, or at least Elder Vwafendal."

"You shouldn't be here, lawman," the lead Terrisman said. "I—"

"It's all right, Razal," a tired voice said from the shadows of a nearby tree.

The three Terrismen turned, then quickly bowed as an old Terriswoman approached. Stately and white-haired, she had darker skin than Wax, and walked with a cane she didn't need. The woman, Vwafendal, studied Wax. He found himself sweating.

Razal, still bowing, spoke with a stubborn tone. "We tried to send him away, Elder."

"He has a right to be here," Vwafendal said. "He has as much Terris blood as you do; more than most."

The Terrisman Brute started, then rose from his bow, peering again at Wax. "You don't mean . . ."

"Yes," Vwafendal said, looking very tired. "This is he. My grandson."

Wayne tipped the rum bottle up and teased the last few drops out into his mouth. Then he tucked the bottle into his coat pocket. It was a good bottle. He should be able to trade it for something.

He hopped off the canal boat, giving a wave to Red, the boatman. Nice chap. He would let Wayne bum rides in exchange for a story. Wayne spat a coin out of his mouth—he'd been keeping it in his cheek—and flipped it to Red.

Red caught the coin. "Why is this wet? Were you sucking on it?"

"Allomancers can't Push on my coin if it's in my mouth!" Wayne called.

"You're drunk, Wayne!" Red said with a laugh, shoving off from the dock with his pole.

"Not nearly drunk enough," Wayne called back. "That cheapskate Wax didn't even have the decency to stock a full bottle!"

Red turned the canal boat, poling it out into the waters, wind rippling his cloak. Wayne walked away from the post marking the canal-side mooring, and was faced with the most intimidating sight a fellow could see. The Elendel University.

It was time for Wayne's three tests.

He reached for the rum, then remembered—a little foggily—that he'd finished it all. "Rust and Ruin," he muttered. Perhaps he shouldn't have downed the whole thing. Then again, it made his sniffles easy to ignore. When he was properly smashed, he could take a punch or two to the face and not even feel it. There was a kind of invincibility to that. A stupid kind, but Wayne wasn't a picky man.

He made his way up to the university gates, hands stuffed in his coat pockets. The etched letters over the top proclaimed, in High Imperial, WASING THE ALWAYS OF WANTING OF KNOWING. Deep words. He'd heard them interpreted as, "The eternal desire of a hungry soul is knowledge." When Wayne's soul was hungry he settled for scones, but this place was full of smart kids, and they were a strange sort.

Two men in black coats leaned casually against the

gates. Wayne hesitated. So they were watching for him out front this time, were they? The first of his three trials was upon him. Rusting wonderful.

Well, after the nature of any great hero from the stories, he was going to do his best to avoid this particular trial. Wayne ducked to the side before the two men could spot him, then followed the wall. The university was surrounded by the thing, like it was some kind of bunker. Were they afraid all their knowledge would leak out, like water from a swimmer's ears?

Wayne craned his neck, looking for a way in. They'd bricked up the broken part he'd used last time. And the tree he'd climbed that other time had been cut down. Drat on them for that. He decided to follow another great tradition of heroes facing trials. He went looking for a way to cheat.

He found Dims on a nearby corner. The young man wore a bowler hat and a bow tie, but a shirt that had the sleeves ripped off. He was head of one of the more important street gangs in the area, but never stabbed people too badly when he mugged them and was polite with the people he extorted. He was practically a model citizen.

"Hello, Dims," Wayne said.

Dims eyed him. "You a conner today, Wayne?"

"Nope."

"Ah, good," Dims said, settling down on the steps. He took something out of his pocket—a little metal container.

"Here now," Wayne said, wiping his nose. "What's that?"

"Gum."

"Gum?"

"Yeah, you chew it." Dims offered him a piece of the

stuff. It was rolled into a ball, soft to the touch and powdered on the outside.

Wayne eyed the lad, but decided to try it. He chewed for a moment.

"Good flavor," he said, then swallowed.

Dims laughed. "You don't *swallow* it, Wayne. You just chew!"

"What's the funna that?"

"It just feels good." He tossed Wayne another ball.

Wayne popped it into his mouth. "How are things," Wayne said, "with you and the Cobblers?"

The Cobblers were the rival gang in the area. Dims and his fellows went about with their sleeves torn. The Cobblers wore no shoes. It apparently made perfect sense to youths of the street, many of whom were the children of the houseless. Wayne liked to keep an eye on them. They were good lads. He'd been like them once.

Then life had steered him wrong. Boys like this, they could use someone to point them in the right direction.

"Oh, you know," Dims said. "Some back, some forth."

"There won't be trouble now, will there?" Wayne asked.

"I thought you said you wasn't no conner today!"

"I ain't," Wayne said, slipping—by instinct—into a dialect more like that of Dims. "I'm askin' as a friend, Dims."

Dims scowled, looking away, but his muttered response was genuine. "We ain't stupid, Wayne. We'll keep our heads. You know we will."

"Good."

Dims glanced back at him as Wayne settled down. "You bring that money you owe me?"

"I owe you money?" Wayne asked.

"From cards?" Dims said. "Two weeks back? Rusts, Wayne, are you drunk? It ain't even noon yet!"

"I ain't drunk," Wayne said, sniffling. "I'm investigatin' alternative states of sobriety. How much do I owe you?"

Dims paused. "Twenty."

"Now see," Wayne said, digging in his pocket, "I distinctly remember borrowin' five off you." He held up a note. It was a fifty.

Dims raised an eyebrow. "You want something from me, I'm guessing?"

"I need into the university."

"The gates are open," Dims said.

"Can't go through the front. They know me."

Dims nodded. That sort of thing was a common complaint in his world. "What do you need from me?"

A short time later, a man wearing Wayne's hat, coat, and dueling canes tried to pass through the front of the university. He saw the two men in black, then bolted as they chased after him.

Wayne adjusted his spectacles, watching them go. He shook his head. Ruffians, trying to get into the university! Scandalous. He walked in through the gates, wearing a bow tie and carrying a load of books. Another of those men—who stood in a more hidden spot, watching his companions chase Dims—barely gave Wayne a glance.

Spectacles. They were kind of like a hat for smart people. Wayne ditched the books inside the square, then walked past a fountain with a statue of a lady who wasn't properly clothed—he idled only a short time— and made his way toward Pashadon Hall, the girls' dormitory. The building looked an awful lot like a prison: three stories of small windows, stonework architecture, and iron grates that seemed to say "Stay away, boys, if you value your nether parts."

He pushed his way in the front doors, where he prepared himself for the second of his three tests: the Tyrant of Pashadon. She sat at her desk, a woman built like an ox with a face to match. Her hair even curled like horns. She was a fixture of the university, or so Wayne had been told. Perhaps she had come with the chandeliers and sofas.

She looked up from her desk in the entryway, then threw herself to her feet in challenge. "You!"

"Hello," Wayne said.

"How did you get past campus security!"

"I tossed them a ball," Wayne said, tucking the spectacles into his pocket. "Most hounds love having somethin' to chase."

The tyrant rumbled around the side of her desk. It was like watching an ocean liner try to navigate city canals. She wore a tiny hat, in an attempt at fashion. She liked to consider herself a part of Elendel upper society, and she kind of was. In the same way that the blocks of granite that made up the steps to the governor's mansion were a part of civic government.

"You," she said, spearing Wayne in the chest with a finger. "I thought I told you not to come back."

"I thought I ignored you."

"Are you drunk?" She sniffed at his breath.

"No," Wayne said. "If I were drunk, you wouldn't look nearly so ugly."

She huffed, turning away. "I can't believe your audacity."

"Really? Because I'm sure I've been this audacious before. Every month, in fact. So this seems a right believable thing for me to do."

"I'm not letting you in. Not this time. You are a scoundrel."

Wayne sighed. Heroes in stories never had to fight the same beast twice. Seemed unfair he had to face this one each month. "Look, I just want to check in on her."

"She is fine."

"I have money," Wayne said. "To give her."

"You can leave it here. You distress the girl, miscreant."

Wayne stepped forward, taking the tyrant by the shoulder. "I didn't want to have to do this."

She looked at him. And, to his surprise, she cracked her knuckles. *Wow.* He reached into his pocket quickly and pulled out a piece of pasteboard.

"One ticket," Wayne said quickly, "admitting two people to the governor's spring dinner and policy speech, occurring during a party at Lady ZoBell's penthouse tonight. This here ticket lists no specific names. Anyone who has it can get in."

Her eyes widened. "Who'd you steal that from?"

"Please," Wayne said. "It came delivered to my house."

Which was perfectly true. It was for Wax and Steris. But they were important enough folk that invitations sent to them had no names, so they could send an emissary if they wished. When it came to someone fancy like Wax, even getting their relative or friend to attend your party could be advantageous.

The tyrant didn't count as either. But Wayne figured that Wax would be happy to not have to go to the blasted party anyway. Besides, Wayne had left a real nice-looking leaf he'd found in exchange. Rusting beautiful, that leaf was.

The tyrant hesitated, so Wayne waved the ticket in front of her.

"I guess . . ." she said. "I could let you in one last time. I'm not supposed to allow unrelated men into the visiting room, however."

"I'm practically family," he said. They made a big fuss about keeping the young women and young men separated around here, which Wayne found odd. With all of these smart people around, wouldn't one of them have realized what boys and girls was supposed to do together?

The tyrant let him pass into the visiting room, then sent one of the girls at the desk to run for Allriandre. Wayne sat down, but couldn't keep his feet from tapping. He'd been stripped of weapons, bribes, and even his own hat. He was practically naked, but he'd made it to the final test.

Allriandre entered a few moments later. She'd brought backup with her in the form of two other young ladies about her age—just shy of twenty. *Smart girl,* Wayne thought, proud. He rose.

"Madam Penfor says you're drunk," Allriandre said, remaining in the doorway.

Wayne tapped his metalmind, drawing forth healing. In a moment, his body burned away its impurities and healed its wounds. It thought alcohol was a poison, which showed that a fellow couldn't always trust his own body, but today he didn't complain. It also washed away his sniffles for the moment, though those would return. It was hard to heal from diseases with a metalmind for some reason.

Either way, sobriety hit him like a brick to the chin. He inhaled deeply, feeling even more naked than before. "I just like to play with her," Wayne said, all hint of slur gone from his voice, eyes focused.

Allriandre studied him intently, then nodded. She did not enter the room.

"I brought this month's money," Wayne said, taking an envelope out and setting it on the low, glass-topped table beside him. He stood up straight, then shuffled from one foot to the other.

"Is that really him?" one of the girls asked Allriandre. "They say he rides with Dawnshot. Of the Roughs."

"It's him," Allriandre said, eyes still on Wayne. "I don't want your money."

"Your mama told me to bring it to you," Wayne said.

"You don't need to bring it in person."

"I do," Wayne said quietly.

They stood in silence, neither party moving. Wayne finally cleared his throat. "How're your studies? Are you treated well here? Is there anythin' you need?"

Allriandre reached into her handbag and took out a large locket. She spread it open, displaying a strikingly distinct evanotype of a man with a wide mustache and a twinkle in his eyes. He had a long, friendly face, and his hair was thinning on top. Her father.

She made Wayne look at it every time.

"Tell me what you did," she said. That voice. It could have been the voice of winter itself.

"I don't—"

"*Tell me.*"

The third trial.

"I killed your daddy," Wayne said softly, looking at the picture. "I mugged him in an alley for his pocketbook. I shot a better man than me, and because of that, I don't deserve to be alive."

"You know you aren't forgiven."

"I know."

"You will never be forgiven."

"I know."

"Then I'll take your blood money," Allriandre said. "If you care to know, my studies go well. I am thinking of taking up the law."

Someday, he hoped he might be able to look into the girl's eyes and see emotion. Hatred, maybe. Something other than that emptiness.

"Get out."

Wayne ducked his head and left.

There should not have been a thatched log hut in the middle of Elendel, and yet here it was. Wax stooped to enter, seeming to step backward in time hundreds of years. The air inside smelled of old leather and furs.

The enormous firepit in the middle would never be needed in Elendel's mild weather. Today, a smaller fire had been constructed at its very center, and over it simmered a small kettle of hot water for tea. However, charred stones indicated that the entire firepit was sometimes used. It, the furs, the ancient-style paintings on the wall—of winds, and frozen rain, and tiny figures painted with simple strokes on slopes—were all fragments of a myth.

Old Terris. A legendary land of snow and ice, with white-furred beasts and spirits that haunted frozen storms. During the early days following the Catacendre, refugees from Terris had written down memories of their homeland, as no Keepers had remained.

Wax settled down beside his grandmother's firepit. Some said that Old Terris waited for this people, hidden somewhere in this new world of Harmony's design. To the faithful, it might as well have been paradise; a frozen, hostile paradise. Living in a land naturally lush with bounteous fruit, where little cultivation was required, could warp one's vision.

Grandmother V settled down opposite him, but did not start the fire. "Did you remove your guns before entering the Village this time?"

"I did not."

She snorted. "So insolent. During your long absence, I often wondered if the Roughs might temper you."

"They made me more stubborn, is all."

"A land of heat and death," Grandmother V said. She crinkled a handful of herbs, flakes dropping into a tea strainer above her cup. She poured steaming water over them, then placed the lid with a gnarled hand. "Everything about you stinks of death, Asinthew."

"That isn't what my father named me."

"Your father didn't have the right. I would demand you remove the weapons, but it would be meaningless. You could kill with a coin, or with a button, or with this pot."

"Allomancy is not so evil as you make it out to be, Grandmother."

"Neither power is evil," she said. "It is mixing those powers that is dangerous. Your nature is not your fault, but I cannot help but see it as a sign. Another tyrant in our future, too powerful. It leads to death."

Sitting in this hut . . . the scent of Grandmother's tea . . . Memories grabbed Wax by his collar and shoved him face-first up against his past. A young man who had never been able to decide what he was. Allomancer or Feruchemist, city lord or humble Terrisman? His father and uncle pushing him one way, his grandmother another.

"A Feruchemist slaughtered people in the Fourth Octant last night, Grandmother," Wax said. "He was a Steelrunner. I know you track everyone in the city with Feruchemical blood. I need a list of names."

Grandmother V swished around her tea. "You've visited the Village on . . . what, a mere three occasions since your return to the city? Nearly two years, and you've made time for your grandmother only twice before today."

"Can you blame me, considering how these meetings usually go? To be blunt, Grandmother, I know how you feel about me. So why torture either of us?"

"You cling to your images of me from two decades ago, child. People change. Even one such as I." She sipped her tea, then added more herbs to the strainer and lowered it back into the water. She would not drink until it was right. "Not one such as you, it appears."

"Trying to bait me, Grandmother?"

"No. I am better at insults than that. You haven't changed. You still don't know who you are."

An old argument. She'd said it to him both times they'd met during the last two years. "I am *not* going to start wearing Terris robes, speaking softly, quoting proverbs at people."

"You will shoot them instead."

Wax took a deep breath. A mixture of scents lingered in the air. From the tea? Scents like that of freshly cut grass. His father's estates, sitting on the lawn, listening to his father and grandmother argue.

Wax had lived here in the Village for only a single year. It had been all his father had agreed to give. Even that had been surprising; Uncle Edwarn had wanted Wax and his sister to both stay away from the place. Before his official heir, the late Hinston Ladrian, had been born when Wax was eighteen, Edwarn had basically appropriated his brother's children and tried to raise them. Even still, it was hard to separate Wax's parents' will in his head from that of Edwarn.

One year among these trees. Wax had been forbidden Allomancy during his days in the Village, but had learned something far greater. That criminals existed, even among the idyllic Terris.

"The only times I've truly known who I am," Wax said, looking up at his grandmother, meeting her eyes, "are when I've put on the mistcoat, strapped guns to my waist, and hunted down men gone rabid."

"You should not be defined by what you do, but by what you are."

"A man is what he does."

"You came looking for a Feruchemist killer? You need only look in the mirror, child. If a man is what he does . . . think of what you've done."

"I've never killed a man who didn't deserve it."

"Can you be *absolutely* certain of that?"

"Reasonably. If I've made mistakes, I'll pay for them someday. You won't distract me, Grandmother. To fight is not against the Terris way. Harmony killed."

"He slew beasts and monsters only. Never our own."

Wax breathed out. This again? *Rusts. I should have forced Wayne to come here instead of me. He says she actually likes him.*

A new scent struck him. Crushed blossoms. In the darkness of that chamber, he imagined himself again, standing among the trees of the Terris Village. Looking up at a broken window, and feeling the bullet in his hand.

And he smiled. Once that memory had brought him pain—the pain of isolation. Now he saw only a budding lawman, remembered the sense of *purpose* he'd felt.

Wax stood up, grabbing his hat, mistcoat rustling. He almost wanted to believe that the scents to the room, the memories, were his grandmother's doing. Who knew what she put into that tea?

"I'm going to hunt down a murderer," Wax said. "If I do it without your help, and he kills again before I can stop him, you will be partially to blame. See how well you sleep at night then, Grandmother."

"Will you kill him?" she asked. "Will you shoot for the chest when you could aim for the leg? People die around you. Do not deny it."

"I don't," he said. "A man should never pull a trigger unless he's willing to kill. And if the other fellow is armed, I'm going to aim for the chest. That way, when people do die around me, it's the right ones."

Grandmother V stared at her teapot. "The one you're looking for is named Idashwy. And she is not a man."

"Steelrunner?"

"Yes. She is not a killer."

"But—"

"She is the only Steelrunner I know of who could possibly be involved in something like this. She vanished about a month ago after acting . . . very erratically. Claimed that she was being visited by the spirit of her dead brother."

"Idashwy," he said. It was pronounced in the Terris manner, eye-dash-wee. The syllables felt thick in his mouth, another reminder of his days in the Village. The Terris language had been dead once, but Harmony's records included it, and many Terris now learned to speak it in their youths. "I swear I know that name."

"You did know her, long ago," Grandmother V said. "You were with her that night, actually, before . . ."

Ah yes. Slender, golden hair, shy and didn't speak much. *I didn't know she was a Feruchemist.*

"You don't even have the decency to look ashamed," Grandmother V said.

"I'm not," Wax said. "Hate me if you must, Grandmother, but coming to live with you changed my life, just as you always promised it would. I'm not going to be ashamed that the transformation wasn't the one you expected."

"Just . . . try to bring her back, Asinthew. She's not a killer. She's confused."

"They all are," Wax said, stepping out of the hut. The three men from before stood outside, glaring at him with displeasure. Wax tipped his hat to them, dropped a coin, then launched himself into the air between two trees, passing their canopies and seeking the sky.

Each time Marasi entered the precinct offices, she got a little thrill.

It was the thrill of bucked expectations, of a future denied. Even though this room didn't look like she'd imagined—as the clerical and organizational center for the octant's constables, it felt more like a business office than anything else—the mere fact that she was here excited her.

This wasn't supposed to have been her life. She'd grown up reading stories of the Roughs, of lawmen and villains. She'd dreamed of six-guns and stage-coaches. She'd even taken up horseback riding and rifle shooting. And then, real life had intervened.

She'd been born into privilege. Yes, she was illegitimate, but the generous stipend from her father had set her and her mother up in a fine home. Money for an education had been guaranteed for her. With that kind of promise—and with her mother's determination that Marasi should enter society and prove herself to her father—one did not choose a profession so lowly as that of a constable.

Yet here she was. It was wonderful.

She passed through the room full of people at desks. Though a jail was attached to the building, it had its own entrance, and she rarely visited it. Many of the constables she passed on her way through the main chamber were the type who spent most of their days at a desk. Her own spot was a comfortable nook near Captain Aradel's office. His room felt like a closet inside, and Aradel rarely spent time there. Instead, he stalked through the main chamber like a prowling lion, always in motion.

Marasi set her handbag on her desk next to a stack of last year's crime reports—in her spare time, she was trying to judge to what extent petty crimes in a region foretold greater ones. Better that than reading the politely angry letters from her mother, which lay underneath. She peeked into the captain's office and found his waistcoat thrown across his desk, right beside the pile of expense reports he was supposed to be initialing. She smiled and shook her head, dug his pocket watch out of his waistcoat, then went hunting.

The offices were busy, but they didn't have the bustle of the prosecutor's offices. During her internship there beneath Daius, everyone had always seemed so *frantic*. People worked all hours, and when a new case was posted, every junior solicitor in the room rushed over in a flurry of papers, coats, and skirts, craning to see who had posted the case and how many assistants they would be taking.

The opportunities for prestige, and even wealth, had been bountiful. And yet she hadn't been able to shake the feeling that nobody was actually *doing* anything. Cases that could make a difference languished because they weren't high-profile enough, while anything under the patronage of a prominent lord or lady was seen to immediately. The rush had been less about fixing the city's problems, and more about making certain the senior solicitors saw how much more eager you were than your colleagues.

She'd probably still be there, if she hadn't met Waxillium. She'd have done as her mother wanted, seeking validation through her child. Proof, perhaps, that she *could* have married Lord Harms, if it had been in the cards, despite her low birth. Marasi shook her head. She loved her mother, but the woman simply had too much time on her hands.

The constables' offices were so different from the solicitors'. Here, there was a true sense of purpose, but it was measured, even thoughtful. Constables leaned back in chairs and described evidence to other officers, looking for help on a case. Junior corporals moved through the room, delivering cups of tea, fetching files, or running some other errand. The competition she'd felt among the solicitors barely existed here. Perhaps that was because there was little prestige, and even less wealth, to go around.

She found Aradel with sleeves rolled up, one foot on

a chair, bothering Lieutenant Caberel. "No, no," Aradel said. "I'm telling you, we need more men on the streets. Near the pubs, at nights, where the foundry workers congregate after the strike line breaks up. Don't bother guarding them during the day."

Caberel nodded placidly, though she gave Marasi a roll of the eyes as she walked up. Aradel *did* tend to micromanage, but at least he was earnest. In Marasi's experience, they were almost all fond of him, eyerolls notwithstanding.

She plucked a cup of tea off the plate of a passing corporal, who was delivering them to the desks. He quickly moved on, eyes forward, but she could almost feel him glaring at her. Well, it wasn't *her* fault she'd landed this position, and the rank of lieutenant, without ever having to deliver tea.

All right, she admitted to herself, sipping the tea and stepping up beside Aradel. *Maybe there is a* bit *of competition around here.*

"You'll see this done, then?" Aradel asked.

"Of course, sir," Caberel said. She was one of the few in the place who treated Marasi with any measure of respect. Perhaps it was because they were both women.

There were fewer women in the constabulary than among the solicitors. One might have guessed that the reason for this was that ladies weren't interested in the violence—but having done both jobs, Marasi felt she knew which profession was bloodier. And it wasn't the one where people carried guns.

"Good, good," Aradel said. "I have a debriefing with Captain Reddi in . . ." He patted at his pocket.

Marasi held out his watch, which he grabbed and checked for the time.

". . . fifteen minutes. Huh. More time than I expected. Where'd you get that tea, Colms?"

"Want me to have someone fetch you some?" she asked.

"No, no. I can do it." He bustled off, and Marasi nodded to Caberel, then hurried after him.

"Sir," she said, "have you seen the afternoon broadsheets?"

He held out his hand, which she filled with paper. He held up the stack of broadsheets, and almost ran over three different constables on his way to the stove and the tea. "Bad," he muttered. "I'd hoped they'd spin this against us."

"Us, sir?" Marasi asked, surprised.

"Sure," he said. "Nobleman dead, constables not giving the press details. This reads like they started to pin the death on the constables, but then changed their minds. By the end, the tone is far more outraged against Winsting than us."

"And that's worse than outrage at *us* for a cover-up?"

"Far worse, Lieutenant," he said with a grimace, reaching for a cup. "People are used to hating conners. We're a magnet for it, a lightning rod. Better us than the governor."

"Unless the governor deserves it, sir."

"Dangerous words, Lieutenant," Aradel said, filling his cup with steaming tea from the large urn kept warm atop the coal stove. "And likely inappropriate."

"You know there are rumors that he's corrupt," Marasi said softly.

"What I *know* is that we are civil servants," Aradel said. "There are enough people out there with the mindset and the moral position to monitor the government. *Our* job is to keep the peace."

Marasi frowned, but said nothing. Governor Innate *was* corrupt, she was almost sure of it. There were too many coincidences, too many small oddities in his policy decisions. It wasn't by any means obvious, but trends were Marasi's specialty, and her passion.

It wasn't as if she'd wanted to discover that the leader of Elendel was trading favors with the city's elite, but once she'd spotted the signs, she'd felt compelled to dig in. On her desk, carefully hidden under a stack of ordinary reports, was a ledger in which she'd assembled all the information. Nothing concrete, but the picture it drew was clear to her—even though she understood that it would look innocent to anyone else.

Aradel studied her. "You disagree with my opinion, Lieutenant?"

"One doesn't change the world by avoiding the hard questions, sir."

"Feel free to ask them, then. In your head, Lieutenant, and not out loud—particularly not to people outside the precinct. We can't have the men we work for thinking we are trying to undermine them."

"Funny, sir," Marasi said. "I thought we worked for the people of the city, not their leaders."

Aradel stopped, cup of steaming tea halfway to his lips. "Suppose I deserved that," he said, then took a gulp, shaking his head. He didn't flinch at the heat. People in the office figured he'd seared his taste buds off years ago. "Let's go."

They wove through the room toward Aradel's office, passing Captain Reddi at his desk. The lanky man rose, but Aradel waved him down, pulling out his watch. "I still have . . . five minutes until I have to deal with you, Reddi."

Marasi shot the captain an apologetic smile. She got a scowl in return.

"Someday," she noted, "I'm going to figure out why that man hates me."

"Hmmm?" Aradel said. "Oh, you stole his job."

Marasi missed a step, stumbling into Lieutenant Ahlstrom's desk. "What?" she demanded, hurrying after Aradel. "Sir?"

"Reddi was going to be my assistant," Aradel said as they reached his office. "Had a damn fine bid for the job; I was all but priced into hiring him, until I got your application."

Marasi blushed deeply. "Why would *Reddi* want to be your assistant, sir? He's a field constable, a senior detective."

"Everyone has this idea that in order to move up, you need to spend more time in the office and less on the street," Aradel said. "Stupid tradition, even if the other octants follow it. I don't want my best men and women turning into desk slugs. I want the assistant position to be for nurturing someone fresh who shows promise, rather than letting some practiced constable gather moss."

The realization made a lot of things lock into place for Marasi. The hostility she felt from many of the others wasn't just because she'd skipped the lower ranks—many with noble titles did that. It was because they'd solidified behind Reddi, their friend who'd been slighted.

"So . . ." Marasi said, taking a deep breath and grasping for something to keep her from a panic. "You think I show promise then?"

"Of course I do. Why would I have hired you otherwise?" Corporal Maindew walked by, saluting, and

Aradel threw the wadded broadsheets into his face. "No saluting indoors, Maindew. You'll knock yourself unconscious slapping your forehead every time I walk past." He glanced back at Marasi as Maindew mumbled an apology and rushed off.

"There's something in *you*, Colms," Aradel told her. "Not the gloss and glint of the application. I don't care about your grades, or what those zinctongues in the solicitors' office thought of you. The words you wrote about changing the city, those made sense. They impressed me."

"I . . . Thank you for the praise, sir."

"I'm not flattering you, Colms. It's just a fact." He pointed toward the door. "That broadsheet said the governor was going to address the city later this afternoon. I'll bet the Second Octant constables ask us for help managing the crowds; they always do. So I'm going to send a street detail. Go with them and listen, then report back to me what Governor Innate says, and pay attention to how the crowd reacts."

"Yes, sir," Marasi said, stopping herself from saluting as she snatched her handbag and ran to follow the orders.

THE HOUSE

Market Opening

EBSE stocks +0.5
Commodities -2.1

1st of Doxil, 342
Morning Edition
Copyright 342, Lean Calour & Daughters & Sons

THE JOURNAL OF CIVILIZATIO

"GENTLEMAN JAK IN THE CITY OF FOUNTAINS"

Part Six

"The Sinister Soiree!"

I need not remind my astute readers of the precarious situation in which I was left at the end of last week's column, but for those of you whose heightened tastes have just now led them from the gutters of disgraceful journalism to the noble pages of The House Record, let me present a short recapitulation.

Through the efforts alone of my silver tongue and tin-quick mind, I gained access to Lady Lavont's private party in New Seran wherein she planned to auction the only remaining buttons from the Lord

Mistborn's favorite smoking jacket. Handerwym, my faithful Terrisman steward, had prised the information that the leader of the Cobblesguilders planned to steal the buttons by swapping them with impeccable forgeries at some point during the night.

As Handerwym watched the tin buttons from the hors d'oeuvres table, I rubbed elbows with Lady Lavont, and her inner circle, who found me completely enchanting. That was when the man in the striped white suit pointed a gun at me. *(Continued Below!)*

ELENDEL FEELS E OF CORBEAU FLO

Higher commodities prices to impact marl

As one of the Basin's key grain-producing regions struggles to rebuild following the breaking of the dam near Corbeau, unanswered questions still threaten the comfort of those at the heart of the Basin. The Argien-Ohr Financial Circle, Elendel's largest and most prestigious committee of bankers and other financial leaders, has called an emergency meeting to discuss sending aid to the flood-ravaged area. The biggest question haunting the Circle is if the investment of boxings and resources will be enough to affect the commodities markets, which are just now beginning to founder under the predictions of grain harvests half as large as last year's.

"There are enough supplies in reserve to meet most demands over the next four months," says Lord Chapmot Heviers, a Circle member with strong ties to Corbeau. "But after that, most grain will start going to the highest bidder. If you own bakeries, you will think twice about selling loaves at five clips each when you could be selling whiskey at forty clips a bottle."

GUEST EDITORIAL:

THE NUISANCE OF NEGLIGENT COINSHOTS!

In the last sixteen months I have replaced three lamposts, an iron gate, and two steeple spires, all at my Madion Ways house. My residence in the 6th Octant, much nearer the Hub, has needed twice that

VISITORS from other WORLDS

The Sinister Soiree!

I described my assailant as wearing a striped white suit, but that is not as specific as it may seem. In Elendel, someone dressed as described would stick out like afternoon tea among koloss,

for
Ha
at t
I n
tale
with
it I
fab

The
said
for
up

6

Wax soared through the air above Elendel, hat held by its strings to his neck, mistcoat waving behind him like a banner. Below, the city bustled and moved, people swarming through its roadway arteries. Some glanced at him, but most ignored him. Allomancers were not the rarity here they had been in the Roughs.

All these people, Wax thought, Pushing off a fountain shaped like mists condensing into Harmony with arms upraised, bracers glittering golden on the otherwise green copper statue. Women sat on its stone edge; children played in its waters. Motorcars and horse carriages broke around it, sweeping to the sides and charging down other roads, going about the ever-important business of city life.

So many people—and here, in the Fourth Octant, a frightening percentage of them were his responsibility. To begin with he paid their wages, or oversaw those who did; on the solvency of his house rested the financial stability of thousands upon thousands. But that was only part of it; because through his seat in the Senate, he represented any who worked for him, or who lived on properties he owned.

Two divisions within the Senate. One side, the representatives of the professions, was elected and came and went as people's needs changed. The other side, the seats of the noble houses, was stable and immutable—not subject to the whims of voters. The governor, elected by the seats, presided over them all.

A good enough system, except it meant that Wax was supposed to look after tens of thousands of individuals he could never know. His eye twitched, and he turned, Pushing off some rebar sloppily left sticking from a tenement wall.

Towns were better in the Roughs, where you could know everyone. That way you could care for them, and really *feel* you were doing something. Marasi would argue that statistically, leading his house here was more effective in creating general human happiness, but he wasn't a man of numbers; he was a man who trusted his gut. His gut missed knowing the people he served.

Wax landed on a large water tower near a glass dome covering his octant's largest Church of the Survivor. People were worshipping inside, though a greater number would come at dusk to await the mists. The Church revered the mists, and yet with that glass dome they still separated themselves from it. Wax shook his head, then Pushed off along the nearby canal.

He's probably finished by now, Wax thought. *He'll be on one of the nearby docks, listening to the lapping water. . . .*

He continued along the canal, which was cluttered with boats. Tindwyl Promenade, which ran along this canal, was crowded—even more so than usual. Dense with life. It was difficult not to feel subsumed by the great city, engulfed, overwhelmed, insignificant. Out in the Roughs Wax hadn't just enforced the law; he had interpreted it, revised it when needed. He had *been* the law.

Here he had to dance around egos and secrets.

As Wax searched for the right dock, he was surprised to eventually find the reason for the traffic on the promenade. It was all bunched up, trying to get through a large clot of men with signs. Wax passed overhead, and was shocked to see a small cluster of constables from the local octant amid the picketers—they were being pressed on all sides by the shouting men, waving signs in an uncomfortably violent manner.

Wax dropped through the air and Pushed lightly on the nails in the promenade boards here, slowing his descent. He landed in a crouch in an opening nearby, mistcoat flaring, guns clinking.

The picketers regarded him for a long moment, then broke apart, taking off in different directions. He didn't even have to say a word. In moments the beleaguered constables emerged, like stones on the plain as the soil washed away in a sudden rain.

"Thanks, sir," said their captain, an older woman whose blonde hair poked down straight about an inch on all sides around her constable's hat.

"They're getting violent?" Wax asked, watching the last of the picketers vanish.

"Didn't like us trying to move them off the promenade, Dawnshot," the woman said. She shivered. "Didn't expect it to go so bad, so fast. . . ."

"Can't say I blame them much," one of the other constables said, a fellow with a neck like a long-barreled pistol. His fellows turned to him, and he hunched down. "Look, you can't say you don't have mates among them. You can't say you haven't heard them grumble. Something needs to change in this city. That's all I'm saying."

"They don't have the right to block a main thoroughfare," Wax said, "no matter their grievances. Report back to your precinct, and make sure you bring more men next time."

They nodded, hiking off. The promenade's knot of pedestrians slowly unwound itself, and Wax shook his head, worried. The men running the strikes *did* have a grievance. He'd found some of the same problematic conditions among the few factories he owned—long hours, dangerous environments—and had been forced to fire a few overseers because of it. He'd replaced them with overseers who instead would hire more men, for shorter shifts, as there was no shortage of laborers in the city who were out of work these days. But then he'd needed to up wages, so that the men could live on the shorter-shift income—making his goods more costly. Difficult times. And he didn't have the answers, not to those problems.

He hiked along the promenade a short distance, drawing more than a few stares from people he passed. But he soon found what he'd been looking for. Wayne sat on a narrow dock nearby. He had his shoes and socks off, feet in the water, and was staring off down the canal. "Hello, Wax," he said without looking as Wax stepped up.

"It went poorly?" Wax asked.

"Same as always. It's strange. Most days I don't mind being me. Today I do."

Wax crouched down, resting a hand on the younger man's shoulder.

"Do you ever wonder if you shoulda just shot me?" Wayne asked. "Back when you and Jon first found me?"

"I'm not in the habit of shooting people who can't shoot back," Wax said.

"I coulda been faking."

"No. You couldn't have been."

Wayne had been a youth of sixteen when Wax and Jon Deadfinger—a lawman who had been mentoring Wax—had found him curled up in the crawl space under a house, hands over his ears, cloaked in dirt and whimpers. Wayne had thrown his guns and ammunition down a well. Even as Deadfinger had dragged him out, Wayne had been complaining of the gunfire. Shots only he could hear, echoing from that well. . . .

"Any number of the boys we run across and take down," Wayne said. "Any of them could be like me. Why did I get a second chance, but none of them do?"

"Luck."

Wayne turned to meet his eyes.

"I'd give those lads second chances if I could," Wax said. "Maybe they've had their moments of doubt, regret. But the ones we shoot, we don't find them unarmed, hiding, willing to be brought in. We find them killing. And if I'd found you in the process of armed robbery all those years ago, I'd have shot you too."

"You're not lying, are you?"

"Of course not. I'd have shot you right in the head, Wayne."

"You're a good friend," Wayne said. "Thanks, Wax."

"You're the only person I know that I can cheer up by promising to kill him."

"You didn't promise to kill me," Wayne said, pulling on his socks. "You promised to have killed me. That there be the present perfect tense."

"Your grasp of the language is startling," Wax said, "considering how you so frequently brutalize it."

"Ain't nobody what knows the cow better than the butcher, Wax."

"I suppose . . ." Wax said, standing up. "Have you ever met a woman named Idashwy? A Feruchemist."

"Steelrunner?"

Wax nodded.

"Never met her," Wayne said. "They keep kicking me out of the Village when I visit. Right unneighborly."

So far as Wax knew, that wasn't true. Wayne would occasionally toss on some Terris robes, mimic their accents, then sneak in to live among them for a few days. He'd eventually get into trouble for saying something crude to one of the young women, but he wouldn't get thrown out. He'd baffle them, as he did most people, until he got bored and wandered away.

"Let's see what we can find," Wax said, waving down a canal gondola.

"Five notes, for *one basket* of apples! That's robbery!"

Marasi hesitated on the street. She'd driven the motorcar up to the Hub for the governor's speech, then parked it with the coachmen who took pay to watch and refuel motors, intending to walk the rest of the way on foot. The Hub could be a busy place.

That led her here, near this small street market with people selling fruit. With disbelief, she saw that one vendor was—indeed—selling apples at *five notes* a basket. Those shouldn't cost more than half a boxing per basket, at most. She'd seen them for a handful of clips.

"I could get these at Elend's stand for a fraction of the price!" the customer said.

"Well, why don't you go see if he has any left?" the

cart owner said, nonplussed. The customer stormed off, leaving the cart owner with her sign proudly proclaiming the ridiculous price. Marasi frowned, then glanced down the row of stands, barrels, and carts.

Suspiciously low quantities, all 'round. She walked up to the cart owner with the high prices; the woman stood up stiffly, braids shaking, and shoved her hands into the pockets of her apron. "Officer," she said.

"Five is on the high side, wouldn't you say?" Marasi asked, picking up an apple. "Unless these are infused with atium."

"Am I doing anything wrong?" the woman asked.

"You have the right to set your prices," Marasi said. "One simply wonders what you seem to know that nobody else does."

The woman didn't respond.

"Shipment coming late?" Marasi asked. "Apple harvest gone bad?"

The woman sighed. "Not apples, officer. Grain shipments out of the east. Simply not coming. Floods did them in."

"A little early to be speculating on food prices, don't you think?"

"Pardon, officer, but do you know how much food this city eats? We're one shipment away from starvation, we are."

Marasi glanced down the row again. Food was moving quickly, most of it—from what she could see—being sold to the same group of people. Speculators grabbing up the fruits and sacks of grain. The city wasn't as close to starvation as the cart owner claimed—there were storages that could be released—but bad news moved faster than calm winds. And there was a good chance this woman was right, that she'd be able to sell her apples at a premium until things calmed down in a few days.

Marasi shook her head, setting down the apple and continuing toward the Hub. There was always a press here, people on the promenade, vehicles on the streets trying to force their way into the ring around the Hub. More people today, crowds drawn by the speech causing traffic clots in the regular bustle. Marasi could barely make out the giant statues of the Ascendant Warrior and her husband in the Field of Rebirth peeking out over the throng.

Marasi walked up to join another group of constables who had just arrived, on Aradel's orders, their carriages lagging behind her motorcar. Together they wended their way through the streets on foot toward the executive mansion. The governor preferred to address people from its steps, a few streets up into the Second Octant from the Hub.

They soon reached the large square before the mansion. Moving here was more difficult, but fortunately the constables from this octant were already in attendance—and they had roped off various areas near the front and sides of the square. In one, dignitaries and noblemen sat on bleachers to hear the address. In another, the Second Octant constables clustered and watched the crowd for pickpockets from the steps up into the National Archives. Other constables moved through the crowd, officers readily identifiable by the blue plumes on their hats.

Marasi and Lieutenant Javies, who had command of the field team, made their way toward the National Archives, where their colleagues from the Second Octant let them pass. A mustachioed older constable was directing things here, his helm—under his arm—bearing the double plume of a captain. When he saw Marasi, Javies, and the team, the man lit up.

"Ah, so Aradel sent me reinforcements after all," he exclaimed. "Rusting wonderful. You chaps go watch the east side of the square, down Longard Street. Foundry workers are gathering there, and they don't look too pleasant. This isn't the place for their picket lines, I dare say. Maybe an eyeful of constable uniforms will keep them in check."

"Sir," Javies said, saluting. "Those masses are pushing up against the steps to the mansion! With respect, sir, don't you want us up there?"

"Governor's guards have jurisdiction, Lieutenant," the old captain said. "They brush us back if we try to do anything on the actual mansion grounds. Damn pewternecked bulls. They barely give us warning anytime the governor wants to have a say to the people, then expect us to do the hard work of policing this mess."

Javies saluted, and his team ran off.

"Sir," Marasi said, remaining behind. "Constable-General Aradel wanted me to bring him a direct report on the speech. Do you think I could get a spot on those bleachers to watch?"

"No luck there," the captain said. "Every niece and nanny of a house lord has demanded a spot; they'll gut me if I send someone else over."

"Thank you anyway, sir. I'll see if I can work my way to the front of the crowd." Marasi moved off.

"Wait, constable," the old man said. "Don't I know you?"

She looked back, blushing. "I'm—"

"Lord Harms's girl!" the old captain said. "The bastard. That's it! Now, don't get red-faced. That's not meant as an insult, child. Just what you are, and that's it, simple as day. I like your father. He was bad enough at cards to be fun to play against, but he was careful not to bet so much that I felt bad winning."

"Sir." News of her nature, once kept discreet, had moved through all of high society. Hanging around Waxillium, who created such stirs, did have its drawbacks. And her mother *did* have something of a reason for her angry letters.

Marasi was quite accepting of what she was. That didn't mean she liked having it thrown at her. Old nobleman officers like this, though . . . well, they came from a time when they felt they could say whatever they wanted, particularly about their subordinates.

"There's space with the reporters, Little Harms," he said, pointing. "Up near the north side. Not great for watching, as you'll have steps in your way, but a great place for listening. Tell Constable Wells at the rope I said you could pass, and give my best to your father."

She saluted, still wrestling with a mixture of shame and indignation. He didn't mean anything by his comments. But Rust and Ruin, she had worked most of her life swept under the rug with a few coins in hand, her father refusing to openly acknowledge her. Among the constables at least, couldn't she be known for her professional accomplishments, not the nature of her birth?

Still, she wouldn't turn down the opportunity for a better spot, so she began to work her way around the square toward the section he'd specified.

What was that? Wax thought. He spun to look away from the group of beggars he'd been questioning.

"Wax?" Wayne called, turning away from another group of people. "What—"

Wax ignored him, shoving through a crowd on the street toward the thing he'd seen. A face.

It can't be.

His frantic actions drew annoyed shouts from some people, but only dark glares from others. The days when a nobleman, even an Allomancer, could quell with a look were passing. Wax eventually stumbled into a pocket of open ground and spun about. *Where?* Wild, every sense straining, he dropped a bullet casing and Pushed, instantly popping up about ten feet. Scanning, he whirled, the motion flaring his mistcoat tassels.

The heavy flow of people on Tindwyl Promenade continued toward the Hub, near which the governor would apparently be making a speech. *That's a dangerous crowd,* a piece of him noticed. There were too many men wearing battered coats and bearing battered expressions. The labor issue was becoming a bigger and bigger problem. Half the city was underpaid and overworked. The other half was simply out of work. A strange dichotomy.

He kept seeing men loitering on corners. Now they flowed together in streams. That would create dangerous rapids, as when a real river met rocks. Wax landed, heart thrumming like the drum of a march. He'd been sure of it, this time. He *had* seen Bloody Tan in that crowd of men. A brief glimpse of a familiar face, the mortician killer, the last man Wax had hunted in the Roughs before coming to Elendel.

The man who had caused Lessie's death.

"Wax?" Wayne hurried up. "Wax, you all right? You look like you ate an egg you found in the gutter."

"It's nothing," Wax said.

"Ah," Wayne said. "Then that look I saw . . . you were just contemplatin' your impendin' marriage to Steris, I guess?"

Wax sighed, turning away from the crowds. *I imagined it. I must have imagined it.* "I wish you'd leave Steris alone. She's not nearly so bad as you make her sound."

"That's the same thing you said about that horse you bought—you remember, the one who only bit *me*?"

"Roseweather had good taste. Did you find anything?"

Wayne nodded, leading them out of the press of traffic. "Miss Steelrunner settled down nearby, all right," he said. "She got a job doing bookkeeping for a jeweler down the road. She hasn't come in to work in over a week though. The jeweler sent someone to her flat, but nobody answered the door."

"You got the address?" Wax asked.

"Of course I did." Wayne looked offended, shoving his hands in the pockets of his duster. "Got me a new pocket watch too." He held up one made of pure gold, with opaline workings on the face.

Wax sighed. After a short trip back to the jeweler to return the watch—Wayne claimed he figured it had been for trade, since it had been sitting out on the counter with naught but a little box of glass around it—they made their way up the road to the Bournton District.

This was a high-quality neighborhood, which also meant it had less character. No laundry airing in front of buildings, no people sitting on the steps. Instead the street was lined by white townhouses and rows of apartment buildings with spiky iron decorations around their upper windows. They checked the address with one of the local newsboys, and eventually found themselves in front of the apartment building in question.

"Someday I'd like to live in a fancy place like this," Wayne said wistfully.

"Wayne, you live in a mansion."

"It ain't fancy. It's *opulent*. Big difference."

"Which is?"

"Mostly it involves which kinds of glasses you drink out of and what kind of art you hang." Wayne looked offended. "You need to know these things now, Wax, being filthy rich and all."

"Wayne, you're practically rich yourself, after the reward from the Vanishers case."

Wayne shrugged. He hadn't touched his share of that, which had been paid out mostly in aluminum recovered from Miles and his gang. Wax led the way up the steps running along the outside of the building. Idashwy's place was at the top, a small apartment on the rear, with a view only of the back of other buildings. Wax slipped Vindication out of her holster, then knocked, standing to the side of the door in case someone shot through it.

No response.

"Nice door," Wayne said softly. "Good wood." He kicked it open.

Wax leveled his gun and Wayne ducked inside, sliding up against the wall to avoid being backlit. He found a switch a moment later, turning on the room's electric lights.

Wax raised the gun beside his head, pointing at the ceiling, and swept in. The apartment wasn't much to look at. The pile of folded blankets in the corner probably served as a bed. With steelsight, Wax saw no moving bits of metal. Everything was still and calm.

Wax peeked into the bathroom while Wayne moved over to the only other room in the apartment, a kitchen. Indoor plumbing for the bathroom, electric lights. This *was* a fancy place. Most Terris claimed to prefer simple lives. What had led her to pay for something like this?

"Aw, hell," Wayne said from the kitchen. "That ain't no fun."

Wax moved over, gun out, and glanced around the corner into the kitchen. It was just large enough for one person to lie down in. He knew this because of the bloody corpse stretched out on the floor, her chest bearing a large hole in the center, eyes staring sightlessly into the air.

"Looks like we're going to need a new prime suspect, Wax," Wayne said. "This one downright refuses to not be dead already."

Marasi's position at the speech turned out to be exactly as advertised: nestled into a narrow gap in the crowd formed by the side steps of the mansion's forecourt. Around her, the members of the press clutched pencils and pads, ready to jot down bite-sized quotes from the governor's speech that might make good headlines. Marasi was the only constable among them, and her lieutenant's bars didn't earn her much consideration from the reporters.

Their view was obstructed not only by the position of the wide stone steps, but also by the governor's guard—a row of men and women in dark suits and hats, standing with hands clasped behind their backs along the steps. Only a pair of sketch artists, who stood at one corner of the knot of reporters, had anything resembling a good view of the governor's platform, which had been erected on the steps.

That was fine with Marasi. She didn't need to see much of Innate to digest and relate his words. Besides, this position gave her an excellent view of the gathering crowd, which she found more interesting. Dirty men stained with soot from work in the factories. Tired women who—because of the advent of electricity—could now be forced to work much longer hours, well into the night, with the threat of dismissal to keep them at the loom. Yet there was hope in those eyes. Hope that the governor would have encouragement to offer, a promised end to the city's growing strain.

Mirabell's Rules, Marasi thought, nodding to herself. Mirabell had been a statistician and psychologist in the third century who had studied why some people worked harder than others. Turned out a man or woman was much more likely to do good work if they were invested—if they felt ownership of what they did and could see that it mattered. Her personal studies proved that crime went down when people had a sense of identity with and ownership of their community.

That was the problem, because modern society was eroding those concepts. Life seemed more transient now, with people commonly relocating and changing jobs during their lifetime—things that had almost never happened a century ago. Progress had forced it upon them. These days, Elendel just didn't need as many carriage drivers as it did automobile repairmen.

You had to adapt. Move. Change. That was good, but it could also threaten identity, connection, and sense of purpose. The governor's guards studied the crowd with hostility, muttering about miscreants, as if seeing the crowd as barely contained malefactors who were looking for any excuse to riot and loot.

To the contrary, these people wanted something stable, something that would let them sustain their communities or forge new ones. Rioting was rarely caused

by greed, but frequently by frustration and hopeless-
ness.

The governor finally made his appearance, stepping
from the mansion. Marasi caught a few fragmentary
glimpses of him between the legs of the guards. Innate
was a tall, handsome man, unlike his brother, who had
always seemed dumpy to Marasi. Clean-shaven, with a
wave in his salt-and-pepper hair and a trendy set of
spectacles, Innate was the first governor to pose for his
official portrait wearing spectacles.

Would he know? Would he understand how to calm
these people? He was corrupt, but it was a quiet kind
of corruption—little favors done to enrich himself or
his friends. It was quite possible he did care for the
people of his city, even while enriching himself. He
stepped up to his platform, where a diminutive woman
in a green dress skittered around, adjusting devices that
looked like big cones with their wide openings facing
the crowd. Marasi felt she should recognize the young
woman—who was barely more than a girl, with long
blonde hair and a lean face. Where *had* Marasi seen her
before?

She thought for a moment, then sidled up to one of
the reporters to read over her shoulder. *"Breezy day"* . . .
blah blah . . . *"air of violent suspense," whatever that
means . . . There! "Attended by the curious ministra-
tions of Miss Sophi Tarcsel, the inventor's daughter."*

Sophi Tarcsel. She'd been making an uproar, writing
opinion pieces in the broadsheets about her father, who
had supposedly been a great inventor—though Marasi
had never heard or read his name before those articles.

"People of Elendel," Governor Innate said, and Marasi was surprised by how his voice echoed across the
square, loud and clear. Something to do with those de-

vices, apparently. "The papers would have you believe that this evening we stand on the brink of a crisis, but I assure you, no such problem exists. My brother was not the criminal they are condemning him to have been."

Oh, Innate, Marasi thought, sighing to herself as she wrote. *That's not why they're here.* Nobody had come to hear more about Winsting. What about the city's real problems?

"I will not suffer this defamation of my dear brother's character," Innate continued. "He was a good man, a statesman and philanthropist. You might have forgotten the Hub beautification project that he spearheaded just three years ago, but I have not. . . ."

He continued in that vein. Marasi dutifully took notes for Captain Aradel, but she shook her head. Innate's goal was understandable. He hoped to preserve his family's reputation in the eyes of important investors and noblemen, and perhaps deflate some of the public anger. It wouldn't work. The people didn't *actually* care about Winsting. It was the deeper corruption, the feeling of powerlessness, that was destroying this city.

As the speech progressed, laboring with explanations of how good a man Winsting had been, Marasi edged to the side in an attempt to get a better view. How was Innate responding to the crowd? He was charismatic; she could hear that even from the way he spoke. Maybe he *was* doing some good with his oratory alone, even if the speech lacked substance.

"A full investigation of the constables will be ordered," Innate continued. "I am not convinced my brother was killed as they say. My sources posit this might all be the result of a bungled raid, using my brother as willing bait to catch criminals. If that is true, and they put my brother in harm's way and are now covering it up, the responsible parties will answer for it."

Marasi moved to the side, but her view was obstructed by one of the guards, who stepped in front of her. Annoyed, Marasi moved again, and again the guardsman moved. She'd have considered it deliberate if his back hadn't been to her.

"As for the floods in the east, we are sending relief. Your friends and relatives there shall be succored. We stand with them in the face of this disaster."

Not good, she noted. *The people don't want to hear about aid going outside the city, no matter how necessary, not while things are growing worse and worse here. . . .* Marasi moved again. Aradel wanted her to judge the public's reaction, but she needed a better view.

Her shuffling earned a curse of annoyance from one of the reporters, and she finally got a sight of Innate on his podium. He moved into a longer rant against the press. Perhaps that was why the reporter had been so testy. She certainly would be. . . .

Marasi frowned. That guardsman who had been moving and shuffling and blocking her view had turned, and she could see a *very* odd expression on his face, like a grimace of pain. And he was whispering—at least his mouth was moving. Nobody else seemed to notice him, as they were focused on the speech.

So Marasi was the first one to scream as the guardsman pulled a revolver from underneath his coat and leveled it at the governor.

Wayne prowled around the dead woman's room. It was too clean. A room where people lived should have a healthy amount of clutter. Miss Steelrunner hadn't spent much time here.

In the other room, Wax inspected the body. Wayne left him to that; he had no interest in poking at a corpse's insides, even if Wax claimed it was important. Wayne, instead, went looking for more interesting bits of life. His first discovery was a small cache of bottles in the cabinet under the bathroom washbasin. Various forms of alcohol, the harder stuff, each a little gone. All save one, which was empty. Wayne gave it a sniff. Port.

Not surprising, he thought. He took the whiskey and gave it a good swig. Bleh. Too much bite, and far too warm. He took another swig as he spun about in the main room. These fancy neighborhoods were too quiet. People should be shouting outside. That was *right* for the city. He checked the trunk beside her sleeping pallet and found it contained three outfits, each clean and carefully folded. The Terris robes were on the bottom. Creases had set; these weren't worn often. The other two were modern designs, the one on top more daring than the one below.

He took another swig of whiskey and wandered back into the room with the corpse. Wax had removed his hat and coat, and knelt beside the body in his vest and slacks.

"You found the alcohol, I see," Wax said. "How uncharacteristic."

Wayne grinned, offering the bottle to Wax, who took a small swig. "Ugh," he noted, handing it back. "This murder is troubling, Wayne."

"I'm sure she felt so."

"Too many questions. Why did she leave the Village, and why choose to live here? It doesn't feel very Terris."

"Oh, I can tell you why she was here," Wayne said.

"Well?"

"Think of yourself as a sheltered Terriswoman in her forties," Wayne said. "Old enough to have missed the chance to be a wild youth, and starting to wish you'd done something more daring."

"The Terris don't long for wildness," Wax said, taking notes in a little book as he inspected the woman's wound. "They aren't daring. They're a reserved people."

"Ain't we Terris?"

"We're exceptions."

"Everyone's an exception to something, Wax. This girl, she left the Village and found a whole world out here. She must have had an adventurous side."

Whiskey.

"She did," Wax admitted. "I didn't know her well, but she'd sneak out of the Village as a youth. That was long ago."

"And she left again," Wayne said, "on account of the Village being so dull as to bore the sense out of a scribe. Hell, even *Steris* would hate that place."

"Wayne . . ."

"Our miss," Wayne said, waving the bottle toward the dead woman, "she tried to remain conservative at first, so she got a job as a clerk, a good Terris occupation. She convinced herself that a nice apartment— where she was safe from the supposed horrors of lesser neighborhoods—was worth the expense. Simple stuff.

"But then some workers at the jeweler took her out, and she let herself drink. She liked that. Awakened memories of sneaked drinks as a youth. She wanted more, so she bought a whole *mess* of different kinds of spirits to try them all out. She liked port best, by the way."

"Makes sense," Wax said.

"Now we find her with increasingly liberal dresses, showing more skin, spending most evenings out. Give her a few more months, and she'd have turned into a right proper girl to have a good time with."

Whiskey.

"She didn't get a few more months," Wax said softly. He took something from his own pocket and handed it out to Wayne. A book, bound in leather, pocket-sized. "Have a look through this."

Wayne took it, flipping through some pages. "What is it?"

"The book that Death gave me."

Marasi's shout was lost in the roar as the governor ended his speech. Polite applause from the nobility, shouts and curses from most of the workers. The noise swallowed her shout like a single splash in a breaking tide.

She fumbled for her handbag as the guard in the dark coat sighted with his gun at the governor. No. There wasn't time for her gun. She had to do something else.

She jumped for the man and slowed time.

She had metal in her this time—she'd made sure, after being embarrassed this morning. Her Allomancy created a bubble of greatly slowed-down time, enveloping herself, the would-be assassin, and a few by-standers.

She grabbed the man around the legs, but her speed bubble did the real work, trapping him inside—as everyone *outside* became a blur. The man squeezed his gun's trigger, and the crack of a gunshot rang amid the strange warping of sounds that she heard inside a bubble from those outside. One of his fellow guards, also caught in her bubble, shouted in alarm.

The fired bullet hit the perimeter of the speed bubble and was deflected. It shot out over the blur of the crowd, the governor's figure vanishing as—she assumed—he was rushed away. Marasi's lunge wasn't enough to topple the would-be assassin, and so she lay there half on the steps, holding on to his legs and feeling foolish, until one of his companions hit him harder, knocking him down.

She dropped the speed bubble and jumped back, the sudden roar of the crowd washing over her. The captured man struggled, shouting, as other guards piled onto him.

"So basically, with this . . . Hemalurgy," Wax said, "you can *make* someone Metalborn."

Wayne sniffled as he flipped through the book, and his cheeks were breaking out in some kind of rash. *Storing health,* Wax thought. Wayne often ended up with odd rashes when he did that. They sat in the main room of Idashwy's apartment, away from the corpse, which they'd draped with a sheet. They'd paused briefly in their inspection to send the newsboy for the local constables.

Wax ground his teeth. Idashwy's wound . . . it was just like those described in the book. Somebody had killed this woman with a spike through the chest, stealing her Feruchemical talent. The book described the process as "tearing off a chunk of someone's soul." Using the spike, one could effectively *attach* that piece of soul to one's own, granting the powers of the deceased.

In the old days, Inquisitors had driven the spike right through the body of the one to be killed into the body of the person to gain the powers. That prevented any power from being lost. Apparently, coating the newly made spike in blood could achieve a similar effect.

He knew, Wax thought. *Ironeyes knew something like this was going to come.* The book had been written by the Lord Mistborn long ago to leave some record of the art known as Hemalurgy. Lestibournes's book said he considered it a crime that the Words of Founding—Harmony's own record—omitted references to the dark art.

"So our killer knows this Hemalurgy stuff?" Wayne said.

"Yes," Wax said. "The killer used a spike to steal Idashwy's Feruchemical talent, then employed that ability to kill Lord Winsting and his guests. We have to assume that our killer could also have numerous other powers at their disposal: any combination of Allomantic or Feruchemical abilities. Or all of them."

Wayne whistled softly.

"Did you discover anything else in your search of the room?" Wax asked.

"Not much."

"I understand the motive here," Wax said, glancing back toward the kitchen with the body. "But I don't yet have one for Winsting's murder. Or . . . well, I know of too *many* possibilities. I don't have the right motive."

"What did you find in the stiff's pockets?"

Wax hesitated.

"You didn't rifle through the pockets?" Wayne asked, aghast. "Wax, you're a *terrible* grave robber!"

"I was distracted by the manner of death," Wax said, rising. "I'd have gotten to it."

The word "distracted" didn't really do justice to his emotions—to the profound shock, the numbness. For months that book had been only an object of study, but now its contents had abruptly ceased being mere words on a page and had become a motive for murder.

We're out of our depth, Wax thought, returning to the kitchen. *We've crept into the realm of the gods. Harmony, Ironeyes, the Lord Mistborn . . .*

Wayne pulled back the sheet, exposing that gaping hole in the woman's chest—right at the sternum. Who would know how to do something like this? Who would Harmony *let* know how to do something like this?

"Here," Wayne said, fishing in the woman's skirt pockets. He came out with a folded-up piece of paper. He unfolded it, then grunted. "Huh. It's for you."

Wax's stomach plummeted. Wayne slowly turned the paper around. It was a sheet ripped from a ledger, filled with numbers and sums. Scrawled across it in a different hand was a single sentence—a familiar sentence. The very words Bloody Tan had said before jerking Lessie right into the path of Wax's bullet, making him kill the woman he loved.

Someone else moves us, lawman.

7

"Look, Wax," Wayne said as the two of them entered Ladrian Mansion, "I saw Tan's body. You shot him square in the head. That bloke was deader than a stuffed lion in a hunting lodge. It ain't him."

"What if he was secretly Metalborn?" Wax asked. "Miles could have survived a shot to the head."

"Doesn't work that way, mate," Wayne said, shutting the door and tossing his coat at Darriance. It hit the butler in the face. "If you're a Bloodmaker, you've got to heal a head wound *right as* it's happening. Once a bloke is actually dead, no power—Allomantic or Feruchemical—is bringin' 'im back."

"I *saw* him, Wayne. Twice." *Once while chasing the Marksman, and then just earlier today.*

"Master," Darriance said, folding Wayne's coat. "New equipment has arrived for you from Miss Ranette. She asked if you'd be willing to test it."

"Aw, Ruin!" Wayne said. "I missed her? What did she leave for me?"

"She . . . said I was to slap you," Darriance admitted.

"Aw. She does care. See that, Wax, she cares!"

Wax nodded absently as Wayne tried to force Darriance to slap him across the rear—which he doubted was what Ranette had intended.

"Sir," Darriance said, turning away from Wayne's proffered posterior. "In addition to the package, Lady Harms awaits you in the sitting room."

Wax hesitated, impatient to go upstairs. He needed time to think—preferably with his earring in—and to go through Ranette's package. They were always very interesting.

But he couldn't simply ignore Steris. "Thank you, Darriance," Wax said. "Send a note to my grandmother at the Village that says we found the missing Terriswoman, but someone had gotten to her—and regretfully killed her—before we arrived. Say the constables will explain the rest, and may have questions for her."

"Very well, my lord."

Wax pushed his way into the sitting room. Steris rose to greet him, and Wax kissed her hand. "I don't have a lot of time, Steris."

"You've sunk your teeth in, then," she said, eyeing him up and down. "I suppose this could be useful. If you catch the murderer of the governor's brother, it will be politically favorable."

"Unless I drag some corpses out into the light."

"Well, perhaps we can prepare for that," she said. "Lady ZoBell's party. You are still planning to attend with me?"

Rusts. He'd forgotten all about it.

"Our invitation has gone missing—I suspect Wayne is to blame—but it doesn't matter. You're lord of a Great House. They won't turn us away."

"Steris. I don't know if I have the time . . ."

"The governor is attending," Steris said. "You could speak with him about his brother."

More meaningless conversation, Wax thought. *More dances and political games.* He needed to be working, hunting.

Bloody Tan. His eye twitched.

"There was some talk of the governor not attending," Steris said, "considering what happened today. However, I have it on the best authority that he *will* come. He doesn't want to appear to have anything to hide in these parlous times."

Wax frowned. "Wait. What happened today?"

"Assassination attempt on the governor," Steris said. "You really don't know?"

"I've been busy. Rusts! Someone tried to kill him? Who?"

"Some deranged man," Steris said. "Not in his right mind. They caught him, I'm told."

"I'll need to talk to the suspect," Wax said, walking for the door. "It might be connected."

"He wasn't a credible threat," Steris said. "By all reports, the man's aim was terrible. He didn't come close to hitting his intended victim. Waxillium?"

"Wayne!" Wax said, shoving open the door. "We've got—"

"On it already," Wayne said, holding up a broadsheet from the table. Evening edition; Wax had a subscription. The top line read, "Bold Attack on the Governor in Daylight!" Wayne tossed Wax his hat off the rack, then snapped his fingers toward the butler—who was in the process of hanging Wayne's duster in the coat closet. Darriance sighed, getting it back out and carrying it over.

"I'll try to make the party," Wax said to Steris, pulling his hat on. "If I'm not back, feel free to go without me."

Steris folded her arms. "Oh? I suppose I should take the butler instead, then?"

"If you like."

"Be careful about that, Steris," Wayne added. "Wax's butlers have a tendency to explode."

Wax gave him a glare, and the two of them charged out the door toward the coach.

"You still need private time for that thinkin' of yours?" Wayne asked.

"Yes."

"Never touch the stuff myself," Wayne said. "Causes headaches. Hey, Hoid. Can I catch a ride up there with you?"

The new coachman shrugged, making room for Wayne on top of the carriage. Wayne climbed up, and Wax stepped inside. This wouldn't be ideal, but it would have to do. He pulled down the window shades, then settled back as the coach began rolling.

He took his earring out of his pocket—the earring of the Pathian religion. His was special. He'd been hand-delivered it under mysterious circumstances. Lately, though, he had avoided wearing it, as the book made clear what it must be. Long ago, a small spike of metal like this had allowed people to communicate with Ruin and Preservation, gods of the ancient world. It was Hemalurgy.

Had this earring, then, been made by killing someone?

Hesitantly, he slipped it in.

Unfortunately, a voice said in his mind, *your fears about the earring are correct. It is a Hemalurgic spike.*

Wax jumped, throwing open the carriage door with Allomancy—preparing his escape—while pulling out Vindication. Rusts! He'd heard that voice as if someone were sitting beside him.

Firing that gun would not have the effect you want, I think, the voice said. *Even if you could see me, shooting at me would merely ruin the furnishings of your coach, costing precisely eighty-four boxings to repair when Miss Grimes takes it to the shop next week. You'd be left with a new wood panel on the coach body just behind me which would never quite match those around it.*

Wax breathed in and out. "Harmony."

Yes? the voice said.

"You're here, in my coach."

Technically, I am everywhere.

Wax trembled, mouth going dry. He forced himself to close the door and sit back down.

Tell me, the voice said in his head, *what were you expecting to happen when you put in the earring, if not this?*

"I . . ." Wax slid Vindication back into her holster. "I wasn't expecting an answer so . . . promptly. And my reflexes tend to be on the jumpy side lately. Um, Your Deificness."

You may call me Harmony, or "Lord" if you must. The voice sounded amused. *Now. About what do you wish to speak?*

"You know."

Better to hear you say it.

"Better for You to hear me say it," Wax said, "or for me to hear myself say it?"

Both.

"Am I insane?" Wax asked.

If you were, speaking to a figment of your delusion would certainly not diagnose that fact.

"You're not helping much."

Then ask better questions, Waxillium.

Wax leaned forward. "I . . ." He clasped his hands before him. "You're real."

You've heard my voice; you've followed my Path.

"A few whispered words when I was in a moment of great stress, when I was gravely wounded," Wax said. "Words I've doubted ever since. This is different. This is . . . more real."

You need to hear it then, do you? the voice said. It sounded as clear and ordinary as if someone normal, someone *visible,* sat there talking to him. *Very well. I am Harmony, the Hero of Ages, once called Sazed. At the end of one world, I took upon myself the powers of protection and destruction, and in so doing became the caretaker of the world to come. I am here, Waxillium, to tell you that you are* not *insane.*

"Bloody Tan lives."

Not exactly.

Wax frowned.

There are . . . beings in this world who are neither human nor koloss. Something related to both. You call them the Faceless Immortals.

"Kandra," Wax said. "Like TenSoon, the Guardian. Or the person who gave me this earring."

They can take the corpses of the dead and use their bones to mimic a person who has died—they wear bodies like you wear clothing, changing back and forth as they wish. They were created by the Lord Ruler using Hemalurgy.

"Your Holy Books give few details about their organization," Wax said. "But everyone knows that the Faceless Immortals are *your* servants. Not murderers."

Any being has choice, Harmony said. *Even koloss have the power to choose. This one . . . the being who wears Bloody Tan's body . . . has not made very good choices.*

"Who is he?"

She is a member of the Third Generation, and you should know better than to assume everyone dangerous to be a male. Paalm was what we called her, but she has chosen the name Bleeder for herself. Waxillium, Bleeder is ancient, older than the destruction of the world—almost as old as the Final Empire. Indeed, she is even older than I am, though not older than my powers. She is crafty, careful, and brilliant. And I'm afraid that she might have gone mad.

The carriage turned a corner.

"One of Your ancient servants," Wax said, "has gone mad and is killing people."

Yes.

"So stop her!"

It is not so simple.

"Free will?" Wax said, annoyed.

No, not in this case. I can directly control a being who has pierced herself with too much Hemalurgy. In this case I would act, for Bleeder has disobeyed her Contract with me and opened herself up for my intervention. Something is wrong, unfortunately.

"What?" Wax asked.

God was silent for a time. *I don't know yet.*

Wax felt cold. "Is that possible?"

It appears so. Somehow, Bleeder has figured out how to hide from me. At times I can spot her, but only when she takes direct and obvious action.

Unfortunately, she has removed one of her Blessings—one of the two spikes that kandra must keep inside themselves to retain their cognition. I would forcibly control her if I could, but one spike does not pierce the soul sufficiently for me to get in.

"Cognition," Wax said. "Two spikes are required for the kandra to be able to think. But she is going around with only one. Which means . . . ?"

Insanity, Harmony said, His voice softer in Wax's ear. *But something is wrong beyond that. She can hide from me, and while I can speak to her, she doesn't have to listen—and I can't keep track of where she is.*

"Didn't you say you were everywhere?"

My essence is, Harmony said. *But this thing that I am . . . it is more complex than you might expect.*

"Being God is more complex than a mortal can comprehend?" Wax said. "What a surprise."

Harmony chuckled softly.

Wait, Wax thought. *Did I just get sarcastic with God Himself?*

Yes, you did, Harmony said. *It is well. Few act that way toward me, even among the kandra. It feels good to me. Like older times. Since Kelsier . . . well, I haven't had much of that.*

"You can hear my thoughts?" Wax asked.

When you have the earring in, yes. I gain the ability to hear you from Preservation, and the ability to speak to you from Ruin. Each had only one half. I always found it puzzling.

Regardless, I know you have been reading young Lestibournes's book. I am not pleased that he made it, but I could not forbid him. I will trust that Marsh was wise in giving it to you. Bleeder can use Hemalurgy, but in a way she should not be able to. Kandra do not have

Allomantic or Feruchemical powers. She has learned to take these, and to use them to maintain her kandra form.

Fortunately, she is limited. She can only use one spike at a time, otherwise she will open herself to my control. If she trades spikes, she must do it by ripping out her single one and then falling onto another, digesting it and returning her to sapience.

I do not know her game with this city, but I'm alarmed by it. She has spent centuries studying human behavior. She is planning something.

"I'll have to stop her, then."

I will send you help.

"I assume, considering the source, it will be spectacular."

Harmony sighed softly. In Wax's mind's eye, he had a sudden image of a being standing with hands clasped behind Him, eternity extending into darkness before Him. Tall, robed, back to Wax, almost visible and distinct yet somehow completely unknowable at the same time.

Waxillium, Harmony said, *I have tried to explain this to you, but I did not do a good job, I think. My hands are tied, and I am bounded.*

"Who ties God's hands?"

I tied them myself.

Wax frowned.

I hold both Ruin and Preservation, Harmony said. *The danger in carrying these opposed powers is that I can see both sides—the need for life, the need for death. I am balance. And, to an extent, I am neutrality.*

"But Bleeder used to be one of Your own, and now she's acting against You."

She used to be of Preservation. She has moved to being of Ruin. Both are needed.

"Murderers are needed," Wax said flatly.

Yes. No. The potential for murderers is needed. Waxillium, I—the personality you speak to—agree with your indignation. But the powers that I am, the essence of my self, cannot allow me to take sides.

Already I fear that I have made things too easy for men. This city, the perfect climate, the ground that renews . . . You were to have had the radio a century ago, but you didn't need it, so you didn't strive for it. You ignore aviation, and cannot tame the wilds because you don't care to study proper irrigation or fertilization.

"The . . . radio? What is that?"

You don't explore, Harmony continued, ignoring Wax's confusion. *Why would you? You have everything you want here. You've barely progressed technologically from what I gave you in the books. Yet others, who were nearly destroyed . . .*

I made a mistake with you, I now see. I still make many. Does that ruin your faith, Waxillium? Does it worry you that your God is fallible?

"You never claimed to be infallible, so far as I remember."

No. I did not.

Wax felt a warmth, a fire, as if the inside of the carriage were heating to incredible temperatures.

I loathe suffering, Waxillium. I hate that people like Bleeder must be allowed to do what they do. I cannot stop them. You can. I beg you to do so.

"I will try."

Good. Oh, and Waxillium?

"Yes, Lord?"

Do be less harsh with Marasi Colms. You aren't my only agent in the affairs of men; I worked quite hard to maneuver Marasi into a position where she could do

*good in this city. It is taxing to have you continue to
dismiss her because her admiration makes you uncomfortable.*

Wax swallowed. "Yes, Lord."

I will send you help.

The voice vanished. The temperature returned to
normal. Wax leaned back, sweating, feeling drained.

A rapping came at his window. Hesitant, Wax pulled
aside the shade. Wayne's face hung there, upside down,
his hand holding his hat onto his head. "You done talking to yourself, Wax?" he asked.

"I . . . Yes, I am."

"I heard voices in my head once too, you know."

"You did?"

"Sure. Gave me a fright. I banged my head against
the wall until I went unconscious. Never heard *them*
again! Ha. Showed 'em good, I did. If rats move in, best
thing to do is to burn the nest and send 'em packing."

"And the nest . . . was your head."

"Yup."

The sad thing was, Wayne probably wasn't lying. Being unkillable, so long as one had some healing power
stored up, could do strange things to a person's sense
of self-preservation. Of course, Wayne had probably
been drunk at the time. That *also* tended to do strange
things to a person's sense of self-preservation.

"Well, anyway," Wayne said. "We're almost to the
precinct headquarters. Time to go back to being dirty
conners. At least they'll probably have scones inside."

Marasi stood in the precinct station with arms folded,
partially to hide the fact that her hands were still
trembling. That was unfair. She'd been in firefights

numerous times now. She should be accustomed to this . . . but still, after the jolt of it all wore off—the moment of thrill and action—she occasionally found herself feeling drained. Surely she'd get past it eventually.

"He was wearing these, sir," Reddi said, placing a pair of bracers onto the table with a thump. "No other metal on his body save for the gun and a pocketful of rounds. We've called in the First Octant precinct's Leecher to make sure he doesn't have any metal swallowed, but we can't be certain until she arrives."

Aradel picked up one of the bracers, turning it over in his hands. The dim room was a kind of balcony, overlooking the interrogation chamber below, where the assassin Marasi had stopped sat slumped in a chair. His name was Rian; no house, though they'd located his family. He was tied with ropes to a large stone behind his chair. No metal in the room, to make it safe to stow Coinshots or Lurchers. Stone floor, walls made of thick wood joined with wooden pegs. Almost primitive in feel. The balcony had glass walls, letting them look down upon him without being heard.

"So he's Metalborn," said Lieutenant Caberel, the only other person in the room. The stout woman picked up the other bracer. "Why didn't he use his abilities in the assassination? If he killed Winsting with Feruchemical speed, like old Waxillium Dawnshot says, he should have done the same today."

"Maybe he didn't kill Winsting," Aradel said. "The attacks could be unrelated."

"He fits the profile though, sir," Reddi said. "Winsting's bodyguards probably would have trusted a member of the governor's personal guard. He could have talked his way past them and done the deed."

"Hard to imagine Winsting's guards letting even someone like that in alone with their charge, Captain," Aradel said. "After a firefight where others were being killed? They'd be tense. Suspicious."

Down below, the suspect began rocking back and forth on his seat. The vents that would allow them to listen in on him were closed, but she had a sense that he was muttering to himself again.

"So, we just ask him," Caberel said.

"Again?" Reddi said. "You heard before. All he does is mumble."

"Then encourage him," Caberel said. "You're pretty good at that, Reddi."

"I suppose his face could use a few new bruises," Reddi said.

"You know you can't do that," Marasi said from beside the window.

Reddi looked at her. "Don't quote statistics at me, Colms. I've found I can make a man speak the truth, no matter what you claim."

"It isn't statistics this time," Marasi said. "If you actively torture that man, you'll ruin him for prosecution. His attorneys will get him off for sure."

Reddi gave her a scowl.

"So send for his daughter," Caberel said, glancing over the fact sheet they had on the man. "We threaten her in front of him, but don't do anything to harm her. He'll talk."

Marasi rubbed her forehead. "That's *specifically* illegal, Caberel. Do you people know nothing about Article Eighty-Nine? He has rights."

"He's a criminal," Reddi said.

"He's a suspected criminal." Marasi sighed. "You

can't continue to act as you have in the past, Reddi. New laws are in place. They're only going to get stricter, and the defense attorneys are increasingly clever."

"The solicitors have sold out to the other side," Caberel said with a nod. "She's right."

Marasi remained silent on that score. Of course it wasn't really a matter of selling out at all—but she'd settle for the constables learning to follow the rules, regardless of the reasoning.

"I think," Reddi said, "that it's unfortunate we've got someone among us who seems to be more on the solicitors' side than on the side of justice. She knows more about their ways than ours."

"Perhaps she does," Aradel said in a soft, stern voice. "And one might consider that to be exactly why I brought her in among us, Captain Reddi. Colms knows contemporary legal codes. If you paid more attention to the very laws you are sworn to uphold, perhaps Daughnin wouldn't have gotten back on the street last month."

Reddi blushed, bowing his head. Aradel stepped up beside Marasi, looking down at the captive. "How are you at interrogating hostile witnesses, Lieutenant?"

"Less practiced than I'd like to be," she replied with a grimace. "I'm willing to give it a try, but we might as well wait for a few more minutes."

"Why?"

Distantly, a door slammed. "That's why," Marasi said.

A moment later, the door into their observation chamber was flung open, Pushed by Waxillium as he approached. Couldn't the man be bothered to lift a hand from time to time? He strode in, tailed by Wayne, who was for some reason wearing Constable Terri's hat.

Waxillium looked down at the captive. He narrowed his eyes, then glanced at the bracers on the table nearby. One jumped, then fell off the table, Pushed by his unseen Allomantic ability.

He grunted. "Those aren't metalminds," he said. "This man is a decoy. You've been duped." He turned as if to leave. Wayne slouched down in one of the chairs and put his feet up beside the bracers, then promptly started snoring.

"Wait, that's *it*?" Reddi said, glancing at Waxillium. "You aren't even going to interrogate him?"

"I'll talk to him," Waxillium said. "He might give us clues that will help find Winsting's killer. But it wasn't that man."

"How can you be so sure, Waxillium?" Marasi said.

"It takes more effort to Push on real metalminds," Waxillium said, pointing. "And that man is too obvious. Whoever did this has predicted our conjecture that one of Innate's guards was behind the murder, and wants us to jump on this man as a suspect. They want us to assume we have the killer in custody. Why, though? Are they planning something tonight . . . ?" Distracted, he walked toward the door. "I'm going to go talk to the prisoner. Marasi, I wouldn't mind another set of ears."

She started. He was *asking* her for help? That was a change from making her feel guilty every time she showed up at a crime scene. She glanced at Aradel, who gave her leave, and she hurried after Waxillium.

In the stairwell down, Waxillium stopped and turned toward her. He was wearing his Roughs hat. He only did that when he was in full-on "tough lawman" mode. "I hear you brought this guy in."

"I did."

"Nice work."

That should *not* have given her the thrill that it did. She didn't need his approval.

It was nice nonetheless.

He continued to study her, as if on the verge of saying something more.

"What?" Marasi asked.

"I spoke to God on the way over here."

"All right . . ." Marasi said. "I'm glad you're devout enough to say a prayer now and then."

"Yes. Thing is, He spoke back."

She cocked her head, trying to judge the meaning of that. But Waxillium Ladrian was nothing if not earnest. Rusts, often he was too blunt.

"All right," she said. "What did he tell you?"

"Our killer is a Faceless Immortal," Waxillium said, starting down the steps again. "A creature who calls herself Bleeder. She can change shapes by taking the bones of the dead, and she's been driven mad. Even Harmony doesn't know her purposes."

Marasi followed him down, trying to swallow that. Mistwraiths and kandra . . . those were things out of the Historica, not real life. Then again, once she would have said that men like Miles Hundredlives and Waxillium Dawnshot were men out of stories. They'd lived up to the legends to a surprising degree.

"So that *could* be her," Marasi said, gesturing toward the wall separating them from the prisoner. "She could have any shape, any face! Why are you so sure this isn't the killer?"

"Because the governor is still alive," Waxillium said softly. "The creature who's behind this casually murdered Winsting in a saferoom, behind a wall of guards, after intentionally starting a firefight in the room above. She wouldn't be caught like this. It's a taunt." He looked to

Marasi. "But I can't be certain, not a hundred percent. So I need you to know what we're up against."

She nodded to him and he nodded back, then he led the way out of the stairwell and around the corner toward the interrogation room. Marasi took a bit of satisfaction in the fact that the corporal there looked to her for authorization before opening the door for Waxillium.

The poor captive inside sat with his arms tied tight, staring at the table in front of him. He muttered softly. Waxillium walked straight up to the table and took the other seat, settling down and putting his hat on the table. Marasi lingered back, where—in case they were wrong about the prisoner—she'd be out of reach but able to offer aid.

Waxillium tapped the table with his index finger, as if trying to decide what to say. The prisoner, Rian, finally looked up.

"She said you'd come talk to me," Rian said softly.

"She?" Waxillium said.

"God."

"Harmony?"

"No. She said I had to kill the governor. Had to attack him. I tried not to listen. . . ."

Waxillium narrowed his eyes. "You met her? What did she look like? What face was she wearing?"

"You can't save him," Rian whispered. "She's going to kill him. She promised me freedom, but here I am, bound. Oh, Ruin." He took a deep breath. "There is something for you. In my arm."

"In your . . ." Waxillium actually seemed disturbed. Marasi took an unconscious step forward, noticing for the first time a small bulge in the prisoner's forearm.

Before she could quote the legal problems with doing

so, Waxillium stood up and took that arm, making a quick slice in the skin. He pulled something out, bloody. A coin? Marasi stepped forward again as the prisoner reached to his head with his bleeding arm and started humming to himself.

Waxillium wiped off the coin with his handkerchief. He inspected it, then turned it over. Then he grew very still, paling. He stood up suddenly. "Where did you get this?" he demanded.

Rian only continued humming.

"Where?" Waxillium demanded, grabbing the man by the front of the shirt.

"Waxillium," Marasi said, running up, hand on his arm. "Stop."

He looked to her, then dropped Rian.

"What is that coin?" Marasi asked.

"A message," Waxillium said, shoving the coin in his pocket. "This man won't know anything of use. Bleeder knew we might capture him. Do you have plans for tonight?"

She frowned. "What . . . why are you asking?"

"Governor's attending a party. Steris says he won't cancel despite what has happened, and this is the sort of thing she's always right about. He'll want to put up a strong front, and won't want his political enemies to think he has anything to either hide or fear. We need to be at that party. Because I guarantee Bleeder will be."

8

Young Waxillium, age twelve, looked from one coin to the other. Both bore a picture of the Lord Mistborn on the front, standing with his left arm outspread toward the Elendel Basin. On the back, each displayed a picture of the First Central Bank, in which his family owned a large stake.

"Well?" Edwarn asked. He had a stern face and perfect hair. He wore his suit like he'd been born in it—and to him it was a uniform of war.

"I . . ." The youthful Waxillium looked from one to the other.

"It is understandable you can't spot the difference," Edwarn said. "It takes an expert, which is why so few of these have been discovered. More may actually be in circulation; we can't know how many. One of those is an ordinary coin; the other has a very special defect."

The carriage continued rattling through the streets as Waxillium studied the coins. Then he unfocused his eyes. It was a trick he'd been taught by a friend at a party recently, used for making two drawings spring to life by overlapping them.

Eyes unfocused, coins before him, he crossed his eyes

intentionally and let the images of the two coins overlap one another. When they locked into place, the element of the picture that wasn't the same—one of the pillars on the bank building—fuzzed as his eyes were unable to focus on that point.

"The mistake happened," Uncle Edwarn continued, "because a defective coin striker was used. One worker at the mint brought home a pocketful of these curiosities, which were never supposed to enter circulation. You won't be able to see it, but the error—"

"It's the pillars," Waxillium said. "On the right side of the bank picture. They are spaced too closely."

"Yes. How did you know that? Who told you?"

"I saw it," Waxillium said, handing the coins back.

"Nonsense," Uncle Edwarn said. "Your lie is not a believable one, but I can respect your attempt at hiding your source." He held up one of the coins. "This is the most valuable defective coin in Elendel history. It's worth as much as a small house. Studying it taught me something important."

"That rich people are foolish? They'll pay more money for a coin than it's worth?"

"All people are foolish, just in different ways," Uncle Edwarn said offhandedly. "That lesson I learned elsewhere. No, this coin showed me a harsh but invaluable truth. Money is meaningless."

Waxillium perked up. "What?"

"Only expectation has value as currency, Waxillium," Uncle Edwarn said. "This coin is worth more than the others because people *think* it is. They *expect* it to be. The most important things in the world are worth only what people will pay for them. If you can raise someone's expectation . . . if you can make them *need* something . . . that is the source of wealth. Owning things of value is secondary to creating things of value where none once existed."

The carriage stopped. Outside, an intimidating flight of stone steps led up to the very bank pictured on the coin. Uncle Edwarn waited for the coachman to open his door, but Waxillium hopped down on his own.

Uncle Edwarn met him on the steps. "Your father," Uncle said, "is hopeless with economics. I have worked on him for years, but he cannot—or will not—learn. I have great expectations of you, Waxillium. Banking is not your only option for serving your house. However, after today I suspect you will recognize it as the best one."

"I'm not going to be a banker," Waxillium said, climbing the steps.

"Oh? You have your eye on administering the teamsters after all?"

"No," Waxillium said. "I'm going to be a hero."

His uncle chose not to reply immediately as they approached the top of the steps. Finally, he said softly, "You are twelve years old, and you still speak of this? I expect such foolishness from your sister, but your father should have beaten it out of you by now."

Waxillium turned defiant eyes up at his uncle.

"The day of heroes has passed," Uncle Edwarn said. "The stories of people breaking out of history belong to another world. We have reached an era of modernism, both louder and more silent at the same time. You watch. Where once kings and warriors shaped the world, now quiet men in offices will do the same—and do it far, far more effectively."

They entered the bank lobby, which had a low ceiling and a wall of cagelike bars with hunched-over people inside who received or disbursed cash from or to those who waited in lines. Waxillium's uncle led him around to the back. The dark wood furnishings and mold-colored rug made it feel like dusk in the room, even with windows open and gas lamps burning.

"There are two appointments today I wanted you to observe," Uncle Edwarn said as they entered a long, unadorned room. The chairs faced the wall; this was a viewing room, a place to spy upon meetings in the bank. His uncle gestured for him to sit, then pulled aside a panel in the wall, revealing a glass slit that let them see the two people in the next room. One was a male banker in a vest and slacks. He sat at an imposing desk, speaking with a middle-aged man in dusty cloth- ing, holding a felt cap in his fingers.

"The loan will help us move up," the dirty man said. "Get a place out of the slums. I have three sons. We'll work hard, I promise you we will."

The banker looked down his nose at the man, then riffled through papers. Uncle Edwarn closed the slit, surprising Waxillium with the abrupt motion. His un- cle rose and Waxillium followed, moving to another set of chairs along the same wall. A second spy slit let them look in on another room similar to the first. A female banker in vest and skirt sat behind a similarly intimi- dating desk. The patron, however, was tall, clean, and relaxed.

"Are you certain you need *another* boat, Lord Niko- lin?" the banker asked.

"Of course I'm certain. Would I bother coming here if I weren't serious? Honestly. You people should allow my steward to make these arrangements. That's what stewards are *for,* after all."

Uncle Edwarn closed the slit with a quiet snap, then turned to Waxillium. "You are watching a revolution."

"A revolution?" Waxillium asked. He'd studied banking—well, he'd been forced to study it by his tutors. "This sounds like what happens every day at a bank."

"Ah," Uncle Edwarn said. "You know all this already. And to which of these men will we give a loan?"

"The rich one," Waxillium said. "Assuming he's not lying or acting somehow."

"No, Nikolin is legitimately wealthy," Uncle Edwarn said. "He has banked with us numerous times in the past, and he never misses his payments."

"So you'll loan money to him and not the other."

"Wrong," Uncle Edwarn said. "We'll lend to both."

"You'll use the good credit of the rich man to underwrite the risk of helping the poor man?"

Uncle Edwarn seemed surprised. "Your tutors have been diligent."

Waxillium shrugged, but inwardly he found himself growing interested. Perhaps this was a way to become a hero. Maybe Uncle Edwarn was right and the frontier was shrinking, the need for men of action vanishing. Maybe this new world wasn't at all like the one that the Ascendant Warrior and the Survivor had lived in.

Waxillium could carefully balance risks, and give money to those who needed it. If men in suits would someday run the world, couldn't they also make it a better place?

"Your assessment is correct on one hand," Uncle Edwarn said, oblivious to the direction Waxillium had been thinking, "but flawed on the other. Yes, we will lend to the poor man—but we will not accept risk to do so."

"But—"

"The papers our banker is now presenting will tie

the laborer in debt that is impossible to escape. If he fails to meet payments, his signature on that paper will allow us to go directly to his employer and take a percentage of his wages. If that isn't enough, we can do the same for his sons. The rich man has banked with us many times, and his house negotiated favorable terms. We will earn barely three percent on what we lend him. But the laborer is desperate, and no other bank will consider him. He'll pay us *twelve* percent."

Uncle Edwarn leaned in. "The other banks don't see it yet. They lend safely, and safely only. They have not changed as the world has. Workers earn more now than they ever did, and they're hungry to pay for things once outside their reach. In the last six months we have pushed aggressively to lend to the common people of the city. They flock to us, and will soon make us very, very wealthy."

"You'll make slaves of them," Waxillium said, horrified.

His uncle took out the error coin and set it on the counter beside Waxillium. "This coin is a mistake. An embarrassment. Now it is worth more than thousands of its companions combined. Value created where none once existed. I will take the poor of this city and make of them the same thing. As I said, a revolution."

Waxillium felt sick.

"The coin is for you," Uncle Edwarn said, standing. "I wish it to be a reminder. The gift that will—"

Waxillium snatched the coin off the counter, then bolted out the door.

"Waxillium!" his uncle called.

The bank was a labyrinth, but Waxillium found his way. He burst into the small room where the poor man sat in consultation with the loan officer. The laborer looked up from the stack of papers; he'd be barely literate. He wouldn't even know what he was signing.

Waxillium set the coin down on the desk before him. "This is a misprinted coin, something that collectors covet. Take it, sell it at a curiosities shop—don't take less than two thousand for it—and use the money to move your family out of the slum. Don't sign those documents. They'll be like a chain around your neck."

Wax paused in his story. He held the coin in front of him, studying it as he and Steris rode toward the party.

"Well?" Steris asked, sitting across from him in the carriage. "What did your uncle do?"

"He was livid, of course," Wax said. "The laborer signed the papers; he couldn't believe that I'd actually give him something so valuable. My uncle came in, wove lies in the air like pretty puffs of colored smoke, and got his documents."

Wax turned the coin over, looking at the image of the Lord Mistborn pressed into the front. "The laborer—his name was Jendel—killed himself by jumping off a bridge eight years later. His sons are still in debt to the bank, though House Ladrian no longer owns an interest in the First Central Bank; my uncle sold it off for capital before gutting the house and faking his death."

"I'm sorry," Steris said softly.

"It's part of what drove me away," Wax said. "Events like that—and what happened in the Village, of course. I told myself I was setting out to find adventure; I never intended to be a lawman. I think I knew, deep down, that I couldn't change anything in Elendel. It was too big, the men in suits too crafty. Out in the Roughs, one man with a gun meant something. Here, it's hard to see him as anything other than a relic."

Steris pursed her lips, and obviously didn't know what to say. Wax didn't blame her. He'd thought often of the events in that bank, and he still didn't know what—if anything—he could have done differently.

He flipped the coin over in his fingers. Scratched onto the back, in tiny letters, were the words *Why did you leave, Wax?*

"How did Bleeder get the coin?" Steris asked.

"I can't fathom," Wax said. "I sold it before going to the Roughs. My father had cut me off by then, and I needed money to outfit myself for the trip."

"And those words?"

"I don't know," Wax said, pocketing the coin. "Thing is, remembering that story bothers me. I told myself at the time that I was trying to help the man, but I don't think that was true. Looking back, I was just trying to anger my uncle.

"I'm still like that, Steris. Why did I leave for the Roughs? I wanted to be a hero—I wanted to be seen and known. I could have done a great deal of good by taking a position in my house here in Elendel, but I'd have had to do it quietly. Leaving, then eventually trying to make a name for myself as a lawman, was ultimately selfish. Even joining the constables here sometimes seems like an act of insufferable hubris to me."

"I doubt that you care," Steris said, leaning in, "but I consider your motives to be irrelevant. You save lives. You . . . saved *my* life. My gratitude is not influenced by what was running through your head as you did so."

Wax met her eyes. Steris was prone to this—startling moments of pure honesty, where she stripped everything away and laid herself bare.

The carriage slowed, and Steris's eyes flicked toward the window. "We have arrived, but it will take us time to get in. There are many carriages in front of us."

Wax frowned, opening his window and leaning his head out. Indeed, a line of carriages and even a few motors clogged the way into the coach portico of ZoBell Tower. The skyscraper towered some twenty stories up into the night sky, its top disappearing in the dark mists.

Wax pulled back into the carriage, mist tumbling in through the now-open window beside him. Steris glanced at it, but did not ask him to close the shade.

"I guess we'll be late," Wax said.

Unless, of course, he improvised.

"This is the first party in the space atop the tower," Steris said, taking a small planning notebook out of her handbag, "and the coach attendants aren't accustomed to this heavy traffic."

Wax smiled. "You accounted for this delay, did you?"

Steris stopped on a page in her notebook, then turned it around. There, in her neat handwriting, was a detailed agenda for their evening at the party. The third entry read, *8:17. Way into the building likely blocked by traffic. Lord Waxillium carries us up to the top floor by Allomancy, which is completely inappropriate and at the same time breathtaking.*

He raised an eyebrow, checking his pocket watch, which he carried in his gunbelt—not his vest—to be easily dropped with his other metals. "It's 8:13. You're slipping."

"Traffic on the promenade was lighter than I expected."

"You really want to do this the hard way?"

"I believe this will actually be the easy way," Steris said. "Completely inappropriate though."

"Completely."

"Fortunately, you have a reputation for that sort of thing, and I can't be expected to keep you reined in. I did wear dark undergarments, though, so they won't be as visible from below while we are flying."

Wax smiled, then reached under his seat, getting out the package that Ranette had sent him. He tucked that under his arm, then pushed open the door. "People underestimate you, Steris."

"No," she said, stepping out onto the misty sidewalk. He saw she wore shoes that fastened securely. Good. "They simply presume to know me when they do not. Understanding social conventions is not the same as condoning them. Now, how is it that we are to—*Oh!*"

She said the last part as Wax gathered her to him in a close embrace, then unholstered Vindication and shot a bullet into the ground—between three cobblestones—at their feet. He grinned as heads popped out of carriages all down the line. He'd have to leave Wayne and Marasi to fend for themselves this way, but that was likely better. Might keep eyes off those two.

Wax decreased his weight, oriented himself and Steris at the correct angle to the bullet, and *Pushed.* They shot into the air at a slant, soaring over the coaches in a line. He landed them on one of the skyscraper's decorative outcroppings a few stories up. Steris clung to him with the grip of a cat hanging above an ocean, her eyes wide. Then, cautiously, she released him and stepped up to the edge of the stonework, leaned out, and peered through the misty depths. Lights bobbed below: coaches, streetlamps, lanterns held high by footmen. In the mist, most were just bubbles and shadows.

"I feel like I'm afloat in a sea of smoke and fog," she

said. The mists twisted and churned as if alive. Eddies and swirls seemed to move against the currents of air, always in motion.

Wax opened Ranette's package, getting out the length of tightly twined rope inside. He looked upward. Ranette's note said she wanted him to experiment with using a tether as he jumped with Allomancy, then provide her with feedback.

"You were eager to come tonight," Steris said. "It's more than wanting to meet the governor. You're working. I can see it in you."

Wax hefted the rope—which was weighted at one end with a hooked steel spike—getting a feel for what throwing it would be like.

"I can tell, you see," she said, "because you are fully awake. You are a predator, Waxillium Ladrian."

"I *hunt* predators."

"You are one too." She looked at him through the translucent mists dancing between them. Her eyes were alight, reflecting the glow from the sea of fog below. "You are like a lion. Most days you're only partially present, with me. Lounging, half asleep. You do what you must, you fulfill the needs of the house, but you don't thrive. Then the prey appears. You wake. The burst of speed, the fury and power; the pounding, pulsing, rush of the hunt. This is the real you, Waxillium Ladrian."

"If what you say is true, then all lawmen are predators."

"True lawmen, perhaps. I don't know that I've met another." She followed his gaze as he looked upward. "So, my question. What do you hunt tonight?"

"Bleeder will be here."

"The murderer? How do you know?"

"She is going to try to kill the governor again," Wax said. "She'll want to test me, to see if she can get close, judge how I'll react."

"You act as if it's personal, between the two of you."

"I wish it were." *Someone else moves us.* "I wish I knew Bleeder well enough for it to be personal, as that would give me an edge. But she certainly is interested in me, and that means I can't skip this party. Otherwise she might take it as a sign that she should strike."

Wax finished coiling the rope in one hand, then held it with the spiked end dangling free. He held out his hand, and Steris readily stepped up to him.

He searched out a metal line that pointed toward one of the steel girders in the stone under his feet. With so much rock separating them, it wouldn't be as strong an anchor as otherwise—but it was large and solid, so it would work for his purposes. Holding Steris, he Pushed off it into the night air. Skyscrapers like this one presented a problem for him, since they tapered as they grew taller. In addition, many of the footholds he used were narrow ledges, which made it hard to get a Push directly upward—those Pushes often sent him slightly outward, away from the building at an angle. Either way, the higher he went, the farther from the wall he got. Usually, he could counter this with his shotgun and his ability to make himself lighter. That wouldn't work while carrying Steris.

Ranette's rope and spike might. He reached a height where he started to slow, his anchor getting too far to give him further lift. As usual, he'd drifted out some ten feet from the building. So, as he slowed, he flipped the spiked end toward a balcony and Pushed on it, shooting the tether toward the balcony frame. The hooked spike shot between the metal bars of the balcony, but then pulled free. He drifted to a stop, precarious, in danger of falling sideways away from the building. He cursed and tried again, and this time got the hook to lock in place.

He pulled them inward, like a fish reeling itself in. That got them to the balcony. He set Steris down and coiled the rope again, looking upward.

"That was well performed."

"Too slow," Wax said absently.

"Oh dear."

He smiled, gathered her again, and Pushed them upward off the balcony. This time, as he drew near the halfway point to the party, he launched his hook toward a passing balcony at speed, hooking in place. He continued Pushing himself, moving up past the balcony on his right. Then a sharp pull on the rope made him pivot in the air as he flew, and he swung toward the building.

Wax hit the side of the building boots first, rope in one hand, the other arm wrapped around Steris. He then dropped them the few feet to the balcony. Better, better. The great liability of a Coinshot like himself was that he could only Push away from things, never Pull toward them. A tether could be useful indeed.

He wiggled the hook free. This was awkward. What if he needed to unhook it while flying, or fighting? Could Ranette make that hook able to unhitch on command somehow? He Pushed on the balcony, sending them upward again. Steris dug her fingers into his shoulders. Mists streamed lazily about them. A Coinshot grew very comfortable with heights—no matter how far he fell, dropping a single piece of metal and Pushing carefully let him land unharmed.

"I forget how disorienting this can be," Wax said, slowing their ascent. "Close your eyes."

"No," Steris said. She seemed breathless. "This is . . . this is wonderful."

I don't think I'm ever going to understand that woman, he thought. He could have sworn she was terrified. The next few leaps went well as he got used to the tether. *The rope is way too bulky,* he thought. *Lugging this around would be a serious pain.* And the hook could easily get tangled. If he were using this in a fight, he'd probably have to leave the rope tether behind after the first leap.

Tonight it worked well enough though, and a moment later he swung them onto the top-floor balcony in a flurry of skirts and mistcoat tassels. A small group of partygoers stood here, and Wax's arrival caused surprised exclamations and one dropped glass. Wax straightened, letting Steris down. Despite what she'd been through, she quickly composed herself, settling her skirts and pulling back her hair to smooth straggling locks.

"I believe," she said softly, "that was an entrance befitting your station."

"Alerted the guards, at least," Wax said, nodding to the men who stood at the sides of the balcony, watching them. The men were doing their job, which was good to see. A Coinshot couldn't enter this party unnoticed. They didn't stop him, however. He was too important to bother.

Wax wound up the rope and spike, tying it at his waist within his coat, which made Steris roll her eyes. Then she rested her hand on his arm. Before leaving Ladrian Mansion, she'd coached him with precision on how to walk and stand—her sixth such coaching during their time together. Perhaps that was because he never did it as he was supposed to. Indeed, tonight he took her by the arm in a more familiar way than she'd explained. They were betrothed. Rusts, he could hold her by the arm.

Steris eyed him, but said nothing as Wax Pushed open the balcony doors with an Allomantic shove and they entered the party.

9

Standing at the foot of ZoBell Tower, Wayne watched Wax and Steris disappear into the mists. He shook his head, then took a ball of gum from the tin in his pocket. He'd gotten himself some of the stuff. It was actually fun to chew.

He popped it into his mouth and thought about what a rusted fool his friend was. Obviously, Wax persisted with this whole engagement-to-Steris mess because he missed Lessie so much. So Wax had chosen a marriage that demanded no emotional investment. That was easy to see as the bottom of your own glass at a pub with watered-down ale, that was.

Wayne held out his hand to help Marasi down from their coach. "You look nice," she told him. "I'm surprised you agreed to wear that."

Wayne glanced down at his sharply tailored suit, chewing absently. Marasi acted amazed that he had a suit, matched by a fancy bowler on his head and a dark green cravat. Why wouldn't he have a costume like this? He had beggar costumes, constable costumes, and old lady costumes. A fellow needed to be able to blend with his surroundings. In the Roughs, that meant having some pale brown cowhand's costume. In the city, that meant having a fancy twit costume.

The stupid line was so long that aluminum could have rusted in the time it took them to reach the halfway point. *Rusting Wax and his cheating ways,* Wayne thought. The man could have at least taken Wayne instead of Steris.

Up ahead, oddly, a couple was turned away, forced to trudge back toward their carriage despite all the waiting. *What's going on up there?* Fancy people like this didn't get turned away from parties, did they? Everyone had an invitation, even if his was forged. It was just like the one he'd given to the old tyrant at the school though.

Well, no telling until they arrived. And this line was still moving *slooooooooowwwww.*

"That fellow you caught ever say anything useful?" he asked Marasi.

"No," Marasi said. "He isn't all there, mentally. We did find what seems to be a Hemalurgic spike in him though."

"Rusts. You know 'bout that too?"

"I got to read the book," Marasi said absently. "Death *did* give it to me first, and Waxillium let me make a copy. Our captive had a piercing on some skin in his chest. After we removed that, he calmed. But he still won't talk."

Eventually, after seven crop rotations or so, they reached the front of the line. Marasi presented their invitation. The bouncer here looked it over, his face grim. "I'm afraid that we've been ordered to deny any nameless invitations not in the possession of the people they were sent to. With the attempt on the governor's life, only guests named on our list can be allowed in."

"But—" Marasi said.

"Here now," Wayne cut in. "We're important people. Don't you see how fancy my cravat is?"

Near the door, men in black coats stepped forward, threatening. Rusting government security. Constables, they were real people—oh, they might bust a man's neck now and then, but they came from the streets same as anyone. These spooks though . . . they barely had any soul to them.

"I saved the governor's life today," Marasi said. "Surely you won't turn *me* away."

"There's nothing I can do, I'm afraid," the bouncer said, his stern face completely expressionless.

Yeah, something was going on here. Wayne grabbed Marasi's arm, towing her aside. "Let's go. Rusting fools."

"But—"

Wayne glanced over his shoulder and, just at the right moment, tossed up a speed bubble. "Alrighty, then," he said. "New plan!"

"You sound excited," she said, glancing at the borders of the speed bubble. It was more distinct than usual, as the mist inside the bubble continued to shift and move while that outside hung frozen in the air like gauze.

"I'm an excitable type," Wayne said, hurrying back to the lectern where the bouncer stood. Wayne had managed to catch the lectern in his speed bubble, but not the bouncer. Right fine precision on his part. That little pedestal had a name manifest on it.

"I think you gave up too easily on getting in the ordinary way," Marasi said, folding her arms.

"Our names are on here," Wayne said, careful to keep moving as he read it over. "In a column of people specifically to be kept out. Wouldn't have mattered how well you argued."

"What?" she demanded, shoving up beside him. "Damn. I saved his *life,* the bastard."

"Marasi!" Wayne said, grinning. "You're startin' to talk normal-like."

"Because of you," she said, then paused. "Bastard."

He grinned, chewing his gum loudly. "You saved the governor's life, yeah, but it's probably his security who want to keep you out, not him. They've got mud on their faces because one of their own went rotten, and you embarrassed them by noticing first."

"But that's petty! They're playing with the governor's life!"

"Men are petty." He danced to the side.

"Why are you moving like that?"

"If I stay too long in one place, they have a chance of seeing me, even with how fast we're moving inside this bubble. If we keep moving we'll be a blur, and out in the mists that should be unnoticeable."

She reluctantly started moving.

Wayne glanced over the lists again, recognizing a name. "Here now. That one will work."

"Wayne, you're going to get us into trouble, aren't you?"

"Only if we get caught!" He pointed. "They have two lists—people they're to turn away no matter what, and people they're to allow. See the notes? Fourth name down? Says he sent word he might not come, and they're to make certain nobody else uses his invitation."

"Wayne," Marasi said, "that's Professor Hanlanaze. He's a brilliant mathematician."

"Hm," Wayne said, rubbing his chin. "From the university."

"No, from New Seran. He's been behind some of the discoveries in combustion technology."

Wayne perked up. "From outside the city. So people might not know him."

"They will by reputation."

"But personally?"

"He's somewhat reclusive," Marasi said. "He often gets invited to things like this, but rarely comes. Wayne, I see that look in your eye. You *can't* imitate him."

"What's the worst that could come of it?"

"We get caught," she said, still walking with him around the speed bubble. "We get thrown in prison, prosecuted for conspiracy, embarrass Waxillium."

"Now that," Wayne said, striding back to where he'd been standing when he'd sped up time, "is the best damn argument for trying this that anyone could make. Come back so I can drop this speed bubble. After that we're gonna need to find us some weapons."

Marasi paled, joining him. "If you are thinking of sneaking guns in—"

"Not guns," Wayne said with a grin. "A different kind of weapon. *Math.*"

"So that kandra is in here," Steris said softly from her place on Wax's arm as she scanned the party room. "Somewhere."

The penthouse of ZoBell Tower encompassed its entire top floor, with windows ringing the outside. Light from a dozen dim chandeliers played off wineglasses, diamond jewelry, sequins on sleek dresses. The dress style was new. Was he so oblivious to fashion that he had missed such a dramatic shift?

Steris wore more traditional attire—a kind of gauzy,

draping white dress with a very small bustle and a distinct waist. However, it had sequins lining the collar and cuffs, and was more filmy—lighter than what she normally wore, and actually quite pretty on her. With the sequins, it shared something with these modern gowns.

The party attendees moved around several bars and numerous small displays set up on the red-carpeted floor. Wax and Steris passed one, a stand with a glass box enclosing a raw copper nugget as big as a man's head. Light glimmered on its surface.

Allomantic metals, Wax thought as they passed another display. Dozens of specimens, with plaques talking about where the nugget or vein had been mined. They provoked conversations around the room, clusters of people chatting as light played off the colorful drinks in their fingers.

"You're drawing attention," Steris noted. "I'm not certain wearing the coat was a wise move."

"The mistcoat is a symbol," Wax said. "It is a reminder." She'd talked him out of the hat, but not this.

"It makes you look like a ruffian."

"It's supposed to. Maybe they'll think twice about lying to me; I don't want to be part of their games."

"You are *already* part of their games, Lord Waxillium."

"Which is why I don't like coming to the parties." He held up his hand, cutting her off. "I know. It's important that we be here. Let's go chat with the partygoers you've planned for us to approach."

She always had a list, carefully prepared. Steris was the only person he'd ever heard of who brought an agenda to a cocktail party.

"No," she said.

"No?"

"That is what we commonly do," Steris said, giving a specific smile—she practiced different ones—to Lady Mulgrave as they passed. "Tonight's purpose is yours. Let us be about it and find that killer."

"Are you certain?"

"Yes," she said, waving to another couple. "It behooves a wife to be interested in, if not involved in, the passions of her spouse."

"You don't need to do that, Steris. I—"

"Please," she said softly. "I do."

Wax let the argument drop. Truth was, he was pleased. With the possibility that Bleeder was here somewhere, Wax wouldn't be able to relax anyway.

So how to find the creature? More importantly, how would he beat someone who could move in a blur? Unlike Allomancy—which burned at a few standard rates—Feruchemical powers could be used up all at once. Bleeder could drain her metalminds in a single burst of speed—and could probably take down dozens of people in an eyeblink. Maybe even hundreds. And Wax wouldn't be able to do a thing.

But perhaps she wouldn't have enough left for that. She couldn't just pop more metal in, like an Allomancer, and refill her reserves. She'd have to rely on what speed she had been able to store up, and she'd only stolen her spike recently. Killing the people at Winsting's party would have expended a large amount of what she'd theoretically been able to save up over the last few weeks.

So he had two options. Kill her before she moved, or somehow get her to waste her Feruchemical reserve without hurting anyone.

He stepped up to the bar, ordering drinks, then

turned to scan the crowd. It had been two decades since he'd been a part of high society, and his two years back in Elendel hadn't yet polished off all the rust. Everyone here had the same counterfeit way about them—they chatted with a studied air of merriment while secretly pursuing their own agendas. There was no better place for a murderer to blend in than this.

Drinks in hand, Wax stepped down from the bar and turned on his steel bubble.

It wasn't something he'd always been able to do, and he wasn't entirely certain how he did it. Oh, the basic mechanics were obvious: he burned steel, then Pushed lightly outward from himself in all directions at once. But how had he learned to exempt metal he himself carried? He still didn't know. It was just something that had happened, over time.

With the bubble on, his Allomantic instincts searched out any bits of metal moving quickly toward him, and would Push on those with increasing force as they drew closer. He was getting better and better at that. Standing and letting Darriance shoot at his chest while wearing about twelve inches of padding and armor had helped. He couldn't dodge bullets, but the bubble helped.

"What did you just do?" Steris asked as he reached her. "My bracelet wants to leap off my arm."

"Remove it," Wax said. "If there's an Allomantic fight, I don't want you wearing any metals."

Steris raised an eyebrow, but took off the bracelet and dropped it in her handbag. Wax mentally added an exception for it.

"I don't know that it will matter," Steris said. "This place is positively teeming with metal. What are you doing with your drink?"

Wax looked up. He'd just finished covertly dumping a bit of brown powder into his cup. "I got water," he said. "The powder will make it look like I'm drinking brandy. If I can feign drunkenness later, it might give me an edge."

"Fascinating," Steris said. She seemed genuinely impressed.

They moved through the room, passing under a chandelier. The separate bits of crystal—which had wires suspending them—moved subtly away from Wax, like the needle of a compass confronted by a magnet's matching pole. He accidentally knocked a nugget off a pedestal as they passed. Rusts. Against his better judgment, he dampened his steel bubble.

"Let's find the governor," Steris said.

Wax nodded. He couldn't shake the feeling that no matter which way he turned, someone had a gun pointed at his back.

Someone else moves us, lawman.

Red on the bricks. Lessie in his arms, already dead. His hands stained with her blood. . . .

No. He'd moved past that. He'd *grieved*. He wouldn't be sucked down into that spiral again. As they continued through the party, a pair of lesser nobles wearing dark colors moved to intercept them, but Wax gave them a glare, which was enough to get them to back off.

"Lord Waxillium . . ." Steris said.

"What?" Wax asked. "You said we were going to the governor."

"That doesn't mean you can growl at everyone else."

"I didn't growl." Did he?

"Let me handle it next time," Steris said, guiding them around a pedestal displaying—oddly—nothing at all. The plaque read: ATIUM, THE LOST METAL.

As they neared the governor—who stood holding court near the windows on the north side—a man in a bright yellow bow tie noticed Wax. Great. Lord Stenet. He would want to talk about textile tariffs again. But of course he wouldn't *say* that, not at first. People never said what they meant around here.

"Lord Waxillium!" Stenet said. "I was just thinking about you! How are your wedding arrangements proceeding? Should I look forward to an invitation soon?"

"Not too soon," Steris said. "We've only just settled on a priest. What of you? Your engagement is the talk of the city!"

His face fell. "Oh. Now, about that . . ." He cleared his throat. Steris prodded, but in a moment Stenet had found an excuse, changed the topic, then politely retreated.

"What was that about?" Wax said.

"He's been cheating on her," Steris said absently. "Naturally, the topic makes him uncomfortable."

"Nice work," Wax said. "You're very good at this."

"I'm proficient at it."

"I believe that's what I said."

"There is a distinction," Steris said with a shake of her head. "In this room there are true masters of social interaction. I am not one of them. I studied social norms, researched them, and now I execute them. Another woman might have sailed through that conversation and left him happy, but distracted. I had to use blunt force, so to speak."

"You are a bizarre woman, Steris."

"Says the only man in the room with guns on his hips," she replied, "a man who is unconsciously trying to Push the earrings out of the ears of every woman we pass. You didn't notice Lady Remin losing her ring into her drink, did you?"

"Missed that."

"Pity. It was entertaining. Here, step this way; we don't want to get into a conversation with Lord Bookers. He is dreadfully boring."

Wax followed her down three steps, passing a display shining with nuggets of tin that rattled at his passing, alongside pictures of famous Tineyes, including several sketches of the Lord Mistborn—who had been a Tineye before the Catacendre. *Funny, that Steris would remark on someone being boring. . . .*

"You're thinking," Steris said, "that it is ironic that I would note that someone is a bore—as I myself have a reputation for the same personality flaw."

"I would not have phrased it like that."

"It's all right," Steris said. "As I have said many times before, I am aware of my reputation. I must embrace my nature. I recognize another bore as you might recognize a master Allomancer—as a colleague whose arts I don't particularly wish to sample."

Wax found himself smiling.

"As a side note," Steris said softly as she steered them toward where the governor was speaking with the lord of House Erikell, "if you do find the murderer, steer me in her direction. I shall endeavor to fascinate her with details of our house finances. With luck, she'll fall asleep in her drink and drown, and I shall have my first kill."

"Steris! That was actually amusing."

She blushed. Then she got a conspiratorial look on her face. "I cheated, if you must know."

". . . Cheated?"

"I know you enjoy witty conversation," she said, "so

I prepared earlier, writing myself a list of things I could say that you would find engaging."

Wax laughed. "You have plans for everything, don't you?"

"I like to be thorough," she said. "Though admittedly, sometimes I can be *so* thorough that I end up needing to plan how to best make my plans. My life ends up feeling like a beautiful ship in dry dock, built with eighteen rudders pointing in different directions to be *extra* certain that a steering mechanism is in place." She hesitated, then blushed again. "Yes. That quip was on my list."

Wax laughed anyway. "Steris, I think this is the most genuine I've ever seen you."

"But I'm being fake. I prepared the lines ahead of time. I'm not *actually* being diverting."

"You'd be surprised at how many people do the same thing," Wax said. "Besides, this *is* you. So it's genuine."

"Then I'm always genuine."

"I guess so. I just didn't realize it before."

They stepped toward Innate, putting them close enough that the governor would notice them waiting. Nearby, other couples and groups shot them covert looks. As the lord of a major house, Wax outranked almost everyone in the room. Old noble titles were coming to matter less and less, but with Steris's money backing him, he'd been able to dig himself out of many of his debts. That in turn had allowed him to avoid foreclosures, and he'd been able to hold out until other investments came through. House Ladrian was again one of the wealthiest in the city. Increasingly, that was more important than a noble pedigree.

He found it unfortunate, though not surprising, how

often noble birth aligned with economic and political power. The Lord Mistborn's laws, based upon the Last Emperor's ideal, were supposed to put power into the hands of common men. And yet the same groups just kept on ruling. Wax was one of them. How guilty should he feel?

Already I fear that I have made things too easy for men. . . .

Drim, the governor's chief bodyguard and head of security, stepped up to Wax. "I suppose you'll be next," the thick-necked man growled. "My men at the doors let you keep your guns, I hear."

"Let me tell you, Drim," Wax said, "if the governor is in the slightest bit of danger, you *want* a gun in my hands."

"I suppose. A gun doesn't mean much to you anyway, does it? You could kill with the spare change in your pocket."

"Or a pair of cuff links. Or the tacks holding the carpet to the floor."

Drim grunted. "Too bad about your deputy."

Wax snapped his attention on Drim. "Wayne. What about him?"

"He's a security threat," Drim said. "Had to turn him away down below."

Wax relaxed. "Oh. All right, then."

Drim smiled, obviously feeling he'd won something from the conversation. He backed up to take his place by the wall, watching those who came to speak with the governor.

"You're not concerned about Wayne?" Steris asked softly.

"Not anymore. I worried he'd find the party so boring, he would wander off. Instead, the good man there kindly gave Wayne a challenge."

"So . . . you're saying he'll sneak in?"

"If Wayne isn't in here somewhere already," Wax said, "I'll eat your handbag and try to burn it for Allomantic power."

They continued to wait. The governor's current interlocutor, Lady Shayna, was a long-winded blowhard, but after the political and financial support she'd given him, even the governor couldn't turn her away. Wax looked around, wondering where Wayne would be.

"Lord Waxillium Ladrian," a feminine voice said. "I've heard about you. You're more handsome than the stories say."

He raised his eyebrows toward the speaker, a tall woman waiting to see the governor. Very tall—she had a few inches on him at least. With luscious lips and a large chest, she had creamy skin and hair the color of gunpowder, and she was wearing a red dress missing most of its top half.

"I don't believe we've met," Steris said, her voice cool.

"I'm called Milan," the woman said. She didn't bother to look at Steris, but inspected Wax up and down, then smiled in a mysterious way. "Lord Waxillium, you wear sidearms and a Roughs-style mistcoat to a cocktail party. Bold."

"There is nothing bold about doing what one has always done," Wax said. *Flirting with a man while his fiancée stands beside him, however . . .*

"You have an interesting reputation," Milan continued. "Are the things they say about you true?"

"Yes."

She pursed her lips, smiling, expecting more. Instead,

he met her eyes and waited. She shuffled, moving her cup from one hand to another, then excused herself, walking off.

"Wow," Steris said. "And they say *I* can make people uncomfortable."

"You learn the stare early," Wax said, returning his attention to the governor. In the back of his mind, he assessed the woman Milan and decided to keep an eye on her. Had that been Bleeder in disguise, trying to feel him out? Or had it been just another foolish partygoer with a bit too much wine in her and an inflated opinion of how men would respond to her?

Rusts, this is going to be tough.

Wayne sauntered about the party, his tiny dining plate stacked with food as high as he could get it. Why did they always use such tiny plates at fancy parties? To keep people from eating too much? Rusts. Rich folk didn't make sense. They gave away the most expensive booze in the city, then worried about people eating all of the little sausages?

Wayne was a rebel. He refused to play by their rules, yes he did. He quickly laid out a battle plan. The ladies with the little sausages came out from behind the east bar, while the west bar was preparing the salmon crackers. Tiny sandwiches to the north, and desserts of various sorts to the south. If he made a round of the penthouse room in exactly thirteen minutes, he could hit each station just as the servants were entering with fresh platters.

They were starting to give him glares. A fellow knew he was doing his job right when he got those kinds of glares.

Marasi stayed nearby, playing the part of Professor Hanlanaze's assistant. Wayne scratched at his beard. He didn't like beards, but Marasi said the few evanotype pictures of Professor Hanlanaze showed him wearing one. Hanlanaze was far thicker at the waist than Wayne was too. That was great. You could hide all kinds of stuff in padding like that.

"I still can't believe you had all of this in the carriage," Marasi whispered, then she stole one of his sausages. Right off his plate. Outrageous!

"My dear woman," Wayne said, scratching his head, where he wore a colorful Terris cap, a proud emblem of Hanlanaze's lineage. "Being a qualified academic depends, before anything else, upon suitable preparation. I would no sooner leave my home without appropriate equipment for every eventuality than I would work in my lab without proper safety precautions!"

"It's the voice that truly *makes* the disguise, you know," Marasi said. "How do you do it?"

"Our accents are clothing for our thoughts, my dear," Wayne said. "Without them, everything we say would be stripped bare, and we might as well be screaming at one another. Oh look. The dessert lady has chocolate pastries again! I *do* find those irresistible."

He stepped toward them, but a comment cut him off. "Professor Hanlanaze?"

Wayne froze.

"Why, it *is* you!" the voice said. "I didn't believe you'd actually come." A tall man approached, wearing so much plaid that you could have strung him up on a pole and made a war banner out of him.

On one hand Wayne was pleased. He'd only had Marasi's description of Hanlanaze to go on in creating his disguise, so the fact that he fooled someone who had obviously seen the professor's picture was impressive.

On the other hand . . . damn.

Wayne handed Marasi his plate, giving her a stern glare that said "Don't eat these." Then he took the newcomer's hand. That suit's fabric really was something. The mill that made it must have used up an entire year's quota of stripes.

"And you are?" Wayne asked, pinching his voice. He'd found that big men like Professor Hanlanaze often had voices that sounded smaller than the person was. He was glad he'd been studying southern accents. Of course he also injected some of a university accent into it, and set both on a base of Thermolian "v" sounds, from the outer village where the professor had grown up.

Getting a good accent was like mixing a paint to match one already on a wall. If you didn't blend just right, the flaws could look much worse than if you'd chosen a different color entirely.

"I'm Rame Maldor," the man said, shaking Wayne's hand. "You know . . . the paper on the Higgens effect?"

"Ah yes," Wayne said, releasing the hand and stepping back. He gave a good impression of being nervous around so many people, and it sold better than twopenny drinks the day after Truefast. Indeed, Maldor was perfectly willing to give the supposed recluse plenty of space.

That let Wayne speed up time around him and Marasi only.

"What in Harmony's wrists is he talking about?" Wayne hissed.

From her bag, Marasi retrieved the book that she'd

purchased at a nearby shop while Wayne was getting into his costume. She soon found the page she wanted. "The Higgens effect. Has to do with the way a spectral field is influenced by magnets." She flipped a few pages. "Here, try this. . . ." She rattled off some gibberish to Wayne, who nodded and dropped the speed bubble.

"The Higgens effect is old news!" Wayne said. "I'm much more interested in the way that a static *electric* field produces similar results. Why, you should *see* the work we are near to completing!"

Rame got pale in the face. "But . . . But . . . I was going to study that effect myself!"

"Then you're behind by at least three years!"

"Why didn't you mention this in our letters?"

"And reveal my next discovery?" Wayne said.

Rame stumbled away, then dashed for the lift. Wayne had never seen a scientist move so quickly. You'd have thought someone was handing out free lab coats in the lobby.

"Oh dear," Marasi said. "You realize the chaos this might cause in their field?"

"Yup," Wayne said, taking his plate of food back. "It will be good for them. It'll stop them from sittin' around and thinkin' so much."

"Wayne, they're scientists. Isn't that their *job*?"

"Hell if I know," Wayne said, stuffing a little sausage in his mouth. "But rusts, if it is, that would explain *so much*."

Governor Innate finished his conversation and turned toward Wax. Drim, the bodyguard, waved them forward. He didn't like Wax, but from what Wax knew of the man, Drim was solid, loyal and dependable. He understood that Wax wasn't a threat.

Unfortunately, Drim didn't know the threat they *were* facing. A kandra . . . it could be anyone. Wax wouldn't have been so trusting.

Wouldn't I? he thought, shaking the governor's hand. *What if the kandra is Drim? Have I considered that?*

That was how Bleeder had gotten in to kill Lord Winsting, after all. She had been wearing the face of someone Winsting's men trusted. *Rusting iron on a hillside,* Wax thought. *This is going to be very, very hard.*

"Lord Waxillium?" Innate asked. "Are you well?"

"I'm sorry, my lord," Wax said. "My thoughts were called away for a moment. How is Lady Innate?"

"She had a moment of passing nausea," the governor said, kissing Steris's hand. "And went home to lie down. I will tell her you asked after her. Lady Harms, you look lovely this evening."

"And you are ever a gentleman," Steris replied, giving him a genuine smile. Steris liked the governor, though politically they were opposites—Steris calculatedly progressive, as she figured would be expected of new money looking to advance, while Innate was conservative. But that sort of thing didn't bother Steris. She liked people whose motives made sense, and she felt Innate's political record was orderly. "I hope Lady Allri will recover soon."

"It is an ailment of nerves more than anything else," Innate said. "She did not react well to what happened today."

"You seem to be doing remarkably," Wax said. "All things considered."

"The would-be assassin was one of our newer guards, and was mentally unhinged. He had terrible

aim, and likely didn't even *actually* intend to kill me."
The governor chuckled. "Would that the Survivor would
always send such enemies to me, and often around election season."

Wax cracked a forced smile, then glanced to the side.
That woman from before, the pretty one with the large
eyes, stood nearby. Who else was suspiciously near?

Bleeder won't be someone I can spot easily, Wax
thought. *The Faceless Immortals have centuries of
practice blending into human society.*

"What is your take on it, Lord Waxillium?" Innate
asked. "What were the man's motives?"

"He was provoked to the attack," Wax said. "It was
a distraction. Someone else killed your brother; they
will try again for you."

Nearby, Drim stood up straight, glancing at him.

"Curious," Innate said. "But you're known for jumping at shadows, are you not?"

"Every lawman follows a bum lead on occasion."

"I believe you'll find Lord Waxillium to be right far
more often than he is wrong, my lord," Steris said. "If
he warns of danger, I would listen."

"I will," Innate said.

"I want to meet with you," Wax said, "so we can
discuss important matters. Tomorrow at the latest. You
need to hear what we're dealing with."

"I will schedule it." From Innate, that was a promise. Wax would have his meeting. "Lady Harms, might
I ask after your cousin? I've yet to thank her for what
she did today, even if the man's aim was off, and I
would have been safe anyway."

"Marasi is well," Steris said. "She should be coming
up here tonight to—"

Look at them.

The thought forced its way into Wax's head. Steris and the governor continued to speak, but he froze.

They dress in painted sequins. They drink wine. They laugh, and smile, and play, and dance, and eat, and quietly kill. All part of Harmony's plan. All actors on a stage. That's what you are too, Waxillium Ladrian. It's what all men are.

A chill moved over Wax, like ants running across his skin. The thoughts in his head were a voice, like Harmony's, but rasping and crude. Brutal. A terrible whisper.

Wax was still wearing his earring. Bleeder had found out how to communicate with someone wearing a Hemalurgic spike.

The murderer was in his head.

10

Wayne turned as the sausage lady passed. He intended to reach for another handful. Instead he got slapped.

He blinked, at first assuming that the servers had finally gotten tired of him outthinking them. But the slapper hadn't been one of them. It was a child. He fixed his stare on the young girl as Marasi hurried back to his side. Why, this child couldn't be more than fifteen. And she'd *slapped* him!

"You," the girl said, "are a *monster*."

"I—"

"Remmingtel Tarcsel!" the girl said. "Do you think anyone in this party has heard that name before?"

"Well—"

"No, they haven't. I've asked. They all stand here using my father's incandescent lights—which he toiled for *years* to create—and nobody knows his name. Do you know why, Mister Hanlanaze?"

"I suspect I don't—"

"Because you stole his designs, and with them his life. My father died clipless, destitute and depressed, because of men like you. You aren't a scientist, Mister

Hanlanaze, whatever you claim. You're not an inventor. You're a thief."

"That part's right. I—"

"I'll have the better of you," the girl hissed, stepping up to him and poking him right in the gut, almost where he'd hidden his dueling canes. "I have *plans*. And unlike my father, I know that this world isn't just about who has the best ideas. It's about the people who can market those ideas. I'm going to find investors and change this city. And when you're crying, destitute and discredited, you remember my father's name and what you did."

She spun on her heel—long, straight blonde hair slapping him in the face—and stalked away.

"What the hell was that?" Wayne whispered.

"The price of wearing someone else's likeness, I guess," Marasi said. Rusting woman sounded *amused*!

"Her daddy," Wayne said. "She said . . . I killed her daddy . . ."

"Yeah. Sounds like Hanlanaze has some dirt in his past."

Hanlanaze. Right. Hanlanaze. The professor.

"I've read broadsheet columns by that girl," Marasi said. "It's a real shame, if it's true those inventions were stolen."

"Yeah," Wayne said, rubbing his cheek. "Shame." He eyed the plate of little sausages as it passed, but couldn't find the will to chase it down. The fun was gone, for some reason.

Instead he went looking for Wax.

"Excuse me," Wax said to the governor and Steris.

Both turned astonished eyes on him as he walked

away. A rude move. He didn't let himself care. He stepped into the center of the room, instincts screaming at him.

Guns out!

Firefight coming!

Find cover!

Run.

He did none of those things, but he couldn't keep his eye from twitching. With his steel burning, a spray of small, translucent blue lines connected him to nearby sources of metal. He was in the habit of ignoring those.

Now he watched them. Quivering, shifting, the rhythm and pulse of a hundred people in a room. Trays for food, jewelry, spectacles. Metal parts in the tables and chairs. So much metal that made the framework for the lives of men and women. They were the flesh of civilization, and steel was now its skeleton.

So, you realize what I am, the voice said in his mind. Feminine, but rasping.

No, what are you? Wax sent back. A test.

Harmony spoke to you. I know that he did.

You're a koloss, Wax said, using the wrong word on purpose.

You dance for Harmony, the voice replied. *You bend and move at his direction. You don't care how poor an excuse for a god he is.*

Wax wasn't certain—there was no way to be certain—but it seemed that Bleeder couldn't read his mind. The kandra could only send out thoughts. What was it Harmony had said? That hearing thoughts had come from Preservation, but inserting them from Ruin?

Wax turned slowly about the room, watching those lines. Bleeder wouldn't have any metal on her. People who were metallically aware were more careful about things like that. The governor's guards, for example. Half of them carried guns, but the other half only dueling canes.

How do you stand it, Wax? Bleeder asked. *Dwelling among them. Like living up to your knees in sewage.*

"Why did you kill Winsting?" Wax asked out loud.

I killed him because he had to die. I killed him because nobody else would.

"So you're a hero," Wax said, turning about. *She's close by,* he thought. *Watching me. Who? Which one?*

And if he thought he'd figured it out . . . did he dare fire first?

The strike of lightning is not a hero, Bleeder said. *The earthquake is not a hero. These things simply exist.*

Wax started walking through the room. Perhaps Bleeder would try to move along with him. He kept his hands to the sides, a coin in each fist. No guns yet. That would provoke a panic. "Why the governor?" Wax asked. "He is a good man."

There are no good men, Bleeder said. *Choice is an illusion, lawman. There are those created to be selfish and there are those created to be selfless. This does not make them good or evil, any more than the ravaging lion is evil when compared to the placid rabbit.*

"You called them sewage."

Sewage is not evil. That does not make it desirable.

Bleeder's voice in his mind seemed to take on more personality as she spoke. Soft, haunting, morose. Like Bloody Tan had been.

Someone else moves us. . . .

"And you?" Wax asked. "Which are you? Wolf or rabbit?"

I am the surgeon.

The woman, the beauty in red, followed him. She

tried to be surreptitious about it, walking over to a group to meet them and chat—but she moved parallel to Wax. There was another person following too. A short man in a server's outfit carrying a tray of food. He made his rounds, but the other servers moved clockwise. Wax was going counterclockwise.

Were they close enough to hear him speaking? Not with natural ears. Perhaps Bleeder could burn tin. If that was the power she'd chosen for the evening.

You are a surgeon too, Bleeder said. *They call you lord, they smile at you, but you aren't one of them. If only you could be truly free. If only . . .*

"I follow the law," Wax whispered. "What do you follow?"

Bleeder gave no reply to that. The whisper, perhaps, had kept her from hearing.

The governor is corrupt, Bleeder said. *He spent years covering for his brother, but in truth he would have done better covering for himself.*

Wax looked to the side. He'd circled the room at this point, almost back to where he'd started. That server had followed all the way.

I have much work to do, Bleeder said. *I need to free everyone in this city. Harmony crushes his palm against society, smothering it. He claims to not interfere, but then moves us like pieces on a board.*

"So you'll kill the governor?" Wax said. "That will somehow free the city?"

Yes, it will, Bleeder said. *But of course I can't kill him yet, Wax. I haven't even murdered your father yet.*

Wax felt suddenly cold. But his father was already dead. He spun, hand on his gun, and met the eyes of the server. The man froze, his eyes wide.

Then he ran.

Wax cursed, dashing after and flipping a coin out in front of himself. It spun in the air, but the waiter ducked behind a group of people. Wax gritted his teeth and let the coin drop without Pushing on it, instead unslinging Vindication. This prompted cries of worry from those in the party. The waiter ducked behind groups of people, ready to dodge Wax.

Fortunately, he—or she, or whatever—wasn't ready for Wayne, who surged out between two plump women with cups of wine and flung himself at the waiter. Both went down in a heap. Wax slowed, raising his gun, taking aim. He couldn't give Bleeder a chance to use Allomancy or Feruchemy, particularly if he was wrong about her using tin right now. A shot to the head wouldn't kill a kandra, he guessed, but it should slow her down. Wax just had to be certain not to hit Wayne in the wrong—

The governor's guards piled on top of Wayne and Bleeder. Wax cursed, dashing forward, Vindication up beside his head and mistcoat flapping behind him. He leaped over cowering partygoers—Pushing off tacks in the floor to get some height—and came down near the group of struggling guards.

Wayne, wearing a false beard and swearing like a canal worker with a headache, flailed about as five security guards held him.

"Let him go!" Wax said. "That's my deputy. Where's the other one?"

The guards stumbled about, all but one, who lay on the floor. Bleeding from the gut.

Wax snapped his head up, spotting a man in a waiter's outfit pushing his way toward the room's outer wall nearby. Wax leveled Vindication and took aim.

You should know, Bleeder said, *that I was sad about your lover's death. I hated that it was necessary.*

Wax's hand froze. Lessie. Dead.

Damn it, I'm past that! Wax squeezed the trigger anyway, but Bleeder ducked, skidding to the ground. The bullet punched a hole in the window above the man's head.

Bleeder threw a chair at the weakened window, shattering it. Then, as Wax fired again, he leaped through.

Twenty-plus stories in the air.

Wax bellowed, charging toward the window. Wayne joined him, grabbing Wax by the arm. "I'll hold on tightly, mate. Let's go."

"Stay," Wax said, forcing himself to think through his turmoil of emotions. "Watch the governor. This might be a distraction, like the attempt earlier."

Wax didn't give Wayne a chance to complain. He shook out of the man's grip, then threw himself into the mists.

SE RECORD

The Weather

Gentle westerly winds will pick up by the evening.

ATION, SOCIETY, AND CULTURE

3₵/Issue
20₵/Week

S EFFECTS FLOODING

act market performance

Reckless Roughian Apprehends, Kills Marksman

A year has passed since the Fourth Octant Constabulary's unpopular Decision to deputize the controversial former Roughs lawman Lord Waxillium Ladrian, and the Octant continues to run from a long List of Embarrassments the man has caused.

Foremost are Waxillium "Wax" Ladrian's reckless Efforts to apprehend the notorious Marksman, who stole from institutions essential to the Commerce of our Grand City and took the life of an Innocent Child.

"Wax's" latest caper, though successful, also ended in the death of the accused (as well as an unidentified Bystander), robbing the City of the chance to see Justice done with a proper Trial. In the process Ladrian destroyed the motorcar of Lady Dorise Chevalle who was enjoying a leisurely Drive, and shot up the accounting offices of Linville & Lyons, doing over 400 Boxings of damage. Both have retained solicitors.

Lord Waxillium "Wax" Ladrian

DISTURBANCE At Lord Winsting Innate's cottage—*See Back, Column 8.*

CADMIUM MISTING slows time to "pulse" through stodgy board meeting—*See Back, Column 4.*

FAMOUS BAKER decorates exquisite pastries with flakes of atium—*See Back, Column 5.*

"Street Racing" Threatens Grand Old Sport

What do you hear the closer one gets to the Hub and the hour gets later? Motorcar engines growling like Roughs beasts and the yell of tires ripping up the roads. It has been half a decade at least since one could hear the nighttime clip-clop of horseshoes on cobble and the chirping of crickets. In the last six months, young ladies and lordlings—some of them the very children of our readers!—have taken to racing each other through some of our best-known streets. The betting and exchange of boxings began not long after, and the youths began paying gangs of street urchins to de-

liberately lead the constables away from these so-called street races at predetermined times.

Hardest hit is the 3rd Octant with its slurry of parallel roads and long straightaways,

and in a little under a month young Lady Carmine Feltry will be opening a motor-cars only circuit at the old fairgrounds abutting the Irongate River.

(Continued on Back.)

onic!

El
vest Vif
wsiness
animal-
utrition.

ors Soy!
onic

DE

SNACK
nly 10
lad you
ADE!

Aluminum Doorknobs & Locks. Don't leave yourself vulnerable to Allomantic ruffians. We install within the week! 42 Adamus St.

Can you tell a story? Calour Publications is looking for novels in the alloy of Dechane's *The Horribles* and Ausdenec's *Fear & Ferociousness.* Apply with samples at Calour & D. & S. 211 Morise, The Hub, 6th Octant.

Investors Wanted. Investing in electrics will grow your wealth. Contact S.T., 15 Stranat Place.

r

ilant as
ite suit,
pecific
lendel,
as de-
ut like
koloss,
e men
vibrant

for any person in the room. Had I not bested the tribes at the Pits of Eltania? Was I not the first to bring back tales of the slopes of the Ashmounts, now gone green with vegetation? And wasn't it I that had domesticated the fabled long-necked horses of the Plains of Kaermeron?

"I shall not lower this gun," said the man, "until you pay for your crimes."

My enhanced senses picked up a faint tremor in the man's speech. I noticed the almost imperceptible flicks

11

Falling felt natural to a Coinshot. That sudden moment of acceleration, gut lurching but spirit leaping. The rush of wind. The chill of mist on the skin.

He opened his eyes to spinning white upon black, mist dancing about him, inviting, eager. All Allomancers shared a bond with the mists, but the other types never knew the thrill of jumping through them. Of nearly becoming one with them. During moments like this, Wax understood the Ascendant Warrior. Vin—they rarely called her by name. Her title, like those of the other Preservers, was used to show reverence.

The Historica, a section of the Words of Founding, said she had melded with the mists. She had taken them upon herself, becoming their guardian as they became her essence. As the Survivor watched over all who struggled, Vin watched over those in the night. Sometimes he felt he could see her form in their patterns: slight of frame, short hair splayed out as she moved, mistcloak fluttering behind her.

It was a fancy, wasn't it?

Wax fired Vindication, slamming a bullet into the ground and Pushing on it to stop his descent. He hit the street in front of the building lobby, going down on one knee. Nearby, some hopefuls still waited to be allowed into the party.

"Where?" Wax demanded, looking at them. "Someone fell before me. Where did he go?"

I haven't even murdered your father yet. . . .

Rusts. Could she mean Steris's father, his soon to be father-in-law?

"There . . . there was nobody," said a man in a black suit. "Just that." He pointed to a smashed chair.

In the distance, a motorcar roared to life. It tore away with a frantic sound.

Bleeder might be a Coinshot now, Wax thought, running toward the sound, hoping it was her. *But she wouldn't need a motorcar if that were the case.* Maybe she'd chosen the Feruchemical power to change her weight, so she could drift down on the wind.

Wax launched himself upward, watching the steel lines for movement. In the mists ordinary vision was of limited use, but steelsight's blue lines pierced the mists like arrows. He could easily make out the motorcar speeding away, but he didn't know for certain Bleeder was in it. He took a moment to watch the movements of other vehicles nearby. A carriage pulled to a stop one street away. He could tell from the way the lines quivered—those would be the metal fittings on the horse's harness. People on foot walked slowly along Tindwyl Promenade. Nothing suspicious.

Decision made, he Pushed against some streetlamps, sending himself after the speeding motorcar. He bounded from lamp to lamp, then launched himself over the top of a building as the motor turned a corner. Wax crested the building in a rush of swirling mists, passing only a few feet over the top. A group of young boys playing on the roof watched him pass with dropped jaws. Wax landed on the far edge of the rooftop, mistcoat tassels spraying forward around him, then leaped down as the motor passed below.

This, he thought, *will not work out as well as you hoped, Bleeder.*

Wax increased his weight, then Pushed on the motor from above.

He didn't crush the person inside—he couldn't be absolutely sure he had the right quarry. His carefully pressed weight did pop the wheels like tomatoes, then squashed the roof down just enough to bend the metal doors in their housings. Even if Bleeder had access to enhanced speed, she wouldn't be getting out through those doors.

Wax landed beside the motorcar, Vindication out and pointed through the window at a confused man wearing a cabbie's hat. Motorcar cabbies? When had that started happening?

"He got out!" the cabbie said. "Two streets back. Told me to keep driving; didn't even let me stop as he jumped!"

Wax kept perfectly still, gun right at the cabbie's forehead. It could be Bleeder. She could change faces.

"P-please . . ." the cabbie said, crying. "I . . ."

Damn it! Wax didn't know enough. *Harmony. Is it him?*

He was returned a vague sense of uncertainty. Harmony didn't know.

Wax growled, but lifted his gun away from the frightened driver, trusting his gut. "Where did you let him off?"

"Tage Street."

"Go to the Fourth Octant precinct station," Wax

said. "Wait for me, or constables I send. We'll likely have questions for you. Once I'm satisfied, we'll buy you a new motor."

Wax Pushed himself into the air to the corner of Tage and Guillem, which put him at the edge of a maze of industrial alleyways linking warehouses with the docks where canal boats unloaded. Steelsight on and Pushing bubble up, he crept through the mists, but didn't have much hope. He'd have a devil of a time finding one man alone here, in the dark.

All Bleeder had to do was pick one place and hide there. Many criminals didn't make the wise choice in this situation, however. It was hard to remain perfectly still, not moving any metal, while an Allomancer prowled about looking for you.

Wax persisted, walking down a dark alleyway, checking the rope at his waist, making sure he could unwind it quickly in case Bleeder was a Coinshot or a Lurcher and he needed to dump his metals. Soon the mists filling in behind him made him feel as if he were in an endless corridor, vanishing into nothingness in both directions. Above as well, only dark, swirling mists. Wax stopped in an empty intersection, silent warehouses like leviathans slumbering in the deep on all four corners, only one of which held a streetlight. He looked about with steelsight, waiting, counting heartbeats.

Nothing.

Either the cabbie had been Bleeder in disguise, or Wax's prey had slipped away. Wax sighed, lowering his gun.

One of the large warehouse doors fell outward with a crash, revealing a dozen men. Wax felt a sweeping wave of relief. He hadn't lost his quarry—he'd simply been led into a trap!

Wait.

Damn, Wax thought, leveling Vindication and pulling his Sterrion from his hip. He Pushed on the men in the same movement, which flung him backward toward the cover of a half-finished building.

Unfortunately, the men opened fire before he arrived. Wax's steel bubble deflected a number of the shots, bending them away to cut empty air. The bullets trailed streaks in the mist. One, however, clipped him on the arm.

Wax gasped as his Push slammed him against an incomplete wall. He fired a shot into the ground, then Pushed on it, backflipping himself over the brick wall and behind cover.

Bullets continued to pelt the bricks as Wax dropped a gun and pressed his left hand to the underside of his right upper arm with a flare of pain and blood. The men on the other side of the wall kept firing, and some of the bullets didn't have blue lines. Aluminum bullets. Bleeder was far better funded than Wax had expected.

Why keep firing so rabidly? Were they trying to bring the wall down with the force of their shots? *No. They're trying to hold my attention so I can be flanked.*

Wax grabbed Vindication, holding his bleeding arm as he raised it—it *hurt*—just as several shadows wearing no metal ducked into the other side of the building site. Wax plugged the first one in the head, then dropped the second with a shot to the neck. Three others knelt, raising crossbows.

Something pulled one of them into the shadows. Wax faintly heard an *urk* of pain just before he fired at the second. He turned his gun toward the third to find it slumping down, something stuck into its head. A knife?

"Wayne?" Wax asked, hurriedly reloading Vindication with bloody fingers.

"Not exactly," a feminine voice said. A tall figure crawled through the mists, moving over a pile of bricks to reach him. As she drew closer, he could make out large eyes, jet hair, and a sleekly elegant gown—that was now missing the bottom half, below the knees. The woman from the party, the one who had tried flirting with him.

Wax flipped Vindication, reloaded, up in a smooth motion, pointing it at the woman's head. The bullets outside stopped pounding the wall. The silence was far more ominous.

"Oh please," the woman said, pulling up beside the wall with him. "Why would I save you if I were an enemy?"

Because you could be Bleeder, Wax thought. Anyone could.

"Um . . . you're hurt," the woman said. "How bad is that? Because we should *really* start running right now. They're going to come charging in here shortly."

Damn. Not much choice. Trust her and potentially die, or not trust her and almost certainly die.

"Come here," Wax said, grabbing the woman and pulling her close. He pointed Vindication at the ground.

"They have snipers," she said. "On five roofs, watching for you to Push into the mists. Aluminum bullets."

"How do you know?"

"Overheard those fellows with the bows whispering as they moved around to come get you."

Wax growled. "Who are you?" he said through gritted teeth.

"Does it matter right now?"

"No."

"Can you run?"

"Yes. It's not as bad as it looks." Wax took off, the woman running at his side. The wound hurt like hell, but there was something about the mists. . . . He felt stronger in them. It shouldn't be so—he was no Pewterarm—but there it was.

In truth, getting shot was bad, but not as bad as people often made it out to be. This shot had gone through the skin and muscle under his arm, making it difficult to raise, but he wouldn't bleed out. Most bullets wouldn't actually stop a man; psychologically, the panic of being shot did the most harm.

The two of them charged out the back side of the building, past the man with a knife in his head. Behind them shouts rose in the mist, and a few of the ambushers trying to get into the building took wild shots.

The woman ran well despite being in a gown. Yes, she'd ripped off the bottom half, but she still seemed to run too easily, without seeming to break a sweat or breathe deeply.

Blue lines. Ahead.

Wax grabbed Milan by the arm, yanking her to the side into an alleyway as a group of four men burst out of a cross street, leveling guns.

"Rusts!" Wax said, peeking around the corner. This short alleyway ended at a wall. The thugs had him surrounded.

"How many men does Bleeder have?" Wax muttered with another curse, under his breath.

"These can't be Bleeder's men," Milan said. "How would she have recruited such an army? In the past she's always worked on her own."

Wax looked at her sharply. How much did she know about all this?

"We're going to have to fight," Milan said as shouts sounded from behind them. She reached to her chest, where her gown exposed considerable cleavage.

Waxillium had seen some odd things in his life. He'd visited koloss camps in the Roughs, even been invited to join their numbers. He'd met and spoken with God himself and had received a personal gift from Death. That did not prepare him for the sight of a pretty young woman's chest turning nearly transparent, one of the breasts splitting and offering up the hilt of a small handgun.

She grabbed it and pulled it out. "So convenient," she noted. "You can store all sorts of things in those."

"Who *are* you?"

"MeLaan," she said, rising and holding her gun in two hands. The pronunciation was slightly different this time when she said her name. "The Father promised you help. I'm it."

A Faceless Immortal. As soon as she stopped speaking, he heard a rustling in his mind. *You can trust this one.* Harmony's voice, accompanied by a sense of endlessness, a vision like he'd seen before. It was as good a confirmation as he could get that this wasn't Bleeder.

Wax narrowed his eyes at the woman anyway. "Wait. I think I know you."

She grinned. "We've met once before tonight. I'm charmed you remember. You want the ones in the back or the front?"

At least a dozen chasing them. Four ahead. He had to trust someone, sometime. "I'll take the ones behind."

"Such a gentleman," she said. "By the way, technically I'm not supposed to kill people. I . . . uh . . . think I already broke that rule tonight. If we happen to survive, please don't tell TenSoon that I murdered a bunch of people again. It upsets him."

"Sure. I can do that."

She grinned—whoever she was, this side of her was completely different from what she'd displayed previously. "Say when to go."

Wax peeked around the corner. Dark figures moved in the mist behind them, coming up on their position. If she was right, and this wasn't Bleeder, then who . . .

Aluminum bullets. Snipers to watch for his escape.

It was his uncle. Somehow Wax had been played. Oh, Harmony . . . If Bleeder and the Set were working together . . .

He tossed a bullet casing to the side, against the wall to his right, and held it in place with a light Allomantic push. He flexed his wounded arm, then raised both guns. "Go."

Wax didn't wait to see what MeLaan did. He Pushed against the casing, throwing himself out into the street, churning the mist. Men fired, and Wax increased his weight, then *Pushed* with a sweeping blast of Allomantic power. Some weapons were thrown backward, and some bullets stopped in the air. Men grunted as his Push sent them away.

Two men's weapons weren't affected by the Push. Wax shot them first. They fell, and he didn't give the other men time to go for the aluminum guns. He decreased his weight greatly and Pushed against the men behind him, hoping that the shove helped MeLaan.

His Push sent him into the middle of the men he was fighting. He landed, kicking one of the aluminum guns away into the mists, then lowered Vindication and drilled a thug in the head, just at the ear. The cracks of his gunfire rang in the night.

Wax kept firing, dropping the men around him as he spun through the mists. Some came at him with dueling canes while others fell back with bows. No Allomancers that he'd spotted. In the night, he could finally prove the worth of the mistcoat. As he dodged between the thugs—kicking the other aluminum gun away—the tassels on his coat spun in the air, seeming to meld with the mists. Men attacked where he had been, the tassels confusing them as they churned the fog.

He twisted between two of the thugs and raised a gun to either side and fired, sending them to the ground. Then he turned and leveled both weapons at the man who had been sneaking up on him.

Both out, I believe. He pulled the triggers anyway. The weapons clicked.

The terrified man stumbled back, then paused. "He's out! Move! He's defenseless!" The man charged forward.

Wax dropped the guns.

Why, exactly, would they assume that I need guns to be dangerous?

He reached into his coat and undid the rope at his waist. He pulled it free, draping the rope from his fingers. Ranette's hook clinked as it hit the ground.

The man in front of him hesitated at the sound, dueling cane held nervously.

"This," Wax said, "is how it used to be done."

He yanked the rope, whipping the metal end into the air, then Pushed the spike at the man's chest, letting the rope move through his fingers to give it more slack. It hit, cracking ribs, and Wax yanked the rope back, holding it on a tight leash and spinning the hook through the air as he turned. He Pushed again, slamming the metal into the man raising a bow.

Wax twisted and knelt, whipping the rope around. It spun before him in a grand arc, stirring the mist as he gave the rope more slack, then Pushed it, slamming the spike-hook past one man and into another's chest. Wax yanked the spike-hook back, catching the other man on the thigh, tripping him as he came forward with a dueling cane.

Wax caught the hook in one hand and turned, Pushing the hook forward into the shoulder of an ambusher. Wax ripped it free with a yank, then Pushed it directly back into the man's face.

One more, he thought. Wax whirled, pulling the hook back into his hand, searching.

The last man scrambled for something on the ground. He looked up, raising one of the fallen aluminum guns. "The Set sends its regards, law—"

He cut off as a shadow behind him rammed a knife into his back.

"Here's a tip, kid," MeLaan said. "Save the wise-cracks until your foe is dead. Like this. See how easy it is?" She kicked the corpse in the face.

Wax looked around at the fallen and groaning men. He held the rope tightly. Those sharpshooters on the roofs might reposition soon and start firing. "We need to move fast. I think Bleeder is going after Lord Harms, my betrothed's father."

"Damn," MeLaan said. "You want to try to climb up and go after those sharpshooters?"

"No time," Wax whispered. He pointed down the street. "You go that way; I'll go the other way. If you get out, head back to the Counselor's Cup, a tavern over on Edden Way. I'll meet you there after I go for Lord Harms. If I or someone I send talks to you, first say the words 'all yellow pants.' "

"Sure thing."

"Good luck."

"I'm not the one who needs help, lawman," MeLaan said. "*I'm* basically bulletproof." She gave him a kind of mock salute, then took off down the street, charging through the mists.

Wax recovered Vindication, but didn't holster her. Instead, he grabbed one of the corpses nearby and lugged it up onto his shoulder, stuffing bullets into its pocket. Then he pulled off his gunbelt. He didn't know if those sharpshooters might be Metalborn, set to watch for lines of metal in the mists.

Just in case, he heaved the corpse overhead and Pushed, lobbing it upward through the mists. Then he Pushed on his gunbelt, sending it flying ahead of him down the street.

Finally he ran, chasing after the gunbelt and using Allomancy to knock it up and forward again as it started to fall. A gunshot broke the night, but he couldn't pinpoint its origin. He didn't know if the sharpshooter was trying to hit the corpse, his gunbelt, or him. Another shot followed.

He burst out of the alley, snatched his gunbelt off the ground, then leaped, soaring over the walkway and coming down in the frigid blackness of the canal. Dark water surrounded him, the guns towing him down as his mistcoat billowed outward.

He kicked downward, seeking the floor of the canal. And then, still submerged, he Pushed on the mooring rings on either side of the canal behind him. Most people, even seasoned gunmen, underestimated the stopping power of a good foot of water. Wax surged through the canal like a fish swimming downstream, continuing to Push on new mooring rings as they passed, staying centered in the canal and remaining submerged. He scraped the bottom of a boat overhead, but kept Pushing, praying he wouldn't ram himself into anything in the depths.

By the time his breath ran out, he must have traveled a number of blocks. He burst out of the water and, coughing, crawled to the side of the canal and heaved himself out onto the walkway. He stumbled to his feet. Nobody shot him, which was a good sign.

He paused just long enough to catch his breath and roughly bind his arm, then took to the skies, heading for the Harms mansion.

12

T hat's good," Wayne said, notepad out. "You're sure that fellow wasn't acting strange, then? Nothing odd?"

The serving woman shook her head, sitting with her arms wrapped around herself. They'd finally managed to get down from the top floor, following the panicked exodus by the rich types. The governor was surrounded by a bubble of guards over to Wayne's left, and a set of strong electric lanterns illuminated the misty night.

The green in front of the skyscraper felt right empty, now that so many people had left. He figured that would soon change, when Marasi returned with some more constables. She'd run off to fetch them, and give a report. That meant Wayne was the sole officer of lawkeepin' in the vicinity. A frightening thought.

"I've got one more question for you," Wayne said to the woman.

"Yes, officer?" she asked.

"Where'd you get those shoes?"

The woman blinked, then looked down. "Um . . . My shoes?"

"Yeah, your shoes," Wayne said. "Look plenty comfortable, they do. Can never have too many pairs of black pumps. They go with *rusting* everything."

She looked back at him. "You're a man."

"Sure am," Wayne said. "Checked last time I pissed. The shoes?"

"Rousseau's," she said. "Third Octant, on Yomen Street." She paused. "They were on sale last week."

"Damn!" Wayne said. "That's beautiful. Thanks. You're free to go."

She gave him that look that people seemed to give only to Wayne, the one he hadn't quite figured. Ah well. He wrote down the name of the shop. If he had to wear those awful pumps from his disguise box *one* more time, he'd probably go insane.

He popped a ball of gum into his mouth and wandered over toward the pile of guards, going over his notes. *That server up above,* he thought, tapping his pad with his pencil, *was not the kandra.* Wayne had talked to a dozen of the staff. All knew the fellow and said he hadn't been acting strange at all. But none of them liked him. He was a screwup, and none were surprised that he'd turned out to be rotten.

An amateur might think that picking the new guy made for a good disguise, but this Bleeder, she could be *anyone.* Why would she pick the low man on the list, someone who had only joined the staff a few weeks back? Sure, being new would give you an excuse to not know people's names, but by reports, this fellow hadn't forgotten anyone's name tonight. And picking a habitual klutz with a bad reputation would just lead to everyone watching over your shoulder. A terrible choice for an imitator.

That guy had been some other kind of mole. He shook his head.

"Where's Drim?" he asked the guards. "I wanna show him what I've got."

The guard leaned over, looking at Wayne's notepad. "All that's on there is a bunch of scribbles."

"It's for show," Wayne said. "Makes people talk more if they think you're writin' stuff down. Dunno why. I sure wouldn't want anyone rememberin' the slag I say. . . ." He hesitated, then shoved aside the guard, looking into the middle of the pile. Drim wasn't there, and neither was the governor.

"What'd you do with him!" Wayne said, turning on the others. A smug group of bastards, they were.

"It was best everyone thought he was still here," the guard said. "In truth, he and Drim headed to a secure location ages ago. If we fooled you, then hopefully we fooled the assassin."

"Fooled . . . I'm supposed to be protectin' the guy!"

"Well, you're doing a rusting good job of that, mate, ain'tcha," the guard said, then smirked.

So Wayne did the only reasonable thing. He spat out his gum, then decked the fellow.

Wax rarely appreciated the city as much as he did when he needed to get somewhere quickly.

To the eyes of a man burning steel, Elendel was alight and full of motion, even while shadowed by darkness and mist. Metal. In some ways, that was the true mark of mankind. Man tamed the stones, the bones of the earth below. Man tamed the fire, that ephemeral, consuming soul of life. And combining the two, he drew forth the marrow of the rocks themselves, then made molten tools.

Wax passed among the skyscrapers like a whisper, the motion drying his clothing. He became just another current in the mists, and moving with him in radial spokes was a majestic network of blue lines—like a million outstretched fingers pointing the way to anchors he could use along his path. When even a galloping horse was too slow, Wax had steel. It burned in him, returning to the fire that gave it shape.

From it he drew power. Sometimes that wasn't enough.

But this night, he exploded through the lit upper windows of the Harms dwelling, rolling and coming up with guns leveled. Lord Harms swiveled in the chair of his writing desk, knocking over his pot of ink. The red-faced older man had a comfortable paunch, an easy manner, and a pair of mustaches that were in competition with his jowls to see which could droop farthest toward the floor. Upon seeing Wax, he started, then scrambled to reach into his desk drawer.

Wax scanned the room. Nobody else there. No enemies in the corners, no moving bits of metal in closets or the bedroom. He'd arrived in time. Wax let out a sigh of relief, standing up as Lord Harms finally got his desk drawer open. The man whipped out a pistol, one of the modern semiautos that were popular with the constables. Harms leaped to his feet and rushed over to Wax, holding his gun in two hands.

"Where are they!" Harms exclaimed. "We can take them, eh, old boy?"

"You have a gun," Wax said.

"Yes indeed, yes indeed. After what happened last year, I realized that a man has to be armed. What's the emergency? I'll have your back!"

Wax carefully tipped the point of Lord Harms's gun

downward, just in case a bullet was chambered—because, fortunately, the man hadn't locked a magazine into the pistol. Wax glanced behind at the windows. He'd flung them open with a Push as he approached, but they were meant to open outward, *not* inward. He'd ripped both right off their hinges, toppling one while the other hung by its corner. It finally gave way, crashing to the floor, cracking the glass inside the wooden frame.

Mist poured in through the opening, flooding the floor. Where was Bleeder? In the house somewhere? Impersonating a maid? A neighbor? A constable passing on the street?

Standing in the room with him?

"Jackstom," Wax said, looking to Lord Harms, "do you remember when you first met me, and Wayne was pretending to be my butler?"

Harms frowned. "You mean your uncle?"

Good, Wax thought. An impostor wouldn't know that, would she? Rusts . . . He'd have to suspect everyone.

"You're in danger," Wax said, sliding his guns into their hip holsters. His suit was basically ruined from the swim in the canal, and he'd tossed aside his cravat, but the sturdy mistcoat had seen far worse than this. "I'm getting you out of here."

"But . . ." Lord Harms trailed off, face blanching. "My daughter?"

As if he had only one.

"Steris is fine," Wax said. "Wayne is watching her. Let's go."

The problem was, go where? Wax had a hundred places he could take Harms, but Bleeder could be lurking at any of them. The odds were certainly in Wax's favor, and yet . . .

Bleeder is ancient, Harmony had said. *Older than the destruction of the world. She is crafty, careful, and brilliant. . . . She spent centuries studying human behavior.*

Any option Wax chose could be the very one Bleeder had predicted he would choose. How did you outthink something so old, so knowledgeable?

The solution seemed easy. You didn't try.

Steris left ZoBell Tower to find Wayne sitting across the street from a huddle of bruised and obviously angry men. Wayne was eating a sandwich.

"Oh, Wayne," she said, looking from the hostile, wounded men and back to him. "Those are the governor's guards. He's going to need them tonight."

" 's not my fault," Wayne said. "They was bein' unaccommodating." He took a bite of his sandwich.

She sighed, settling down beside him and looking up through the mists toward the tower. She could make out the lights on various floors glowing like phantoms above, leading all the way up to the very top.

"This is how it's going to be, with him, isn't it?" she asked. "Always being left behind in the middle of something? Always *half* feeling as if I'm part of his life?"

Wayne shrugged. "You could do the noble thing, Steris. Give up on the whole marriage. Let him loose to find someone he actually likes."

"And my family's investment in him and his house?"

"Well, I know this here is revolutionary words, Steris, but you can loan a chap money *without* him havin' to jump you in appreciation, if you know my meanin'."

Good *Harmony* he could be shockingly unmannered. He wasn't like this to others. Oh, he was crass and whimsical, but rarely blatantly rude. He saved that for her. Was he expecting her to fight back, prove herself somehow? She'd never been able to figure this man out. Preparing what to say to him only seemed to make him more vulgar.

"Did he say where he was going?" she said, trying to remain polite.

"Nah," Wayne said, taking a bite of his sandwich. "He's chasin' Bleeder down. Means he could have gone anywhere, and so tryin' to find him is useless. He'll come back for me when he can. If I leave, I'll just end up missing him."

"I see." She settled back, crossing her feet on the curb and staring up at those lights. "Do you hate me because of what I represent, Wayne? The responsibilities that called him back?"

"I don't hate you," Wayne said. "I find you repulsive. That there is an important distinction, it is."

"But—"

Wayne stood up. He shoved the rest of the sandwich into his mouth.

Then he walked over to the guards that were glaring at him and sat down. The implication was obvious.

I'd rather be here.

Steris closed her eyes, squeezing them shut, and tried to pretend she was someone other than herself for a time. Eventually, sounding bells announced the arrival of constable carriages. She stood up and composed herself, relieved when Marasi exited one of them and hurried over.

"Waxillium?" she asked.

Steris shook her head.

"Get in," Marasi said, pointing to one of the carriages. "I'm sending you someplace safe."

"I think the danger has passed here," Steris said. "Unless Wayne is picking fights again."

"No," Marasi said. "The danger has only just started."

Something in the younger woman's tone gave Steris pause. Other constables weren't piling out of the carriages. In fact, they seemed to be waiting for Marasi. They weren't coming here to investigate the man Waxillium had chased off.

"Something's happened, hasn't it?" Steris asked.

"Yeah," Marasi said. "Wayne, get over here! We've got work to do."

Wax stashed Lord Harms at the very top of Feder Tower. He'd chosen its location on the city map by picking random numbers; hopefully Bleeder wouldn't be able to outthink a plan with no thought involved. Harms had instructions to lie low, hide in the darkness and stay quiet. Even if Bleeder could Steelpush and search in the night, the chance of her happening upon Harms was ridiculously low verging on impossible. That didn't stop Wax from worrying. Steris's father was a silly man, but good-natured and amiable.

It was the best Wax could do, as he needed to locate the governor. That hunt took Wax longer than he'd have assumed, which was actually a good thing. It meant that Drim, despite his dislike of Wax, was doing his job properly. Best Wax could determine, they had sent at least three unmarked carriages away from ZoBell Tower: two decoys, and one with the governor inside. He spotted one on Stanton Way, and dismissed it. Too obvious, with the guards riding on top. Guessing that another had gone east, he found it driving around in a circle in the Third Octant, also trying to draw attention. It was moving too slowly.

Besides, the governor wouldn't go that way. Innate was a fighter. He wouldn't want to be seen hiding. So it was that Wax found himself perched on the top of a building near Hammond Promenade, a few streets from Innate's own mansion. He'd return here, eschewing safehouses in the city. He'd want to be in his center of power and authority.

The mists seemed to glow here in the city, lit by a thousand lights—an increasing number of them electric. It took long enough for the carriage to arrive that Wax was starting to second-guess himself. But arrive it did: a tall-topped enclosed coach with red curtains. Yes, it was quite nondescript. The horses, however, were from the governor's prized breeding stock. Just like the two decoys.

Wax shook his head as he jumped and Pushed his way to the top of the stone archway outside the First Insurance Bank. The coach moved at a fair clip and held no obvious guards. They must have taken a very round-about way to take so long to reach here. Wax leaped off the bank's facade and Pushed on a streetlight, hurling himself after the governor's coach. He landed on its top and nodded to the surprised coachman, then swung down alongside the vehicle and knocked on the coach's door, hanging by one arm above the blur of cobblestones beneath. They were certainly running the animals hard.

After a few moments the window shade opened, revealing Drim's surprised face. "Ladrian?" he said. "What the hell are you doing?"

"Being polite," Wax said. "May I come in?"

"What if I refuse?"

"Then I *stop* being polite."

Drim sneered, but glanced to the side, where the governor rode with his hat in his lap. The man nodded, and Drim sighed and turned back to the door.

They didn't stop the carriage. So Wax had to let go, drop a bullet casing, and Push back to the carriage as Drim opened the door. He grabbed it by the handle, Pushing off a passing light, and ducked into the vehicle, ending up seated opposite Drim and the governor.

Drim would be a perfect person to imitate. As would the carriage driver, as would basically anyone with access to the governor, including his wife and family.

"Lord Ladrian," Innate said with a sigh. "Breaking up the party wasn't enough for you? You have to harass me on the way home from it as well?"

Wax shrugged, then moved to climb back *out* of the carriage. He had the door half open before Innate, sputtering, snapped, "What are you doing now, you fool?"

"Leaving," Wax said. "There are thousands of places I could be right now, most of them more pleasant." He hesitated, then pulled out one of his Sterrions and flipped it in his hand, holding it grip-first to the governor. "Here."

The governor's eyes bulged. "Why would I need a gun? I have bodyguards."

"So did your brother," Wax said. "Take it. I'll feel guilty when you get shot, if I haven't done *something*."

". . . Shot?" Innate blanched. "My brother was killed

because of his flirtations with the underbelly of Elendel. They wouldn't dare touch me."

"I'm sure they wouldn't," Wax said, leaning out the door, then hesitated again and looked back in. "You know how to spot a kandra, right, Drim?"

"A what?" the thick-necked bodyguard said.

"Those are myths," Lord Innate said.

"Are they?" Wax said. "Then the one I met tonight must have been lying. Not sure how she made her skin transparent though. Oh well. Guess you have it in hand."

"You mean to tell me," Innate said, stopping Wax with a touch before he could move out the door again, "that one of the *Faceless Immortals* was at my party tonight?"

"Two, actually," Wax said. "One came to help. I would introduce you, have her prove her nature to you, but it does seem that your mind is made up. The other one at the party was the person who killed your brother. You sure you don't want a gun? No? All right, I'll just be—"

"You've made your point, Lord Waxillium," Innate said, sour-faced. He settled back beside the carriage's lantern, which burned gas with a proper light.

"My lord," Drim said, looking to Innate. "This is stupid. The Faceless Immortals? Every second person claims to have met one, just to get their stories in the broadsheets! You're not really considering these claims, are you?"

Innate studied Wax.

"He is," Wax said. "Because he knows *something* strange happened to his brother. Killed in his saferoom, guards murdered from behind by someone they trusted—and Winsting Innate took his security *very* seriously. More seriously than you do, I'd suspect, Mister Governor."

"You can introduce me to one of the creatures?" Innate asked. "Offer me proof of their existence?"

"Yes."

"But why," Drim said, "would one of Harmony's own servants kill Lord Winsting?"

"The kandra has gone insane," Wax said softly. "We don't know her motives yet, but she does seem to want you dead, Mister Governor. So my job is to keep you alive."

"What do we do?" Innate asked. "How do we prepare?"

"Well," Wax said, "first I take over your security."

"Like hell you do!" Drim said.

"You taking over is impossible," Innate agreed. "Drim has served me well for years. He . . . Where are you going?"

Wax turned back from the door. "There's a play I wanted to see tonight," he said, gesturing. "Figured I'd go catch the tail end while you two discuss this."

"And if this creature comes for me while you're gone?" Innate demanded.

"I'm sure your head of security can deal with it," Wax said. "He knew the kandra were at the party tonight, didn't he? And he most certainly didn't miss Wayne slipping in wearing a disguise. And—"

"You may review my security protocols," Innate said with a sigh. "And offer advice."

"Fine," Wax said, pulling the door closed as the carriage turned a corner and approached the governor's mansion. "But you have to agree to one thing right now. I'm going to give you both a passphrase, and I want you both to vow not to share it with *anyone*. Not even each other or Lady Innate. You'll also give me a passphrase. When we meet, we'll exchange them in a whisper, which will prove that none of us have been replaced."

"You honestly think I wouldn't know my own wife?" Innate asked tiredly.

"I'm sure you would," Wax said, softening his tone. "But this is a requirement of my aid, and you must humor me. It will put my mind at ease."

The family was most dangerous. Bleeder had sounded so confident, as if she had the governor in hand, which made Wax think the creature had already gotten to one of the family. Lady Innate hadn't been at the party, but Harmony had said Bleeder could swap bodies whenever she wished. Rust and Ruin, what an awful spot to be in. Bleeder could have killed a niece or nephew, a toddler even, and be planning to imitate one of them to get to the governor. In the Historica, kandra imitated animals. The house pets could secretly be assassins.

Wax glanced at the governor, who looked profoundly disturbed, his hands clasped, eyes staring as if to see a thousand miles. The implications of it were sinking in. Innate wasn't an idiot. Just an egotist and possibly a crook.

The carriage pulled up to the mansion and Drim climbed out. As Wax followed, the governor took him by the arm. "I will want to see this proof of yours, Roughian."

"I'll arrange a meeting tomorrow."

"Tonight."

Wax nodded.

"If this is true," the governor said, still holding his arm, "what do we do? I've read the Words of Founding. I know what the Immortals were capable of. Ruin . . . this creature could be anyone. Passphrases won't be enough. Not nearly."

"They won't," Wax admitted. "Sir, the thing has access to the Metallic Arts too. At any time, she could be anything from a Pulser to an Archivist. Though she can only carry one at a time without risking loss of control, she can swap the powers out at will."

"Great *Harmony*," the governor whispered. "How do you stop something like that?"

"Frankly, I don't know. You should probably already be dead."

"Why am I not?" the governor asked, waving back Drim, who had peeked in to check on them. "This creature could have killed me as easily as she did my brother."

"She seems to have some kind of agenda. Bigger than you. She might not want to bring you down until doing so topples the city government entirely." Wax hesitated, then leaned closer. "Sir, you might want to leave Elendel."

"Leave?" Innate said. "Have you *seen* what is going on in the city?"

Wax nodded. "I—"

"Labor strikes," Innate continued as if he hadn't heard Wax. "Food prices skyrocketing. Too many men from one job out of work, too many from another demanding to be treated better. Rusts, there are practically riots in the streets, man! And the *scandal*. I can't leave. My career would be over."

"Better than your life being over."

The governor glanced at him. He didn't seem to see it that way. "Leaving is impossible," Innate reiterated. "It would look like I'm abandoning the people—they'd think the scandal drove me into hiding. I'd be perceived as a coward. No. Impossible. I will send Lady Innate to safety, as well as the children. I must stay and *you* must deal with this thing, whatever it is. Stop it before it can go any further."

"I'll try," Wax said, leaning in. "Give me a passphrase to authenticate myself. Something memorable, but nonsensical."

"'Leavening on sand.'"

"Good. Mine for you is 'bones without soup.' You have a saferoom?"

"Yes," Innate said. "In the bottom of the mansion, beneath the sitting room."

"Set up in there," Wax said, climbing out of the carriage, "and if you lock the door, *don't* let anyone in until I arrive, and can give you the passphrase."

Soon after stepping down, Wax found himself pulling out Vindication.

He'd leveled the gun before he registered what had set him off. Cries of alarm, but not pain. A servant hastened out of the governor's mansion, passing pillars on the front lit stark white, like a line of femurs.

"My lord governor!" the woman cried. "We've had a telenote through the wire; something has happened. You're going to need to prepare a response!"

"What is it?" Wax demanded as the governor climbed from the carriage.

The servant hesitated, eyes widening at Wax's gun. She wore a sharp black suit, skirt to the ankles, red scarf at the neck. A steward, or perhaps one of the governor's advisors.

"I'm a constable," Wax said. "What is the emergency?"

"A murder," she said.

Harmony, no . . . "Not Lord Harms. Please tell me!" Had he left the man to be killed, in his haste to get to the governor?

"Lord who?" the woman asked. "It wasn't a nobleman at all, constable." She glanced at Drim, who nodded—Wax could be trusted. She looked back to Wax. "It was Father Bin. The priest."

Marasi stared up at the corpse, which had been nailed to the wall like an old drapery. One spike through each eye. Blood painted the man's cheeks and had soaked into the white ceremonial robes, forming a crimson vest. Almost like a Terris V. Blood stained the wall on either side of the corpse as well, smeared there by thrashing arms and fingers. Marasi shivered. The priest had been alive as this happened.

Though constables poked and prodded at the large nave of the church, Marasi felt alone, standing before that corpse and its steel eyes. Just her and the body, a disturbingly reverent scene. It reminded her of something out of the Historica, though she couldn't remember what.

Captain Aradel stepped up beside her. "I've had word of your sister," he said. "We've got her in one of our most secure safehouses."

"Thank you, sir."

"What do you make of it?" he asked, nodding toward the body.

"It's ghastly, sir. What exactly happened?"

"The conventicalists aren't being very helpful," he said. "I'm not sure if they're in shock, or if they see our intrusion here as offensive."

He gestured for her to go before him and they passed

Wayne, who sat in one of the pews chewing gum and looking up at the body. Marasi and Aradel exited the domed nave and entered a small foyer where a row of ashen-faced people sat on some benches. They were conventicalists—those who worked in a Survivorist church aside from the priest.

A grey-haired woman sat at their head, wearing the formal dress of a church matron. She wiped her eyes, and several youths huddled against her, eyes down. Constable Reddi stood nearby; the lean man tucked his clipboard under his arm and saluted Aradel. Normally, this wasn't the sort of thing a constable-general would be involved in, but Aradel had been a detective for many years.

"Will you be handling the interrogation yourself, sir?" Reddi asked. The conventicalists stiffened visibly at the word "interrogation." Marasi could have smacked him for his tone.

"No," Aradel.

"Very good, sir," Reddi said, pulling his bow tie tight and taking out his clipboard. He stepped up to the conventicalists.

"Actually," Aradel said, "I was thinking we'd let Lieutenant Colms try."

Marasi felt a sharp spike of panic, which she smothered immediately. She wasn't afraid of a simple interrogation, particularly with amiable witnesses. But the way Aradel said it, so seriously, made her suddenly feel as if it were some type of test. Wonderful.

She took a deep breath and pushed past Reddi, who had lowered his clipboard and was eyeing her. The assembled group of eight people sat with slumped shoulders. How to best approach them? They'd described to a sketch artist what had happened, but details could separate Ruin from Preservation.

Marasi settled down on the bench between two of them. "My condolences on your loss," she said softly. "My apologies too. The constabulary has failed you this day."

"It's not your fault," the matron said, pulling one of the children tight. "Who could have anticipated . . . Holy Survivor, I knew those Pathians were a miscreant bunch. I always *knew* it. No rules? No precepts to guide their lives?"

"Chaos," a shaven-headed man said from the bench behind. "They want nothing but chaos."

"What happened?" Marasi said. "I've read the report, of course, but . . . rusts . . . I can't imagine . . ."

"We were waiting for evening celebration," the matron said. "The mists had put in quite the appearance! Must have been almost a thousand people in the dome for worship. And then he just sauntered up to the dais, that Pathian *mongrel*."

"Did you recognize him?"

"Course I did," the matron said. "It was that Larskpur; we see him at community functions all the time. People feel they have to invite a Pathian priest, as if to not show favoritism, though nobody wants them around."

Behind her, the underpriest nodded. "Little wretch of a man, barely fit his robes," he said. "Nothing ornate. Really just a smock. They don't even dress up to worship."

"He started talking to the crowd," the matron continued. "Like *he* was going to give the mistdawn sermon! Only it was vile stuff he spouted."

"Such as what?" Marasi asked.

"Blasphemy," the matron said. "But it shouldn't matter. Look here, constable. Why are you even talking to us? A *thousand* people saw him. Why are you treating *us* like we did something wrong? You should be off arresting that monster."

"We have people hunting for him," Marasi said, and rested her hand on the shoulder of one of the children; the little girl whimpered and clamped on to her arm. "And I promise you, we'll catch and punish the one who did this. But every detail you can remember will help us put him away."

The matron and the underpriest glanced at each other. But it was one of the others—a lanky altarman in his twenties—who spoke. "Larskpur said," the man whispered, "that the Survivor was a false god. That Kelsier had tried, and failed, to help humankind. That his death hadn't been about protecting us or Ascending, but about stupidity and bravado."

"It's what they've always thought," the matron said, "but don't say. Those Pathians . . . they claim to accept everyone, but if you push you can see the truth. They mock the Survivor."

"They want chaos," the underpriest repeated. "They hate that so many people look to the Survivor. They hate that we have standards. They have no meetings, no churches, no commandments. . . . The Path isn't a religion, it's a *platitude*."

"It stunned us, I'll tell you that," the matron said. "I thought at first that Father Bin *must* have invited Larskpur to speak. Why else would he be so bold as to step up to the pulpit? I was so horrified by what he said that I didn't notice the blood at first."

"I did," the underpriest said. "I thought he was wearing gloves. I stared at those fingers, waving, bright red. And then I noticed the drops that he was flicking across the floor and the pulpit as he gestured."

They all were quiet for a moment. "There isn't anything more to say," the matron finally said. "Larskpur gestured one last time, and the back draping fell down. There he was, our blessed father, nailed there in a terrible parody of the Survivor's Statemark. Poor Father Bin had been . . . hanging the whole time. Might have been still alive, bleeding and dying while we all listened to that blasphemy."

Marasi doubted that. Though the priest had obviously struggled at first, the spikes would have ended that quickly. "Thank you," she said to the distraught group. "You've been very helpful." She carefully pried the little girl's hands from her arm and passed her to the matron.

Marasi stood, walking to Aradel and Reddi, who stood on the other side of the room.

"What do you think?" Marasi asked softly.

"About the information," Reddi said, "or your interrogation techniques?"

"Either."

"That wasn't how I'd have done it," the short constable said. "But I suppose that you did put them at ease."

"They didn't offer much," Aradel said, rubbing at his chin.

"What did you expect?" Marasi asked. "Captain, this had to be the same person who killed Winsting."

"Don't jump to conclusions," Aradel said. "What would be the motive?"

"Can you explain this any other way?" Marasi said,

gesturing toward the room with the dead priest. "A Pathian? Murdering? Sir, their priests are some of least aggressive people on the planet. I've seen toddlers more dangerous."

Aradel continued rubbing his chin. "Reddi," he said, "go get those conventicalists something to drink. They could use a warm mug right now, I'd suspect."

"Sir?" Reddi said, taken aback.

"You been spending so much time at the gun range you've gone deaf?" Aradel said. "Be about it, Captain. I need to talk to Constable Colms."

Reddi's glare at Marasi could have boiled water, but he moved off to do as ordered.

"Sir," Marasi said, watching him go, "I can't help noticing that you're determined to see the rest of the constables hate me."

"Nonsense," he said. "Just giving the boy a nudge. He's useless when he isn't trying to show off for me—those weeks when he thought he had the assistant's position sewn up were miserable. He's a better officer when he has somebody to compete with." He took Marasi by the shoulder and steered her away from the seated conventicalists. A junior corporal had just shown up with blankets and mugs of warm tea. Hopefully Reddi wouldn't be too put out at having that job stolen from him too.

"I," Aradel said, drawing her attention back to him, "can't fight mistwraiths and spirits in the night. I'm a watchman, not an exorcist."

"I understand that, sir," Marasi said. On their ride over here, she'd told him what Waxillium had said about Bleeder. She wasn't about to keep information like that from her superior. "But if the criminal is supernatural, what option do we have?"

"I don't know," Aradel said, "and that frustrates me to no end. I've got a city dry as a pile of autumn leaves, Lieutenant, and it's about to go up in flames. I don't have the manpower to hunt down a fallen immortal; I need to have constables on the streets trying to keep this city from consuming itself."

"Sir, what if the two are related?"

"The two murders?"

"The murders and the unrest, sir." She closed her eyes, remembering the chapel with its dome and pews, and tried to imagine it as it had been earlier. Larskpur standing in front and waving his hands, horrified parishioners fleeing and bearing the story that the Pathian leader had murdered a Survivorist priest . . .

"Bleeder, or whoever is behind this, has distracted the government with a scandal," Marasi said opening her eyes. "Now she strikes at one church leader in the guise of another? Sir, whatever her real motives are, she's obviously trying to strain Elendel. She *wants* this city to break."

"You might be ascribing too much to one person, Lieutenant."

"Not just a person," Marasi said. "A demigod. Sir, what started the worker strikes?"

"Hell if I know," Aradel said, patting at his pocket and taking out his cigar case. He opened it and found only a little folded note. He grimaced and showed it to her. *There's a banana in your drawer.* "Damn woman will be the death of me. Anyway, I suspect the strikes have been building for a while. Harmony knows I sympathize with the poor fools. Get paid like dirt while the house lords live in mansions and penthouses."

"But why now?" Marasi asked. "It's the food, right?

Suddenly spiked prices, worry that even when the strikes end, there won't be food to be bought?"

"That certainly hasn't helped," Aradel agreed. "Those floods are going to be a strain."

"A broken dam. Did we investigate that properly?"

Aradel paused, little paper half folded to return to his pocket. "You think that could have been sabotage?"

"Could be worth checking," Marasi said.

"Could be indeed," Aradel said. "I'll see if I can spare some men. But if you're right, what's this creature's endgame?"

"General mayhem?" Marasi asked.

Aradel shook his head. "Maybe it's different for mistwraiths, but men who do things like this, they do it to *prove* something. They want to show how clever they are, or they want to stop an injustice. Maybe she wants to bring someone down. Isn't the governor a Pathian?"

"I think so."

"So this murder tonight could be an attempt to discredit his religion." Aradel nodded. "Kill his brother, expose a scandal, undermine his faith, cause riots during his tenure . . . Rusts, this could be about making sure that Innate doesn't just die, he gets *stomped* to the *ground*."

Marasi nodded slowly. "Sir. I . . . might have proof that the governor is corrupt."

"What? What kind of proof?"

"Nothing definitive," she said, blushing. "It has to do with his policies, and when he's changed his mind on bills, when he's voted irregularly following visits with certain key individuals. Sir, you said you hired me in part because of my ability to read statistics. I'll show you what I have once it's all arranged, but the story the governor's record tells is of a man who is offering himself up for sale."

Aradel ran a hand through his hair, red flecked with grey. "Harmony. Keep this quiet, Lieutenant. We'll worry about it another time. Understand?"

"Yes, sir. And I agree."

"But good work," he noted, then jogged over to take crime scene reports. Marasi couldn't help feeling a thrill that he'd listened to what she said, even when all she could offer was half explanations. At the same time, however, a disturbing thought struck her. What if *Aradel* was secretly the kandra, somehow? How much damage could Bleeder do if she had an entire octant's constables under her thumb?

No. Aradel had been around people when the priest was murdered. Rusts . . . the creature would have Marasi jumping at shadows, wondering if everyone she met was a kandra. She went to get herself a cup of that tea, hoping it would help her banish the image in her head of poor Father Bin hung from the wall. She wasn't halfway to the table with the flasks before the doors to the foyer slammed open and Waxillium strode in.

He trailed tassels like the curling mists, his powerful stride prompting lesser constables to scuttle out of his way. How was it that he could so fully encapsulate everything the constables *should* be, but weren't? Noble without being pandering, thoughtful yet proactive, unyielding yet inquisitive.

Marasi smiled, then hurried after him. It wasn't until they reached the chapel, with its large glass dome and the dead priest hanging on the far side, that she realized she'd forgotten entirely about getting tea. A headache still thumped inside her skull.

Aradel stood inside the nave, accompanied by two

young constables. "Lord Ladrian," he said, turning toward Waxillium. "We'll have a report on the body ready for you in—"

"I'll see for myself, constable," Waxillium said. "Thank you." He dropped a bullet casing and rose into the air, soaring over rows of pews beneath the dome to land on the dais.

Aradel sighed and muttered a curse under his breath, then turned to one of the corporals. "See that His Lordship gets whatever he needs. Maybe he can make something of this damn mess—assuming he doesn't just shoot the place up instead."

The young constable nodded, then ran to join Waxillium, who was saying something to Wayne, who had stepped up to join him. Whatever Waxillium said sent the shorter man scuttling out the doors on some errand.

The constable-general shook his head, a sour grimace on his lips.

"Sir?" Marasi said. "You're upset with Lord Waxillium?"

Aradel started, as if he hadn't seen—or hadn't registered—her standing there. "Pay no heed, Lieutenant. His Lordship is a great resource to this department."

"Sir, that has the sound of a practiced answer to it."

"Good," Aradel said, "because it took me a long time to learn to say it without cursing."

"Could I have the non-practiced version?"

Aradel looked her over. "Let's just say that it must be damn nice, Lieutenant, to have other people to clean up your messes for you." He nodded to her, then stalked from the room.

Rusts. Was that how Aradel saw Waxillium? A rogue

nobleman accustomed to getting what he wanted, blunt in ways that Aradel could never be? The constable-general wasn't a nobleman, and had to worry about funding, politics, the future of his men. Waxillium could just butt in and do what he liked, shooting and letting his status—both as an Allomancer and a house lord—get him out of it.

That perspective was eye-opening. Waxillium was a *trouble*. A worthwhile trouble, as he did get things done, but almost as bad as the problems he solved. But for that brief moment he seemed less an ally and more a storm that you had to prepare for and clean up after.

Disturbed, she walked up through the room to join him beside the body.

"Those spikes give off strong lines," Waxillium noted to her, pointing at Father Bin's ruined face. "To my Allomantic senses, I mean. From what I've read, I think that means they're not Hemalurgic spikes. Those are supposed to be tough to see and Push on, like metalminds."

"What would spiking him accomplish?" Marasi asked.

"No idea," Waxillium said. "Still, when you get that body down, send me a sample of metal from each spike. I want to run some tests on their composition."

"All right," Marasi said.

"We should have seen it. She's trying to drive a wedge between the Pathians and the Survivorists."

"The governor is Pathian," Marasi said. "We think Bleeder is trying to get at him."

"You're right," Waxillium said, narrowing his eyes. "But that's not her true goal. She wants to overthrow the city. Perhaps the governor's murder will be the capstone. But what does this have to do with me?"

"Everything doesn't *have* to be about you, you know."

"Not everything," Waxillium agreed. "Just this."

Annoyingly, he was probably right. Why else would Bleeder be parading around the city wearing the body of the man who had killed Waxillium's wife? Waxillium left the corpse, pushing out of the building though the rear exit. There a narrow alleyway led out to the street. Marasi followed, joining Waxillium in the darkness and mists.

"What are you doing?" she asked.

"You don't plan a dramatic murder like this one without preparing an escape route," Waxillium said. "From the discarded handkerchiefs and handbags left behind, I'd guess the room was full when she revealed the body. The worshippers ran out the main doors, and the murderer would have expected this. She would have come out the back, getting away while everyone was either fleeing or stunned."

"Okay . . ."

"Narrow alley," Waxillium said, kneeling to inspect the wall. "Look at this."

Marasi squinted. The bricks along the wall here had been scraped, leaving behind something that had rubbed off on them. "Looks metallic. Silvery."

"Paint, I'd guess," Waxillium said. "Where it came from is a small question, unfortunately, compared to the larger ones. Why would she kill this priest in the first place? She warned me she was going to. I thought she meant your father. Not Father Bin."

"Waxillium," Marasi said. "We need more information. About what this creature can do, and what its motives might be."

"Agreed," Waxillium said. He rose and stared down

the alleyway. "I'd like to ask God a few hard questions. I doubt He's going to make Himself available, however, so we'll have to settle for someone else."

"Who?" Marasi asked.

"I had some help tonight," Waxillium said. "From an unexpected source. I have a feeling that an interview with her will be illuminating. Want to come?"

"Of course I do," Marasi said. "Why wouldn't I?"

"Well," Waxillium said, "I'm worried that interacting with her might prove . . . theologically difficult."

13

Wayne didn't consider himself to be a particularly religious man. He figured that Harmony didn't pay much attention to fellows like him, for the same reason a master painter didn't often wonder what his mom had done with the pictures he'd given her as a toddler.

That said, Wayne *did* like to visit the temple of the common man now and then. It made him feel better and forget his problems for a spell. So he knew the place when Wax sent him on ahead to check it over.

The temple huddled on the corner of an intersection, a stately old building, squat and stubborn. Newer tenements perched on either side, some six stories tall, but the temple had the air of an old gaffer in his chair who hadn't the inclination to look higher than a fellow's knees. As Wayne had expected, the door was open and friendly, still spilling out light, though it was starting to get late. He strolled down the lane and nodded to the temple guard, who wore a cap and overalls for his uniform and bore a ceremonial stick what seemed to have bits of hair sticking out of the end, likely from clubbing men upside the head for being too rowdy.

Wayne tipped his hat to the man and chanted the proper invocation to gain admittance. "Hello, Blue. How watery's the beer today?"

"Don't make trouble at the pub tonight, Wayne," the man intoned in response. "My temper is really short."

"Temper?" Wayne said, passing him. "That's a funny name for it, mate, but if the ladies like you givin' silly names to your body parts, I ain't gonna say nothin'."

Ritual introductions finished, Wayne stepped into the temple proper. Inside, men and women bowed at their places, heads drooping as they considered the deep complexities of the cosmere. Their prayers were made in mumbled exchanges to friends, and their incense in the burning of pipes. A picture of Old Ladrian himself hung over the altar, a man with a ripe paunch and a cup thrust forward, as if to demand attention.

Wayne stood in the doorway, head bowed in respect, and dabbed his fingers into a trail of beer dripping from a nearby table, then anointed himself on the forehead and navel, the mark of the spear.

The scent marked him as a pilgrim upon this holy ground, and he passed among the penitent seeking forgiveness on his way to the altar. The air of the place was odd tonight. Solemn. Yes, the temple was a place of contemplation, but it should also be a place of joy. Where were the hymns, sung in a holy slur? Where was the laughter, the joyful noise of celebration?

Not good, he thought as he settled onto one of the pews—in this case a rough, circular table with scriptures carved into it, like *Mic is a total git* and *The sausages is rubbish.* He'd always liked that one. It brought up real theological implications, it did. If the food they ate was trash, were they ultimately trash? Were they all nothing in the end? Or should one instead see even trash as something to be elevated, as it had been created by the God Beyond like everything else?

Wayne settled back in his seat and drew a few looks from nearby tables. As a lovely young conventicalist in a plunging top passed by carrying mugs, he took her arm. "I'll haaave . . ." he blinked. "Ahll have some whiskey." He had the accent and tone of a man who had been very, *very* pious already this night.

The maid shook her head and continued on her way. Those nearby ignored him. Wayne closed his eyes and listened to their prayers.

"They're just gonna let us starve. You heard the governor, Ren. All he cares about is his rusting reputation."

"We're supposed to have the good life. Harmony made this land for us all. But do we get to enjoy it? No. Its riches only mean that the fine folk get more outfits and big houses."

"Something needs to change in this city. I ain't out of work like those fellows at the steel mill, but Harmony . . ."

"Sixteen-hour shifts. I leave before my little girl gets up, and she's in bed before I get back. See her once a week, I do."

"We work and die so we can give it all up to the same people. They own the building we live in. Ain't that the scam? Work for them all day, then give it all back at night for the privilege of bein' able to survive another day to keep workin'."

Weighty prayers, those were.

Wayne kicked back away from his table and walked to the altar at the front of the room, with its bottles on the rack behind shining in the light. Gas lights. Real traditional, this temple was. He settled down at the altar between a fellow with suspenders and another with arms so hairy he had to have some bear in him. Grandfather, at least.

"Whhiskey," Wayne said to the priest behind the altar.

The man gave him a cup of water with a lemon in it instead. Rusts. Might have laid the accent on a little too thick. Wayne settled back, sipping his water.

The men here at the altar, they didn't complain. They just stared, holding their cups. Wayne nodded. Those were silent prayers, the kind that you could read in their eyes. He reached out and plucked the cup from the next man's hands and gave it a sniff. Plain rum. What fun was that?

He reached over to bear-fur and plucked his drink from his fingers as well, and gave it a sniff. Both men turned toward him as he downed the rest of his water, then mixed their drinks together in his cup. He gave it a squeeze of his lemon and a pinch of sugar from behind the altar, then added some ice, placed a coaster on top, and shook like his life depended on it. Which it might, since the fellow with rugs on his arms had just stood up and cracked his knuckles.

Before he could start pounding, Wayne spun a cup toward each man and settled back in thought. The cups settled into place, and the altar fell silent. Hesitant, the men reached out and tried their drinks. Suspenders tried his first.

"*Wow*," the man said. "What did you do?"

Wayne didn't reply, tapping the table with one finger as hairy-arms tried his drink and nodded appreciatively. Living among the fancy folk had taught Wayne a few things. Fancy folk couldn't ever do anything the ordinary way. Sometimes he thought they acted strange just so they wouldn't be like regular folk.

But they *did* know how to get drunk. He'd give them that.

The priest came over to investigate the disturbance, but both men just wanted more of what Wayne had made. The priest listened to them try to explain it, and then nodded—looked like he'd worked some fancy parties, or had some rich folk come in.

Wayne slipped something onto the altar. A couple of bullet casings.

"What's this?" the priest asked, setting down the cup he'd been wiping. "Is this . . . is this *aluminum*?"

Wayne stood up and gathered a few things from behind the altar, then piled them in the priest's arms. He had ice, fortunately, from a delivery earlier. That was getting cheaper and cheaper these days, with shipments down from the mountains. The fellow also had a nice collection of spirits and some fixings. Enough for Wayne to make do.

Wayne pointed for the man to follow him, then began working his way through the room. He stopped at each table, taking their drinks and reworking them. Those with beer got juice or soda water, mixed carefully and transformed. He always left them with something like what they'd started with, but new. Fresh. He added ginger to some—worked real nice with lemon—and bitters to others. He tried to use something from every table, and only got cussed at a couple of times. Before too long, he had the temple feeling far more companionable. In fact, he'd drawn something of a crowd.

The group cheered as he settled down at a table in front of a tall, pretty woman with large eyes and long fingers. The drink he made for her wasn't actually anything special—gin and lime, with some soda water and a hint of sugar—but the secret ingredient . . . well, that *was* something special. A pouch of blue powder he'd found at the party earlier that night. He'd traded some sand for it.

He mixed the powder into the drink with a hidden twist of the fingers, shaking, before finally adding the lime. As he slid the cup in front of the woman, the drink's blue liquid swirled and moved, then blushed to a deep violet, the color moving through it like growing mists.

Those around him hushed in awe, and the woman smiled at him. He gave her a grin back. He was taken, yes, but he needed to keep practicing his flirtin' or Ranette was likely to start ignoring him.

And then the skin of the woman's cheeks shifted to *blue,* then *violet,* just like the drink had. Wayne jumped back from the table as her skin returned to normal. She took the drink with a sly smile and sipped at it. "Nice," she said, "but I usually like something with more kick to it."

The others in the temple were retreating to their pews. They'd enjoyed the show, but were looking forward to enjoying their liquor even more. They didn't seem to have noticed what the woman's skin had done. Perhaps Wayne had been mistaken. He hesitantly took the seat back and looked at the woman, whose eyes— clear as daylight—shifted from blue to violet, then once again to blue.

"Well hang me," Wayne said. "You're that immortal, ain't you?"

"Sure am," she said, sipping her drink and holding out her hand for him to shake. "Name's MeLaan. Waxillium told me to say 'all yellow pants' to prove it. You did well here tonight. When I first arrived, I felt like the place was going to burst from all the anger. You might have stopped a riot."

"It's just one pub," Wayne said, shaking her hand, then settling back in his chair. "One outta hundreds. If a riot is brewin', I can't stop it with some girly drinks."

"True, I suppose."

"What I need to do," Wayne said, "is get the whole *city* drunk."

"Or, you know, advocate workers' rights to bring down working hours, improve conditions, and meet a base minimum of pay."

"Yeah, yeah," Wayne said. "That too. But if I could get *everybody* drunk, think how much happier this city would be."

"So long as you get *me* drunk first, I'd be fine with it." She held out her cup to him. "Top a lady off, will you?"

Wayne frowned. "Now, this ain't right. You're some kinda demigod or something. Shouldn't you be moralizin' at me?"

"Lo, behold," MeLaan said, wiggling her cup, "bring an offering to your deity in the form of one blue sunset, extra gin. And ye shall be blessed."

"I think I can do that," Wayne said. "Bloody hell, maybe I *am* religious after all."

The immortal demigod took a throaty slurp of her beer, then slammed the mug down onto the table, grinning like a four-year-old who had been paid in cookies to rat out her sister. Wax studied her as she looked Wayne in the eyes and let out a belch that could have woken the dead. Beside Wax, Wayne nodded in appreciation, looking quite impressed. He then downed his own beer and belched back at MeLaan, easily twice as long and loud.

"How do you *do* that?" MeLaan asked.

"Years of trainin' and practice," Wayne said.

"I've been alive for well over half a millennium," MeLaan said. "I am *certain* I have more practice than you."

"You don't have the *will*, though," Wayne said, wagging his finger. "You gotta *want* it." He downed the rest of his mug and let out a protracted belch.

Marasi, who sat next to Wax in their booth at the pub, looked horrified by the exchange. Wax had allowed her to drive them here, if only so he could rebind his wound and check it over. The painkillers were doing their job, though. He could barely feel the hit.

After the short ride, he and Marasi had walked in on these two in the middle of their belching . . . contest? Wax wasn't certain if it was a contest, or more a matter of mutual appreciation, like two virtuosos playing their favorite songs.

MeLaan finished her beer, then dramatically held up her hand. The palm split, forming lips, which then let out a soft belch.

"Cheating," Wayne said.

"Just using what Father gave me," MeLaan said. "Don't tell me you wouldn't belch out of other body parts if you could."

"Well," Wayne said, "now that you mention it, I *can* make a real interestin' sound wif—"

Wax cleared his throat. "Not to defer a conversation about which parts of Wayne's body can and can't make noise, but I have to admit that you aren't what I expected, Your Grace."

"Bloody hell," MeLaan said. "Please don't call me that."

"You're a servant of Harmony," Wax said.

"I'm from one of the later generations," MeLaan said. "In kandra terms, I'm basically still a kid."

"You lived through the Catacendre," Wax said. "You knew the Originators."

"I spent the Catacendre underground," MeLaan said. "I was an adolescent, and didn't know the land when it was covered in ash. You really don't need to be intimidated by me."

"You're over *six hundred* years old," Marasi said.

"So is dirt," MeLaan said. She leaned forward. "Look, I'm just here to help. If you want someone to fawn over, I'll send VenDell or one of the really ancient ones to you. They like it. I just want to see Paalm stopped, then helped."

Wax leaned forward on the table. He could sense in the way MeLaan smiled at people passing by—the way she tapped her finger to the tavern song a group of drunk men sang in the corner—that she liked people. She liked being here, among them. She wasn't aloof, as he'd expected, or withdrawn. Not even that alien, despite the fact that she'd just made a mouth in her hand. "You're the one who brought me my earring," he said, fingering his ear with its tiny spike. "All those years ago."

MeLaan's smile widened. "I was wearing the same body, but I'm still surprised you remember."

"And whose body is it?" Marasi asked. "Where did you get those bones?"

"I made them," MeLaan said, raising her chin. Her face went transparent, suddenly, revealing the skull underneath—one made of carved crystal of a vivid emerald color. "I prefer True Bodies, though if I need to I can take another form. I'll warn you, as far as kandra go, I'm only so-so at impersonation."

"And this one we're huntin'?" Wayne asked. He'd started building a houselike tower using the thin wooden coasters strewn around the tavern table, balancing them on their ends.

"Paalm?" MeLaan said, turning her face back to normal. "She was one of our best. Of all the kandra I know, only TenSoon is better at it than she is."

"But she'll be erratic," Wax said. "She's gone mad. That should help us spot her, even in disguise, right?"

"Maybe," MeLaan said, grimacing. She took a few of the coasters and started her own tower. "Paalm is good, and imitation . . . well, it's kind of *ingrained* in us, particularly the older kandra who worked back in the days of the Final Empire. Some of them don't feel like they have personalities of their own; they don't know how to live unless they're being someone else."

"You seem to find the idea disturbing," Wax said, curious.

"I'm a youngster," she said with a shrug. "Never really had to serve the Lord Ruler. I've always served Harmony, who seems like a generally nice fellow."

An odd way to refer to God. Wax glanced at Marasi, who cocked an eyebrow at him and shrugged. Around them, the pubgoers chattered with a low hum of energy and enthusiasm. Wax and the others had settled into a secluded booth at the side. The warm gas lighting was somehow friendlier, more alive than the electric lights back at his mansion.

"All right," Wax said to MeLaan. "Let's talk about what Bleeder can do. And about how to kill her."

"You don't need to kill her," MeLaan said quickly, getting her tower to a second story. She glanced at Wayne, who already had his up to three levels. "Just remove her remaining spike, which will basically immobilize her. She's confused; we can deal with her once we have her in custody."

"Confused?" Wax said. "She killed a priest by *nailing him through the eyes.*"

MeLaan's smile faded. "She only has one spike. She's not thinking straight."

"Yes," Wax said, "but she pulled the other spike out herself, right?"

"We think so," MeLaan admitted. "We're weaker than other Hemalurgic creatures. Only two spikes, and we can be taken. So she removed one."

"She wanted freedom to kill," Wax said. "She's not 'confused,' MeLaan. She's destructive and possibly psychotic. Tell me how to kill her."

MeLaan sighed. "Acid works, but that's horribly inefficient. If you crush her skeleton, she'll have a hard time moving, so maybe use that. Gunshots will be useless, as will most forms of physical damage. The spike—it's the key. Pull it out, and she'll revert to her primal state. It *is* the best way."

"Her primal state," Marasi said. "A mistwraith."

MeLaan nodded.

Wax tapped the table in thought. "If I can get the spike out, chances are that I've already immobilized her. If she's tied up, what good will it do to remove the spike?"

"Waxillium," MeLaan said, leaning forward, "you *do* realize what you're dealing with? Paalm was trained by the ancients, and served the Lord Ruler *himself*. She quashed rebellions and overthrew kingdoms in his service, and she is intimately familiar with the intricacies of Hemalurgy. By your own accounts, she's learned to use spikes to grant herself Allomancy and Feruchemy—something we thought impossible. If you have her captured, that is a state she's not likely to remain in for long. *Remove that spike.*"

Wax felt a chill. "Right," he said. "Will do."

"Rusts," Marasi whispered. "I thought you didn't want us to be intimidated by you."

"Me?" the kandra said. "I'm harmless." She waved at the barmaid, then pointed at her mug. "I'm far less crazy than Paalm."

"Great," Wax said. He glanced at Wayne. "You look concerned."

"Me?" Wayne said, placing a fourth level onto his tower. "Sorry. Tryin' to think of how to get everyone in the city drunk."

"I . . . I'm not going to ask." Wax grabbed a few of the coasters as a barmaid dropped more on the table, noticing that they were playing with them. He started building a tower of his own. "So we get the spike out. How?"

"Easiest way is to call me," MeLaan said. "I can get it out. But if I'm not there, don't wait on me. Break her bones, start pulling them out, and eventually you'll find the spike. It will take a strong stomach."

Great. "Is there a way to spot a kandra? Wound patterns? Blood samples?"

MeLaan dug into her pocket. "Once we've shifted shapes, we lock into that body and *are* that person. We'll bleed, and if you take off a finger, our prints will remain that of the person we're imitating. Even another kandra will have trouble spotting a duplicate. Haven't you read the Historica?"

"Several times," Wax said, "but the kandra sections are kind of dull."

"I feel like I should be offended by that."

"Then you aren't drunk enough," Wayne responded. Five levels. Wax shook his head and concentrated on getting his second level built.

"Anyway," MeLaan, "locating other kandra was a problem in the past. So we did something about it, just in case. The more scientifically minded among us developed this."

She slid something onto the table. A pair of needles, about as long as a man's palm is wide, attached to metal syringes. Wax held one up.

"Inject that into a kandra," MeLaan said, "and the liquid inside will make her shape droop for a bit. The skin briefly goes clear, reveals who she really is."

"Nifty," Wayne said.

"One problem though," MeLaan said. "If you stick it into someone who *isn't* a kandra, it will kill them."

"Inconvenient," Marasi said, examining the other one.

"Yeah," MeLaan said. "We're working on that part. This is a last resort, obviously, but it *will* immobilize her briefly. If you want to find Paalm before using it, you can try to catch her in a lie. She won't have the actual memories of the person she's imitating. Conversely, if you see someone who isn't Metalborn use a power, that outs her too."

"I've got a feeling that if she's using her powers right in front of me, I'm dead anyway," Wax said.

The group fell silent. Wax took both syringes and tucked them into the pouch on his gunbelt. Marasi scribbled on a note pad, transcribing the conversation—he'd have to ask her for a copy. Drink refills arrived, and no payment was requested. What had Wayne done here before Wax arrived? He was afraid to ask.

What help is this? Wax thought, frustrated, his tower falling to pieces. A weapon he could use only when he was already a hundred percent certain who the impostor was? It felt like so little. Bleeder could be anyone. Bleeder could manifest any of the powers. Bleeder was ancient, brilliant, and crafty. . . .

"She has a plan," Wax said. "She's *not* simply crazy, MeLaan. There is more to this."

"You're still determined to kill her," MeLaan said, sighing.

"If I have to. Why are you so hesitant? I'd think that the kandra would be determined, more than anyone, to see this problem dealt with."

"She's not a 'problem,'" MeLaan said. "She's a person. Yes, I want to see her stopped. She *needs* to be stopped. But . . ." She settled back, then knocked over her small tower of coasters with a flick of the finger. "There's so few of us left. Hell, there weren't ever more than five or six hundred of us, and we lost a lot in the days before the Final Ascension. Imagine if your entire race consisted of three hundred people, lawman. Maybe you'd be a little more hesitant to see one of them slagged."

"A person's species shouldn't matter," Wax snapped. "I don't care if there are three hundred of you left or just three; when one of you starts nailing people to walls in my city, I'm going to—"

"Wax," Wayne interrupted, balancing his *sixth* story of beer-mat coasters. "Check your pulse, mate."

Wax took a deep breath. "Sorry," he said.

"What was that," Marasi said, wagging her pencil from Wayne to Wax. "Pulse?"

"Sometimes," Wayne said, "Wax forgets he's a person and starts thinkin' he's a rock instead."

"It's Wayne speak," Wax said, grabbing some coasters and starting another tower. "For times when he thinks I should be a little more empathetic."

"You can be single-minded, mate."

"Says the man who once collected eighty different kinds of beer bottles."

"Yeah," Wayne said, smiling fondly. "Did that mostly to annoy you, I did."

"You're kidding."

He shook his head. "Started to hate all those rusting bottles, but each morning you'd curse when you tripped over a new box o' them, and it was just so melodious . . ."

"You know," MeLaan said, taking a pull on her drink, "you two aren't *anything* like I was led to believe."

"Tell me about it," Marasi said.

"For one thing," MeLaan added, "I had no idea that Kid Wayne was so talented with beer-mat sculptures."

"He cheated," Wax said. "He stuck some of the coasters on his lower level together with that gum stuff he's been chewing."

Marasi and MeLaan turned to Wayne, who grinned. He picked up his sculpture, knocking down the top levels, but revealing that the bottom three had—indeed—been stuck together.

"Wayne," Marasi said, aghast. "Are you that concerned with impressing us?"

"It wasn't about impressing anyone," Wax said. "The contest wasn't about how high the towers got—it was about if I'd spot what he did. He always cheats somehow. Back to the matter at hand, MeLaan. Your rogue kandra friend is planning something. If her plot gains momentum, it will roll over us and crush this city."

"I agree," MeLaan said. "So what do we do?"

"We outthink her," Wax said. "I need to know her motive. *Why* is she doing this? What drove her to pull out her spike in the first place?"

"I wish I knew," MeLaan said. "We've been trying to figure out the same thing."

"Tell me about her, then," Wax said, tapping at his empty shot glass. "What is she like? What are her passions?"

"Paalm was the ultimate blank slate," MeLaan said. "Old-style kandra. Like I said, she spent so much time out on missions that she barely had a personality of her own. She had real trouble with that at the dawn of a new world. Some of the older generations, they liked to spend time in the Homeland, only left for a mission when forced to. Not Paalm. She was the Father's own, the kandra reserved specifically to do missions for the Lord Ruler." She hesitated. "She might know things from him. Things the rest of us weren't told. I think he may even have had her imitate Inquisitors at times, act as a mole among them.

"Anyway, she wouldn't have been able to imperson-ate an Inquisitor without a good grasp of Allomancy and Feruchemy. So maybe that's where she got the knowledge. She was loyal to the Lord Ruler, and then when he was gone, she became loyal to Harmony. Fanatical about it. Insisted on being given mission after mission, and never spent time with the rest of us. Kept to herself. She was almost always in character. Until . . ."

"Murderous rampage," Wayne said softly. "It's always the quiet ones. Well, and the psychopathic ones. That too."

So what does that tell me? Wax thought, leaving his little tower at three stories. *How would I approach this if it were any other criminal?*

MeLaan leaned back for a moment, as if lost in thought, then flipped a coaster at Wax's tower to knock it down. She grunted.

"What?" Wax said.

"I was just curious to see if you were cheating too."

"Wax never cheats," Wayne said, face halfway in his mug. Wax had never figured out how he could talk and drink at the same time without choking.

"That's incorrect," Wax said. "I cheat *infrequently*. That way nobody's expecting it." He stood up. "Can you think of a reason Bleeder would target the governor in particular?"

MeLaan shook her head.

"Do any of the other kandra know her better than you do?"

"Maybe one of the older ones," MeLaan said. "I'll see if I can get one of them to come talk to you."

"Good," Wax said. "But first I want you three watching the governor."

"I've got to report in to the precinct offices first," Marasi said. "I want to follow up on something there."

"Fine," Wax said. "Wayne, you head to the governor's mansion first."

"He ditched me last time."

"He won't again," Wax said. "I've persuaded him to listen, though we'll need him to meet MeLaan soon."

"Sure, all right," Wayne said. "It wasn't like I was planning to, you know, *sleep* tonight or anythin'."

"Sleep might be in short supply going forward," Wax said.

"You want me to go with him, Dawnshot?" MeLaan asked.

"Depends. Marasi, would you like some backup?"

"Yes please," she said.

"Watch her," Wax said, nodding toward Marasi. "And maybe give Aradel a glimpse of your nature. It's probably time to inform him what we're up against."

"Already done," Marasi said. "Though I'm sure he'd like proof."

Wax grunted. He hadn't ordered her to do that. "Be quick about your errand," Wax told her. "And get to the governor. I want more than one set of eyes on him. And before we split, I want each pair of us to exchange codes, individual and unknown to the others, so we each have a way to authenticate ourselves to one another. I've done the same with the governor and his top staff." Harmony, this was going to be a nightmare.

"Watching the governor isn't going to be enough, Wax," Marasi said, standing up from the table. "You yourself said it. Too reactive. So what else are we going to do?"

"I'll come up with something."

The others stood, and Wax towed Wayne by the arm to check to see that they were square with the pub manager. Surprisingly, Wayne had indeed paid for everything he should have. On their way toward the door, Wax explained to his friend a little idea he had for protecting the governor.

They stepped into the entryway of the pub, where

MeLaan was waiting while Marasi fired up her beast of a motorcar. Wayne hiked off to catch a carriage to take him to the governor's mansion, and Wax took Me-Laan by the arm.

"I hate this," he noted, soft enough to keep the bouncer outside from hearing. "Not being able to trust people I should always be able to. Second-guessing myself."

"Yeah," she replied. "But you'll handle it. There's a reason He came to you for this." She stepped in closer. Rusts, she was attractive—but then, it would be odd if she weren't, all things considered. "You and I aren't the only ones hunting Paalm, lawman—every kandra in the city is searching for her. Thing is, I don't think many of my brothers and sisters will be of use. They're timid about hurting others, particularly after what TenSoon was forced to do during the Remarked Duplicity. And beyond that, they can be an . . . inconsistent group."

"They're God's servants," Wax said.

"Yes," MeLaan replied, "and they've had centuries upon centuries to refine their eccentricities. Getting older does *not* tend to make you more normal, let me tell you. We don't think like killers. We've been too closely in contact with Harmony. What Paalm is doing, it baffles us. It goes against everything we've believed and lived for centuries. I don't think we'll be able to find her, not in time. But you . . . you can."

"Because I think like a killer."

"I didn't—"

"It's all right," Wax said, releasing her arm. "I am what I am." He took his mistcoat from the peg by the door and shrugged it on before stepping out into the night. "Thanks, by the way," he said.

"For?"

He tapped his ear, and the earring he wore in it. "This."

"I was just the delivery girl."

"Doesn't matter. It was what I needed. When I needed it." He dropped a bullet casing, then stilled it with his foot. "I'll meet you all at the governor's mansion."

14

I f you want to know a man, dig in his firepit.

The phrase was from the Roughs, maybe koloss in origin. Basically, it meant that you could judge a lot about a man's life by what he threw away—or by what he was willing to burn in order to stay warm.

A loud church clock rang eleven as Wax moved through the mists on Allomantic jumps. The sound echoed in the night, the bell tower hidden in the darkness. Eleven was not late these days, particularly not in the heart of the city, but it *should* have marked a time when most men and women had begun to seek their beds. Labor started early in the morning.

Only, a sizable portion of the laborers in the city didn't have a job to get up for right now. That was reflected in the busy streets and busier pubs, not to mention the Soothing parlors he passed, still open well into the night. Those were places where the downhearted could seek a different kind of relief, in the form of an Allomancer who—for a small fee—would wipe away their emotions for a time and leave them numb.

Rioting parlors were a different beast. There, you could choose the emotion you wanted and have it stoked within you. Those might be even more popular, judging by the line he saw outside one.

Wax delayed on a rooftop, listening, then headed for the sound of men shouting. He ran along the peaked roof and Pushed off the nails in the shingles, launching himself over a set of apartments in a quiet flutter, coming down and landing on a street beyond.

Here, he found a small Pathian sanctuary. Not the church with the bell he'd heard earlier; Pathian structures were too small for that. Built to resemble old Terris huts, they were often empty save for two chairs. One for you. One, ostensibly, for Harmony. The religion forbade worship, in a formal way. But talking to God was encouraged.

Tonight, the little sanctuary was under siege.

They shouted and threw rocks: a group of shadows in the mist, probably drunk. He could make them out well enough; a misty night was never too dark in the city, not with all the ambient light reflecting off the vapors.

Wax yanked Vindication from her holster and stalked forward, mistcoat flaring behind him. His profile was enough. The first man who spotted him emerging from the mists yelled a warning and the men scattered, leaving the detritus of their tiny riot. Fallen stones. A few bottles. Wax watched their metal lines to make sure none of them rounded back on him. One stopped nearby, but kept his distance.

He shook his head, stepping up to the sanctuary. He found the missionary cowering inside, a Terriswoman in intricate braids. Pathian clergy was a strange thing. On one hand, the religion emphasized man's personal connection to Harmony—doing good, without formality. On the other hand, people needed direction.

Someone to explain all of this. Pathian missionaries—called priests by outsiders, though they rarely used the term for themselves—set up in places like this, explaining the Path to all who came. A clergy, yes, but not in the formal way of the Survivorists.

He'd always found it curious that the small Pathian sanctuaries—with large doorways on eight sides—let in the mists, while Survivorist churches observed the mists from behind domes of glass, comfortable in their ornate rooms full of golden statues and fine wood pews. The woman looked up at him as he knelt, smelling oil. Her lantern lay broken nearby.

"Are you all right?" he asked.

"I . . . Yes," she said. "Thank you."

Her eyes flicked toward the gun. On principle, Wax didn't holster the thing. "It would be best if you retired for the night," Wax said.

"But I live in the loft upstairs."

"Go to the Village then," Wax said. "In fact, gather any of your colleagues you can in a short time and take them as well. A Survivorist priest has been brutally murdered by someone posing as a Pathian missionary."

"Sweet Harmonies," the woman whispered.

Wax left her to gather her things and, hopefully, do as he told her. He struck out into the night, following a few lines of metal toward where the man he'd scared off earlier had hidden. Wax studied the darkened alleyway in the mists, then dropped a shell casing and launched himself into the air. A careful Push let him drop straight into the alleyway, where he landed and leveled a gun at the head of the person hiding there.

Who immediately soiled himself, judging from the stench and the liquid pooling at the young man's feet. Wax sighed and lifted Vindication. The young man scrambled backward, stumbling over a box of trash, adding to his humiliation.

"You're going to leave that missionary alone," Wax said. "She had nothing to do with the murder."

The youth nodded. Wax dropped a shell casing and prepared to launch himself back into the night.

"M-murder?" the youth asked.

"Of the . . ." Wax hesitated. "Wait. Why were you here, attacking that sanctuary?"

The boy whimpered. "They came into the pub, two of them in those Pathian robes, and cursed out the Survivor an' us."

"*Two?*" Wax said, advancing on the boy, making him cringe. "There was more than one?"

He nodded, then—crying—scrambled away and ran into the night. Wax let him go.

I should have guessed, he thought, launching himself into the air. *The news of the murder couldn't have traveled this quickly.* There was more to the plot than the one killing. Rusts. Were other priests in danger?

Two people. Bleeder and someone else? Or two helpers? MeLaan had seemed confident that Bleeder would be working alone, but this offered evidence to the contrary. And the attempt to kill Wax earlier, the ploy involving the server at ZoBell Tower, matched too well with his fears of an assassin to be coincidence. Bleeder had help, likely from Wax's uncle. He'd look into that later. For now, however, there was a different lead he wanted to chase.

He eventually reached the location he'd set out to find: Ashweather Carriage and Coach, a large open yard at the northern edge of the octant where a fleet of carriages of various styles was stored. Rich-looking landaus with retractable tops. Conventional buggies, with less lavish upholstery and wood, to attract a modest clientele. A few surrey-style, with frilled tops.

By far the most common in the carriage park was the standard road coach: the four-wheeled vehicle with a completely enclosed passenger compartment, and room at the top front for a driver. They called them Barringtons in the city, after Lord Barrington, and though the paint jobs could vary wildly, the style was pretty much standardized. Wax's own coaches were Barringtons.

He counted seven in a line here, all lit by electric lamps atop towering stanchions high enough to light the whole yard and adjacent large, low buildings. Those were stables, of course, as his nose confirmed. All of the Ashweather Company's carriages were painted a shiny black, common for vehicles used as cabs in the city, and they had a round shield on the side proclaiming the Cett family heritage.

A shield painted silver. The color that had scraped onto the bricks in the alleyway outside the church. Bleeder had likely fled in a coach just like one of these, one that had been told to wait while Bleeder killed the priest.

Wax inspected each vehicle in turn, running his fingers over the silver-painted shields on the sides. No scrapes.

"Can I help you?" a curt voice demanded. Steelsight indicated a person walking up the row of vehicles. No weapon held, but metal buttons on his coat, a ring on each hand, some change in the pocket, and a watch in his waistcoat. A few pins in the collar of his shirt— very small lines—gave Wax an idea of how tall the man was.

Wax turned toward the voice. The man turned out to be a pudgy fellow in a distinctive formal suit with long tails, identifying him as the establishment's proprietor. Wax had known more than a few Cetts in his time. He'd never gotten along with any of them. Lean or fat, rich or scrawny, they all got the same calculating look on their faces as they tried to estimate how much money Wax would be willing to part with.

This Cett's eyes flicked toward Wax's suit, which was rumpled, swum-in, and missing the cravat. With the duster on, he likely didn't look very distinguished—and the man's expression hardened. Then he saw the tassels on the duster.

His entire demeanor changed immediately. His posture went from "Stay away from my coaches" to "You look like the type who will pay extra for velvet pillows." "My lord," he added, nodding his head. "Would you like to hire a coach for the evening?"

"You know me?" Wax said.

"Waxillium Ladrian, I believe."

"Good," Wax said, digging into his pocket and removing a small steel sheet, engraved on one side. His credentials, proof that he was a constable. "I'm on constabulary business. How many of these coaches do you have?" Wax nodded toward the line.

Cett's expression fell as he realized Wax wasn't likely to be paying him for anything tonight. "Twenty-three," the man finally said.

"Lots of coaches still in service for the night," Wax said. "Considering the hour."

"We work as long as people are out, constable," Cett said. "And tonight, people are out."

Wax nodded. "I need a list of the drivers who are still

working, their routes, and any prearranged clients they picked up today."

"Of course." Cett seemed more relaxed as he led Wax toward a small building in the center of the carriage yard. As they walked, a coach arrived—no scraped sides—drawn by a pair of sweaty horses with drooping heads and a bit of froth at the mouths. Long hours for the beasts too, it seemed.

Inside the building, Cett fetched some records from a desk. *Too eager,* Wax thought as the man hurried over and offered them. Whenever someone worked with the authorities too easily, it made Wax's eye twitch. So he took his time browsing through the lists Cett proffered and kept an eye on the man as he did so. "What percentage of your pickups are impromptu, and what percentage are arranged ahead of time?"

"Half and half, for the black coaches," Cett said. "The open carriages are more spur-of-the-moment." He had a good game face, but something *was* bothering him. What was he hiding?

You think everyone is hiding something, Wax told himself, flipping through the pages. *Stay on the task at hand.*

Wax dug into the list, hoping Bleeder had decided to hire a coach for a pickup to be certain she had her escape planned, rather than just grabbing a cab on the street. Finding the one who had driven her would be useful either way. He looked over the records for the drivers still out for the night. Each had a few prearranged pickups over the course of the day, but only three had been scheduled around the time of the murder. And two of those were repeat customers with a long list of pickups in the past.

That left one. A person to be picked up in the Fourth Octant, and to be driven "at liberty," meaning they were to be driven as long as the client wished. Shanwan was the name listed. A Terris name. The word meant "secret."

"I need to find this driver," Wax said, holding up the list and pointing. *If they're still alive.*

"Coach sixteen," Cett said, rubbing his chin. "That's Chapaou's. No telling when he'll be back; you probably don't want to wait. I can send you a message when he returns."

"Maybe," Wax said, but dallied.

The door slammed open and a young woman in trousers and suspenders burst in. "Boss," she said, "late-night play getting out on Bonnweather. They're going to want rides."

"We sent coaches there already."

"Not enough," the young woman said. "Boss, there are *lots* of men on the streets. Common men, the type that will make the rich folk nervous. Playgoers will want carriages."

Cett nodded. "Wake Jone and Forgeron. Send them and anyone else you can rouse. Anything more?"

"We could have more wheels out for certain, particularly near the pubs."

"Coinshot," Wax guessed, noticing the bag of metal bits—probably pieces of scrap—the young woman carried. "You've been using Allomancer runners to scout for busy areas to send drivers."

"Is that surprising?" Cett asked.

"It's expensive."

"You have to spend money to make money, constable," Cett said. "And as you can see, I'm having a very busy night. Perhaps you could leave me to it, if I promise to—"

"Coinshot," Wax said to the girl. "You see coach number sixteen out there? I assume your boss has you checking in on the drivers, make sure they're doing their jobs?"

"How—" she began.

"You don't hire an Allomancer just for traffic reports," Wax said. "Coach sixteen?"

She glanced at Cett, who nodded. So whatever Cett was hiding, it probably didn't have to do with this driver. In fact, it probably didn't have anything to do with Bleeder. Just your average, run-of-the-mill law-breaking.

At least one Allomancer on staff, Wax thought.

"I didn't see sixteen on the streets," the young Allomancer said, turning to Wax. "But that's because Chapaou is at a Soothing parlor over on Decan Street. His coach is around the corner."

"At a *Soothing parlor?*" Cett demanded. "He's on the clock!"

"I know," the Allomancer said. "I thought you'd want to hear."

"Hm, yes," Wax said. "And what of the Rioter you have on staff. Are they there too?"

"Nah," the Allomancer said. "He's on—" She cut off, and grew pale. The entire room fell still.

"Using emotional Allomancy," Wax said, "to drum up customers. Riot passing people, make them feel tired or urgent, and more willing to take the coach conveniently parked right across the street."

Cett looked sick. Yes, that was it. Flagrant use of a Rioter to drum up business, a violation of the Allomantic Agreement of '94. There were entire departments in the government that watched for this sort of thing. Fortunately, while it was a dangerous crime, it wasn't one that worried Wax at the moment.

"You don't have any proof . . ." Cett said, then thought better of it. "I'll be speaking with my attorney. I'll have you know that my people are off-limits for interrogation without a judicial order to—"

"Take it up with the constable-general," Wax said. "I'm sure you'll be hearing from him soon. For now, I need a description of this carriage driver of yours, along with the names of any pets he owns."

Marasi walked along a counter topped with a row of rifles, each accompanied by a domed steel helmet, a folded heavy jacket, and a box of ammunition. Rusts! She hadn't realized the constabulary had access to these kinds of weapons.

"Well," she said, looking back at MeLaan, "we're ready if a koloss warlord decides to invade again."

A pair of corporals, both men, were looking over each weapon to confirm it was in good repair. Though she spotted more than one pair of bleary eyes, the place was alive with activity. More and more constables were arriving, called in for extra duty. As they entered through the main doors they tended to stop as Marasi had, looking at the row of weapons. Perhaps that was why Aradel had ordered them set out like this. A quick visual reminder of how dangerous things were growing in the city.

Marasi rounded the front counter and entered the offices behind. A young woman corporal passed by, handing Marasi a warm cup of dark tea. It smelled strong, cooked down to increase the concentration of caffeine. She tried a sip.

Yup. Awful. She drank another sip anyway. She wasn't going to embarrass herself by asking for honey when everyone else was chugging the stuff like it was some kind of contest. MeLaan trailed after her, looking around the room with interest. The voluptuous kandra drew glances. And, well, stares. It wasn't often that a gorgeous, six-and-a-half-foot-tall woman strode into the constabulary offices clad in trousers and a tight shirt. She seemed to like the attention, judging by the way she smiled at the men they passed.

Of course she likes the attention, Marasi thought. *Otherwise she wouldn't have chosen a body so exquisitely proportioned.* It seemed blatant to Marasi. After all, technically MeLaan wasn't even *human*.

"I didn't expect to find women in uniform here," MeLaan noted. "I'd assumed you to be an oddity."

"The constabulary is very egalitarian," Marasi said. "The Ascendant Warrior serves as a model for all women. You won't find as many of us here as in, say, the solicitors' offices, but it's hardly considered an unfeminine profession."

"Sure, sure," MeLaan said, smiling at a young lieutenant as the two of them made their way to the back rooms, where the records office was. "But I've always found humans to be rather sexist. A natural result of your sexual dimorphism, VenDell says."

"And kandra aren't sexist?" Marasi said, blushing.

"Hmm? Well, considering that a male kandra you're talking to today might decide to be a woman tomorrow, I'd say we have a different perspective on all that."

Marasi blushed further. "Surely you're exaggerating."

"Not really. Wow, you blush easily, don't you? I'd have thought you'd find this natural, considering that your God is basically a hermaphrodite at this point. Both good and evil, Ruin and Preservation, light and dark, male and female. Et cetera et cetera."

They reached the doors to the records office and Marasi turned away to hide her blush. She really wished she'd just find a way to get over her embarrassment. "Harmony's not my god. I'm a Survivorist."

"Oh, yeah," MeLaan said, "because *that* makes sense. Worship the guy who died, rather than the one who saved the world."

"The Survivor transcended death," Marasi said, looking back, hand on the door, but not entering. "He survived even being killed, adopting the mantle of the Ascendant during the time between Preservation's death and Vin's Ascension."

Rust . . . was she arguing theology with a demigod?

MeLaan, however, just cocked her head. "What, really?"

"Um . . . yes. Harmony wrote of it *himself* in the Words of Founding, MeLaan."

"Huh. I really ought to read that thing one of these days."

"You haven't . . ." Marasi blinked, trying to fathom a world where one of the Faceless Immortals didn't know doctrine.

"I keep meaning to," MeLaan said, shrugging. "Never can find the time."

"You're over six hundred years old."

"That's the thing about having an eternity, kid," MeLaan said. "It gets *really* easy to procrastinate. Are we going in that room or not?"

Marasi sighed, pushing into a room filled with filing cabinets and tables piled high with ledgers and broadsheets. This was Aradel's doing; he liked to keep his thumb on what people were saying and writing in the city. So far, he didn't do much with the collection besides watch for reports of crimes his men had missed, but Marasi had plans.

Unfortunately, Constable Miklin—who ran the records office—was one of Reddi's closest friends. As Marasi entered, Miklin and the other two people working there looked up, then immediately turned back to their files.

"Who's the civilian?" Miklin asked from his desk in the corner. How *did* he get his hair to stand up straight like that? Almost like a patch of grass growing from a pot.

"Special investigator from another jurisdiction," Marasi said. "Lord Ladrian sent her."

Miklin sniffed. "I'm led to believe this wisp hunt is your doing? I barely got to the offices tonight before I was sent back here to dig up information on that dam breaking."

"What did you find?" Marasi said eagerly, slipping between two large filing cabinets—he had them arranged like sentries—and stepping up to his desk.

"Nothing," Miklin said. "Dead end. Waste of my time."

"I'd like to see what you found anyway," Marasi said. "If it's not too much trouble."

Miklin rested his hands on the table. He spoke softly. "Why are you here, Colms?"

"I thought Aradel told you," Marasi said. "The dam breakage might—"

"Not that. Here. In the constabulary. You had an offer to join the octant's senior prosecutor on a permanent basis, with a letter of commendation on your internship with him. I looked into it. And now . . . what? You suddenly want to chase criminals? Strap on some six-guns like you're from the rusting Roughs? That's not what police work is like."

"I'm well aware," Marasi said dryly. "But thank you for the information. What did you find?"

He sighed, then tapped a folder with the back of his hand. "Rusting waste of my time," he muttered.

Marasi took the folder and retreated between the filing cabinets. She wished it were only Miklin she had to deal with, but the two other constables made their opinions known with quiet sniffs of disdain. Marasi felt them glaring at her as she led MeLaan out of the room, clutching her folder.

"Why do they treat you like that?" MeLaan asked as they slipped out.

"It's complicated."

"People tend to be. Why do you *let* them treat you like that?"

"I'm working on it."

"You want me to do something?" MeLaan said. "I could scare the cynicism right out of those people, show them you've got friends that—"

"No!" Marasi said. "No, please. It's nothing I haven't dealt with before."

MeLaan followed her as she scurried to her desk outside of Aradel's office. A lanky female constable stood there, one foot on Marasi's chair, chatting with the man one desk over and sipping her tea. Marasi cleared her throat twice before the woman—Taudr was her name, wasn't it?—finally looked at her, rolled her eyes, and moved out of the way.

Marasi settled down. MeLaan pulled over a chair. "You sure you don't want me—"

"No," Marasi said immediately, digging into the folder. She took a deep breath. "No, please."

"I'm sure your friend Waxillium could come on over, fire off a few slugs, force them to stop being such sourlips."

Oh, Survivor, no, Marasi thought, the image of it making her sick. But MeLaan obviously wasn't going to let this go without an explanation.

"I'm beginning to realize that Waxillium is part of the reason why they treat me as they do," Marasi said, opening the folder Miklin had prepared. "Life in the precinct follows a hierarchy. The sergeants start as corporals, work the streets, put in ten or fifteen years doing a hard beat and finally earn a promotion. The captains start out as lieutenants, and mostly come from noble stock. Once in a while, a sergeant works his or her way up. But everyone's expected to put in their time at the bottom."

"And you . . ."

"I skipped all that," Marasi said. "I applied for—and got—an important position as Aradel's chief aide. Waxillium makes that worse, as I'm associated with him. He's like a whirlwind, blowing through and messing everything up. But he's also good at what he does and a high-ranking nobleman, so nobody complains too loudly. I, however . . ."

"Not noble."

"Not noble enough," Marasi said. "My father is low-ranked, and I'm illegitimate. That makes me the available target, when Waxillium is off-limits."

MeLaan leaned back in her chair and scanned the room. "Spook was always droning on about things like this—that bloodline shouldn't matter as much as capability. You doing what you did should be impressive to everyone, not threatening. Hell, you said the place was egalitarian."

"It is," Marasi said. "That's why I could get the job in the first place. But it doesn't stop people from resenting me. I'm the way the world is changing, MeLaan, and change is frightening."

"Huh," the kandra said. "And the lower ranks just go along with this? You think they'd like you showing that someone can jump in line."

"You don't know a lot about human nature, do you?"

"Of course I do. I've studied, and imitated, dozens of people."

"I suspect you understand individuals, then," Marasi said. "The interesting thing about people is that while they might seem unique, they actually play into broad patterns. Historically, the working class has often been *more* resistant to change than the class oppressing them."

"Really?" MeLaan asked.

Marasi nodded. She started to reach for some books on the small shelf beside her desk, but stopped. This wasn't the time. In fact, they might be witnessing one of the exceptions to this rule, outside on the streets. And, like many upendings of the status quo, when it *did* happen, it could be violent. Like a steam engine's boiler that had been plugged up, given no release until suddenly . . . everything exploded.

Nobody liked to realize they'd been had. People in Elendel believed they were living the good life—they'd been told all their lives that Harmony had blessed them with a rich and lavish land of bounty. You could listen to that sort of talk only so long before starting to wonder why all the incredible orchards were owned by someone else, while you had to work long hours just to feed your children.

Marasi dug into the contents of the folder, which listed the events surrounding the flooding to the east. MeLaan settled back in her seat. What a curious creature she was, sitting with head held high, meeting the glances of people who passed without the least concern about what anyone thought of her.

Miklin was annoying, but he hadn't let his displeasure undermine his work, which was meticulous and thorough. He'd included constable reports on the dam breakage, a piece written by the engineer who had investigated the problem, and broadsheet clippings from Elendel regarding the disaster.

Most importantly, there was a transcript of the recent trial and execution of the farmer who had caused the flood. He claimed he'd wanted to ruin his neighbor's harvest in an "accident." But the saboteur had packed too much dynamite, and had blown a hole in the dam large enough to cause the entire thing to fail. Dozens dead, and crops destroyed throughout the region, causing grain shortages.

The defense had called witnesses who claimed that the saboteur, a man named Johnst, had been acting erratically. They claimed he was obviously mad. And the more she read, the more Marasi was convinced he *was* mad—if only because Bleeder was.

"Look at this," Marasi said, handing a sheet to MeLaan.

The kandra took it and read, then grunted. "He couldn't remember the names of his children at the trial?"

"Seems like good evidence that Johnst had been replaced, wouldn't you say?"

"Yes and no," MeLaan said. "The old guard, they are *really* good at interrogating people and doing research before taking a new form. We don't have to do that so much anymore—most of the forms we take are personas we've made up ourselves. If this *was* Bleeder, she must have been pressed for time." MeLaan pointed at a section farther down the page. "This is much better proof, if you ask me."

Marasi scooted over, looking at the paragraphs indicated.

Report of the execution. Prisoner was hanged until dead. Rejected a final meal, and demanded it be "over with quickly." Grave desecrated two nights later; suspected to be the work of those who lost family in the flood.

"Wow," Marasi said, taking the paper back. She hadn't reached that section yet. "Yeah. Escaping the grave, eh? She actually let them *bury* her?"

"Undoubtedly," MeLaan said. "Paalm is nothing if not dedicated to her craft."

"Then why forget the names of the children?"

MeLaan shook her head. "No idea."

Either way, this seemed to be enough to take to Aradel. "Come on," she said.

15

One thing that Wax's life in the Roughs had taught him was that men would monetize anything. The first time he'd seen someone selling water, he'd been surprised. Who sold something that literally fell from the sky?

Now, more than twenty years later, he was surprised nobody in Elendel had found a way to charge a tax on collecting rainwater. If someone wanted it, you could charge for it. That went double for Allomancy, though there were some conservatives who decried the increasing commercialization of the Metallic Arts. Feruchemists for hire were much scarcer than Allomancers, perhaps because Terris traditions viewed their powers with such reverence.

Wax walked up the steps toward the building, which stood alone on the street in a fairly nice neighborhood of town, even if this was the darker end of the lane, so to speak. The place was two stories tall, and had the window shades drawn, though light inside gave them a warm glow. A black coach—with a silver crest, scraped across its face—was parked in the drive to the right.

The Soothing washed over him right as he reached

the door. A calm, gentle feeling—like emotional anesthetic. Like someone had pressed a pillow against his emotions in an attempt to lovingly smother them.

Sloppy, he thought. *Should have brought my hat.* It had an aluminum lining, and Bleeder could have access to a spike letting her Soothe or Riot. Well, he'd have to fetch it later. He pushed into the building, entering a room dimly lit with lamps in red shades. A scattering of men and women lounged on cushions inside, smoking cigars or incense pipes, staring at the ceiling, which was painted like a stained-glass window in a pretty, abstract pattern.

Most businesses would be closed by this hour, but not the Soothing parlors. Visiting one was more expensive than a night at the pub, but had none of the side effects. Or to be more precise, it had different side effects. A woman in a matronly gown—and a hat, likely aluminum-lined—approached Wax, probably to take payment, but Wax flashed his credentials.

"If you think credentials will get you in free," the proprietor said, "then you must be new to the force."

Wax gave her a dry smile, tucking away the metal plate. She ran a low-grade Soothing parlor. While what she did wasn't illegal—amusingly, it was fine to manipulate people's emotions so long as they were paying for it—she'd be used to the constables checking up on her. Not only did these sorts of places tend to attract people who were hiding from something, it was very possible for a disreputable Soothing parlor to take advantage of its clients.

None of the people here matched Chapaou's description, but Soothing parlors often had more than one room. "Short man," Wax said, "balding. Known as Chapaou, but may not have given that name."

The proprietor nodded and gestured for Wax to follow as she crossed the room, weaving between the people lounging on the floor. The dim, smoky building should have left Wax jumpy—this was just the sort of place where accidents or ambushes happened—but the Soothing was difficult to pierce. It tore away the top layers of his concern, exposing those beneath—his worry for Wayne and Marasi. Beneath that, a surprising frustration—even anger—at God. Then those emotions too became as fluttering wings, leaving him hollow. Not calm, just empty.

He wanted to settle into one of the chairs, close his eyes, and let out a sigh of relaxation. Bleeder would wait. Surely she wouldn't try to kill again tonight. Why worry if she did? He probably couldn't stop her anyway.

He found he hated that sensation. These emotions were his; they were a core of his self. Taking them away didn't make him happy or help him forget. It just made him feel sick.

He picked up his pace, trying to urge the proprietor faster as they left the room with the cushions and stepped into a long hallway. Here, they passed several other rooms: A completely white chamber with people sitting cross-legged on the floor. Another that was completely black, no lights at all, the people inside barely visible. There was even a room with painted trees on the walls, the ground covered in thatch, like a Terris meeting hut. A lone man sat in this one, on a solitary chair, eyes closed.

The proprietor led Wax up a set of steps. Perhaps the man in the Terris room had been one of the Soothers— the parlor would have at least one in here somewhere, extending out a small bubble of Soothing. Parlors were supposed to have aluminum sheets in the walls to keep the emotional Allomancy contained from the neighborhood, but the rule wasn't uniformly enforced.

The proprietor led Wax to a small room on the second floor, unadorned save for a couch at the center for massages. Chapaou didn't lie on that. Instead, he paced by a latched window in the far wall, frustrating the masseuse who stood nearby with her arms folded. An old man sat in a chair by the wall. The metal vials in his pocket—visible to Wax as small, diffuse lines pointing at the suspended flakes—marked him as an Allomancer.

Wax raised his eyebrow. Chapaou had paid for a private session. Where had he found that kind of money? The coach driver stopped in place, looking toward Wax. His eyes flicked toward the guns at Wax's hips, then he fell to his knees, weeping.

The aged Soother rose with audible cracks from his joints. "I've done what I can, Mistress Halex," he said to the proprietor. "But this man doesn't need Allomancy. He needs a physician."

"He's yours," Mistress Halex said to Wax. "Get him out of here. He's disturbing my people."

Wax crossed the room to kneel beside Chapaou. The short man shivered, holding his legs. "Chapaou," Wax said. "Look at me."

Chapaou turned toward him.

"What's the name of your dog?" Wax asked.

"My ... I don't have a dog. He died a few years back."

Good enough. This wasn't Bleeder in disguise, unless she'd thought to interrogate a random cabdriver about his pets before killing him and taking his shape.

"What's wrong?" Wax said. "Why are you here?"

"To forget what I saw."

"Soothing doesn't work like that," Wax said. "It doesn't take your memories."

"But it should make me feel better, right?"

"Depends on the emotions you're feeling," Wax said, "and the skill of the Soother." He held the man by the shoulder. "What did you see, Chapaou?"

The man blinked reddened eyes. "I saw . . . myself."

Aradel wasn't in his office, of course. That place was there, as he put it, "for giving house lords somewhere to sit when they come to complain at me."

Marasi found him on the roof of the constabulary offices listening to reports from the two precinct Coinshots who had been scouting the city. Marasi politely waited with MeLaan and several constable lieutenants standing nearby, and was able to hear most of the latest report. *Thousands still on the streets, my lord. They're congregating at pubs. Not going home . . .*

Aradel stood with one booted foot up on the short wall around the rooftop as he took the reports. Mist curled around each Coinshot in a distinct vortex; it responded to the use of Allomancy. Finally, Aradel dismissed the two. They weren't true constables—more contractors. Their loyalties would be to their houses. Or in some cases to their pocketbooks.

As they left—jumping off the building—the constable-general turned to the waiting lieutenants. "Get the men ready to clear out the pubs," he said softly.

"Sir?" one of the women asked.

"We're going to close them down," Aradel said, pointing. "First on the promenades, then work down the smaller streets. We can't start until I get authority from the governor to institute martial law in the octant, but I want the constables ready to move as soon as we have word."

The lieutenants ran to obey. Aradel glanced toward Marasi, and she thought she saw something of his ancestor in him, a soldier who had died a martyr during the days of the Ascendant Warrior. In another era, would this man have been a field general rather than a policeman?

"What do you have for me, Lieutenant Colms?" he said, waving her forward. MeLaan lingered by the stairwell down, hands in her trouser pockets.

"Our assassin, sir," Marasi said, proffering the folder. "She dug her way out of her own grave after being executed for causing the floods in the east. They found the bones nearby a few days later, and called it desecration of the grave. After all, why would they guess that one of the holy Faceless Immortals had been inhabiting the body of a murderer and criminal?"

Aradel breathed out quietly in a hiss. Shadows moved beneath the streetlights, despite the hour, on the promenade behind him. "So this is all her doing?"

"Pardon, sir," Marasi said, "but I'd say this is rather the fault of the city's unpleasant working conditions. That said, Bleeder is most certainly shoving it along. She wanted this city to be on the brink of cracking when she made her move."

"Ruin . . ." Aradel whispered. "In the face of that, it seems almost trivial whether the governor is corrupt or not, doesn't it?"

"I suppose that depends on whom you ask." Shouts rose from the street down below; a group of men passing along the canal, speaking riotously to one another. She couldn't make out their words, just their tone.

"I still want proof," Aradel said. "Not to diminish your efforts, Lieutenant. But I'm not going to jump at wraiths in the mist unless I can see for myself. That goes for the governor too. Keep your eyes open. If you can find me something concrete, we'll use it once this all blows over. And I still want some kind of proof regarding your supernatural assassin."

"I understand, sir," Marasi said, nodding toward MeLaan, lit by the lanterns hanging on poles near the door to the stairs. "And I have some proof for you there. But it would be best if we could do this in private."

Aradel slowly shifted his weight backward, lowering his foot from the top of the parapet he'd been leaning on. He glanced at Marasi, who nodded.

"Below," he said to the two remaining constables attending him. Junior corporals, for message running. They obeyed, and once they were gone, Aradel crossed the distance to MeLaan. "I hope," he said, after clearing his throat, "that my questions aren't offensive, er, Your Grace."

"Sincere inquiries never offend, human," MeLaan said, "for it is thy duty to seek truth. True questions return only truth." Her skin shimmered, growing transparent as it had before, but somehow also giving off a kaleidoscopic sheen. She spread her hands to the sides, and her blouse somehow split and slid down her shoulders, exposing a transparent torso with an emerald skeleton that glittered in the lamplight.

Marasi blinked. Well, *that* hadn't been what she'd been expecting. Beside her, Aradel inhaled sharply, then didn't seem to be breathing at all as he took in the sight. MeLaan's head—completely transparent—cocked, and she looked down at them with a maternal cast.

"Speak," she whispered.

"What . . ." Aradel cleared his throat. "Is what Constable Colms has told me true? Could one of your kind really be behind this?"

"Paalm is a lost soul," MeLaan said, "tortured by a broken mind and a twisted spirit. Yes, she is of us, human. Thy task is not easy, but we shall aid thee in thy desperation."

"Great," Aradel said. "I guess . . . I guess that's the confirmation I needed." He hesitated. "Could you, by any chance, put in a good word for me with Harmony?"

"Thy deeds are thine own good words, human," MeLaan said. "And thy God knows of them. Go and protect this city. Worry not for thyself, but instead for thy fellows."

"Right, right," Aradel said. "I'll just be about it, then. Unless there's anything more you can tell me . . ."

"Thy snoring," MeLaan said, "is rather loud."

"I . . . What?"

"It doth be like unto an hundred angry koloss," MeLaan said, "in the middle of a rockslide. Lo, and it doth come near to waking the dead."

"Right . . ." Aradel said.

"Be on thy way, human," MeLaan said.

"As commanded. Lieutenant Colms, a moment?" He bowed his head to MeLaan, walking around her to the side, and had trouble tearing his eyes off her. Granted, Marasi had trouble doing the same. MeLaan was overwhelming even when she wasn't transparent and half naked. MeLaan nodded Marasi onward. No need to come back up for her.

When they were halfway down the stairs, Aradel let out a deep breath. "Well, that was strange."

"I did warn you," Marasi noted.

"That you did. The bit about snoring . . . a metaphor, I assume. But for what? The constables, we're too loud, perhaps?" He nodded to himself. "We're supposed to serve the people, but the complaints of brutality, and of officers ordering people around as if they were lords . . . Yes, I can see. I'll need to make some changes. Do you think that's what she meant?"

"I don't know," Marasi said carefully. "Meeting her does tend to affect one in profound ways."

"Very true." Aradel hesitated on the steps, turning as if he longed to return up above. He held himself back. "The question I had earlier remains. We've got an immortal killer out there, potentially trying to overthrow the government. How in Preservation do we fight something like that?"

"You don't," Marasi said. "Lord Waxillium will handle the kandra. We should focus on keeping the city from exploding."

Aradel nodded. "I want you to do something for me."

"Sir?" They still stood in the stairwell, lit by a solitary electric light above them.

"You mention Lord Ladrian," Aradel said. "He seems to trust you, Lieutenant."

"We have become good friends over the last year."

"He's a wildcard, Lieutenant," Aradel said. "I appreciate the work he does, but his methods . . . let's just say I wouldn't mind having a little more information on what he's doing and when."

"You're asking me to spy on him."

Aradel shrugged. Another man might have been embarrassed to be confronted with it so bluntly, but he didn't seem so. "I won't lie to you, Colms. I think you can be a resource for this department in more ways than one. It's my job to see that the law in this octant is served, and I'll feel a hell of a lot better if I know what Lord Ladrian is doing. If only so I can get the proper warrants—and if necessary, apologies—ready."

"I see," Marasi said.

Aradel waited for something more. She could practically hear the implication. *You're a constable, Lieutenant. This is your job. Do as you are assigned.*

"You could just ask him," she said. "He's been deputized. He is technically under your jurisdiction."

"And you don't think I've tried? He always promises a report. If I'm lucky, that consists of a letter telling me where he left a suspect hanging by his ankles—do you remember that one?—or a quick rundown at a party of something he's hunting, if only so he can ask me for the loan of some resources. I don't mean to turn you into his chaperone, but honestly, a little more information would be *wonderful*."

Marasi sighed. "I'll write you a weekly report. More frequently if an investigation is ongoing, as it is now. But I will inform him that I'm doing so."

"Great. Fantastic." Aradel started down the stairs again, stepping quickly and speaking almost as fast. "Get to the governor's place and tell him I need an executive order for martial law tonight so I can clear the pubs. Suggest he send one to each of the octants. Then check in on your friend Ladrian and tell me anything he's learned about this immortal who thinks she can bring down our city."

He reached the floor below and strode out into the main chamber, shouting for a report on the number of constables they'd been able to call up for duty this night. Marasi followed more slowly, legs feeling like they bore hundred-pound bracers.

You can be a resource for this department in more ways than one. . . .

She reached the ground floor and walked out the precinct's back door. She'd always known that her involvement with Waxillium had helped her obtain this job. If she hadn't joined his hunt for Miles Hundredlives, she'd never have gained enough notability. That said, she'd assumed her understanding of historical crime rates, her letters of recommendation, and her interview had been more important.

Was that even the case? Had Aradel given her the job instead of someone like Reddi because she knew Waxillium? Did her studies even matter?

She settled with her back against the wall, waiting for MeLaan. Rusts . . . did everything always *have* to be about Waxillium? Of course, thinking that made her feel like a child, jealous that someone else had more blocks than she did.

MeLaan strolled into the alleyway a short time later, disturbing the mists. "Well?" MeLaan asked. "How did I do?"

"We shall aid thee in thy desperation?" Marasi asked.

"Hey, it's what he expected."

"Not what *I* expected."

MeLaan sniffed. "I can be divine when I need to be. I've had a *long* time to practice."

"Then why don't you use the act around me and the others?"

"Who says this isn't the act?" MeLaan said. She met Marasi's eyes. "Perhaps my duty as one of Harmony's servants is to show people what they need to see, whatever will bring them the most peace."

Marasi felt cold, suddenly, a shiver running through

her. Not at the words, but at the look in MeLaan's eyes, which had faded to a faint translucence. As if . . . in reminder?

Then MeLaan threw her head back and started laughing. "Nah, I'm just rusting you, kid. I don't show you that side because it's too hard to keep a straight face while talking with all those 'thee's and 'whatfore's."

"Hence the snoring wisecrack?" Marasi said.

"Yeah. I had to check on the guy when Harmony was first looking for Paalm. He snores like a *steam engine*, that one. Anyway, where to now?"

"The governor's mansion," Marasi said.

"Along we go, then," MeLaan said, striding toward the exit of the alleyway.

"We pulled to a stop," Chapaou said, hunched up next to his carriage in the mists outside the Soother's place. "And I'd been hearing things inside the coach. I didn't like how he'd come out of that church, with hands all red."

Wax knelt in the back of the coach, listening while he carefully unwrapped a bundle of black cloth. A lantern hung on the side of the coach, giving him light, but also turning the mists into a bloom of illumination. He could still feel the Soother's touch from the nearby building, but it was far less pronounced now. He felt almost like himself. That was both good and bad, for there was nothing to hold back his sense of revulsion as he unwrapped the bloody mallet that had been used to pound the spikes into Father Bin.

"I shouldn't have looked into the coach," Chapaou said. "He told me not to look, you know? But I couldn't help it. So I turned softly and peeked in the coachman's slot, the one they have so you can see if the person inside is ripping the upholstery or whatnot.

"I found I hadn't been carrying a man, but a monster. A mistwraith, with bones and sinew exposed, and a face of stretched muscle and grinning teeth. It looked at me, all smiles, and scrambled up toward the hole. It pressed that exposed eye against the slot, and then it *changed*. It *changed*. Skin growing over its face, like mine. A twisted, broken version of me."

He started weeping again. Wax unrolled bones from the bundle, the corpse of the Pathian whom Bleeder had imitated in order to kill Father Bin. Bleached, picked clean, and under them a pile of cloth. Pathian robes? Yes, the colors were right.

"Hands all red . . ." Chapaou whispered.

"You ran, after that?" Wax asked, lining up the bones carefully.

"No, I drove," Chapaou said. "I whipped the horses forward, bearing that demonspawn in my coach. A driver for Ironeyes himself. What good would it do to run? It had my soul. Harmony . . . it *has my soul*."

"No," Wax said. "It is a trickster, a false face, Chapaou. It was a twisted version of yourself, you say?" MeLaan had said that older kandra could often approximate a face without having the right bones, but it was always noticeable.

"Yeah." The man huddled down lower in the alleyway. "I know what you think, lawman. I killed that priest tonight, didn't I? I went mad, and I killed him, and those bloody hands are mine. Shoulda killed myself, jumped off that bridge . . ."

"No," Wax said. "You've been taken in by a charlatan, Chapaou. It wasn't you."

The man just whimpered.

Wax continued, methodically laying out the evidence, though a part of him wondered what good it would do. Did traditional detective work have any place in a fight against a creature like this? How did you fight mythology with a microscope? Harmony . . . what if he *did* find a clue? If he chased her down? Could he even defeat something like this?

He stared at the bones, then shook his head. He would send for a crime-scene team to look this over. He needed to get to the governor's mansion and check in.

Wait, he thought, then leaned forward. There, on the hem of the robe. What was that? He shielded the lantern, causing Chapaou to groan and huddle down farther.

With the lantern dimmed, Wax spotted it better. The corner of the robe's hem *glowed* with a soft blue light, easy to miss. Wax reached down, taking a substance off the robe and rubbing it between his fingers. A powder of some sort? What kind of powder gave off its own light, faint though it was?

"Did you see anything glowing back here, Chapaou?" he asked, turning toward the man. Wax had to unshield the lantern to get him to respond. Even then, the only reply he got was a confused shake of the head.

"Where did you drive the coach?" Wax asked.

"Lestib Square," Chapaou whispered. "Where I'd been told to drop the creature off. Then I squeezed my eyes shut and waited. It . . . it climbed up to me, as it left. Hands on my shoulders, head beside mine, cheeks touching. I could feel the blood, though it left none staining my shirt. It . . . it *whispered* to me, lawman. 'I will make you free.' When I opened my eyes it had gone, leaving those bones in the passenger compartment along with a small pile of coins. I thought for sure I'd gone mad."

Wax downed an extra vial of metals to refill his stores, then dried the vial out and took a sample of the dust. Lestib Square, named after the Lord Mistborn. It was worryingly close to the governor's mansion. "Don't worry. I'm on the thing's trail. I intend to stop it."

"It said it would make me free," Chapaou said. "If I'm not mad, then that means . . . that means that thing was *real*."

"It is," Wax said.

"Honestly, sir, I'd rather be crazy."

"Eh," Wax said, rising and pushing Chapaou toward his coach. "The thing probably doesn't want you dead anyway."

"Probably?"

"No way to tell for certain," Wax said, checking his ammunition. "But I'd bet money against it—at least, it no more wants you dead than it wants everyone in the city dead. Maybe. Not sure yet what its endgame is."

Chapaou looked sick. Damn. He was sure that last part had been comforting.

"Go home," Wax said, then tossed the man a few banknotes. "Or go find a hotel. Get some sleep. She isn't going to come for you."

She had much bigger game to hunt.

GUEST EDITORIAL:
THE NUISANCE OF NEGLIGENT COINSHOTS!

In the last sixteen months I have replaced three lamposts, an iron gate, and two steeple spires, all at my Madion Ways house. My residence in the 6th Octant, much nearer the Hub, has needed twice that attention due to it being on the main route of Coinshot couriers. Motor cars, carriages, bronze statues. None of these is safe from similar fates. Must our fine neighborhoods look like a return to the World of Ash?

No! Let us take back our dignity! *(Continued on Back.)*

AND IT'S BEDTIME WITHOUT SUPPER, TOO.

VISITORS from other WORLDS

Rarely does The House Record bring news of the sensational, but the reputable Lady Nicelle Sauvage of New Seran has contacted us with a report that will shock you.

"I was lost in the mountains south of the Southern Roughs," said Sauvage. "And my fellow travellers had either left me or died. That's when I came upon a mountain pool of the most perfect blue, fed by the melting snows of the heights. Harmony, but I thought I'd reached Paradise."

As twilight struck early, as it is wont to do in the mountains, Sauvage saw a hunched figure by the pool. "Just a shadow, really," she said. "Piercing eyes, and a face like some otherworldly beast from one of those hideous pulp stories. I regret to say I hadn't the courage to engage this Visitor. Instead, its horrible visage struck right at my heart. I let preservation instinct take over and ran for an hour before making camp elsewhere."
(More on Back, Column 4.)

The Sinister Soiree!

I described my assailant as wearing a striped white suit, but that is not as specific as it may seem. In Elendel, someone dressed as described would stick out like afternoon tea among koloss, but in New Seran the men run about in such vibrant suits that one would almost think they are all performers late for the circus. So I will be more specific. The gunman also wore mustaches waxed straight horizontal to a perfect point. The women on both sides of him stood back not only because he had brandished a gun, but also because they feared losing eyes to the sharp and glistening facial hair.

I burned what little tin reserves I had left. (You will recall that I detailed the episode last week in "A Sport of Spirits" where I'd been forced to flare most of my tin to counteract the effects of winning a gentlemanly impromptu wine-sipping contest earlier in the evening.)

"Stand down, sir," I said, cursing myself for leaving Glint in my outer jacket taken by the servant when I'd entered the party. Had I become so soft since leaving the Roughs that I felt comfortable enough without Glint on my very person? Never! Unconsciously I knew that even without my trusty sidearm I was a match

16

Wax perched on an electricity pylon, overlooking the governor's mansion—a clean white building, brightly lit in the mists by floodlights. Those didn't shine so strongly every night, and their brightness tonight seemed to indicate that Innate was worried. The crowds were not dispersing. Men roamed the streets; there seemed to be *more* of them than there had been earlier, though the clock had struck midnight soon after Wax had left the Soothing parlor.

He'd stopped by his house to rebind his arm wound, chew down some painkillers, and pick up some supplies: his hat, his short-barreled shotgun, and his thigh holster. He'd considered sending someone for Lord Harms, but honestly, Wax wanted him safe where Bleeder couldn't use the man against him. Better that he stay hidden on his rooftop. In fact, he'd been half tempted to go fetch Steris and drop her somewhere similar. Time was short, unfortunately. He had to trust that the constables watching her would keep her hidden.

From there, he'd walked the streets a short time, listening. He'd overheard anger at the government. Vitriol for the Pathians. Those complaints were bad enough, but mixed with them was a more disturbing trend. Anger, but with no focus. General discontent. The grumbling of men over their beers, of youths out on the street throwing rocks at cats. Hiding amid it all was a murderer, like a lion in the grass.

At least the governor's mansion looked calm. He'd come fearing the worst, a strike on Innate while he was away. *She's got me pinned,* Wax thought with dissatisfaction, as the breeze rustled his mistcoat. *I can't stay and protect the governor because I have to follow leads and try to figure out her plan. But I can't be as effective in that hunt because I keep worrying that I'm leaving Innate exposed.*

Could he convince the governor to hide? Beneath his feet, electricity ran like an invisible river through the suspended cables. Spirits that moved like Allomancers in the sky, hopping from building to building . . .

Ah, lawman, a voice intruded upon his thoughts like a nail into a board. *There you are.*

Wax reached to his waist for Vindication. Where? This had to mean Bleeder was close, right? Watching somewhere?

Do you know, the voice said, *about the body's re-markable defenses? Inside, there are tiny bits of you that men never see. Even surgeons don't know of them, for they're too small. It takes a refined taste to distinguish them, know them. What is it that your friend likes to say? Ain't nobody what knows the cow better than the butcher?*

Wax dropped down from his perch, slowing himself by Pushing on a discarded bottle cap. Mists churned around him, drawn by his Allomancy.

If a tiny invader enters your blood, Bleeder said, *the entire* body *begins to spin around it, to fight it, to find it and eliminate it. Like a thousand fingers of mist, like a legion of soldiers all too small to see. But what is very interesting is when the body turns upon itself, and these soldiers run wild. Free . . .*

"Where are you?" Wax asked loudly.

Close, Bleeder said. *Watching. You, and the governor. I will need to kill him, you know.*

"Can we talk?" Wax asked a little softer.

Isn't that what we're doing?

Wax turned, walking in the night. Either Bleeder would have to follow—which might let him catch motions in the mists—or he'd get far enough away that she couldn't hear to reply to him, which would tell him which direction to search in.

"Are you going to try to kill me?" Wax asked.

What good would it do to kill you?

"So you want games."

No. Bleeder sounded resigned. *No games.*

"What, then?" Wax asked. "Why bother with all of this showmanship?"

I'll free them. Every one of them. I'll take this people, and I'll open their eyes.

"How?"

What are you, Waxillium? Bleeder asked.

"A lawman," Wax said immediately.

That's the coat you're wearing right now, but it's not who you are. I know. God knows I've seen the truth in you.

"Tell me, then," Wax said, still walking through the mists.

I don't think I can. I might be able to show you.

Bleeder didn't seem to have trouble hearing, though Wax had softened his voice. Allomancy? Or did she just have the ability to make ears that worked better than human ones? He kept searching. Perhaps one of those dark windows in the government building nearby? Wax headed that way. "Is that why you're targeting the governor, then?" he asked. "You want to bring him down, free the people from the government's oppression?"

You know he's just another pawn.

"I don't know that."

I wasn't talking to you that time, Waxillium.

He hesitated in the mists. The office building loomed before him, the windows a hundred hollow eyes. Most of those windows were closed—a common practice at night. No need to invite the mists in. Religion could say what it wished, and people believed, mostly. But the mists still made them uncomfortable.

There, Wax thought, picking out an open window on the second floor.

Very good, Bleeder said, and Wax saw something shift just inside the window, ambient light barely sufficient to let him discern it. *Ever the detective.*

"I'm not much of one, actually," Wax said. "In the Roughs, you solve fewer cases with investigation than with a good pair of guns."

That's a fun lie, Bleeder said. *Do you tell that one at parties to youths who've read too many stories about the Roughs? They don't like hearing about interrogating family members of a man gone bad? Tracking down gunsmiths to see who fixed an outlaw's rifle? Digging through an old campfire after days spent on the road?*

"How do you know about things like that?" Wax asked.

I do my homework. It's a kandra thing, which I assume MeLaan explained. Whatever you claim, you're a good investigator. Maybe an excellent one. Even if you are, by definition, a dog chasing its own tail.

Wax walked right up to the base of the building, the mist thinning between him and Bleeder, who skulked just inside the window about ten feet up. Her face, though enveloped by the shadows, seemed wrong to Wax. Shaped oddly.

"Have you asked him?" Bleeder whispered from above, barely audible in the night. She had a rasping, dry voice, like the one in his head.

"Who?"

"Harmony. Have you asked why he didn't save Lessie? A whisper at the right time, telling you not to split up. A warning in the back of your mind, telling you not to prowl down that tunnel, but instead circle around behind? You could have saved Lessie so easily with his help."

"Don't speak her name," Wax hissed.

"He's supposed to be God. He could have snapped his fingers and made Tan drop dead on the spot. He didn't. Have you asked why?"

Vindication was in Wax's hand a moment later, pointing up toward that window. His other hand felt at his gunbelt for the pouch that held the syringes.

Bleeder chuckled. "Ever quick with the gun. If you speak to Harmony again, ask him. Did he know the effect Lessie had on you, that she was what kept you out in the Roughs? Did he know, perhaps, that you'd never return here—where he needed you—as long as she was alive? Did he, perhaps, *want* her to die?"

Wax fired.

Not to hit Bleeder. He just needed to hear a *crack* in the night. That sound, so familiar, of breaking air. The bullet left a trail in the mist, and the wall beside Bleeder popped, scattering flakes of brick.

Rusts . . . he was shaking.

"I'm sorry," Bleeder whispered. "For what I have to do. Cleaning the wound is often more painful than the cut itself. You will see, and understand, once you are free."

"No, we—"

The mists churned. Wax stumbled back, swinging his gun toward something that had passed in a blur, leaving a corridor of swirling mist.

Bleeder. Moving with Feruchemical speed.

Toward the governor.

Wax cursed, swinging Vindication behind himself and planting a bullet in the ground, then Pushing in a powerful burst. He launched through the mists toward the blazing light of the governor's grounds, sweeping over the gates, startling a small flock of ravens, which scattered into the air around him.

Two shots rang out in the night. As Wax crossed the grounds, he spotted Bleeder on the mansion's front steps, wearing a body-length scarlet coat. The guards at the front doors lay dead at her feet. In the glow of the electric lights, he could see what was wrong with Bleeder's face now—she wore a black-and-white mask. The Marksman's mask, but twisted, broken up one side.

She ducked into the building, not using her speed any longer. Wax landed beside the bodies—he didn't have time to check them for life—and growled as he shoved into the building, gun out, and checked right, then left. The house steward screamed, dropping a tray of tea in the entryway as Bleeder skidded across the floor and into the next room.

Wax followed, the main door ripping from its frame and flying out behind him into the night as he Pushed against it and its hinges to cross the room in a half run, half skim. He burst into the next chamber—a sitting room—with Vindication out, spinning the cylinder to one of the gun's special hazekiller rounds. A Thug shot, extra-heavy slug, built to deliver as much force as possible.

The room he entered was decorated with the kind of perfect furniture you found only in a house that had too many rooms. According to the blueprint he'd been given, under it would be the saferoom.

Still the gun, Bleeder said in his mind as she leaped over a sofa, heading toward the wall, which hid the steps down to the saferoom. *Useless. I cannot be killed with that.*

Wax raised Vindication and sighted, then fired, Pushing the bullet forward in a burst of extra speed. It hit Bleeder as she landed.

Right in the ankle.

The bone shattered and Bleeder collapsed as she tried to put weight on her ankle. She turned toward Wax, lips raised in a snarl visible through the broken side of the mask.

Wax put a bullet through the eyehole in the mask.

This is meaningless—

He strode forward, shooting her in the hand as she tried to raise her gun. Wax pulled out the syringe, ready to Push it toward her skin, but she growled and became a blur. Wax tried to follow that blur—but at that moment, the side of the room burst open, revealing the hidden stairwell. A group of men in black suits and shotguns piled out, frantic. The governor's special security.

Wax dove for cover as they started firing. He didn't catch much of what happened next, as he put his back to the side of a thick chair. Bleeder moved among the men, firing. They tried to fire back, doing more damage to their friends than they did to her.

It was over by the time the report from the first gunshot had faded in Wax's ears. Men lay groaning and bleeding on the floor, and Bleeder was through the hole and heading down the steps. Wax set his jaw and Pushed himself across the room. He landed, skidding on blood, and leaped into the stairwell. Another Push sent him soaring down the steps.

Gunshots resounded in the narrow confines of the stairwell, coming from just ahead. Wax slowed himself with a shot forward into the ground, landing beside a final handful of guards who lay bleeding on the floor.

The kandra stood alone before the door to the saferoom. She looked at Wax, smiled, and became a blur.

But her speed only lasted a fraction of a second. Soon after she'd begun tapping her metalmind, she slowed back down.

Wax caught sight of her just as she unlocked the door to the governor's saferoom, using a key she shouldn't have. She pulled the door open with a flourish, then glanced back at Wax, shaking her head. She obviously thought she was still a blur moving with incredible speed. And she was.

Wax had simply joined her.

One of the fallen bodies stirred, and Wayne pushed back his hat, showing a grin. Wax raised his hands, a gun in each, and was rewarded by an expression of utter shock on Bleeder's face. She'd regrown her eye, though blood still streamed down the front of her mask. As he had chased her, talked to her, she'd always seemed fully in control.

Until this moment.

Wax blasted away with both guns. That wasn't

usually a good idea, at least if you wanted to hit any-thing, but they were barely ten feet apart—and be-sides, he was inside a speed bubble. His bullets would refract when leaving sped-up time, and so aiming was of questionable value anyway.

At a time like this, you didn't want to be precise. You wanted to be thorough. Steris would be proud.

He fired in a cacophony, empting both weapons. He took advantage of Bleeder's shock, dropping his guns and pulling his other Sterrion out of its under-arm hol-ster and unloading it. His short-barreled shotgun, from the holster on his thigh, followed, belching slugs and thunder as Wax strode to the edge of the speed bubble.

After reaching the rim, the bullets deflected out into normal time, moving painfully slowly. But less than a foot separated Bleeder and the edge of Wayne's bubble. Wax dropped the shotgun and pulled out one of the syringes again, and shoved it toward her, Pushing on the metal, hoping against hope that—stunned from the gunfire—she wouldn't notice it coming.

As the kandra turned to run, the first bullet hit. Oth-ers followed in a storm. Half missed, but Wax had fired almost two dozen shots. Many punched into Bleeder, who dropped her Feruchemical speed as they caught her. She moved lethargically, trying to escape the hail of bullets, sprays of blood bursting silently into the air, like the seeds blown from a dandelion.

She stumbled against the doorframe, and one of the shotgun slugs hit the back of her head, ripping a hole through her face and breaking off the mask. She sagged, gripping the doorframe, draped in her red cloak.

The needle flew from Wax's Push, spinning in the air, but it—like the bullets—had been deflected by the edge of the speed bubble. It impaled itself into the wood of the doorframe just inches from Bleeder.

She righted herself a second later, and sped up again, wounds vanishing. She didn't look at him as her back straightened and she strode through the door. She did flip the needle off the frame, sending it toppling in slow motion toward the ground.

Wax dug a handful of rounds from the pouch on his belt, then leaped out of the speed bubble. He felt an immediate *lurch*—as if the world had been upended—and heard a faint popping sound. The nausea hit him like a punch to the face, but he was ready for it. He'd ducked out of speed bubbles before.

A single gunshot sounded from the saferoom.

He crossed the distance to the door in a rush, throwing the cartridges in front of himself, ready to Push on the ones that he might need to hit Bleeder. Once inside, however, he let the rounds drop to the ground. Bleeder wasn't in the room; an open door at the back led out, presumably through a tunnel to the grounds above.

The plush saferoom—round and rimmed with bookshelves—had a wet bar on one end and was lit by comfortable reading lamps. The governor knelt on the floor, holding a bleeding Drim, frantically trying to stanch the blood coming from the bodyguard's neck.

Wax dashed across the room, stopping at the door into the escape tunnel.

"Lawman!" Innate cried. "Help. Please . . . oh, Harmony. Help!"

Wax hesitated, peering into that empty, dark tunnel. He was reminded of another one like it, dusty and shored up by beams at the sides. Both a tomb and a stage . . .

Behind, Wayne stumbled into the room, then scrambled to help Innate. Wax remained by the door into the tunnel, rolling a few rounds between his fingers.

"He saved me," Innate said, weeping. By this point, he was drenched in Drim's blood. He'd pulled off his shirt, trying to use it to stanch the blood. "He leaped into the way right as the assassin shot," Innate said. "Tell me you can . . . Please . . ."

"He's gone, mate," Wayne said, settling back.

"Other casualties upstairs, Wayne," Wax said, pointing. With reluctance, he shut the door to the escape tunnel. He couldn't give chase, not and leave the governor alone here.

Wayne rushed out of the room to check on the men who had been shot upstairs. Wax walked over to the governor, who knelt before his bodyguard's corpse. He'd never seen Innate look so human as he did at that moment, shoulders slumped, head bowed. Exhausted, wrung-out. Could anyone fake that?

He checked anyway. "Leavening on sand," Wax said.

Innate looked up at him, eyes unfocused. Wax's heart skipped a beat, but then the governor sighed. "Bones without soup."

He knew the passphrase. This was really Innate.

Wax knelt beside the governor, looking over Drim's corpse. Annoying though the man had been at times, he had not deserved this. "I'm sorry."

"She stopped moving at a blur," Innate said, his voice strained. "She appeared inside, gun out, but seemed angry about something. Drim leaped for me right before she shot. She was gone a second later. Surely she could have paused to finish me off, rather than running."

"She obtained Feruchemical powers only two weeks ago," Wax said. "That time frame greatly limits how much speed she can have stored up, and moving as fast as she has been must have drained her metalmind quickly. She needed to escape before it ran out."

Of course, there could be another reason. She might have just wanted to frighten them, and the governor. To prod him to do something. But what? She said she intended to kill him, but not until the time was right.

Why? What was the plan?

"So she's flawed," Innate said. "She can be beaten."

"Of course she can," Wax said. He looked down at the corpse, and the floor stained red. *But at what cost?* He took a deep breath. "I want you to leave the city."

"No."

"That's stupidity," Wax snapped. "She *will* be back."

"Have you looked out there, lawman?" Innate said, waving a bloody hand in a vaguely upward direction. "Have you seen what's happening in this city?"

"You can't do anything about that tonight."

"I most certainly can." Innate stood. "I'm the leader of this city; I'm not going to run away. If anything, I need to be seen—need to meet with the chief instigators of this movement, if any can be found. I need to address the crowds, prepare a speech—I need to gather my cabinet, and with them make sure that there's still a city here in the morning." He pointed at Wax. "You *stop* this creature, Ladrian. I don't have a bodyguard any longer. I'm in your hands."

He strode out then. Whatever else he thought of the man, Wax had to respect Innate's grit.

You stop this creature. . . .

Wax glanced at the syringe, still lying on the floor near the doorframe. So close. If it had hit, he might have been able to depress the metal plunger and send the liquid into her veins. Feeling powerless, he fetched that syringe and brought it back to Drim's corpse, dead with a bullet right in the neck. Wax plunged the syringe into the corpse's arm and emptied it into the flesh.

Nothing happened. He hadn't expected it to—it seemed very implausible that Bleeder would have managed to get Drim's face on and fool the governor this way. But it still made Wax feel more comfortable.

He stumbled to his feet. Rusts, he was tired. Why *hadn't* she killed the governor? There was more to this.

Wayne peeked in. "Two guards might make it. We have a surgeon helpin' them now."

"Good," Wax said. "Wait for me upstairs."

Wayne nodded, ducking back out. Wax instead walked to the escape route and pulled open the door. He lit a candle and stepped up the slope, cautious, hand on his gun. What did undermining the governor, inciting a riot against the Pathians, and Wax's own "freedom" have to do with one another? What was he missing?

He didn't find Bleeder in the tunnel, though halfway up it he found her red cloak. She'd tossed it, bloodied, to the side. There, scrawled on the wall, was a crude picture shaped like a man, drawn with a fingernail into the wood.

Dabs of dried blood marked the figure's eyes, and another marked its mouth. The words scrawled beneath in blood gave Wax a chill.

I rip out his tongue to stop the lies.
I stab out his eyes to hide from his gaze.
You will be free.

17

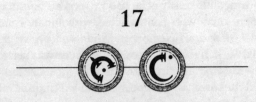

About a half hour after Bleeder's attack, Wayne walked into the governor's fancy washroom. Only in his head it wasn't the washroom. He just knew to call it that here.

You see, Wayne had figured out the code.

Rich folks, they had this *code*. All of them knew it, and they used it like a new language to weed out everyone who didn't belong.

Regular folk, they called something after what it was.

You'd say, "What's that, Kell?"

And they'd say, "That? That there's the crapper."

And you'd reply, "What do you do with it?"

And they'd say, "Well, Wayne, that's where you put your crap."

It made sense. But rich folk, they had a different word for the crapper. They'd call it a "commode" or a "washroom." That way, when someone asked for the crapper, they knew it was a person they needed to oppress.

Wayne did his business and spat his gum into the bowl before flushing. It felt good to be wearing his own hat again, dueling canes at his waist. He'd spent a good hour or two wearing the clothing and false face of a guard for Innate. Horribly uncomfortable, that.

He wiped his sniffly nose and washed his hands, drying them on towels embroidered with Innate's name. He was *that* worried people would run off with his towels? Well, the joke was on him. Wayne was perfectly happy to wipe up dirt with the governor's name. He tucked the towel into his pocket, and left in trade a few mints he'd taken from the bar.

He wandered out from there, peeking into the room where the governor was holding a meeting with all kinds of important folks, the type who called the crapper "the facilities."

You know, he thought, *maybe I have it wrong. Maybe it's not code. Maybe they're just so familiar with what comes out of their arses, normal words aren't specific enough.* Like how the Terris language had seven different words for iron.

He nodded to himself. A new theory. Wax was gonna love this one. Wayne passed into the room with the couches, where the guards had been gunned down. Wax stood inside with an envelope, into which he dropped something small and metallic. He sealed it, then handed it to a young messenger from the governor's staff.

"Deliver it quickly," Wax said. "Pound on the door. Wake her up if you have to—and don't get scared off if she cusses at you or threatens to shoot you. She won't actually hurt you."

The young man nodded, though he'd gone pale.

"Tell her it's urgent," Wax said, holding up his finger. "Don't let her toss it aside and read it in the morning.

You stay there until she's read what I wrote, you understand?"

"Yes, sir."

"Good lad. Off with you."

The youth ran out. Wayne strolled over to Wax, passing the open door down to the saferoom. The bodies around it had been removed, though the blood remained.

"Ranette?" Wayne asked hopefully.

Wax nodded. "I thought of something that might help."

"I coulda delivered that, you know. . . ."

"You, she *would* shoot," Wax said.

"Only 'cuz she likes me," Wayne said, smiling. He'd have welcomed an excuse to go see Ranette. This night was getting darker and darker, it seemed.

"Wayne . . ." Wax said. "You know she doesn't actually like you."

"You always say that, but you're just not seein' the truth, Wax."

"She tries to kill you."

"To keep me alive," Wayne said. "She knows I live a dangerous life. So, keepin' me on my toes is the best way to make sure I stick around. Anyway, was that Marasi I saw in there with the governor and his important folk?"

Wax nodded. "She and MeLaan arrived a short time back. Aradel wants to declare martial law."

"And you don't?" Wayne asked, taking a seat on one of the nice couches that didn't have much blood splattered on it. Important people were meeting nearby. He suspected he knew what would come next, and he intended to wait around for it.

Wax stood for a moment, then shook his head. "Bleeder set this all up, Wayne. She's been pushing us toward this. 'I rip out his tongue . . . I stab out his eyes . . .'"

"Now, I'm as for dismemberment as the next fellow," Wayne said, "but that's a mite violent for this time of day."

"Bleeder wrote it on the wall down below. A poem of some sort. It doesn't feel finished to me."

"She nailed that priest through the eyes," Wayne noted.

"And ripped out Winsting's tongue," Wax said. He fished in his pocket and brought something out, tossing it to Wayne.

"What's this?" Wayne asked, turning it over in his fingers. It was a piece of painted wood.

"Remains of the Marksman's mask. Bleeder was wearing it."

"You think she was him all along?" Wayne asked.

"Maybe," Wax said. "It would have served her purpose, riling up the people of the slums, reminding them how rich the houses are. By bringing him down, I put myself at odds with the common people."

"I hate to say it, mate," Wayne said, "but you ain't exactly beloved of them anyway."

"I'm a hero from the Roughs," Wax said.

"You're a conner," Wayne said. "*And* a house lord, mate. Not to mention the fact that you can, yunno, *fly*. You can't treat this like Weathering. You can't convince a fellow you're on his side by slapping him in jail overnight, then playing cards with him until he sees you as a regular chap."

Wax sighed. "You're right, of course."

"Usually am."

"Except that time on Lessie's birthday."

"You always have to bring that up, don't you?" Wayne leaned back, tipping his hat down over his eyes. "Honest mistake."

"You put dynamite in the *oven*, Wayne."

"Gotta hide a gift where nobody'll look for it."

"I need to piece this together," Wax said, starting to pace. "Sketch it out. Write it down. We're missing something very important."

Wayne nodded, but was hardly listening. Wax would figure it out. Wayne just needed to get some shuteye, while the getting was still good enough for . . .

He heard a door click open. He threw back his hat and was on his feet a second later, scrambling for the door. Wax cursed, pulling out one of his guns, following as Wayne dashed into the hallway and intercepted the servant with a plate full of little party foods.

"Aha!" Wayne said. "Thought you could slip by me, didja!"

The kitchen maid looked horrified as Wayne gathered up three of each of the treats. Wax stopped in the doorway, then lowered his gun. "Oh, for Harmony's sake."

"Harmony can get his own," Wayne said, popping a little cake in his mouth. As he turned back to Wax, the maid scuttled away, heading for the meeting.

It was exactly what Wayne had been waiting for. Important folk meeting together always meant snacks. Or canapés, if you knew the code. Wayne popped one in his mouth—candied bacon wrapped around a walnut.

"How is it?" Wax asked.

"Tastes like cotton candy," Wayne said, relishing the flavor, "made of baby."

"I did not need to hear that," Wax said, slipping his

gun back into its holster. "I'm going to need to go back out there, see if I can figure out Bleeder's plan. That leaves you here to protect the governor again."

Wayne nodded. "I'll do what I can, but that's a tall order, mate."

"I've arranged for some help," Wax said, leading the way over to the ladies' crapper. He knocked on the door.

"Still changing!" MeLaan's voice came from inside.

"How long?" Wax said.

The door cracked, and a woman's face peeked out that looked completely unlike MeLaan's. "Not long," she said in MeLaan's voice. "This lady's hair was a real pain." She shut the door.

"I recognize that face," Wayne said, folding his arms and leaning against the wall.

"One of the guards," Wax said. "That got shot a little earlier."

"Oh right." Wayne had a sinking feeling. "Wasn't she one of the ones I tried to save?"

"Died shortly thereafter," Wax said. "MeLaan will keep the arm in a sling—that was where the shot hit first, before penetrating into the woman's lung. We'll keep her on the governor's guard staff, and hopefully Bleeder will be so busy looking for you and me that she'll miss MeLaan."

"I hope you appreciate this," the kandra's voice came from inside the crapper. "I *hate* being short. As a side note, this lady tasted awful. Far too lean and tough." The door cracked, revealing the face again. "Next time, choose a body that's been sitting around awhile, would you? Nice and aged is the best flavor for . . ."

She trailed off, looking from Wayne to Wax, noticing their expressions. "Oh right," she said. "Mortals. I'd forgotten how squeamish you can be."

"Please," Wax said, sounding pained, "show some respect for the dead woman. It's already difficult to let you use her corpse like this."

MeLaan rolled her eyes—rusts, it was strange to see her behave just like before, but in an entirely different body. "It's either me or the worms, kids. Don't you think she'd be happy to go out all at once, munched down in half an hour, rather than sitting there and melting into the ground over the course of—"

"Too much description, MeLaan," Wax said, his voice strained.

"Fine, fine. I'm almost ready; just have to get the clothing on. How is the hair?"

"Good," Wayne said. "I think you forgot an eyebrow though."

MeLaan felt at her face. "Hell," she said. "This is what you get by forcing me to work so quickly." She ducked back into the room.

"Speaking of quickly," Wax said through the door, "is this about what I can expect with Bleeder? A half hour to change bodies?"

Wayne nodded. That would be useful to know.

"No, unfortunately," MeLaan's voice said from inside, muffled. It was still the same voice as she'd had in her other body. Was she going to change that? "Paalm is old-generation, *very* practiced. I don't think anybody is as good as TenSoon, mind you, but Paalm will be fast—particularly swapping into a body she's used before. I've known early-generationers who can change bodies in under ten minutes, and that's going in blind."

"Isn't that tough?" Wayne called. "Like . . . I once hadda eat twenty sausages for a bet. Won five notes, but spent an hour on the ground moaning like a fellow on the pot tryin' to force a mango through his delicate doughnut, if you catch my meaning."

Wax groaned softly, but a short time later MeLaan opened the door again, and was this time clothed in a black suit like the other guards. She was also smiling. "You're cute," she noted to Wayne. "How's my eyebrow?"

"Uh, good." Cute? "But I'm taken."

"In answer to your question," MeLaan said, "it *is* hard, but not for the reason you're implying. We can force-feed and expel excess, which makes doing the transformation near a drain like in here convenient. The tough part is memorizing the muscle patterns as you digest them. That and getting the hair right. You people are practically drowning in the stuff. Fortunately, for a quick change like this, I can ignore the hair under the clothing."

"So . . . wait," Wayne said, rubbing his chin. "You're saying we might be able to check if a person is a kandra by . . ."

". . . Seeing if they put leg and arm hair on?" Me-Laan asked. "That might actually work, but only if the kandra had to change fast."

"*Arm hair*," Wayne said. "Right. I was thinkin' of arm hair."

"That is the most difficult part to get right on short notice," MeLaan said. "We can't make hair, so we've got to use your own, and place each strand in a pore. Arms and legs have thousands of the things. What a pain. Far worse than a mass on the head or whatnot."

"MeLaan," Wax said, digging in his coat pocket and bringing something out. "Do you recognize this?"

"I don't have a lot to go on, chief, but I'd say it's an empty glass vial."

"Take it inside and turn off the lights," Wax said, tossing her the vial as Wayne stepped forward, trying to get a look. That stuff seemed interesting.

MeLaan withdrew, then shoved open the door a second later. She grabbed Wax by the mistcoat, somehow still imposing despite the fact that she was now shorter than either of them. "Where did you get this?"

"Bottom of Bleeder's robes," Wax said. "The ones she was wearing to imitate a priest."

"This is perchwither," MeLaan said. "It's a bioluminescent fungus. It grows in only one place."

"Where?" Wax asked.

"The kandra Homeland."

Wax looked deflated. "Oh. So that's where we'd expect her to be going, right?"

"No," MeLaan said. "The kandra are no longer trapped there. We move in society—we have homes, lives. If we want to meet up with others of our kind, we catch them at the pub. The Homeland is a monument. A holy site. A place of relics. The fact that she's been there recently, wearing the body of someone she killed . . ." MeLaan shivered visibly, letting go of Wax. "It's nauseating."

"I should check it out," Wax said. "She might be staying down there."

MeLaan folded her arms, looking him over. "Harmony says it's okay," she said. "You can get in through the tombs; look for the sign of atium and use your other eyes. We don't use that entrance very often, but it's probably easiest for you. Just don't break anything, lawman."

"I'll do my best," Wax said, turning as a footman peeked in from the hallway, then approached with a small silver tray bearing a card.

"Lord Ladrian?" said the footman, holding out the tray. "Your coach has arrived."

"Coach?" Wayne asked. On a hunt, Wax was usually in full-on "fly through the city like a rusting vulture" mode. Why would he need a coach?

Wax picked up the card on the tray, then nodded and took a deep breath. "Thank you." He turned to Wayne and MeLaan. "Keep the governor alive. I'll send word if I discover anything."

"So what's in the coach?" Wayne asked.

"I sent a note soon after I got here to the mansion," Wax said. "There's one person in this city who might have an inkling of what Bleeder is up to." Wax's face took on a grim cast.

Ah, of course, Wayne thought. He patted Wax on the shoulder. This wouldn't be a pleasant meeting.

"Who?" MeLaan asked, looking from Wayne back to Wax. "What are you talking about?"

"Have you ever heard," Wax said, "of a group called the Set?"

Wax found his uncle waiting comfortably inside the coach. No bodyguards. The coachman didn't even ask for Wax's weapons as he stopped at the door. Contacting his uncle had been easy; the appointment book had listed a few of Edwarn's safe-deposit boxes, kept under false names. After posting watch on one for a few weeks, Wax had found a letter inside, suggesting he try something else.

He'd left his own letter. After that, one had appeared for him. They never said anything useful, and Wax had driven himself crazy trying to find out how they were being placed. But Edwarn seemed to know the moment a new one from Wax arrived.

Wax took a deep breath, then climbed into the coach. Edwarn was a stocky man distinguished by a short, precisely trimmed beard, a beautifully tailored suit, and a cravat so narrow and thin, it lay flat like a bowtie loosened at the end of a long night. Edwarn's hands rested easily on the ornate head of a cane, and his face bore a wide smile.

"Nephew!" he said as Wax settled into his seat. "You can't imagine my joy upon receiving your note, and with a promise that you wouldn't try to arrest me. So quaint! I came immediately; I feel like we've been too distant lately."

"Distant? You tried to have me killed."

"And you've tried to return the favor!" Edwarn said, knocking with his cane on the roof to get the coach moving. "Yet here we sit, both alive and well. I see no reason why we can't be amiable. We are rivals, yes, but also still family."

"You're a criminal, Uncle," Wax said. "Considering the things you've done, I don't feel much familial empathy."

Edwarn sighed, slipping his pipe from his pocket. "Can't you at least try to be pleasant?"

"I'll try." Truth was, Wax wanted information from this man. Antagonizing him would not be smart.

They rolled on silently for a while as Edwarn lit the pipe, and Wax tried to organize his thoughts. How to approach this?

"Dangerous night," Edwarn noted, nodding out the window as they passed a group of men and women holding aloft lanterns and torches while listening to a woman standing on a stack of boxes. She shouted into the mists angry words that Wax couldn't quite make out. Rusts, that group was close to the governor's mansion. He hoped that Innate and the constables could get this under control.

"I wonder," Edwarn said, puffing on his pipe, "if that night long ago felt the same as this one—the night when the Survivor's Gambit played out. The fall of a regime. The start of a new world."

"You can't possibly think this is equivalent," Wax said. "The Lord Ruler's reign was one of terror and oppression. These people are upset, yes, but it's a far different world now."

"Different?" Edwarn said, letting smoke roll from his mouth as he spoke. "Perhaps. But human emotions are the same. It seems that no matter how nice the box is, put a man inside it and he will buck. Fight. *Rail.*"

"And you claim to be on the side of the common man," Wax said dryly.

"Hardly. I want power. Wealth. Influence. Just like the people in the Survivor's crew, actually."

"They were heroes."

"And thieves."

"They were what they had to be."

"And Kelsier himself?" Edwarn said. "In the years before his grand gambit? What of the Ascendant Warrior, living on the street, scamming noblemen and priests for a living? Have you read the Words of Founding, Nephew? The Historica speaks frankly about their ambitions. The Survivor didn't just want to overthrow the Lord Ruler; he wanted to steal the empire's riches. He wanted to rule the world that came about upon the Lord Ruler's fall. He wanted power. Influence. Wealth."

"I'm not going down this road, Uncle," Wax said.

"Have you ever wondered," Edwarn mused, ignoring Wax's objection, "if you'd get along with them? If you'd lived back then, what would you have seen? A bunch of miscreants? Lawbreakers? Would you have trussed up the Ascendant Warrior and tossed her in a cell? The law is not something holy, son. It's just a reflection of the ideals of those lucky enough to be in charge."

"I don't know any constables," Wax said, "who think the law is perfect or the courts infallible. But they're the best damn things we have right now, and I'm not going to entertain for a *second* the idea that you're some kind of secret seeker of justice. You're as rotten as they come, Uncle."

"So pleasant," Edwarn said. "And this is what I get for responding to your invitation? Insults and vitriol. And one wonders why our house is considered a laughingstock these days. I'm told they invite you to parties just to see you strut."

"I sent to you," Wax said through clenched teeth, "because I think we might have a common enemy. I know you want to rule this city. Well, I need you to see reason. I've spoken with the creature. If we don't stop her, there might not be a city *to* rule."

Edwarn didn't respond, holding his pipe and looking through the coach's glass window at the curling mists in the darkness just outside.

"What do you know?" Wax asked, almost a plea. "I'm certain the Set has been watching events with interest. Your attempt to kill me earlier—tell me that was just a strike of opportunity. Tell me you aren't working with her. She'll see it all burn, Uncle. Help me bring her down."

Edwarn mused silently awhile, enjoying his pipe. "Do you realize what your overzealous campaign against us has accomplished, Nephew?" he finally asked. "Half the city's elements are too frightened to work with the Set, for fear that you'll show up on their doorstep and shoot their mothers. The money you've seized hasn't ruined us, but it has made some of our members very, very upset."

"Good," Wax said.

"You say that because you're ignorant," Edwarn spat. "Among the members of the Set, I am conservative. I speak against brashness, against violence. The more you shove, however, the weaker my influence becomes, and stronger grow the voices clamoring for change. At any cost."

"Oh, Harmony," Wax whispered. "You *are* working with her."

"It's more like we're riding the storm," Edwarn said. "Personally, I'd love to see you bring this creature down. It might topple some of my rivals, give me a chance to propose something audacious of my own to the Set. But I'm not going to help you, Nephew. Perhaps this is what needs to be."

"How can you do this?" Wax asked. "You're going to watch it all burn?"

"Ashes are excellent fertilizer," Edwarn said.

"Unless they pile so high they smother everything."

Edwarn drew his lips to a tight line. "You are shortsighted and self-righteous. You were ever so, even during your youth. But still I love you, Nephew. I consider it a sign of that love that I haven't actually had you killed. I keep hoping you'll see we are not your enemy. We are the thieves and miscreants of this day who will someday be hailed as heroes. The men and women who will change the world because . . . what was it you said? . . . this is what we need to be in order to survive."

"And my sister?" Wax said. "Is holding her captive part of what you need to do to survive?"

"Yes, actually," Edwarn said, meeting his eyes. "Because I don't doubt that someday I'm going to need to use her against you. Kill me, and your sister is as good as dead, Waxillium." He knocked again on the ceiling beneath the driver. The carriage slowed to a stop.

"Run along now," Edwarn said. "Go be the toy soldier and pretend you wouldn't have murdered the Survivor's entire crew, if you'd lived under the Lord Ruler. Try to pretend you went out into the Roughs to find justice, and not because you realized life in this city was just too damn *hard* for you."

They sat in the quiet, immobile coach. Wax held himself steady, though Edwarn's eyes flicked toward Wax's shoulder holster, as if he was expecting Wax to draw. He could. He could shoot this man right here and now—he'd broken promises before, and to far better men than his uncle.

Kill me, and your sister is as good as dead. . . .

Wax kicked the door open. "I'm going to go deal with this kandra, but know that I won't forget you, Uncle. One day you're going to find me standing behind you with a gun to your head, and you'll have the sudden, horrible realization that there's nothing left that can protect you."

"I look forward to it!" Edwarn said. "If that day doesn't come before next summer, you should join me for Mareweather dinner. We'll have stuffed pig in your honor."

Wax growled softly, but stepped from the coach and slammed the door.

18

Marasi had spent a great portion of her adult life preparing to be an attorney, and her mother had wished her to someday find her way to politics. Marasi had abandoned aspirations toward politics in her youth, and had recently abandoned the solicitors as well. The thing was, those professions had one important flaw: They were populated entirely with attorneys and politicians.

Despite her best efforts she now found herself in a room full of them. Governor Innate stood by the hearth here, in his private study, one arm resting on the mantel. Arrayed before him were the men and women of his executive staff, a hearty bunch who didn't seem nearly as groggy as the constables and guards who had been called up in the middle of the night.

In fact, the group displayed a distinct energy as they discussed the crisis. Their words tumbled over one another in their eagerness to express their opinions, like children vying for parental approval. Marasi stood beside the window—where the governor had put her, saying he'd get to her later. So she waited, listened, and circumspectly took notes on her pad. If the kandra happened to be hiding among them, she doubted a verbal slip would enable her to recognize Bleeder, but it seemed the best use of her time as long as she was required to stay put.

"It will all blow over," repeated the city sanitation director. He was an attorney who had been through the same program she'd completed, albeit many years ago. Marasi wasn't sure why he needed a law degree to run city sanitation. "Rep, you're taking this too seriously."

"I am taking an attempt on my *life* too seriously?" Innate asked. "An attack that left one of my lifelong friends dead?"

That brought a stillness to the room, and the sanitation director settled back down, red-faced. Innate had changed his shirt from the one stained red with blood, but Marasi knew they all had seen him before he'd done so. She rather thought he'd delayed changing until they had.

"I wasn't talking about the assassination attempt," the sanitation director said. "I meant the ruckus outside. It will blow over."

"They're already looting," the minister of trade noted, a bespectacled woman who had brought two aides to take notes for her. She hadn't offered them seats.

"There will *always* be looting," the sanitation director said. "It happens. We hunker down, let burn what needs to burn. Contain, rather than try to stamp out."

"Foolishness," said the secretary of education, a corpulent woman who sat with her feet up by the crackling fire. "This is a time for decisiveness, my lord governor. You need to show your rivals that you are not easily cowed. You know the Lekals have been getting traction lately, and your brother's scandal will only fuel their ambition. Mark my words, they will present a strong candidate to rival you at the next election, and he will lean on this night's events to discredit you."

"Yes," said the minister of public affairs. "Could they be behind the assassination attempt, perhaps?"

The governor glanced toward Marasi—the first time he'd acknowledged her since the meeting had begun. He knew about MeLaan now; she'd shown her true nature to him just before the meeting started. He believed, and had begun by explaining to the executive staff about the rogue kandra. The others obviously considered it foolishness and, after the way of their kind, were simply ignoring what he'd told them.

Marasi met his gaze calmly. Once upon a time she had dreamed of being a participant in meetings like this one. Gatherings where important decisions were made, where laws were drafted and political strategies adopted. Now, she found herself frustrated by all the talk. Waxillium was rubbing off on her, and perhaps not in ways she should appreciate.

"No, no," the sanitation director said. "The Lekals aren't behind this. An assassin? Are you mad, Donton? They would never be caught engaging in something so potentially damaging."

"Agreed," said the secretary of education. "This was someone far more desperate. I repeat, my lord governor. Decisiveness. Leadership. You asked about martial law? Well, that is the *minimum* you must do, I say. Send the constables out in force. Crush the looters, scatter the rioters, be seen protecting the city."

Others voiced their opinions on this, and the governor quieted them. "I'll consider. I'll *consider*." His tone was sharp, sharper than Marasi had heard from him before. "Out with you all. I need to think."

In that moment he looked haggard. The counselors

quieted, then made their way out. Marasi moved to join them, reluctantly.

"Miss Colms," the governor said, walking to his desk, "a moment."

Marasi obeyed, stepping up before the desk as he settled down. He reached to the floor, pushing back the rug and exposing the top of a small safe, which he absently unlocked with a key from his desk. He reached inside, taking out his seal of office, then settled down to begin writing.

"Tell Constable-General Aradel that he has his writ of martial law," the governor said tiredly. "He's the only constable-general to contact me so far, which I find disturbing. I am appointing him with executive authority as lord high constable, director of all law-enforcement offices in the city until this crisis is over. The other octants' constables-general will need to report to him."

Marasi didn't reply. The others weren't going to like that. The rivalry among the octant precincts was officially characterized as friendly, but in reality had far too much bite to it for her taste. "And your instructions regarding the people of the city?" Marasi asked softly as he wrote. "Should the constables do as your education secretary suggests?"

Innate finished writing. He looked up at her, and seemed to weigh her with his eyes. "You're new to the constabulary, I believe? The . . . cousin of Lord Ladrian's betrothed?"

"I wasn't aware I'd attracted your attention," Marasi said.

"You haven't. *He* has. Damnable man."

Marasi remained silent, feeling awkward before his judgmental gaze.

"Those mobs will end up here sooner or later, you know," the governor said, tapping his pen on the table. "They'll come demanding answers. I must speak to them, turn this tide."

Speak to them? Marasi thought. *As you did earlier?* That speech hadn't shown any particular sense of empathy.

Rusts, had that only been this afternoon? Checking the governor's ornate desk clock, she found it was almost two—so the governor's speech had technically been yesterday. She probably shouldn't have looked at the time; seeing exactly how late it was merely reminded her of her own exhaustion. It was like an angry creditor pounding on her door; she'd be able to ignore it for only so long.

"Tell Aradel," the governor mused, "not to stop the people from converging here at the mansion, but he is to beat down any looters in other parts of the city. Put the fear of the sword into them. I'll need a force of constables here, of course, to keep the masses who come to me in check, but I do want to speak to them. This will be a night for *history* to be made."

"Sir," Marasi said. "I know a thing or two about the mentality of crowds, if you wish—"

Someone outside called for Innate, and he stood in the middle of Marasi's sentence. He shoved the writ toward her, sealed with his stamp, then marched out to deal with the questions.

Marasi watched him go with a sigh. Hopefully Wayne and that kandra woman would be able to assure his safety. She'd happily see Innate incarcerated someday, but she didn't wish him dead. His assassination would be, among other things, terrible for city morale.

She stored the writ beside her pistol in her purse,

then walked from the room and slipped through the hallway, where many of the cabinet members were giving orders to aides and accepting cups of steaming black tea from household staff. Wayne lounged in a corner, feet up on an end table and spinning an expensive gold-and-mahogany pen between his fingers. Harmony knew where he'd stolen *that*.

Unfortunately, her motor needed a refueling, so she'd have to use more mundane methods to run the writ to Aradel. She found the footman and ordered a carriage.

The haggard footman, however, shook his head. "It will be a few minutes, miss, before I can dredge up a coach. The executive staff have half the cabs in the city running notes for them, and on a night like this one no less . . ." He glanced meaningfully toward the open door. Outside, the porch lights barely penetrated the mists. They curled and danced, almost timid. Tiny wisps would creep into the entry hall, then vanish almost immediately like steam over a stove.

"I will wait," Marasi said. "Thank you."

He seemed pleased by her response; perhaps others had been less understanding. As he was called away, Marasi idled in the doorway, staring into the mists. That orange haze over the city wasn't normal. Fires were burning out there. If they were lucky, those flames would only be massed lanterns and torches, not buildings.

Standing there strongly reminded her of something that she couldn't put her finger on. She shook her head and walked back into the mansion with half a mind to find Wayne and see what he thought of recent events. In the large sitting room beyond the entryway, she passed a weary serving man scrubbing the wooden floor. The bloodstains were stubborn, it appeared. The man had already discreetly rolled the rug up against the wall for disposal.

Marasi passed him and, changing her mind about finding Wayne, instead walked down the stairs toward the hidden chamber. *A city close to breaking,* she thought as she reached the bottom. *This has happened before.*

In the confined space, the air still smelled of the soap that had been used to clean up the blood. The empty saferoom had a quiet, scholastic feel about it, with all those books on the walls. There was no overhead lighting, just the lamps, shaded a soft red-orange. She walked around the room, noting the many volumes of the full Words of Founding when she passed it on the wall. The leather-bound books seemed pristine, and on a whim, she pulled the first one out and checked it. The pages were uncut, as sometimes happened in new books. This volume had obviously never been read.

Long ago the Survivor had pushed a city to the brink of destruction, then channeled that fury into a rebellion that had overthrown a millennium-long dictatorship. Every student learned of those days, but Marasi had read the detailed accounts, including of the night when it had all come to a head. She could imagine it had been a night very much like this one.

Only instead of the Survivor, this time it had been induced by a psychotic murderer.

She has to be doing it on purpose, Marasi thought, walking through the room. *Trying to echo that night when the Lord Ruler fell. A people on the brink of insurrection. Noble houses at each other's throats. And now . . .*

Now a speech. The governor would have his moment before the crowd, and they would sense the resonance even if they couldn't put their finger on it. They'd been taught about that night since childhood. They would listen to him, and expect him to be like the Last Emperor, who had spoken long ago on the night of the Lord Ruler's death. The Last Emperor had come to power because of his heartfelt words that night.

But Governor Innate was *not* Elend Venture. Far from it.

Marasi suddenly stopped and backed up a few steps. She'd been walking beside the built-in bookcases, paying little conscious attention to them, but just enough to have noticed something off. Here, on this long shelf of pristine books, were three in a row with spines scuffed at the bottom. What distinguished these books? They were part of a seven-volume collection of dry political treatises written long ago by the Counselor of Gods.

She took one and flipped through it, finding nothing of interest. Perhaps Innate had been studying lately. But . . . why were only the third, fourth, and fifth volumes scuffed? She picked up another and opened it—and here she found the reason. Cut into the center of the pages was a hole containing a key. Innate hadn't been reading Breeze's old essays. He had simply forgotten which volume had the key in it.

Marasi held up the key, then glanced at the room's solitary desk. Dared she?

Of course I dare, she thought, crossing the room with a swish of skirts. Her constable credentials, plus Aradel's concern about the governor, would give her legal grounds for doing a quick search. She knew the law as well as anyone.

She also knew that the law was subject to interpretation by the city's judges, most of whom had noble blood and would not take kindly to someone spying on the governor. That was why her fingers were trembling as she quickly tried the key in the desk drawer. It didn't fit. She paused, then tried a spot on the floor like the one up above, where the governor had gotten out his seal.

Sure enough, there was a hidden safe under the rug. She turned the key in it, and earned a satisfying *click*. She pulled the safe open and quickly scanned the contents.

A pistol.

Cigars. She didn't recognize the brand.

A bundle of banknotes tied with string. Enough to buy a house. Marasi's eyes bulged a little, but she kept searching.

A stack of letters. These she took over to the desk, expecting to find details of an illicit romantic relationship or the like. She skimmed them, then read more deeply, then sank down into the desk's chair, raising her fingers to her lips.

The letters did detail a relationship—or, rather, many of them. These were private communications with house leaders throughout the city. Although couched in euphemism and circumlocution, to her they clearly spoke of corruption.

Marasi grew cold as she flipped through them, letter by letter. The actual writing was opaque. *We agree that certain courtesies will be extended* or *These are acceptable terms as per our previous arrangement*. But they were dated, and her mind quickly related each of them to her notes back at the precinct. This was proof. She flipped through more. Yes, they aligned with her own statistical analysis. These were Innate's promises of political favors in exchange for bribes.

With the obfuscatory language, it might not be a smoking gun—but it was at least a very warm one. Better, Innate had added notations to most of the letters to remind himself of important points. Here was one probably trading a promise by Innate to push for higher tariffs on refined steel from outside the city in exchange for a favorable deal on a land purchase by one of his family. Another more recent one was about a judge's seat, when Innate had appointed a Hammondess scion to a recent opening.

She'd suspected corruption, but this was jarring—seeing it discussed like this in black and white. She sifted through the stack. No letters to the Lekals, his primary rivals. None to Waxillium either, Marasi saw with relief—nor any older ones to Edwarn Ladrian, Waxillium's uncle.

Under the letters was a ledger, which she expected would show what Innate thought he was still owed, and would also record the state of his private accounts. Flipping through quickly didn't tell her enough to be certain, but it did seem reasonable.

Marasi sat holding it all, feeling overwhelmed. *Rusts. The people are right to be in revolt.* Was this the crux of Bleeder's plan? Shove Innate into the limelight, then undermine him by exposing his corruption—indeed, the corrupt nature of virtually every noble family in the city? In revealing these letters, Marasi could be playing into the creature's hands. That made her sick. If he *was* this corrupt, didn't he need to be exposed and removed?

She hurriedly tucked the letters into her purse. Captain Aradel needed to see this. Marasi quickly shut and locked the safe, put back the key, and then started up the steps. She didn't want to be in the basement when the footman came looking for her to announce her carriage.

Innate will claim they were planted by Bleeder, Marasi thought as she reached ground level. *He'll have an easy out.* Beyond that, if he noticed they were gone, he'd have a pretty good idea of who took them. That same servant was still cleaning up, and he'd seen Marasi go down and return.

But Rust and Ruin, she wasn't going to just ignore something like this.

Flying through the air at night let Wax see the distinct presence of humankind, as marked by strict boundaries. Where they dwelled, there was illumination. Pinpricks in the darkness, men and women staking a claim on the night. The lights spread like the roots of a tree.

His uncle had left him far from where he wanted to be. Fortunately, for a Coinshot even the vastness of Elendel was manageable. He didn't immediately turn inward, however, to visit the kandra Homeland. His uncle's words haunted him, and before those Bleeder's gibes. They attacked from two different directions, like pins pushed into either temple.

He needed to think, to be alone. Perhaps then he could sort through what this mess meant. He landed on a rooftop overlooking the vast glowing carpet of lights before him. A cat watched him from a nearby flower box, its eyes alight. Below was another row of pubs. Loud, raucous. Surely it was past two in the morning, yet they showed no signs of quieting down.

Rusts, how he hated that one could never feel truly alone in the city. Even in the privacy of his mansion, the quiet was marred by the incessant passage of carriages outside.

He leaped away into the night, frightening the cat. He soared high in a long arc, trying to get far enough away that he couldn't hear the men shouting drunkenly in the row of pubs. His search took him eastward, toward the edge of the city. As he approached, something emerged from the mists like the bleached spine of some ancient monster. Eastbridge, a massive construction that spanned the Irongate River here.

On one hand, he marveled that humankind could create something like this—an enormous riveted marvel, big enough to let motors pass and also hold railroad tracks. On the other hand, the mists completely engulfed the bridge, giving it an even more skeletal cast. Humankind would create, and take pride in those creations, but Harmony's presence could make it all seem trivial.

Did He know? Wax landed atop one of the bridge's towers, boots clanging. *Could He have saved Lessie?*

The answer was simple. Of course Harmony had known. To believe in a God was to accept that He or She wasn't going to deliver you from every problem. It wasn't something Wax had ever dwelled on. Living in the Roughs, he'd accepted that sometimes you just had to weather things on your own. Help didn't always come. That was life. You dealt with it.

But now, something felt different. He'd spoken to Harmony. Hell, Wax was out here right now because of a request from God Himself. That made it all the more personal. God hadn't saved Lessie, hadn't given Wax warning. And now He expected Wax to just hop to it and do as He demanded?

And what would you do? Wax addressed himself, walking along the bridge's lofty pinnacle. *Let the city burn? Let Bleeder keep killing?*

Of course he couldn't. Harmony knew that too. He had Wax by the throat.

Are you there? Wax asked, sending the thought out. *Harmony?*

He felt at his ear before remembering that he'd taken out his earring. By necessity, yes, but in that moment he was glad not to have it. Not to let God get a purchase on his mind, for the thoughts he had weren't particularly pious.

Wax strode through the mists, while down below a lone motorcar puttered across the bridge. Bleeder was toying with him. He could feel her fingers sneaking in, piercing his skull, wrapping around his mind. He could see exactly what she was doing, yet couldn't banish the questions she raised.

Wax paused at one end of the tower's top. From here he could see the edge of the city, where the lights gave way to the darkness of the countryside. Behind him, the city was a brilliant blaze, thousands upon thousands of lights, but the electric lines hadn't yet come out past the bridge. On the outskirts of Elendel, the lights stopped. The last few hung on the bridge, like lighthouses looking out at the vast blackness of the sea.

He yearned for that darkness. To leap out into it, escape all this responsibility—stop needing to worry about hundreds of thousands of people he couldn't know, and get back to helping the few he could.

Freedom. Freedom, to Wax, wasn't the absence of responsibility. He didn't doubt that if he left again, he'd find himself as a lawman once more. No, freedom was not lack of responsibilities—it was being able to do what was right, without having to worry if it was also wrong.

He didn't contemplate leaving, not seriously. But he did sit for a time, looking out at that darkness. Trying to look past the people, the shadowed suburbs, and see simplicity again. Rusts. What he wouldn't give to trade all the politicians, games, and secrets for an honest murderer calling him out on the street.

Coward.

His own thought. Not from Harmony, or Bleeder. That made it all the more like a punch to the gut, for he knew it to be the truth. Wax took a deep breath and stood up again, shouldering his burdens. He turned away from the darkness and leaped off the bridge, Pushing himself into the night again. He'd come here for a moment's solace, to think.

Turned out, he didn't like where those thoughts were taking him.

19

As much as Wayne appreciated all the fancy treats the governor was providing, he had to admit he wasn't entirely sympathetic to the man's plight. After all, the whole point of having someone in charge—like the governor—was about makin' sure people knew which fellow to kill.

That was why they had elections, wasn't it? Innate got to be in charge and order everybody about, but when the assassins got bored, they didn't go whack the guy what sold fish on the street corner. They went for the guy in charge. You had to take the good with the bad, you did. On one hand, you got fancy sweets any time of day. On the other hand, you might find murderers in your loo. That was the breaks.

And this Innate guy, he seemed to really *want* to meet Ironeyes. Not running away to the country when you *knew* a psychopathic, shapeshifting super-Allomancer was after you? Yeah, he understood he was a target. As Wayne sauntered after him—taking the tray from the serving girl as she tried to retreat with the uneaten cakes—the governor stopped in the doorway to his study.

"I need a few minutes to think, to prepare my remarks," he said to Wayne and the other guards. "Thank you."

"But sir!" MeLaan said. "You can't go in alone. We need to protect you!"

"And what are any of you going to do," Innate said, "about someone who can move at the speed of a thunderclap? We will just have to take our chances that the constables can deal with this . . . creature."

"I don't think—" MeLaan began, but cut off as he shut the door, leaving her, Wayne, and a couple of other guards in the hallway.

Wayne rolled his eyes, then leaned against the wall. "You two," he said to the other guards, "go watch the window from outside that room, whydontcha? We'll set up here."

The two fellows shuffled, looked like they'd object, but then slunk out of the hallway. *I wonder,* Wayne thought, settling down on the floor beside the door, *if they're rethinkin' their career choices. What with most everyone else guarding the governor dead already . . .*

"You mortals," MeLaan said, waving toward the door, "can be surprisingly cavalier with your limited life spans."

"Yeah," Wayne said. "He probably just wants to get me in trouble."

"What?" MeLaan sounded amused. "By getting himself killed?"

"Sure," Wayne said. "The idiot forbade me from goin' to his fancy party earlier, then ditched me afterwise. He's got it in for me. He's gonna get himself killed, and leave me to explain it to Wax. 'Sorry, mate. I let your pet politician get ripped in half.' And Wax'll scowl at me real good, even though 's not my fault."

MeLaan sat down across from him and grinned. "Is that what happened to his horse?"

"Why you gotta bring that up again?" Wayne asked, wriggling down to get comfortable and tipping his hat over his eyes. "That *really* wasn't my fault. I had myself a dehabilitating injury when that happened."

"De . . ."

"Yeah," Wayne said, "made me cuss and drink like a bugger." He settled back, listening, eyes closed. Servants moved through the building. Messengers went over their routes. Important types discussed their opinions just a room over.

They all talked. Everyone had to talk. People couldn't just think something, they had to *explain* it. Wayne was the same. He was people, after all.

This murderer, this kandra, she was people too. She had talked to Wax. She *had* to talk.

Wax would probably catch her. He did things like that, impossible things that nobody thought he could. But just in case he didn't, Wayne listened. You could tell a lot about people from the way they talked. You saw their past, their upbringing, their aspirations—all in the words they used. And this kandra . . . sooner or later she'd slip up and use the wrong word. A word that would be obvious, like a fellow drinking milk in the middle of a rowdy tavern.

He didn't hear anything right off, though oddly he *did* notice MeLaan whispering to herself. As he listened, she modulated her voice, making it deeper—though still feminine. She repeated a few words to herself.

"She woulda been a twofie," Wayne noted, eyes still closed.

"Hm?" MeLaan said.

"Your bones," Wayne said. "Woman you're wearin' right now. Twofie. Second Octant. Raised on the outskirts."

"And how do you know that?" MeLaan asked.

"Heard her curse as I was helpin' her," Wayne said, feeling a stab of regret. The woman had just been doing her job, trying to keep someone from being killed.

She's still doing her job though, he thought, cracking an eye and looking at MeLaan. *Her bones are, at least.* Given the choice, if he died while trying to do something important, he'd rather that his bones get up and see it done right. Hell, with some kandra friends, he could be annoying Steris well into the afterlife.

"Like this?" MeLaan said. "Second Octant, touch of agave farmer?"

"Nice," Wayne said. "Draw out the end of your sentences, pitch them lower. Get some real twofie into that voice."

"Is this better?"

"Yeah, actually," Wayne said, sitting up. "That's damn good."

"TenSoon would be proud," MeLaan said. "I can still get a difficult accent right, when I need to."

"Difficult?" Wayne said. "The twofie accent?"

"With agave farmer."

"Common mix," Wayne said. "Once, I hadda do a guy who grew up on the northwestern coast, raised by deaf parents, only talking once in a while—who had then moved in with the Terris fundamentalists up in the mountains there."

MeLaan frowned as a servant bustled past carrying linen. Some of the executive staff were going to be staying through the night, what was left of it, and guest rooms needed to be prepared. "I don't know if I can do that," MeLaan said, talking in a slow, deliberate way, with a hint of Terris and a lot of slurred words. "But it does sound like fun."

"Ha!" Wayne said, turning on the accent, which was actually more clipped than MeLaan had made it. "Good, but you're trying too hard. Being raised by parents who can't hear doesn't make a chap stupid. He just looks at the world differently, see?"

"Not bad," MeLaan said. The next servant who passed gave them a glare as she had to pick her way over their outstretched legs in the hallway.

"It's better if I have a hat," Wayne said.

"A . . . hat."

"Sure," Wayne said. "Hats is a disguise for your *brain*. Helps you think like the person what wore it last. You wanna know a guy? Put on his hat."

"Has anyone ever told you that you're surprisingly wise?" MeLaan asked.

"All the bloody time."

"They're idiots. You're not wise, you're playing them. You're doing this on purpose." She grinned. "I love it."

Wayne tipped his hat forward, smiling and leaning back again. "I'm not lying 'bout the hats though. They do help."

"Sure," MeLaan said. "Like bones."

He cracked an eye at her. "Does it ever . . . bother you? Knowin' you might live forever?"

"Bother me? Why would it? Immortality is damn convenient."

"Don't know about that," Wayne said. "Seems to me that it would be nice to finally be *done,* you know? It's like . . . like you're running a race, and you don't know quite where the end is, but you got an idea. An' you only need to make it that far. I can do that, I figure. But you, you don't have no end."

"You actually sound like you *want* to die."

"Someday," Wayne said. "Huh. Maybe I should get into politics."

MeLaan shook her head at him, seeming bemused. "It can be daunting," she admitted a short time later, "to consider eternity, as Harmony must see it. But anytime I get bored, I can just live a new life."

"Put on a new hat," Wayne said. "Become someone else."

"Switch it up. Be bold where once I was timid. Be crass where I was respectful. Makes life interesting, dynamic." She paused. "And there's something else. We *can* die, if we want."

"What, just like that?"

"Kinda," MeLaan said. "Don't know if you've read the accounts. They're blurry about this topic anyway, but near the end of the World of Ash, Ruin tried to take over the kandra. Control them directly. Well, TenSoon and those in charge, they were *really* terrified by that. So they planned, and we all talked. And about a century after the Catacendre, we figured out a way to stop our own lives. Takes a little concentration, but sets the body into a spiral where we just . . . end."

"Nice," Wayne said, nodding. "That makes a lot of sense. Always have an escape route planned. Oh, and your 'a's are still off; you carried them over from your own accent. They aren't nasal enough. Draw them out, if you wanna sound like a real twofie."

She cocked her head at him. "You're wasted as a human."

"Nah," Wayne said. "I've barely had a few mouthfuls

today." He reached in his pocket and checked his flask. "Well, maybe a wee more than that."

"No, I meant—"

He grinned at her, and she cut off, then grinned back. He tipped his hat to her, then closed his eyes and continued listening. A short time later, she stood up and started pacing the hall, and he could hear her saying her "a" sounds to herself as she walked.

He listened for a good long while, catching nothing abnormal, though he was pretty sure the sanitation-minister guy was lying about his education. That fellow had never been to the university—or if he had, he hadn't hung around long enough to pick up the proper words. Wayne was mulling this over when he heard something out front. A voice, faint but unmistakable.

He scrambled to his feet, causing MeLaan to jump.

"Gottago," he said. "Watchdaidiot."

"But—"

"Berideback," Wayne said, clutching his hat and running down the hallway, his long Roughs-style duster flaring to the sides. He raced around the corner and dashed toward the front of the mansion.

"He said to deliver it here," the woman was saying to the butler. "So I've brought it. It was a simple task—he just needed something made. Hardly worth waking me . . ."

She turned to him. A radiant, glorious woman, built like a good Roughs fence—just tall enough, lean, but strong too. She had dark hair, which he'd compared to a pony's on several occasions—and it was right unfair that she should get mad, considering she kept it in a tail and everything. She wore trousers, because skirts were stupid, and boots, 'cuz stuff needed to be kicked.

The whole world could be going wrong, but seeing her made him forget. He grinned.

In return she gave him her special scowl, the one just for him. It was how he knew she cared. That, and when she shot him she tended to aim for places that didn't hurt too much.

"She's with me," Wayne said, running up.

"Like *hell* I am," Ranette said, but she let him steer her away from the butler.

"And one wonders," the butler said from behind, "how His Grace's life can be threatened, when we're letting every dust rat in the city saunter up and—"

He cut off as Ranette spun, her pistol out. Wayne caught her arm in time to stop her from firing.

"Dust rat?" she muttered.

"When's the last time you bathed?" Wayne said. Then winced. "Just . . . you know, curious."

"Guns don't care if I stink, Wayne. I have things to do. And I *don't* like being ordered around." She shook a little cloth pouch in her left hand. Behind, the butler had grown very pale.

Wayne got her into the sitting room. She didn't stink, despite what she said—she smelled of grease and gunpowder. Good scents. Ranette scents.

"What is it?" Wayne asked, snatching the pouch once they were out of sight.

"Something Wax asked me to make," Ranette said. "Who got killed over there?" She pointed toward the still-open secret door down to the saferoom. Murder always caught her attention, if only because she'd want to see the bodies and judge how well the bullets tore up the flesh.

Wayne rolled a small metal object from the pouch onto his palm.

A bullet.

His hand started to shake.

"Oh, for Harmony's sake," Ranette said, plucking the bullet from his hand before he could drop it. "It's not a gun, you idiot."

"It's a part of one," Wayne said, shoving his hand in his pocket and breathing deeply. He could hold a bullet. He did that all the time, for Wax. The shaking subsided. Something seemed odd about that bullet though.

"So if I gave you a splinter of wood, and told you it had once been in a rifle stock, you'd go to pieces then too?"

"Dunno," Wayne said. "You think I understand how my brain works?"

"I'd say there's a logical fallacy in that statement," Ranette said. "Maybe two." She tucked the bullet back into the pouch. "Wax here?"

"No. He's off detectiving."

"Then you'll have to take this," she said, handing him the pouch. "His note insisted it was important. Half powder as he asked, piercing bullet, forged not to shatter."

He *could* hold a bullet. He took it, then tucked it away immediately in his duster. See?

"So, uh, want to go get a drink?" he said. "You know, when the city is safe. Or maybe before it's safe? I don't mind none if the pub's a little on fire while we drink."

"You know I'd sooner shoot myself, Wayne," she said with a sigh. "And Misra would shoot me if—by chance—I did go, come to think of it."

Wayne frowned. That was nowhere *near* the vitriol he normally got from her. "What's wrong?" he asked.

She shook her head, glancing back toward the entryway. "It's bad out there, Wayne. People still on the streets, thronging together, shouting. I've seen crowds like this before, in the Roughs. Usually right before a man got strung up, law or no law. Those were towns of five hundred. What happens when it's *five million* who start acting like that . . ."

"Probably the return of the Ashen World," Wayne said. "What better time to finally profess your long-requited love for a certain handsome fellow what don't mind none if you smell like the inside of a barrel of sulfur?"

She gave him the glare again. He grinned. But then she didn't shoot him. Or even punch him. Damn. This was *bad*.

"They're starting to gather outside," Ranette said, distracted. "Chanting slogans about the governor."

"I need to check that," Wayne decided. If the governor wasn't going to let him in and watch him close up, maybe he could learn something about Bleeder's plans out in that crowd. "Get back to your house, lock the doors, and keep your guns handy."

It was telling that she didn't offer the slightest objection to his order as he strode toward the door out into the mists.

Captain Aradel regarded the governor's writ as he would the last will and testament of a beloved family member: with both reverence and obvious discomfort.

"He names me lord high constable," Aradel said. "But . . . rusts, I'm no lord." He looked up at Reddi and his other lieutenants.

"Perhaps," Reddi said, "the appointment conveys a title, sir."

"The governor can't just appoint someone to the peerage," Marasi said. "A new title has to be ratified by a council with a quorum of the major house seats in the city." She bit her lip as soon as she said it. She didn't mean to be contrary.

Aradel didn't appear to mind. He carefully folded the writ and slid it into his jacket pocket. She'd found him gathering a sizable force outside of headquarters, preparing to still malcontents and ring constabulary bells to let the people living nearby know that at least someone was patrolling this night. Phantom sounds floated through the mists. Distant shouts. Clangs. Screams. It felt like hell itself surrounded them, shrouded in a veil of darkness and fog.

"Sir," Marasi said. "The governor said that he wanted you to do two things. First, send a detachment to forcefully quell rioting in the city. Second, bring up a smaller force to guard him as he prepares to address the people near the mansion. You're not to turn protesters away there, but elsewhere in the city . . . sir, he counseled you to be firm of hand. Very firm."

"Rusting idiots deserve it," said Lieutenant Mereline, a woman with short blonde hair.

"No need for bloodthirst, Lieutenant," Aradel said. "I seem to remember you cussing out the Hasting family with some regularity yourself."

"Doesn't mean I'm setting fire to the city," Mereline said. "The high houses being bastards doesn't excuse being bastards ourselves. Sir."

"Well, the mansion seems a good enough center from which to operate," Aradel said. "Chip, you and the messengers run to the other constables-general and ask them to meet me at the governor's mansion with their officers. We'll coordinate the city lockdown from there.

Everyone else, let's double-time it that way. If His Grace wants to talk to the people, I want a nice *thick* barrier of police bodies between him and his constituents, understand?"

The group bustled into motion, the bell ringers setting out in front, the messengers scattering—one even taking to the skies; Chip was one of the Coinshots. The rest of the constables fell into a march. An uneven one—they weren't soldiers—but no less resolute.

"Sir," Marasi said, walking quickly up to Aradel, "there's something else I need to tell you, if you can spare a moment."

"How important is it?" Aradel asked, pausing at the side of the group.

"Very."

Reddi cleared his throat behind them. "Perhaps you should discuss it while traveling to the mansion, sir. If the governor really is planning to address the crowds . . ."

"Yes," Aradel said. "Innate suddenly appointed me lord high constable; that immediately worries me about what other kinds of impulsive things he's capable of doing tonight. Let's do this on the move, Colms. Reddi, bring along the rest of the constables as smartly as you can. I'm going to the mansion ahead of you."

Marasi nodded. The things she wanted to discuss would be best said in the privacy of a carriage anyway.

Except . . .

Idiot, she thought as Aradel jogged over to a group of horses in constable livery, reins held by a corporal. The carriage she'd been contemplating pulled away, loaded with equipment most likely. Reddi grinned at her smugly.

Marasi sighed. She'd been looking forward to

maintaining her decorum tonight. Ah well. She walked over and took a set of reins.

Aradel was already in his saddle. He glanced at her, then raised a hand to his head. "Oh, of course. I didn't think—"

Marasi swung up into the saddle, awkwardly bunching her skirt up between her legs and sitting on part of it, revealing a generous expanse of leg. "It occurs to me, sir," Marasi noted, "that lady constable uniforms could be distinctly more utilitarian."

"We'll . . . make a note of it, Lieutenant Colms." He glanced toward the retreating carriage. "If you wish—"

"Sir," Marasi said, "I believe the city is on *fire*. Perhaps we can discuss feminine modesty on another occasion?"

"Of course." He nodded and they set off in a clatter of hooves, trailed by two corporals with rifles in the scabbards on their saddles. The four horses quickly outpaced the larger group of constables, and even the carriage, as they rode through the mists.

Marasi was glad of the darkness, as it hid her furious blush. In compensation, she had gained the memory of Reddi's stunned expression, utterly shocked by what she'd done.

Well, why *shouldn't* she show her legs? Historical precedent, and simple practicality, demanded that women be allowed into all professions. What lord would turn away a Thug or a Bloodmaker from his guards just because she had breasts? What constable office would pass up the chance to have every Tineye or Coinshot they could get? What bank wouldn't jump at the chance to employ a Terriswoman with copperminds?

The thing was, woman constables were *also* expected

to be models of ladylike behavior. A holdover from the old days, reinforced by the speeches of Lady Allrianne Ladrian soon after the Catacendre. There was just this blunt expectation that you would strive to remain feminine at the same time as you did your job. A heavy double standard to bear. At times Marasi didn't mind. She *liked* dresses, and nice hair, and solving problems with a careful word instead of a fist to the face. To her it was perfectly reasonable to be feminine and a constable. But did the men ever have to worry about being properly masculine while doing their jobs?

One social problem at a time, Marasi, she admonished herself, riding alongside Aradel. Though she *was* going to buy some rusting trousers. Riding this way was *cold*.

"You ride well," Aradel called to her as they slowed slightly from their initial burst away from the others. He led the way across a canal bridge, cutting across the middle of the Third Octant to get to the Second.

"I've had plenty of practice," Marasi said.

"That's uncommon in the city these days," Aradel noted. "A hobby?"

"You could say that," Marasi said, blushing as she remembered her girlish fascination with the Roughs, lawmen, and Allomancer Jak stories. When her friends— well, acquaintances—had been given new coats for their birthdays, she'd begged for a Roughs duster and hat.

Pure foolishness, of course. She'd completely grown out of that.

"What is it you wanted to tell me?" Aradel called.

"Could we slow further for a moment?"

He nodded and obliged, to the point where the horses were maintaining a brisk walk. Marasi opened the purse she'd slung over her shoulder and thrust the letters at Aradel. She hadn't consciously realized how eager she'd been to pass them on to someone else, so that the responsibility they represented wouldn't rest solely on her.

Aradel took them. "What's this?" he asked quietly.

"You remember telling me to snoop around the governor's place, if I got the chance?"

"I remember telling you—with great circumspection—to keep your eyes open, Lieutenant."

"I did, sir. I kept my hands open too. In case something damning *happened* to fall into them."

"Harmony. What did you find?"

"Letters," Marasi said, "from Innate to various ladies and lords in the city, arranging for the purchase of political favors and the suppression of legislation they didn't want. Sir, they're annotated in his own hand, and they match my records of suspicious events during his tenure as governor. During the ride to bring you the writ I read through them, and I'm convinced he's just as corrupt as his brother was."

Aradel gave no outward reaction of either surprise or outrage. He rode in silence, gripping the letters, eyes forward.

"Sir?" Marasi finally asked.

"You put me in a difficult position, Lieutenant."

"Sir. I'd say that the governor has put you in that position, not me."

"How legally did you obtain these?"

"That depends," Marasi said, "on how the courts would interpret your authority to investigate when there is reasonable suspicion of wrongdoing, and whether or not you were justified in authorizing me to act."

"In other words, you stole them."

"Yes, sir."

Aradel tucked them away.

"It doesn't mean we shouldn't protect him, sir," Marasi offered. "Until proven guilty in court, he's still the rightful leader of the city. This isn't the Roughs, where we can just stride up and shoot someone, then publish our reasons later."

"The mere fact that you feel you need to point that out," Aradel said, "means you've been spending too much time with your Coinshot friend, Colms. I'm not considering avoiding my duty. I'm just thinking of all those people, and their rioting. And they're *right*. They *are* being robbed by the system. Ruin . . . we were supposed to be better than this. What if the Lord Mistborn saw us now?"

"I suspect," Marasi said, "he'd tell us to do something about the situation."

Aradel nodded curtly. When he offered no further commentary, Marasi kicked her horse back into a trot, and the lord high constable followed suit.

Tradition held that today's Field of Rebirth looked exactly the same as on that day long ago when humankind had crept from the wombs of stone that Harmony had created. Though the city had claimed all of the surrounding area, this central ring of pleasant grass and gentle hills had been left as a monument to another time.

Marewill flowers brushed Wax's mistcoat as he strode across the springy ground. The tradition that this place hadn't changed was pure stupidity. Surely when Breeze and Hammond had climbed out into the sunlight, they hadn't found grass that was perfectly manicured or flowers that grew in careful lines. Did people who spoke of that tradition just ignore the benches and the pathways? The buildings? Surely Harmony hadn't left *lavatories* on the grassland for the convenience of visitors.

At the center the highest hill was topped by the half museum, half mausoleum sheltering the tombs of the Last Emperor and the Ascendant Warrior. Their giant statues rose above, dominating the area. As Wax approached, he was surprised to find lamps on the low structure spilling light across the grass and flowers. A pair of constables guarded the door.

"Now, just turn on back and don't make trouble," one of them called as Wax approached.

Wax ignored the order, striding out of the mists and up to the men. "The caretakers called for your help, I assume?"

The two constables studied him, then reluctantly saluted. His reputation preceded him, though these men wore the patches of constables from the First Octant. It was a precinct he hadn't often visited, but who else strode through the night in a mistcoat with a shotgun strapped to his leg?

"They're worried about looters," one of the constables said, a squat fellow with a half beard around his mouth. "Um, sir."

"Wise," Wax said, striding past them and pushing into the mausoleum.

"Uh, sir?" one of the constables said. "They said not to let . . . Sir?"

Wax pushed the door shut as the two constables started arguing outside about whether they should stop him or not. He scanned the open foyer, with its murals of the Originators. Hammond, the Lord Mistborn,

Lady Truth, Wax's own ancestor Edgard Ladrian. Portly and self-satisfied, in his portrait he held a cup of wine. He'd always looked like the sort of person Wax would want to punch on sight. The type who was certainly guilty of *something*.

Wax ignored the displays of various relics from the World of Ash, and didn't enter the chamber that held the resting places of the Ascendant Warrior and her husband, though he did raise his gun and spin the cylinder toward them in acknowledgment. A Roughs tradition to respect the fallen.

"What's this?" A bleary-eyed woman stepped out of a nearby room, apparently a small apartment for the caretaker. "Nobody was to be let in!"

"Routine inspection," Wax said, striding past without looking.

"Routine? In the middle of the night?"

"You asked for constable involvement," Wax said. "Codes require that when you ask for guards from the precinct, we have to do an inspection to make sure you don't have contraband."

"Contraband?" the woman asked. "This is the *Originator Tomb*!"

"Just doing my job," Wax said. "You can take it up with my superiors outside, if you wish."

She stormed out toward the front doors in a huff as Wax reached a small room unadorned with relics or plaques. The only thing in here was a hole in the ground.

It was a gaping pit fenced by a railing to keep inquisitive children from tumbling in. There was a ladder, but Wax dropped a bullet casing and jumped, falling freely a short distance before slowing himself and hitting the dark, glassy stone floor at the bottom.

A few lights dangled from the ceiling, like drips of molasses. He Pushed on a nearby light switch, causing the lights to flicker on throughout this enormous cavern. He'd visited here as a youth; every tutor brought their charges to visit, and he understood it was common in the public schools as well. It felt different now, standing alone in the large, low-ceilinged chamber. No jabbering tourists to break the mood or chase away visions of the past. He could hear much better the water rushing in the distance, where the river flowed. Parts of the caverns were supposed to have flooded over time. He could only vaguely remember explanations during his tour here of why others remained dry.

He walked into the cavern, trying to imagine what it had been like to huddle in one of these caves, the world dying outside, wondering if you were going to spend the rest of your short life trapped in darkness. He trailed his fingers on the stone walls as he wound around corners. The place was large and open, but also contained a series of smaller, bulbous chambers at the side. Most were part of the museum, and contained plaques with quotes from the Originators, written in metal. Others contained depictions of the rebuilding of the world, or other relics such as a replica of both Harmony's Bands and the Bands of Mourning.

One entire chamber was dedicated to the Words of Founding, Harmony's books, lore, knowledge, and own holy account of what had happened to the World of Ash. Another chamber contained volumes by other Originators, some of which were considered holy canon by one sect or another—while some, like the Docksithium, were decidedly apocryphal. Wax had tried to read the thing once. Copyright pages were more interesting.

He lingered at a chamber dedicated to the Survivor containing a hundred different depictions of him by various artists, some contemporary, others ancient. There was fervent fascination with his posthumous "apparitions" to people during the final days, though Harmony himself attributed those to the Faceless Immortals.

Echoing voices chased Wax onward. Wayne would probably give him hell for confusing the poor people, rather than just telling them what he was doing. Of course, Wayne would probably have convinced them he was the Lord Ruler, then made them fix him dinner. So he tried not to let Wayne's moral compass influence him too much.

Wax counted down the chambers dedicated to each of the metals until he reached the sign of atium. This little chamber contained documentation and rumors about the mythological metal; Wax didn't have the time to read them. Instead, he followed the blue lines his steelsight showed him. They pointed toward a side wall, where he was able to pry back a decorative piece of wood paneling and push on a lever, popping open a doorway and revealing a cavern beyond.

He slipped in, unhooked an old oil lantern from the wall, and pulled the door shut before kneeling down in the pitch blackness, fishing in his gunbelt for some matches. As he pulled them out, a growling voice sounded in the dimness.

"I've been waiting for you."

20

Wax held very still in the darkness. He flared his steel, seeking guidance from that comfortable fire inside of him. The blue lines pointed exclusively behind him; those pointed toward the hidden doorway and the nails in the wall. There was nothing else.

Except . . . Could he just barely make something out? Two faint lines, tiny as the threads of a spiderweb. He flared his metal, straining, Pushing. The lines quivered in the darkness. Then they were gone.

Wax whipped out his Sterrion and pointed it down the corridor away from the lines, and fired three times in quick succession. The flash of gunpowder lit the room like lightning as he leveled his other gun toward the blue lines and the source of the sound.

In those flashes, he made out something in the darkness crouching nearby. It was inhuman, with bestial eyes and stark white teeth. *Rust and Ruin.* Fingers sweaty on his gun, Wax backed away from the thing, ready to fire.

He didn't pull the trigger. You didn't shoot something for talking to you.

"You're certainly a jumpy one," the voice growled.

"Who are you?" *What are you?*

"Light your lantern, human," the voice said. "And lock that door. Let's be away from here before someone comes to investigate the gunfire."

Wax paused to catch his breath and steady his nerves, but eventually slipped his guns back into their holsters. Whatever it was, it could have attacked him instead of speaking to him. It didn't want him dead.

He lit the small lantern, but when he raised it, the creature had retreated into the corridor until it was just a shadow. Still unnerved, Wax flipped the latches he found on the wall, locking the hidden doorway closed from the inside.

"Come," the voice said.

"You're one of them," Wax whispered, raising the lantern and following the shadowy figure, which walked on all fours. "You're a kandra."

"Yes."

Wax jogged to catch up, his lanternlight finally giving him a good look at his companion. A wolfhound, easily the largest he had ever seen, of a mottled grey coloring. The pelt reminded him of the mists.

"I've read about you," Wax said.

"Thrilling," the kandra growled. "I'm so happy Sazed included me in his little book so that drunk people can curse by my name."

"They . . . do that?"

"Yes." The wolfhound growled quietly in the back of his throat. "There are . . . stuffed toys too."

"Oh yeah," Wax said. "Soonie cubs. I've seen those around."

The growling grew louder, and Wax's nervousness returned. Best not to taunt the immortal hound. He didn't know how many of the legends of this creature were true, but if even a percentage were based in fact . . .

"So," Wax said. "Guardian. You were waiting for me?"

"It was decided," the kandra said, "that allowing a human to wander these caverns alone was unwise. I came myself. The others are busy."

"Hunting Bleeder?"

"Counteracting her," the kandra said, leading him to an intersection, then taking the right fork.

They walked in silence for a short time before Wax cleared his throat. "Um . . . do you mind explaining what you mean by that?"

The dog sighed, a discomforting sound. A talking dog was strange, but the sigh was just so *human*.

"I don't talk much these days," the kandra said. "I've . . . fallen out of practice, it seems. Paalm is trying to spark a revolution, using skills she learned from the Lord Ruler himself. But she is only one kandra. She has disdain for the rest of us, and therefore underestimates us in equal measure. We can do what she does, imitating people, appearing on the streets. For every 'priest' she has commit an atrocity, we will have dozens out tonight, preaching temperance and peace, pleading with the people not to listen to rumors."

"Wise," Wax said. He hadn't considered what the other kandra might be doing, other than vaguely assuming they were tracking Bleeder. This made good sense. Could he use it, somehow, in his investigation?

As they moved deeper into the caverns, Wax noted a crusty white substance growing on the rocks, the source of the powdery residue he'd found on Bleeder's clothing. Presumably, if he extinguished his lantern he'd be able to see the glow. He might not even need the lantern, but thinking of all this stone surrounding him—separating him from the mists above—he felt no urge to extinguish it.

The network of tunnels was far more extensive than he'd expected. He'd thought of this place only as that one cavern underneath the tomb—but that wasn't it at all. Harmony had assembled many different refuges of people as he remade the world, placing them all in the same area that was now Elendel. How much of the city did these tunnels stretch beneath? He passed a number of them that had flooded; what was the difference between those and the ones that remained dry?

As they wound through the tunnels, they passed an opening into a different large cavern. He raised his lantern to give it a glance, then froze in place. Instead of more rough, natural rock, his light illuminated dusty tiles and pillars, with parts of the floor torn up. Past them, there was what appeared to be a small *hut* of all things.

"TenSoon?" he asked as the kandra continued forward.

"Come along, human."

"Is that . . ."

"Yes. Many people hid in the basements of Kredik Shaw, the Lord Ruler's palace. Sazed moved that here, as he did with all other caverns of refuge."

Wax couldn't pull himself away, gaping at history—no, *mythology*—come alive. The Lord Ruler's palace. Places where the Survivor and his followers had walked.

Rusts . . . the *Well of Ascension itself* would be in there.

"Human," the kandra said, insistent. "There is something I wish for you to see. Come."

Another time, Wax thought, turning from the entrance to lost Kredik Shaw and following TenSoon. "MeLaan said that the kandra don't come down here often. Why not? Isn't this your home?"

"It is a sacred place," the wolfhound said. "Yes, it is home, but also a prison—and so much more. Under the Lord Ruler, we needed this place for freedom, to be ourselves. Outside, we were controlled, enslaved by men."

Bitter, Wax thought. Even after hundreds of years, this creature was pained by the life it had led. Did he blame humankind? Did Bleeder?

"We come here," TenSoon said, "when the mood strikes us. Usually we come alone, and infrequently. There are clubs up above where we can socialize now, being ourselves. Homes. Lives. The younger generations almost never visit this place. They prefer their lives as they are now, and don't wish to remember the past. I suppose I'm the same, though for different reasons."

Wax nodded, walking alongside the kandra as they penetrated ever deeper into the twisting tunnels of the Homeland. They passed many empty chambers, but some that held oddities, like two with old baskets and some discarded bones on the floor.

Wax had been in his fair share of tunnels out in the Roughs, but most of those had been some kind of man-made mine. These caverns were different. Those had smelled of dust and dirt, while this place somehow felt *alive.* Of water and fungus. Of patience.

The tunnels were knobby, yet smooth, like wax pooled beneath a long-burning candle. Holy ground. Everything else in the world, so far as he knew, had been completely remade during the Catacendre. But these caverns stretched back to eternity, as old as human memory. Older.

Eventually they reached a small chamber that didn't seem quite as organic as the others. Had it been shaped, somehow, by kandra hands? TenSoon settled down on his haunches in the entrance to the room. Wax's light glittered off the smooth, bulbous rock of the floor, which fell away into a series of pits. Perhaps three feet across, they looked like holes dug by prospectors foolishly hunting metals out in the Roughs.

Wax glanced at TenSoon.

"I passed by here on my way to meet with you," the kandra said in his growling, half-human voice. "I smelled something wrong."

Smelled something? Wax couldn't catch any odd scents—but this whole place smelled strange to him. He stepped into the room, then noted something. One of the small pits was full. Were those sheets of paper?

Yes, they were. As Wax knelt at the rim of the pit, he was surprised to find hundreds of sheets of paper inside, jagged on one edge, as if they'd been ripped from a book. They contained cramped writing, with numbered verses. The Words of Founding.

Besides the normal writing, someone had scrawled all over these in brownish-red ink.

Blood, Wax thought. *It's blood.*

He set down his lantern, then reached down and picked up a page. Book eighty, verses twenty-seven through fifty. Verses about Harmony's quest for Truth.

Someone, likely Bleeder, had written all over them the words *Lies, lies, lies.*

Wax dug up other sheets. Most had something written on them, a word or phrase, though many were just smeared with blood. Something bothered Wax about it all, something that made his eye twitch. He couldn't say what it was.

I was there, one sheet read. *Nobody,* said another. *It was,* said another. He started laying them out. TenSoon—whom he'd almost forgotten—sniffed in the doorway.

Wax glanced back. "Did you see these?"

"Yes," TenSoon said.

"What do you make of them?"

"I . . . did not stay long," the kandra said, then looked to the side. "I do not spend time in this room, human. I am not fond of it."

This room . . . Wax felt cold. Was this the prison that TenSoon had been trapped in, locked away without bones, awaiting execution?

Rusts. He was kneeling in a place that had decided the fate of the world.

Wax stretched down, grabbing more of the sheets. It seemed like Bleeder had ripped apart an entire set of the Words of Founding—the unabridged version. Old edition too, judging by the fact that it had been hand-written instead of printed.

"You really knew her, didn't you?" Wax asked. "The Ascendant Warrior?"

"I knew her," TenSoon said softly. "Near the end, I spent over an hour without my spikes, and so my memories degraded. However, most of what I lost was from the time right before my fall. Most of my memories of her are crisp."

Wax hesitated with stacks of pages in his hands. "What was she like? As a person, I mean."

"She was strong and vulnerable all at once," Ten-Soon whispered. "She was my last master, and my greatest. She had a way of pouring everything of herself into what she did. When she fought, she was the blade. When she loved, she was the kiss. In that regard, she was far more . . . human than any I have known."

Wax found himself nodding as he settled the pages about him, in stacks based on whether they had words or not. The ones with fingerprints he set in their own stack. Perhaps they would be useful. Probably not. Bleeder *was* a shapeshifter, after all.

TenSoon eventually padded up to him. "They look," TenSoon said, inspecting the sheets, "like they might say something if you string them together."

"Yeah," Wax said, dissatisfied.

"What is wrong?"

"It's too much," Wax said, waving his hand at it. "Too convoluted, too sensational. Why would she write on a bunch of pages, then rip them out and leave them here?"

"Because she's mad."

"No," Wax said. "She's not that kind of mad. The way she's been working is too deliberate, too focused. Her *motives* might be insane, but her *methods* have been careful." How could he explain it? This case had his instincts fighting with one another.

He tried again. "When someone leaves something like this behind, it means one of two things. They're sloppy, or they're trying too hard. She's not sloppy, but I don't think she's trying to be cute either, dangling clues and playing games. When I talked to her . . ."

"You *spoke* with Paalm?" TenSoon demanded, his ears perking up. "When?"

"Earlier tonight," Wax said. "There was something regretful about her. She claimed to not be playing games, but this seems like a game. A thousand discarded pages, left to be put back together and form a clue?"

He shook his head. "I don't buy it. Madness or not, she had to know that other kandra would eventually find this."

"Very well," TenSoon said, settling back down. "But she spoke to you as *herself*, not an imitation?"

"Yes. Is that odd? You're doing it right now, and Me-Laan seems to be acting no specific role either."

"We are not Paalm," TenSoon said. "As long as I've known her, she's been subject to the performance. I was like that too, years ago. I didn't know who I was if I was not imitating someone."

Wax looked across the sheets. *Freedom,* one of them said in a scrawl across the page. *Will give you freedom whether you,* said another, only half of a thought.

"What was she like?" Wax asked. "Who *is* she, Guardian?"

"Hard to say," TenSoon replied. "Paalm was the Lord Ruler's pet kandra, a slave to his will and the contract we made with him. She ignored events surrounding the end of the World of Ash; she vanished, didn't return to the Homeland. I assumed her dead, until she appeared among the survivors. Even then she separated herself from us, though she served Harmony as we all did. Until . . . nothing. Absence."

"Freedom," Wax said, tapping the page. "She talked about that with me. What does it mean?"

"I don't know," TenSoon said, voice even more a growl than before. "She has betrayed everything we are. But then, so did I. So perhaps we are a pair, she and I. Two of the oldest monsters remaining on this planet, now that many of the Seconds have taken the escape of ending their own lives."

"Freedom . . ." Wax whispered. "Someone else moves us. . . . She left a note for me in the governor's mansion.

She removed a politician's tongue, to stop his lies. Killed a priest through the eyes, to stop him from looking. Seeing. For who? For what?"

She had been the Lord Ruler's kandra, moved about and danced at his whims. And then . . . Harmony's servant? She lived with his voice inside her head, knowing all along that he could take control of her. How would that feel?

Would it make you remove one of your spikes? Would you be trying to bring that freedom to everyone? Misguided, in your insanity, certain that the world needed saving?

Wax stood up slowly. "It's about Harmony."

"Lawman?"

"She's trying to bring down God Himself."

"That's insane."

"Yes," Wax said, turning to the kandra. "It is." He started to pace in the small room. "Speak to Harmony and find out something for me. Did Bleeder first leave because Harmony tried to take control of her at some point? Did that set her off?"

A moment of silence. "Yes," TenSoon replied. "Harmony says He didn't try to control her directly, but He did push her very hard to do something she didn't want to do."

"She's been persistent about this idea that all people are controlled." *Harmony . . . was she Bloody Tan? Was she wearing his body, even back then? Was she there when I shot Lessie?* "She sees everyone as Harmony's puppets—in her eyes, the politicians are His mouth. She's bringing down the government for that reason. Religion? Harmony's eyes, to watch over the people. She works to undermine that by creating strife between the religious sects."

"Yes . . ." TenSoon said. "In a way, it could be seen as a continuation of the First Contract. Serve the Lord Ruler. Bring down the force that he worked to defeat. Harmony is half of that."

"But what am I in this?" Wax continued, only half listening to TenSoon. "Why me? Why focus on—"

No, wrong question.

What was she going to do next? Eyes, tongue . . . ears, maybe? *Pretend she's a step ahead of you,* Wax told himself. *Prepare for the worst.*

He looked again at the sheets on the floor. She wanted Wax out of the way. An elaborate puzzle? It was a time waster, a distraction. She'd ripped out these sheets not to tease him, but to remove him from the investigation long enough to accomplish the next phase of her plan. She'd *led* him here with that dust on her robe. She'd planted it there for that purpose.

"She knows," Wax said softly. "She knows what you're going to do, TenSoon. What you've *done.*" He felt cold, and met the kandra's inhuman eyes. "She's *planned* that you would send your kandra to try to win back the hearts and minds of the people. That exposes you. Her next step is to bring them down."

Wayne wandered between two bonfires. Inside one, table and chair legs made sharp lines, like the shadowy limbs of corpses being burned. The mists didn't get too close to the fires, though the smoke made a good imitator in the night. Like a beggar dressed up so nice, you only knew him for what he was when you got close enough to catch a proper whiff.

Wayne leaned in to one of the bonfires to light his cigar, though that required him to heal the skin of his arm as it burned. He smelled both of his own singed hair and of the scent of the fire. Polished furniture didn't burn clean. He liked feeling the heat though. Made him feel alive.

He had stopped filling his metalminds, hoping he had enough health for what was coming. He couldn't afford to be weak or sickly right now. Not with what was happening.

He leaned back away from the flames and settled the cigar between his teeth. It was a fancy type, from the governor's own hidden stash. Wayne took a long puff before remembering that he hated the rusting things. Ah well. He hadn't traded anything good for it. Just one of Wax's forks.

The crowd gathering here in the square was the biggest he'd seen this night. They clumped in the bonfire light like a flock of ravens drawn to a kill. Wayne moved up to the back of the crowd and handed his cigar to someone there. He left her standing, baffled, as he dove into the crowd.

With a crowd this big, you couldn't move *through* them, but *with* them. You hadda pull the crowd on like a good coat, snug and tight, then let the cloth give you some direction. Wayne shuffled when the people shuffled, and shouted at the proper points, giving just the right drunken slur to his speech. He gave back a friendly elbow when one nudged him, and before too long he neared the front. Here, above everyone else, a shirtless fellow in trousers and suspenders stood atop a fountain statue, holding on to the Survivor's spear for balance, his other fist raised toward the crowd.

"They rob us blind!" the man shouted.

Aye, that's true, Wayne thought, shouting along with the crowd's roar of agreement.

"They expect us to work long hours every day, but then when it ain't convenient for them, they just cut us loose and don't care none if we starve."

Yeah, they do, Wayne thought, joining in the cursing and shouting.

"They do each other favors," the man bellowed. "They suck us dry, then gather to throw lavish parties!"

I've been to those parties, Wayne thought. *Good sandwiches.*

"Would the Survivor have stood for this?"

Probably not, Wayne admitted. As the crowd surged around him, Wayne folded his arms and thought. Sure, bringing down a homicidal shapeshifter was important and all, but *rusts,* this seemed a bad time to be hanging around with conners and noblemen. Listening to this speech, he was half inclined to string *himself* up, which was really disturbing, since he was generally suicidal only in the mornings.

He was about to turn away and flow back toward the mansion to talk with MeLaan about this when something changed. A new figure climbed up onto the statue: an older, balding man who was a little thick around the waist, but in a friendly-type way. He wore ornate robes that frayed like a mistcoat at the bottom. A Survivorist priest?

The older man held up a pleading hand, and the fellow who had been shouting bowed his head in acknowledgment and stepped back. Beneath the giant image of the Survivor, his priest would be heard. Wayne felt a disturbance stir within him, like his stomach discovering he'd just fed it a bunch of rotten apples. Religion worried him. It could ask men to do things they'd otherwise never do.

"I come to you," the priest said into the night, "understanding and sympathetic. But I implore you, do not invoke the Survivor's name for looting and destruction. There is a way to fight back, and I will join you in it, but these are not the days of the Lord Ruler's tyranny. You have the ability to make your voice heard. You can send advocates to the government for you."

The crowd hushed. A few men shouted out expletives, explaining exactly what they wanted to do to the governor, but most grew quiet.

"The Survivor said that we should smile," the priest pled. "He taught that we should not let our sorrows drag us down no matter how bad life became."

The mood of the crowd was shifting. They shuffled instead of shouted. Wayne relaxed. Well, maybe religion *was* good for something other than fancy clothes and weird hats. If that priest defused this group, Wayne would buy him a drink, he would. And buying drinks for priests was great, because they usually wouldn't drink theirs, so you got two for yourself to . . .

Wait. Why was that fellow in the suspenders—the one who had talked before—sneaking up behind the priest? Raising his hand, as if to—

"No!" Wayne shouted, shoving through the crowd toward the fountain. He froze time, which caused quite a mess of confusion in the people around him, but it didn't do much. All that let him do was stand there feeling helpless, knowing the priest was too far away to save. The fellow in the suspenders stood just behind the gentle old man, hand raised, knife glittering in the firelight.

Except that wasn't no knife. It was a *needle*.

Wayne dropped his speed bubble. The needle plunged down, striking the priest in the back. The round-faced man jerked upright, and then his flesh started to *melt*.

It turned translucent, his eyes drooping out of their sockets, crystal bones beneath glittering in the light of the bonfires.

"Look!" the bare-chested man said. "See what they send to try to placate you? The Faceless Immortals serve the nobility! This was no priest, but one of their minions. They want you to believe you're free, that their democracy works for you, but all that surrounds you is lies!"

Wayne gaped as the priest—no, the kandra—struggled to stand upright and speak, but that made it worse. The protesters shouted, their rowdiness back with renewed strength, save for near Wayne, where the people were still confused as to why time had stopped for them.

A woman in a dirty skirt eyed him. "Hey, aren't you that guy from the Roughs?"

Wayne grimaced, backing away. On the fountain, the leader spotted him and interrupted his diatribe. He pointed right at Wayne. "One of them is here!" he shouted. "They send constables into our midst! They're all around, controlling you!"

Basically the entire crowd turned to look at Wayne.

Well, hell.

The betting and exchange of boxings began not long after, and the youths began paying gangs of street urchins to de-

times.

Hardest hit is the 3rd Octant with its slurry of parallel roads and long straightaways, only circuit at the old fairgrounds abutting the Irongate River.

(Continued on Back.)

ilant as
ite suit,
pecific
llendel,
as de-
out like
koloss,
e men
vibrant
almost
ormers
o I will
e gun-
staches
ntal to
women
stood
he had
ut also
losing
glisten-

ttle tin
(You
iled the
A Sport
d been
of my
effects
mantly
ipping
eming.)
I said,
leaving
jacket
t when
. Had I
leaving
t com-
ithout
erson?
usly I
out my
match

for any person in the room. Had I not bested the tribes at the Pits of Eltania? Was I not the first to bring back tales of the slopes of the Ashmounts, now gone green with vegetation? And wasn't it I that had domesticated the fabled long-necked horses of the Plains of Kaermeron?

"I shall not lower this gun," said the man, "until you pay for your crimes."

My enhanced senses picked up a faint tremor in the man's speech. I noticed the almost imperceptible flicks of his eyes to the right and left. This wasn't one of the Cobblesguilder henchmen as I'd at first thought. He was a man looking for revenge, and he wasn't entirely sure if I was the one from whom he should exact it.

"Let us talk this through peaceably," I suggested. I gently removed Lady Lavont's trembling fingers from my arm. "All will be solved, my lady," I said, detecting a faint gasp in her breathing as my fingers brushed hers for so short a moment.

Mustaches straightened. "You killed my brother three years back in the Roughs near Covingtar," he said.

I needed time to think on his accusation, so I stepped forward, raised my hands in the air, and said, "As you can see, I am unarmed." I turned in a circle, displaying to the crowd that I in fact held no sidearm. And yes, bravely, I turned my back on Mustaches, trusting in his uncertainty of my identity.

As I turned, I thought through my predicament. It was true that some three years back I had found myself in the vicinity of Covingtar. But had I killed someone's brother there? No doubt I had left many a man brotherless, but never intentionally. The very thought of killing a man for the express purpose of leaving another man brotherless is highly repugnant to me.

"I am not the man you seek," I said, raising my glass for another sip because, by the Faceless, if I was going to die I would do it drinking a fine Chamblis Montreau 328.

The gun barrel shook more. If my gambit failed, I would sport yet another bullet scar on my strapping abdomen. Skin and muscle would heal, but the finely-woven shirt had been a gift from the daughter of the owner of Gilles & Gilles—on the corner of Canton Avenue and Troncheau Way—tailors of exquisite and tasteful dress shirts for fashionable and high society types. I did not wish it to be spoiled with my worthy blood.

"Then who are you?" asked Mustaches, his gun's barrel dropping more. The moment of danger was not yet over, but my own breathing evened out. My enhanced senses found Mustache's gazelle-quick heartbeat slowing to a more reasonable pace.

"Gentleman Jak," I said with humility. "Surely you have heard of me."

"So you ain't that Waxillium Ladrian fellow?"

"By the Survivor, no!" My anger rose without warning. Many a man had met the righteous end of my knuckles for such a comment, but here in the barely civilized reaches of the Outer Cities, I knew I musn't punish this ill-informed yokel for his folly.

"My good man, no," I said more calmly and letting out a generous laugh. He shakily reholstered his pistol. A crooked smile began beneath those knifelike mustaches of his. I approached him like I would a prairie lion, but heartbeats later I was slapping him on the back like an old friend (and narrowly avoiding the end of one of his mustaches piercing me through the right earlobe, a hole that no doubt would make the honorable Handerwym jealous of the metalminds I might hang there).

"A drink," I roared. "A drink for my friend! For I too would pull a gun on Waxillium Ladrian were I to meet him in person!"

Danger averted, Lady Lavont came again to my side, a tinkle of laughter on her lips. Then I noticed over the crowd two pairs of waving arms that I immediately recognized as Handerwym's. In trying to get my attention over the pressing crowd in the room, he shook his arms in so aggravated a fashion that one of his metalminds flew from his wrist and landed like an Outer Cities cataract diver into the sparkle punch, spraying red droplets all in a mottle upon Lady Lavont's pastel satin evening gown.

My dependable steward's convulsing could only be interpreted one way. During my diversion with Mustaches, the Lord Mistborn's only remaining buttons had been stolen, swapped for the indistinguishable duplicates, and neither I nor Handerwym had been in a position to intercept the perpetrators.

I needed my enhanced senses to seek out the thieves, but I had just used my last modicum of tin to help defuse Mustaches' desire to bring me face to face with Old Ironeyes.

I pushed through the crowd toward the only source of reliable tin in the room. The Lord Mistborn's clasps of wasing, which I now knew to be counterfeit—

—Continued next week!!—

21

shfalls!" TenSoon said as he ran alongside Wax through the tunnels of the kandra Homeland. "I have told Harmony to pass the word to my fellows. We will stop our efforts immediately, but He says it might be too late."

Wax nodded, holding his lantern and puffing from exertion.

"We're Harmony's ears," TenSoon growled. "That fits with her theme, doesn't it? We listen, move among you, report back to God. She's going to try to deafen Him."

Wax nodded again.

"That's pointless!" TenSoon said. "She can't stop Harmony. Even with all of this, she's just a child throwing rocks at a *mountain* to try to move it."

"Yeah," Wax said, scrambling over some rubble. Pieces of the kandra Homeland had obviously suffered from being shoved about in the earth during the Catacendre. Walls had collapsed, then had lain here, broken, for hundreds of years. "But she's not really trying to *kill* God. She just wants to free people from Him, in her twisted way."

"Free them?" TenSoon said. He was silent for a time. "Emotion. That's it, isn't it? Vin liberated koloss by making them feel powerful emotions. It gave an opening into their souls, let her break through another's control and seize the creatures."

"That's what the old stories say," Wax replied. "Good to have confirmation."

"Humans aren't Hemalurgic creations like koloss. Powerful emotion won't 'free' them from Harmony."

"Sure it will," Wax said. "At least in Bleeder's eyes. If you're in a rage, you're not following Harmony's careful plans. You're out of control. She's going to drive this city to madness in an insane attempt to liberate it."

"Ruin!" TenSoon growled. "I may have to leave you behind, lawman. I must reach my people quickly and speak with them about what is happening."

"Fine," Wax said. "But I might keep up better than you assume, so long as I—"

A shrill howl echoed through the corridor, so chilling that Wax pulled to a stop. He drew Vindication, lantern held high in his off hand. The howl was joined by others, a terrible cacophony, each sound jarring against the others.

TenSoon leaned low, growling as the howls faded.

"What the hell was that?" Wax said.

"I have never heard its like before, human."

"Aren't you over a thousand years old?"

"Something like that," TenSoon said.

"Holy *hell*," Wax repeated. "Another way out?"

The kandra took off, leading him back the way they had come. The howls started up again, louder. The tight tunnels and uneven stones suddenly seemed far more confining.

Wax ran and, despite his earlier bravado, found he

had real trouble keeping up with TenSoon. The stone around them didn't contain any metals, at least not in a pure enough form for him to Push on. Besides, the tunnels twisted and turned too much for long Pushes.

So he ran, holding on to his lantern with sweating fingers, listening as the things behind seemed to grow more excited. Distracted as he was, he almost crashed into TenSoon when he caught up to him standing still in the tunnel.

"What?" Wax asked, panting from his run.

"It smells wrong ahead," TenSoon said. "They're waiting for us."

"Great," Wax said. "What are they?"

"They smell like men," TenSoon said.

More howls came from behind.

"Those," Wax said, "are *men*?"

"Come," TenSoon said, turning and scrambling away, his claws scratching on stone.

Wax followed. "Another way out?" he asked again.

TenSoon didn't answer, instead leading them in a sprint through small caverns, around corners, through tunnels. They stopped at an intersection, TenSoon considering their options while Wax fingered his gun nervously. He swore he could see something moving down the tunnel they'd left behind, the one where TenSoon claimed to have spotted an ambush.

"TenSoon . . ." he said, nervous.

"This way," the kandra said, dashing off.

Wax followed, entering a longer tunnel. Perfect. He let himself lag behind, holding up the lantern, trying to get a glimpse of whatever was following.

His light reflected from eyes in the shadows. Figures that were bent low, scrambling on all fours, moving in a distinctly inhuman way. Sweating, Wax dropped a shell casing and shoved it with his foot into a cleft in the rock. He Pushed, throwing himself down the corridor to catch up with TenSoon, landing just before they took a corner at speed.

"They're *not* human," Wax said. "Not completely."

"Hemalurgy," TenSoon said. "This is terrible. Paalm . . . She has gone further than I had assumed. She doesn't just kill. She Ruins."

"They're almost upon us," Wax said, clutching gun and lantern. "How do we get out?"

"We don't," TenSoon said, ducking to the side and into a small chamber. "We fight."

Wax followed, but stopped in the doorway, gun at the ready. They'd passed this room before, or one like it. It was filled with small baskets—glancing at them now, he could see they were full of bones.

The things chasing them had started yipping, but he could hear them scrambling on the stone—could hear them breathing in excited gasps—as they drew close.

Inside the room, TenSoon transformed.

It happened in a burst, the kandra's skin sloughing off his canine bones and splashing to the ground like a bucket of slop tossed out the back of a kitchen. The muscles and melting skin slapped against one of the baskets, tipping it, dumping bones.

MeLaan had said he was fast, but that word didn't begin to describe the sudden motion as TenSoon absorbed the bones. Arms sprouted from the side of his mass, then lifted it into the air even as legs formed beneath, thick like those of a wrestler. A skull emerged like a bubble rising through molasses, filling in with muscles stretched against bone, a jaw shifting into place.

In seconds, a short but robust figure stood in the

chamber. The face of stretched skin and muscle reminded Wax of a koloss, but those forearms were like
hammers, and the chest superhumanly powerful. It was
nude, though the crotch lacked genitals of either variety.

Wax looked back down the corridor outside and
raised his pistol, sweating. The things prowled closer.
Heads emerged from the darkness, faces that twisted
human features into something more canine. He counted
five total. These creatures were no longer bipedal, but
traces of humanity laced them—fingers that were too
long, hands with opposable thumbs. The joints bent the
wrong way at the elbows and knees, and the eyes . . .
the eyes were dead. Pure black.

"What has she done to you?" Wax whispered at
them.

The creatures didn't respond. Either they could not
think, could not speak, or didn't care to do either.
Wax fired upward, half hoping that the sound would
scare the things away, send them scuttling back into
the night.

The greater part of him hoped they would remain,
so he could finish off every last one of the poor bastards.

The single shot rang loud in the tunnel, but the beasts
didn't flee. Instead they surged forward, their reluctance giving way to frenzy. Wax leveled Vindication
and unloaded at the first creatures, aiming for skulls.
Flashes of gunfire lit the tunnel. Though his bullets tore
off skin and left streaks of bleeding muscle, not one of
the creatures dropped.

Wax ducked back into the room, holstering Vindication and setting his lantern on an outcropping. "Their
skulls have been thickened," he shouted to TenSoon
while reaching for his Sterrion.

The kandra stepped past him, both lithe and powerful. Wax could almost hear the muscles constricting, pulling taught beneath that skin. As the first creature entered, TenSoon smashed it on the side of the head, pinning it to the wall with one hand. Then he stepped back and raised his foot to *crush* the skull against the rocks.

The others leaped over TenSoon, dragging him down, biting his flesh. He grabbed at one, ripping it free by the hind legs and hurling it away. Wax fired, aiming for the eyes.

"They have been created to fight you," TenSoon growled from the ground, where he wrestled with one of the creatures while others tore at him. "Flee. Your modern weapons are useless here, lawman!"

Like hell they are, Wax thought, dropping his Sterrion and reaching to the large holster on his thigh, bringing out his short-barreled shotgun. He pulled out a handful of shells and tossed them to the floor with a sound like rain. Then he waded in, slapping the first monster that came at him across the face with the shotgun. It flinched, then howled—baring rows of uneven teeth.

Wax shoved the shotgun into its mouth and fired.

Bits of it colored the wall, and as it fell—thrashing—it knocked over baskets, spilling bones to the rock floor. The one creature's death caught the attention of others, who turned from the bleeding TenSoon and charged Wax.

Wax naturally preferred the pistol. A handgun was an extension of one's focus, a weapon of precision—like a thrown coin in anteverdant days. The soul of the Coinshot, his will made manifest.

The shotgun was something different; it wasn't an

extension of focus or will, but it *did* do a good job of representing his rage.

Wax shouted, slamming his shotgun across the face of one beast and Pushing on the barrel, giving the swing incredible momentum. The blow flung the creature to the side as Wax spun and pumped his gun, then blasted at the leg of the next one, ripping its arm free at the shoulder and sending it face-first into the stone.

He leaped over the next one that came for him, Pushing on a fallen bullet for lift. He fired a shotgun slug down into the beast's back, stunning it, then multiplied his weight and landed with a crunch.

The thing thrashed and writhed beneath him as another leaped at his throat. He pumped and shot it in the head, then Pushed on the slug. His weight still increased—draining his metalmind at a furious rate—that bullet didn't stop at the skull as the others had. It split bone and made a mess of the brain.

Wax sidestepped that corpse as it flopped beside him, then swung his shotgun upward into the head of the last beast coming for him. It flipped backward, exposing the belly.

Wax fired three times, emptying the shotgun. The underbelly was soft, as he'd hoped. The thing went down.

He stood, breathing deeply, the rhythm of the fight having consumed him. Nearby, TenSoon rolled over, the wounds to his arms and sides resealing. He had killed another of the things by ripping it in half. His eyes were wide as he regarded Wax. His bloodied face looked as inhuman as those of the creatures they'd just fought.

TenSoon climbed to his feet, surveying the wreckage. The lantern still burned calmly, illuminating bones scattered across the floor and masses that had once— horribly—been human, but now just twitched. Wax felt sick. He'd called them "things" in his head, but these had been people. TenSoon was right. What Bleeder had done here was worse, somehow, than even her murders.

"I will need to ask Harmony," TenSoon said, "if I have failed Him in killing this day." His voice was the same gravelly growl as before, when he'd inhabited the wolfhound's body.

"Why would he care?" Wax said, still sick. "He uses me to kill all the time."

"You are His Ruin," TenSoon said. "I am His Preservation."

Wax stood in silence amid the dead and dying and lowered his shotgun, trying to suppress the immediate feeling of *indignation* he felt. Was that all he was to Harmony? A killer? A destroyer?

"Still," TenSoon said, picking his way through the room and speaking as if he didn't realize the insult he'd just offered, "I do not think Harmony will mind what I have done. These poor souls . . ." He knelt and prodded at one of the bodies Wax had killed.

TenSoon came up with a thin piece of metal, silvery and perhaps as long as a finger. Did it have a red cast to it, or was that just the blood? He used steelsight and found that while he could see the spike, the line was duller than it should have been. Hemalurgy.

"One spike," TenSoon said, turning it over. "Any more, and Harmony might have been able to control these beasts. How could such a change be effected by a single spike? This is a level of Hemalurgy beyond my understanding, lawman."

Wax shook his head, checking on the creatures. Not to see if they were still a threat, but to make sure he didn't leave one of them here to die a protracted death. He found one woman still alive, paralyzed by his shot into her back. She watched him with those eyes, shaped like a person's, yet alien and dark. Whatever else had happened to these people, they should have been able to keep their eyes.

Wax put his gun to the woman's eye and fired, up into the brain. Then he closed his eyes and offered . . . what? A prayer to Harmony? Harmony hadn't helped these people.

I have done something to help. . . . The words whispered to him from the past. A memory of the last time Harmony had spoken to him. *I sent you.*

Wax wasn't certain if that was enough this time.

"Tell me you'll see these people buried," Wax said.

"I will," TenSoon said as a howl sounded in the distance. "More come. Do we fight here, or run?"

"Can you get us out?" Wax asked, reloading the shotgun.

"Perhaps. Not by a conventional method, but there could be a way."

"Then let's go," Wax said. "This is another distraction, TenSoon. Those creatures only came for us when we left the other chamber."

TenSoon nodded, dropping his body to the floor and absorbing the wolfhound's bones again. Only seconds passed before he'd restored himself, save for the hair. That started to sprout from the skin as TenSoon moved to the door, coming in waves as the kandra's body arranged it and pushed it out.

Wax grabbed his lantern and they fled, TenSoon again leading the way.

"There he goes, boys!" Wayne yelled, pointing into the darkness. "I saw that dirty conner right ahead. You go that way, I'll head around the other way, and we'll trap 'im between us, we will!"

The small force of men with him—armed with wrenches and brooms—split off in a cheering, clangorous mass of spit and vengeance. Wayne egged them on while backward-jogging in the other direction. Eventually he slowed, finally alone, and shook his head. Not bad fellows, for all the fact that they had the combined wits of a brick.

Wayne spun a dueling cane in his fingers, rounding back through an alleyway and popping out near the governor's mansion. He didn't go toward the front—more and more angry people were gathering there, and some might recognize him from before. On his head he wore a newsboy's cap, his other hat carefully stowed in a bush along the way. That was fine; he liked this new cap well enough, but he felt naked in another way—he was out of bendalloy. Completely dry.

That was bad. No more stopping time unless Wax had an extra vial for him. The fellow often carried one.

Wayne slipped around the mansion, intending to head toward the back doors, where he hoped the guards would let him in. He'd wasted time, far too much, getting away from that crowd. The sight of that poor kandra melting in front of everyone else haunted him.

Rusts. He wasn't sure which side of the argument he came down on, but at least he wasn't going around melting people for an audience. Besides, for the moment he figured he'd choose the side that *wasn't* actively trying to kill him.

He strolled and stuck a new ball of gum into his mouth. Then he hesitated, mists swirling around him, the mansion looming before him like a mesa in the

Roughs, lit up all white. He heard a voice drifting toward him.

The accent was wrong. Just *slightly* wrong, but in a profound way.

And suddenly he knew who Bleeder was impersonating.

The howls were distant from Wax, but they haunted him more than they had during the first chase, for now he knew what made them. If he survived this, he would have to see something done for these creatures.

TenSoon conducted them through the intestines of the Homeland, eventually reaching a wall full of cracks. Wax raised his lantern, inspecting it. The wolfhound beside him had a pelt that was missing hair in patches.

"Well?" Wax said, inspecting the dead end.

"We have been watching this spot," TenSoon said. "It cracked long ago, and the cracks seem to have widened over the years. If it opens, it will provide another path into the Homeland, and we wish to be aware of each of those."

Wax ran his fingers along the cracks in the stone wall. Air moved through them, he thought, catching a whiff of something more . . . rotten. More like the city he knew. Familiar and disgusting all at once.

He tapped his metalmind, increasing his weight, then threw his shoulder against the wall. This was tricky, as his strength hadn't increased except in its ability to lift his own limbs and manipulate his heavier muscles. That lent him some ability, but mostly he had to try to force things just right so that he was *falling* into the wall as much as pushing on it.

He finally got the correct leverage, shoving through the cracked rock and causing a clatter. He was able to pick his way through into a narrow rift, like a very thin slot canyon out in the Roughs. The walls were slick with water, and knobby as in so much of this underground realm.

"What now?" Wax asked.

"Now we climb, human," TenSoon said. He melted again, dumping his bones and fur to the ground, becoming a group of muscles. Here, in these narrow confines, that was an advantage. TenSoon was able to push on both walls and start sliding up the crack, filling holes and clefts with his mass, then using his muscles to propel himself upward. A bag, like a stomach, had formed around the wolfhound bones, and he carted these up behind him.

It was grotesque yet fascinating. This was the natural state of the kandra, the sludgelike collection of muscles that at times acted human.

Of course, Wax thought, starting to climb, *what am I but a pile of blood and meat that gets up and walks around?*

This climb was difficult, particularly with the lantern, though decreasing his weight substantially helped. After only a short time, he heard the creatures come in below, howling and scrambling. His heart beat more quickly, but they didn't seem to have much luck climbing. He continued to inch upward, until—in his haste for a handhold—he fumbled with the lantern and dropped it.

It bumped and clanged against the stones before smashing down below. The light went out.

In that moment, Wax realized he was buried in the earth, clinging to rocks in the darkness. The walls seemed to press against him, and twisted monsters howled below and sought his blood. He gasped in sudden panic.

Then his eyes adjusted and a soft blue light revealed the world to him. He wasn't trapped. There was a way out above. He could see it by the patina of blue fungus growing on the walls, giving a gentle light to everything.

"Harmony made sure it spread here," TenSoon's voice said from above. "He wanted to make certain that no person was ever trapped in darkness in this place again."

Wax forced himself to continue upward. He recognized where he was now, from the stories. The holes in the walls that he used as handholds had once been overgrown with crystals, and within, geodes containing a bead of the lost metal. Legendary atium.

He was climbing the Pits of Hathsin themselves.

"Peace, lawman," TenSoon said from above. "Keep climbing."

Had he heard Wax's breathing quicken? He steadied himself and continued. This place was no longer a prison. No more did it cut and lacerate, as it had done to the Survivor's arms. The climb was actually easy, with all those holes. The sounds from below grew softer.

Finally, he crawled from the crevice into a section of man-made tunnel. One of the city sewers; the crack behind him was just a thin cleft in the rock that gave no hint of its ancient origin. Wax shivered, breathing in the awful stench of the sewers, but still glad to be free. TenSoon convulsed as a mass nearby, then formed into a wolfhound again. "I can see why Paalm might want me distracted and unable to stop my people from being caught in her trap," he said. "But what happened below, that was not for me, but you, human. What was she trying to distract you from?"

Wax didn't reply, but could think of only one reason. Once she dealt with the kandra, her plan would be ready for the final steps. She'd need to drive the people of the city further into a frenzy, freeing them, as she saw it, sending them forth as a mob to rage and hate, destroying Elendel.

The governor was planning to speak to the people of the city. Bleeder hadn't succeeded in killing him yet, and Wax suspected he knew why.

Because when she murdered him, she wanted an audience.

PART THREE

22

M ist seemed to burn in the night, like clouds before the sun. Wax dropped through it, slamming to the steps of the governor's mansion, surprising the guards there. Constables, by the uniforms, rather than the normal guards. Good. They'd been running low on the latter.

Wax stood up straight, turning and regarding the crowd gathering in front of the mansion. Constables with rifles made an uneasy barrier between them and the building. Nearby, workers erected a small stage on the steps. Aradel supervised, though judging from his sour expression, he was rather displeased with the governor's plan.

Wax agreed. Addressing the crowd would be playing right into Bleeder's hands. He grabbed one of the constables. "I assume there hasn't been another attempt on the governor's life?"

"No, sir," the constable said. "He's in his study, sir."

Wax nodded and barged into the mansion, trailing wisps of mist behind him. He stalked toward the back, and in the hallway Marasi intercepted him, taking him by the arm. "Kolossblood," she said, giving him the password he'd given her, proving she wasn't a kandra.

"Nighttime Summer," Wax said back, authenticating himself. "You need to do something about that crowd, Marasi. They're going to rip this city down."

"We're working on it. Have you seen Wayne?"

"No. Why?"

"MeLaan says he went out to inspect the protesters. That was over half an hour ago. Nobody has seen him since."

"He'll turn up," Wax said. "I need to talk to the governor."

Marasi nodded, but held on to his arm as he tried to walk toward the study. "Wax," she said softly, "he's corrupt. *Really* corrupt. I've found proof."

Wax drew in a deep breath. "Let's survive this night. Then we'll do something about that."

"My thoughts are similar," Marasi said, "but I think Bleeder wants to put us in a difficult position—perhaps she wants to force us to let the governor die."

"Not going to happen," Wax said. "We'll hand him over to the courts, but not a mob. Have you checked on your sister?"

"No," Marasi said. "But I've been intending to."

"Do so," Wax said. "I'll look in on your father after talking to the governor. I don't want either showing up as an unexpected hostage."

"As long as it isn't me, for a change," Marasi said with a grimace. "MeLaan is wearing the body of the guard with the sling. She's furious the governor won't let her or the others in. I'm going to go see if I can track down Wayne; wouldn't be surprised to find him on the front row of the mob."

She let go of his arm and headed toward the exit.

"Marasi," Wax said after her.

"Hm?"

"The uniform," he said. "It suits you. Don't know if I've had a chance to mention that."

She blushed—she *was* Marasi after all—before continuing. Wax turned and strode down the hallway toward the door to the governor's study. MeLaan lounged there with a group of three other guards.

"Nobody is to enter, lawman," one of them said with an annoyed tone. "He's been in there composing a speech for the last hour. He won't—"

Wax walked past them and tried the door, which was locked. He could hear Innate's voice inside, going over a speech. Wax increased his weight and flung the door open with Allomancy, splintering the doorframe. Innate stood inside, holding a pad of paper and pacing as he talked. He froze midstride and spun on Wax, then relaxed visibly.

"You could have knocked," the governor said.

"And you could have ignored a knock," Wax said, walking in and swinging the door shut behind him. It didn't latch, of course, after what Wax had done. "What do you think you're doing, Innate? You could have been killed in here, quietly, alone without anyone to help."

"And what would they have done?" Innate demanded, tossing his pad onto his desk. He walked up, then spoke more softly: "Wind's whisper."

"Drunken steam," Wax said back, latest passphrases exchanged. Innate was authentic. "Locking your guards out was foolhardy. They would have fought for you, protected you. We chased her off one time before."

"*You* chased her off," Innate said, walking back to his desk and picking up his pad. "The rest were useless.

Even poor Drim." He went back to his pacing, speaking the lines of his speech to himself and practicing emphasis.

Wax fumed, feeling dismissed. This was the man they struggled to protect? Wax made his way to the window. It was open, surprisingly, letting in wisps of mist. They didn't travel far. He'd heard legends of the mists filling rooms, but that rarely happened.

He leaned against the window, looking out at the darkness, listening with half an ear to Innate's speech. It was inflammatory and dismissive. He claimed to feel the problems the people had, but called them peasants.

This would just make things worse. *She wants that,* Wax thought. *She wants to free the city from Harmony by making it angry.*

She knew what Innate was going to say. Of *course* she knew. She'd been leading them around this entire time. Every clue Wax had found so far had been carefully planted for him. So what did he do? Stop Innate's speech? What if *that* was what she wanted?

He tapped his finger on the windowsill. Tap. Tap.

Squish.

He looked down, then blinked. A wad of chewed gum had been stuck here. Wax lifted his finger, and—as he contemplated it—something started to fall into place. Something he'd been missing. Bleeder had set this all up from the start.

Wax's suspicions had begun because she'd deliberately alerted him by wearing Bloody Tan's face. That had been a conscious ploy on her part, a way to start the festivities. Everything was moving on her timetable.

Bleeder had had everything already in place when this night arrived. She'd been planning this for a long time. Far longer than he'd assumed.

So where was the best place to hide?

Rusts.

Wax reached for his gun and spun.

He found himself facing down Governor Innate, who had taken out a sidearm and leveled it. "Damn it, Wax," the governor said. "Just a few minutes more and I'd have had this. You see too far. You can always see a *little* too far."

Wax froze there, hand on his gun. He met the governor's eyes, and hissed out slowly. "You knew the passphrase," Wax whispered, "but of course you did. I gave it to you. When did you kill him? How long has the city been ruled by an impostor?"

"Long enough."

"The governor wasn't your target. You think bigger than that—I should have seen. But Drim . . . He was in the saferoom when you entered below. Is that why you killed him? No. He'd have known you were gone."

"He knew all along," Bleeder said. "He was mine. But tonight, I killed him because of you, Wax. You'd shot me up . . ."

"You had on the governor's clothing underneath the cloak," Wax said. "Rusts! I'd bloodied you. So you needed an excuse for why the governor was covered in blood, an excuse to pull off your shirt and stanch a wound."

She held the gun on him, immobile. The weapon didn't register to his Allomancy. Aluminum. She was prepared, of course. But she seemed torn. She didn't want to kill him. She'd never wanted to kill him, for some reason.

So Wax yelled for help.

It was risky, but nothing ever ended well when you obeyed the person with the gun on you. As he'd suspected, Bleeder didn't shoot at him as the door burst open. Wax pulled out his gun and fired at Bleeder, to distract her as he dug in his gunbelt for the last needle that MeLaan had given him.

The guards turned their guns toward Wax and started firing.

Idiot, he thought, throwing himself toward the governor's desk for cover. Of course they'd do that. "Wait!" he said. "The governor has been taken. Don't—"

Bleeder gunned down the guards. Wax rolled behind the desk, but still heard it as they cried out in shock, their own governor—so far as they knew—shooting them down. Wax winced, cursing. Those deaths were upon him.

"I guess the rest of the constables will be upon us soon," Bleeder said. "They're not free yet. Neither are you, despite how I've tried. . . ."

Wax peeked up over the desk, then ducked down again as she swung the gun toward him. The governor's face was twisted in a mask of anger and frustration.

"Why couldn't you have given me a little longer?" she demanded. "So close. Now I have to kill you, claim you were the kandra, and blame you for shooting my guards. That way I can still talk to the crowd, free them. . . ."

Yet she didn't come for him. She still seemed upset. Best to take advantage of that.

"MeLaan, go!" Wax shouted, then Pushed on the nails in the floor, flinging himself up into the air.

One of the corpses at Bleeder's feet grabbed her around the legs.

Wax Pushed off the wall, leaping toward Bleeder. She growled, then slapped his hand as he landed, knocking the needle free. Rusts, she was *strong*. She kicked MeLaan off as Wax dove for the fallen needle.

She became a blur. As he tried to grab the needle, Bleeder snatched it and spun around, slamming it down into MeLaan's shoulder. It was done in an eyeblink.

Then she lurched to a stop. She seemed jarred by the motion. Her metalmind storage, at long last, had run dry.

Wax pulled out his gun and fired, lying with his back on the floor. The bullets ripped her skin, but did nothing else. Nearby, MeLaan's shape distorted—face drooping and the skin going transparent.

Wax lay on the ground, his emptied gun pointed at Bleeder, whose skin re-formed from the wounds. They stared at one another for an extended moment before boots in the hallway outside made Bleeder curse, then dash for the window. Wax grabbed his other gun, following, then threw himself down as shots sounded outside.

He waited a moment, then glanced up, but didn't spot her in the swirling mists. Wax cursed, rolling his arm in its socket. Rusts. That bullet hole he'd taken earlier in the night was bleeding again, and the pain was returning. He thought he'd chewed enough painkiller to keep it away.

"You all right?" he asked MeLaan, who had managed to sit up.

"Yeah," she said, though the word was mangled by her melted face. "I made them do this to me once to test it out. I'll be fine in a few minutes."

"Thanks for the save," Wax said, anxiously scanning the room for hidden compartments with his steelsight. Quivering lines in the closet. Could he be so lucky? He rushed over and yanked it open.

Wayne—tied securely and gagged—tumbled out and hit the floor with a thump. He was alive, thank

Harmony. Wax knelt down, sighed in relief, and loosened the gag. Wayne looked like he'd been stabbed in the leg, and his metalminds had been stripped away so he couldn't heal, but he was alive.

"Wax!" Wayne said. "It's the governor. Bugger's got the same 'a' as MeLaan!"

"I know," Wax said. "You're lucky. She probably wanted to harvest your Metalborn abilities with spikes, otherwise she'd have killed you right off. Why didn't you warn anyone?"

"Was going to, but I needed to check first. Got too close to the window, and she rusting came right out for me. Had knocked me upside the head, stripped off my metalminds, and had me over her shoulder all in an eyeblink. Drug me up here after, real quiet-like. You get her?"

"No," Wax said, working on Wayne's bonds. "She ran off."

Gunshots sounded outside.

"And you ain't chasin' her down?"

"Had to check on you first."

"I'm fine," Wayne said. "Stop untying me and look in my pocket."

Wax felt at Wayne's pocket, pulling out a small pouch.

"From Ranette," Wayne said.

Wax removed a single bullet cartridge. He held it up as a tense set of constables, led by Marasi, piled into the room.

The newcomers called for an explanation. Wax left them to interrogate Wayne, instead seeking the mists once more.

23

Wax was a bullet in the night, rushing through the mists and disturbing them with his passing. He had become the hunter rather than the game, though the transition might have taken too long. He soared upward first to get a view of the area. An ever-growing crowd surrounded the governor's mansion. Roaring. Calling for change, or perhaps just blood.

Would he bring down Bleeder only to find her victorious in a city destroyed?

He couldn't worry about that at the moment. Instead he sought signs, clues, a story. Nobody passed, even at night, without leaving a trail. Perhaps it would be too faint for him to locate, but it would exist.

There. A group of people pulling *away* from the mansion, instead of crowding toward it. Wax landed in a storm, mistcoat flaring. This was the mansion's garden, near a large workers' shed. Wax studied the pattern of people moving away.

The gunfire just a moment ago, he thought. *It wasn't to shoot someone, but to clear the crowd.* She was out of Feruchemical speed and fleeing frantically, and had opened fire into the air to clear this pocket of people. As he listened he picked out cries of confusion, some people claiming the constables had opened fire on the crowd. Others claimed they'd seen the governor himself running, trying to escape the mansion.

Wax loaded Vindication with the single bullet Ranette had sent, placing it in one of the special chambers he could quickly spin to at will. Then he inched open the door to the shed, crouching beside the doorway so as to not present a profile. The mists were bright with torchlight this night, but that light didn't penetrate to the dark shed. Wax searched through the shadows, until he saw something.

A bone? Yes, and draped over it cloth. He picked out a fallen cravat, a white buttoning shirt . . . the governor's clothing. Bleeder had stashed another body in here, and had fled to swap into it. How fast was she? MeLaan had said that Bleeder could change faster than she could, but that nobody was as quick as TenSoon.

That didn't tell him much. MeLaan had taken minutes, TenSoon seconds. Wax held Vindication beside his head and slipped through the doorway. If he could find Bleeder in midtransformation . . .

"I can still free you," a voice whispered from the darkness inside. "Perhaps I have lost the city, but I didn't come here for them. Not at first. I came for you."

"Why me?" Wax asked, searching furiously through the darkness, palm sweating as he held Vindication. "Damn it, creature, *why me*?"

"I have deafened him," Bleeder whispered. "I have cut out his tongue, pierced his eyes, but still he can act. You are his hands, Waxillium Ladrian. He may be deaf, blind, and mute . . . but still, with you, he can move his pawns."

"I'm my own man, Bleeder," Wax said, finally spotting what he thought was her silhouette, crouched at the back of the dusty chamber, beside a rack of shovels. "Perhaps I serve Harmony, but I do so because I wish it."

"Ah," she whispered. "Do you know, Wax, how long he cultivated you? How long he teased you, led you by the nose? How he sent you to be hardened by the Roughs, so he could draw you back in once you had aged properly, like leather being cured. . . ."

Wax raised Vindication, but the side of the building burst outward, showering pieces of wood across the lawn. Wax tried to draw a bead on her, but didn't fire, and Bleeder ducked out. He had to be very careful with this shot. Ranette had sent but one bullet, and only it would matter in this fight.

Bleeder fled into the night and launched into the air. The breaking wall had been an indication, but this was confirmation. Her metalmind, drained of the speed she'd stored up, was now useless. She'd left it on the ground beside the governor's bones, and had become a Coinshot instead.

Wax followed, Pushing on the same nails, sending himself into the sky. He could see why she'd chosen to become a Coinshot; Steelpushing lent great maneuverability and speed, and logically gave her the best chance of escaping.

There was a problem with that, of course.

Steel was *his* domain.

The pile of bones on the floor of the little shack proved that at least one person was having a worse night than Wayne was. He nudged the pile with his toe, then grimaced at his wounded leg. Rusting inconvenient, that was. He had to grab the wall for support.

He looked toward Marasi. "I can't decide," he said, "if the governor already bein' dead means we did a really terrible job, or a really good one."

"How," Marasi replied, kneeling beside the corpse, "could you see this as anything *other* than terrible?"

"Well, see, we weren't the ones what was in charge of keepin' him alive when he died." Wayne shrugged. "Guess anytime I find a corpse and it ain't *my* fault they're dead, I feel a little relieved."

MeLaan strolled into the cottage, still wearing the body of the guardswoman—though she had moved back to speaking with her own voice now. "It's getting rough out there. We'll want to get back into the mansion soon."

Marasi continued to kneel by the bones, which were lit by Wayne's lantern. His wrists still chafed from his confinement, and his leg smarted something fierce. Rusting kandra. She'd known just how to take him out: a quick burst of speed, tie his legs together, gag him, steal his metalminds—even though it didn't matter none how quickly he could heal if he was tied up.

Course, she should have checked his hands for gum as she towed him into the room.

"The governor is dead," Marasi whispered.

"Yeah," Wayne said, "havin' your skeleton removed tends to do that to a guy."

"What does it mean?" Marasi said, looking out the side of the shack, in the direction they'd seen Wax escape.

"Well, it means he won't be makin' it to his tap-dancing lessons this—"

"Wayne?"

"Yeah?"

"Shut it."

"Yes, ma'am."

Marasi closed her eyes, and Wayne leaned back against the wall, looking out at that crowd. Angry, waiting for the governor to give them his speech. The speech that was supposed to stop all this.

"Bleeder was planning to outrage them," MeLaan said. "I heard some of his speech. Maybe we can make them disperse?"

"No," Marasi said, standing. "We can do better than that." She turned to MeLaan, then nudged the governor's skull with her foot. "How long will it take you to imitate him?"

"I didn't digest his corpse—and don't wince like that, it's not my fault you people happen to be edible. If it helps, you taste terrible, even if you're properly aged. Anyway, it will be tough. TenSoon's pretty good at re-creating a face from a skull, but I'm way less practiced."

Wayne didn't say anything. He could shut it. Damn right he could shut it, when he needed to. Even if there was jokes that practically *begged* to be said.

"You have us to help you get it right," Marasi said to MeLaan. "Plus, it will be dark. You won't need to fool Innate's mother, just a crowd of angry citizens, most of whom haven't seen him up close."

MeLaan folded her arms, inspecting the remains. "Fine. If you think you can come up with something for me to say that will placate that crowd, I'll do it."

Wayne stood still, jaw clenched. *No jokes about . . . well, the obvious things.* Besides, he'd just learned something far worse. Something that was *no* cause for laughter.

Marasi looked at him, then frowned. "Wayne, what's wrong?"

He sat down, shaking his head.

"Wayne?" Marasi said, rising, sounding genuinely concerned. "I didn't mean to snap at you. It's just that—"

"I don't mind what you said," Wayne said.

"Then what?"

"Well," he said, looking at MeLaan, "I'd just always assumed . . . you know . . . that humans tasted *wonderful*."

"Nope," MeLaan said.

"You're really woundin' my self-esteem," Wayne said. "Maybe I'm different. Wanna gnaw on my arm a bit? It'll grow right back, least once we find out what that monster did with my metalminds. . . ."

Marasi sighed loudly. "MeLaan, work on those bones. I need to rewrite your speech. . . ."

24

Bleeder had obviously practiced with steel. She knew how to Push on passing latches or lampposts to adjust her course. She knew how to drop low before shoving on a parked motorcar to give herself lateral speed, rather than just Pushing herself higher. She was capable.

Wax was more than capable. He followed as a shadow, never more than a half leap behind her. He sensed an increasingly frantic quality to her motions, flared steel trying to Push herself out of his reach.

He let her, at first, trying to run her out of steel. They bounced through the city, two currents in the mist, leaping over roadways clogged with angry rioters, past middle-class neighborhoods full of closed shutters and extinguished lights, over the grounds of the rich—whose security forces stood tensely by gates, waiting for this hellish night to end.

Wax confirmed to himself as they flew that Bleeder had not been the Marksman. She'd worn one of his masks earlier—and seemed to be doing so again, from the quick glance he got as she passed a burning building in the night—but she did so to consternate and confuse him. Marks had sought the insides of rooms as he ran, trying to set up an ambush. She kept to the open spaces, as if frightened of the indoors. No running toward skyscrapers, no seeking the cramped confines of the slums. Instead, she headed directly east from the governor's mansion, toward the freedom of the outer city.

There wouldn't be nearly so much metal out there, making it difficult for her to flee—but also removing some of his advantage. He couldn't let that happen.

As they chased past a late train, Wax redoubled his efforts. He anticipated her turn as she cut away from the train toward an industrial quarter, and he cut sideways, earning a few seconds. As she leaped over a squat, burning building—passing protesters who threw rocks at her from below—Wax skimmed between it and the building beside it, coming around the other side in a precise turn. He passed through boiling smoke and emerged, gun out, as she came down from a more graceful arc.

That earned a curse from her as she saw him. She flung herself down a street, using each passing light as another source to Push off, increasing her speed. It was done with deftness, but Wax had an advantage. He decreased his weight, filling his metalmind. As always, though the change was sometimes subtle, this increased his velocity. If he decreased his weight while in motion, he got a little burst of speed. He didn't know why.

In a chase such as this, shoving off each light that passed, little advantages like that added up. Each cut corner, each careful judge of an arc, each use of the speed boost in flight after landing for a moment, sent him closer to her. To the point that as they neared the edge of the city, she glanced backward and found him about to grab her heels.

She cried out, a feminine exclamation of surprise. She shoved herself to the side, passing out over the river, and managed to land on the roadway portion of the Eastbridge, holding on to one of the support wires.

Wax landed gracefully before her, gun out. "You can't run from me, Bleeder. Let me remove your spike and take you prisoner. Perhaps the others can find a way, someday, to heal your madness."

"And become a slave again," she whispered behind the red and white mask. "Would you clasp the manacles willingly on your own hands?"

"If I had done the horrible things that you have, then yes. I would demand to be taken in."

"And what of the god you serve? When will Harmony accept *his* punishments? The people he lets die. The people he *makes* die."

Wax raised his gun, but Bleeder launched herself upward.

Wax trailed her with his weapon, but she bounced back and forth between massive bridge support beams, and he did not fire. Instead he lifted himself with a Push, soaring up—coat flapping—until he reached the top of one of the bridge's suspension towers. Bleeder waited here, atop the pinnacle, dressed in her red shirt and trousers, a loose cape blowing around her.

Wax landed and leveled the gun.

Bleeder dropped the mask.

She wore Lessie's face.

Marasi didn't tell the other constables, even Aradel, the truth about Innate. What would she have said? "Sorry, but the man we've been protecting was actually the killer"? "Oh, and the city has been *run* by an insane kandra for who knows how long"? She'd make a report soon, once she knew how to explain it, but for now she didn't have time. She needed to save the city.

She still felt a stab of guilt as she stood near the flimsy stage at the front of the steps, where she watched Captain Aradel pass her. The lord high constable looked visibly sick as he paced. The predicament she'd placed him in, with regards to thinking the governor was a crook, troubled him deeply.

Nearby, MeLaan stepped up onto the stage to address the crowd. Though she critiqued her own shortcomings, in Marasi's estimation her imitation of the governor was excellent.

The crowd grew quiet. Marasi frowned. Had Aradel's men prompted that somehow? No . . . the constables stood in a tight line between the crowd and the mansion, but weren't doing anything to quell the crowd.

How odd. Though there were a few jeers, for the most part everyone fell silent—watching through the mists, which seemed thinner than they had before, now that lights had been set up all around the square in front of the mansion. The former rioters genuinely wanted to hear what the governor had to say. Well, why *shouldn't* they?

Marasi felt their mood, one of hostile curiosity. She felt a calmness too. MeLaan's speech would work. Everything was fine. Why had she been so worried earlier? It . . .

Rusts. She was being Soothed.

She snapped alert, suddenly tense. She knew crowds. She'd studied mob dynamics. It was her specialty—and she could tell, easily, that something was wrong here. But who was Soothing? Why? How?

Suit, she thought. Waxillium had said the Set was involved. His uncle had access to Allomancers, and an inclination to see that Bleeder's plans came to fruition. It didn't matter what Marasi had written for MeLaan to say; when Suit's men discovered that "the governor" was deviating from the script, they'd drive the crowd to a frenzy.

Suddenly frantic, Marasi didn't listen to the beginning of MeLaan's speech. Could she get to Aradel? No, he was standing on the rusting stage, near MeLaan. Wayne, putting on a brave face despite his wound, hovered near the two of them, ready to help if something went wrong.

Marasi had to move quickly, and quietly, not alerting the Set. She spotted Reddi standing near the base of the steps, watching the crowd with arms folded. Marasi scrambled over to him and seized his arm.

"Reddi," she said. "There's a Soother in this crowd somewhere."

"What?" he asked absently, glancing at her. "Hmm?"

"A Soother," Marasi said. "Dampening our emotions. Probably a Rioter waiting too, to drive the crowd into a frenzy once they hear the speech."

"Don't be silly," Reddi said with a yawn. "Everything is fine, Lieutenant."

"Reddi," she said, tightening her grip. "How do you feel?"

"Fine."

"Not annoyed at me?" she said. "Not angry that I hold the position you should? Not jealous at all?"

He glared at her, then cocked his head. Then he hissed out softly. "Damn it, you're right. I usually *hate* you, but all I feel is a mild dislike. Someone's playing with my emotions." He hesitated. "No offense."

"Can't feel offense," Marasi said. "I'm having trouble feeling any strong emotion or urgency. But Reddi, we *have* to stop them."

"I'll get a squad," he said. "How will we find them though? They could be anywhere."

"No," Marasi said, scanning the crowd. Her eyes found a carriage parked discreetly in a small alleyway across from the governor's square. "Not anywhere. They won't want to mix with the masses that they're planning to turn into a murderous mob. Too dangerous. Come on."

25

Upon seeing Lessie's face, Wax growled in a guttural, primal sound. The sound of a man getting hit straight in the stomach with a well-driven punch. He held the gun on Bleeder, but his hand wavered, and his vision shook.

It's not her. It's not her.

"Again with the guns," Bleeder said softly. Rusts! It was Lessie's voice. "You lean on them too much, Wax. You're a Coinshot. How often do I have to point that out?"

"You dug up her corpse?" Wax asked in a pleading voice. He was having trouble seeing straight. "You monster. You *dug up her corpse*?"

"I wish I hadn't been forced to do this," Les—*Bleeder* said. "But strong emotion frees us from him, Wax. It's the only way."

She stared down that gun. Of course she would. She was a kandra. He had to remind himself of that forcibly. The gun meant nothing to her.

Lessie . . . How often had he dreamed of hearing that voice again? He'd wept for the wish to tell her one last time of his love. To explain the hole, gaping like the wound from a shotgun blast, left in him by her death.

To apologize.

Harmony. I can't shoot her again.

Bleeder had outthought him after all.

"I worried about using Tan's body," Lessie said, stepping toward him. "Worried it would make you figure out who I really was."

"You're *not* Lessie."

She grimaced. "Yeah, I guess that's true. I was never Lessie. Always Paalm the kandra. But I *wanted* to be Lessie. Does that count for anything?"

Rusts . . . she had Lessie's mannerisms down exactly. MeLaan had said she was good, but this was so real, so *believable*. He found himself lowering his gun, wishing. Wishing . . .

Harmony? he begged.

But he didn't have his earring in.

Marasi and Reddi wrapped around, moving over a block before coming back in behind the suspicious carriage. They hadn't been able to gather as large a force as she'd wanted—not only did they worry about the Soother noticing the motion, Reddi was concerned about leaving too few people watching the crowd.

MeLaan's voice carried through the voice projectors, audible even as Marasi and her team of eleven men set up near the far end of the alleyway containing the carriage. How long before the Set noticed they'd been had? Probably not long. Marasi had left in some of the beginning part of the speech, in order to not sound *too* different from Innate, but the speech would take a turn very soon.

Reddi pulled off his constable's helmet—Marasi's own pressed against her hair, an uncomfortable weight—then nodded to the rest of them in the darkness. With his aluminum-lined helmet off, he could feel the Soother's touch more powerfully here than he had out in the crowd. That carriage really was the source of it.

He put the helmet back on. The precinct owned only a dozen of these, all donated by Waxillium. Reddi had just enough clout to requisition the task force that had them. He secured his helmet, then reached to his side, taking out a thick dueling cane like a long baton with a knob on the end. The others did the same. There would be no gunplay this close to a crowd of civilians.

"We go in quickly and quietly," Reddi whispered to the team. "Hope to Harmony they don't have a Coinshot with them. Keep your helmets on. I don't want that Soother taking control of any of you."

Marasi cocked an eyebrow. Soothers couldn't control people, though many mistook that. It didn't help that the Words of Founding spoke vaguely of kandra and koloss being controlled by Allomancy, but Marasi now knew that was only possible for someone who bore Hemalurgic spikes.

"Colms," Reddi said, still speaking in a low voice, "stay at the back. You're not a field agent. I don't want you getting hurt or, worse, messing this up."

"As you wish," she said.

Reddi counted softly. On ten, the group of them surged into the misted alleyway. Marasi hung near the back, walking with hands clasped behind her. Almost immediately after entering the alleyway, the constables pulled to a stop. A force of men in dark clothing piled out of a doorway inside the alley, blocking off access to the little carriage.

Marasi's heart pounded as the two groups regarded one another. At least this proved she'd been right about the carriage. A few of the newcomers carried guns, but a barked word from one of the dark-clothed men made them tuck those away.

They don't want to draw the crowd's attention from the speech, Marasi thought. *They still think what the governor is saying plays into their plans.*

Keeping this fight quiet would serve both sides. The two groups stood waiting, tense, before Reddi waved his dueling cane.

The two forces crashed into one another.

Bleeder stepped closer to Wax in the mists. Atop this high platform, this tower on the bridge, nothing else seemed to exist. It was as if they stood on a tiny steel island rising from the sea. Grey all around, darkness extending into vastness above.

"Maybe I should have come to you," Lessie's voice said. "And had you help me with my plan. But he was watching. He's *always* watching. I'm glad you took the earring out. At least my words meant something to you."

"Stop," Wax whispered. "Please."

"Stop what?" Lessie asked, mere inches from him. "Stop walking? Stop talking? Stop loving you? My life would have been a lot easier if I'd been able to do *that*."

Wax seized her with his open hand, grabbing her by the neck, thumb along her jaw. She met his eyes, and he saw pity in them.

"Perhaps," she said, "the reason I didn't come to you had no connection to Harmony at all. I knew this would hurt you. I'm sorry."

No, Wax thought.

"I'm going to have to do something about you," she said. "Keep you safe, somehow, but out of the way. Might have to hurt you, Wax. For your own good."

No, this isn't real.

"Still don't know what to do about Wayne," she said. "Couldn't bring myself to kill him, poor fool. He followed you here, to help you in the city. For that I love him. But he's still Harmony's, and so he's probably better dead than the way he is now."

NO!

Wax shoved her back, lifting Vindication again. The gun, however, leaped from his fingers—Pushed by Bleeder. It tumbled into the mists.

Wax growled, ramming his shoulder into Bleeder, trying to toss her off the tower. She seized him as he hit, throwing them both off balance.

As they fell together, she raised her aluminum gun and shot him in the leg.

He cried out as they fell from the tower, dropping through the mists. A frantic Push on the bridge below slowed Wax, but when he hit, his leg gave out and he screamed, dropping to one knee.

Gun. Find the gun.

It had fallen this way. Rusts. Would it even work after dropping so far? He hadn't heard it hit. Did that mean it had plunged into the waters?

Bleeder landed hard nearby. She spun on him, lit now by the garish electric lights that lined the roadway of the bridge. It was empty of carriages and motorcars, and behind her, a greater light hovered over the city. Red, violent light, seeming to burn the mists.

Looking out of the city, he saw darkness and peace. But inward, Elendel burned.

Marasi edged along the outside of a battlefield.

It was a very *small* battlefield, true, but the ferocity of the conflict stunned her. She felt she could—for the first time—imagine what it had been like to live during the War of Ash, so long ago.

But surely wars back then had been more thought-out, more deliberate. Not this mixed jumble of figures beating on one another, breaking bones, cursing, stepping on the fallen. Watching it made her sick, anxious. Those men were her colleagues, struggling frantically to push through the Set's thugs. All night they'd been forced to stand and watch the city decompose around them, the situation growing worse and worse as they felt helpless.

This was something they could fight, so fight they did, cracking heads, shoving down enemies, grunting in the dirty, dark alleyway in an effort to reach the carriage. Thankfully, the Set troops here didn't appear to include any Coinshots or Pewterarms.

Her men were still outnumbered, and for all their determination they weren't making much headway. Outside the alleyway, the crowd was growing restless. The kandra's speech turned toward the words Marasi had written for her, words promising social reform, legislation to cut down work hours and improve conditions in the factories. What Marasi was able to hear of the echoing voice, unfortunately, had a sense of desperation to it. It sounded fake, inauthentic.

That wasn't MeLaan's fault. She had said she didn't have time to prepare this imitation properly, and it wasn't her specialty in the first place. Rusts. The crowd started to shout, cursing the governor's lies. MeLaan's voice faltered. Was this the Rioter, whipping the crowd into a frenzy? Or were the people so angry, they were overcoming the Allomancy?

Either way, Marasi couldn't help feeling desperate as her men struggled and fell, the crowd building toward a full-on riot. She made her way along the side of the alley, hoping that if she got to that carriage she could make a difference. Unfortunately, the alley's confines were too narrow, and combatants filled the entire thing. Already half her men were down. Those who fought looked like wraiths, shifting and undulating in the mists. Shadows trying to consume shadows.

Nobody on either side seemed to pay her much attention. That was common. For most of her life, her father had wished that she would vanish. Those in high society were very good at pretending she didn't exist. Even Waxillium seemed to forget she was along sometimes.

Well, so be it. She took a deep breath, and strode directly into the fight. As she neared two struggling men, she dodged in, as if trying to do something to help—then flung herself to the side as if she'd been hit. It was a fair impression, in her opinion.

She heard Reddi curse her name from somewhere in the alleyway, but nobody came to her rescue. They kept trying very assiduously to kill one another, and so Marasi crept along the ground, crawling in the shadows until she neared the carriage.

Two guards stood here. Drat. She needed to get past them. How?

She glanced back toward the fight. It had moved farther up the alley, the constables being forced to retreat before superior numbers. They were probably far enough away that Marasi could try something truly desperate.

She used her Allomancy.

For a brief moment, she engaged a speed bubble that caught herself and just the two guards. She extinguished her metal immediately. Only seconds had passed outside.

It was still jarring. The mists seemed to zip with sudden speed around them, and the combatants lurched in their motions. The two guards jumped in surprise, looking around. Marasi did her best impression of a corpse.

Then she flicked on the Allomancy again.

"Ruin!" one of the guards said. "You see that?"

"There's Metalborn among them," the other said. They both sounded very nervous.

Marasi gave them another jolt of distorted time. The two guards held a hushed, frantic argument; then they knocked on the door of the carriage and spoke through the window. Marasi waited, sweating, her nerves taut. Her men didn't have much time. . . .

The two guards ran down the alleyway, leaving the carriage and carrying orders to the other combatants to be wary of Metalborn. Marasi got to her feet and slipped around to the other side of the carriage, which had no driver, then pulled open the door and slipped inside, seating herself.

A pudgy woman sat on the bench within, wearing a lavish gown of three silken layers. A man beside her sat with a hand on her wrist, his eyes closed, his suit very stylish and modern. The handgun Marasi leveled at them was, on the other hand, quite traditional. And quite functional.

The woman blinked, breaking her concentration to regard Marasi with a look of horror. She nudged the man, who opened his eyes, startled. One Soother and one Rioter, Marasi would guess.

"I have a theory," Marasi said to them, "that a gentlewoman should never need to resort to something so barbarous as violence to achieve her goals. Wouldn't you agree?"

The two quickly nodded.

"Yes indeed," Marasi said. "A true gentlewoman uses the *threat* of violence instead. So much more civilized." She cocked the gun. "Stop those pewterheads in the alley from beating up my friends. Then we'll talk about what to do with this crowd. . . ."

"Stop it, Wax!" Bleeder screamed. "Stop obeying him!"

There. Vindication! He spotted the gun near Bleeder, peeking out of a gutter alongside the roadway.

Wax leaped for it, rolling painfully on his wounded arm, using a Push to skid forward. Bleeder leveled her gun at him, but didn't fire. Perhaps, deep down, a part of the creature had adopted the feelings of the body it wore. Perhaps it no longer could tell the difference between its mind and its face.

Wax snatched up Vindication.

"Please," Bleeder whispered. "Listen."

"You're wrong about me," Wax said, spinning the chamber, feeling the trigger, hoping the gun still worked. He looked up at Bleeder and leveled the weapon.

Looking down those sights, he saw Lessie. His stomach turned again.

"How am I wrong?" Bleeder asked.

Rusts, she was crying.

"I'm not Harmony's hands," Wax whispered. "I'm His sword."

Then he fired.

Bleeder didn't dodge. Why would she? Guns barely inconvenienced her. This shot took her right in the forehead. Though her head flinched at the impact, she didn't fall, barely even moved.

She stared at him, a little dribble of blood running down beside the bridge of her nose, onto her lips. Then her eyes widened.

Her gun dropped from trembling fingers.

We're weaker than other Hemalurgic creatures, Me-Laan had said. Wax struggled to his feet, holding on to the bridge's side wall for support. *Only two spikes, and we can be taken.*

"No!" Bleeder screeched, falling to her knees. "*No!*"

One spike allowed her to be sapient. And a second—delivered into her skull in the form of a bullet forged from Wax's earring—let Harmony seize control of her again.

26

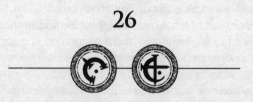

M arasi towed the female Soother after her, holding the woman's collar with one hand, her gun in the other. They were accompanied by a battered Reddi, who regarded the surging crowd with displeasure. They'd left the other captives with the rest of the constables, and she prayed to Harmony that wasn't tempting fate.

"Stop them," Marasi hissed at the woman as they reached the edge of the crowd, which was throwing things at the stage. Poor MeLaan soldiered onward with the speech, growing more and more testy that they weren't listening.

"I'm trying!" the Soother complained. "It might be easier if you weren't *choking* me!"

"Just Soothe!" Reddi said, raising his dueling cane.

"I can't control their minds, silly man!" the Soother said. "And beating on me won't accomplish anything. When do I get to speak to my solicitor? I've broken no laws. I was simply watching the proceedings with interest."

Marasi ignored Reddi's angry response, instead focusing on the crowd. MeLaan stood before them, lit by electric lights from behind, but by bonfires from the front. The rage of the crowd, an ancient fire, against the cold sterility of the new world.

"You should be grateful!" MeLaan shouted at the crowd. "I've come to talk to you myself!"

Wrong words, Marasi thought. Her annoyance was leading her to deviate from the script.

"I'm listening!" MeLaan yelled over the crowd. "But you have to listen back, you miscreants!"

She sounds just like him. Too much, perhaps? Me-Laan was playing a *part.* She was the governor, the role Marasi had given her. It seemed that the kandra had let the form dictate her reactions. Rusts . . . it wasn't that she was doing a bad job. She was doing a good job—of being Innate. Unfortunately, Innate had always had trouble connecting with the crowds.

"Fine," MeLaan said, waving a hand. "Burn the city! See how you feel in the morning without homes to live in."

Marasi closed her eyes and groaned. Rusts, she was tired. How late was it, now?

The crowd was growing violent. Time to grab MeLaan and Wayne and leave. Their gambit had failed. It had been a long shot in the first place, perhaps impossible. This crowd had come for blood. And . . .

The crowd shouted a new set of jeers. Marasi frowned, opening her eyes. She stood at the south edge of the crowd, near one of the bonfires, and was close enough to the front to make out Constable-General Aradel, who had stepped up beside MeLaan. Likely, he was going to get "the governor" to safety.

Instead Aradel took out his pistol and *pointed it at the governor.*

Marasi gaped for a moment. Then she spun on the Soother. "Soothe them!" she said. "Now. With everything you have. Do it, and I give you immunity for what you did tonight."

The woman eyed Marasi, displaying a craftiness that belied her earlier whining. She seemed to be weighing the offer.

"I promise it," Marasi said, "by the Survivor's spear."

The woman nodded, and a wave went through the crowd—a sudden hush. It didn't quiet them completely, but when Aradel spoke, his voice carried.

"Replar Innate," Aradel said. "In the name of the people of this city, and by the authority of my station as lord high constable, I arrest you for gross corruption, personal exploitation of this city's resources, and perjury of your oaths as a civil servant."

The crowd finally stilled completely.

"What idiocy—" MeLaan began.

"Men, turn around," Aradel said. He looked down at his constables. "Turn *around*."

The feeble line of soldiers reluctantly turned to face him, putting their backs to the crowd.

"What is he *doing*?" Reddi demanded.

"Something brilliant," Marasi said.

Aradel looked over the crowd, still holding a gun to the governor. "Tonight, the governor himself declared this city to be in a state of martial law. That puts the constables in charge, with him at the head. Unfortunately, it turns out the governor is a lying bastard."

Some of the people began hesitant shouts of agreement.

"He's no longer in control," Aradel said. "Best I can figure, *you're* in control. So if you're willing, tonight, the constables stand with you.

"Now, you all came here to start a riot. Listen! Stop your shouts. I won't stand for rioting or looting. You start burning this city, and I'll fight you up to my last breath. You hear me? We *aren't a mob*."

"Then what are we?" a call went up, along with a handful of others.

"We're the people of Elendel, and we're tired of being led by a pack of rats," Aradel yelled. "I have proof of at least seven house lords who are corrupt. I mean to see them arrested. Tonight." Aradel hesitated, then spoke louder, voice carrying and amplified by the cones set up before the stage. "I could use an army to help me, if you're willing."

As the crowd roared its agreement, Aradel shoved MeLaan into the hands of a pair of corporals waiting nearby. They seemed utterly stunned. In truth, Aradel himself seemed a little overwhelmed by what he'd just done.

"Pure Preservation," Reddi cursed softly, looking over the excited crowd. "They're going to turn into a lynch mob."

"No," Marasi said. "They won't."

"How can you be sure?"

"Because a river is easier to channel than to stop, Reddi," Marasi said.

This could work. She didn't have much hope for holding the house lords and ladies Aradel wanted to arrest, but the governor himself . . . With those letters and MeLaan playing the role . . . Yes, this could *really work*.

She released the Soother. "You're free; get out of here. And tell Suit he might want to take an extended vacation during what is coming."

Wax crossed the bridge limping. Life had taught him never to underestimate an enemy you thought you'd downed. One hand on his bleeding leg, he kept his gun trained on the writhing figure until he could sweep her gun away. Then he went down on his good knee and rolled her over, making certain she wasn't covering up another weapon.

He found tears streaming from her eyes, mixing with the trickling blood from the bullet wound. "He's in my head again, Wax," she whispered, trembling. "Oh, *Ruin,* he's in my head. He's taking me. I won't go back to him."

"Hush," Wax said, pulling a second gun from her side and tossing it away. "It's all right."

"No," she cried, grabbing his arm. "No, it's not. I won't be his again! I *will be me,* at the end!"

Bleeder's trembling increased, her body bucking, as she held to his arm. He frowned as she kept her head thrust forward, meeting his eyes, weeping and shudder- ing. Thrashing.

"What are you doing?" Wax demanded.

"Dying. We decided it! We won't fall again. We found a way out." She could no longer meet his eyes, and she fell backward, spasming. Eyes dilating quickly, skin trembling against the bone.

Wax watched, horrified. He seized her arm. No pulse. She *was* dying. Killing herself.

Could he stop it?

Why would he care to? She was a murderer many times over. This was a fitting end. In truth, he empa- thized with her. Let her take this route, rather than suf- fering under Harmony's control. Hesitant, but feeling there was little else he could do for this poor creature, he picked her up and held her close. Let her die in someone's arms. It revolted him to do so, after what she had done. But damn it, it was *right.*

Bleeder turned her head toward him, and her expression softened as she shook, smiling through bloodied lips. "You're . . . you're as surprising as a . . . dancing donkey, Mister Cravat."

Wax grew cold. "Where did you hear that? How did you know those words?"

"I think I loved you even on that day," she said. "Lawman for hire. So ridiculous, but so . . . earnest. You didn't try to shelter me, but seemed so eager to impress. . . . A lord with a purpose."

"Who told you of that day, Bleeder?" Wax demanded. "Who . . ."

"Ask Harmony," she said, the trembling growing more violent. "Ask him, Wax! Ask why he sent a kandra to watch over you, all those years ago. *Ask him* if he knew I would come to love you!"

"No . . ."

"He moved us, even then!" she whispered. "I refused. I wouldn't manipulate you into returning to Elendel! You loved it out there. I wouldn't bring you back, to become his pawn. . . ."

"Lessie?" Harmony, it *was* her.

It was *her*.

"Ask him . . . Wax," she said. "Ask him . . . why . . . if he knows everything . . . he'd let you kill me. . . ." She grew still.

"Lessie?" Wax said. "Lessie!"

She was gone. There in his lap, he stared at her body. It kept its shape. Her shape. He clutched her, and let out a low-pitched howl, from deep within, a raw shout that echoed into the night.

It seemed to drive the mists back.

He still knelt there, holding the body, an hour later when a figure loped out of the mists and approached on four legs. TenSoon the kandra, Guardian of the Ascendant Warrior, approached with a reverent step, wolfhound's head bowed.

Wax stared out into those shifting mists, holding a corpse, hoping irrationally that his heat would keep it warm.

"Tell me," Wax said, voice cracking and rough from his shouting. "*Tell me,* kandra."

"She was sent to you long ago," TenSoon said, sitting back on his haunches. "The woman you knew as Lessie was always one of us."

No ...

"Harmony worried about you in the Roughs, lawman," TenSoon said. "He wanted you to have a bodyguard. Paalm had exhibited a willingness to break prohibitions the rest of us held sacred. He hoped that you two would be good for one another."

"You didn't tell me?" Wax spat, his grip tight. Hatred. He didn't think he had ever felt *hatred* so intense as he did at that moment.

"I was forbidden," TenSoon said. "MeLaan didn't know; I was only informed a few days ago. Harmony foresaw a disaster if you were told whom you hunted."

"And this *isn't* a disaster, kandra?"

TenSoon turned away. They sat there on that empty bridge, electric lights making pockets in the mist, a dead woman in Wax's lap.

"I killed her," Wax whispered, squeezing his eyes closed. "I killed her *again.*"

EPILOGUE

Wax sat alone in a room full of people. They'd done everything to make him comfortable. A warm fire on the hearth, a small lamp on the table beside it, for Steris knew he preferred flame to electricity. Broadsheets lay untouched in a roll beside a cup of tea that had long since grown cold.

They talked and celebrated, led by Lord Harms, who laughed and exclaimed about his minor part in it all. A disaster averted. A new governor—the first ever who was not of noble blood. Even the Lord Mistborn, long ago, had been part nobleman. The Last Emperor had been full-blooded, and the Survivor half nobleman. All great people, everyone agreed, to be lauded.

But Claude Aradel had none of the same lineage. Not a drop of noble blood in him. Those at the party congratulated one another for being so progressive as to speak favorably of one who was common-born.

Wax stared into the fire, fingering at the stubble on his chin. He spoke when it was required of him, but mostly they allowed him his peace. He was wrung out, Steris told them. Fatigued by the terrible things he'd seen. She diverted them from him when she could, telling them—when they inevitably asked—that she and he had decided to delay the wedding so Wax could take a short vacation to recuperate.

Partway through the event, Wayne sauntered over on crutches. He couldn't heal without storing up more health—and he couldn't do that while healing from his wound, or it would defeat the purpose. For now, he had to deal with the fragility of the body, just like a normal person.

We're all so fragile, when you consider it, Wax thought. *One little thing goes wrong, and we break.*

"Hey, mate," Wayne said, settling down on the footstool by Wax's feet. "Wanna hear how I'm a rusting genius?"

"Shoot," Wax whispered.

Wayne leaned forward, spread his hands before himself dramatically. "I'm gonna get *everybody* drunk."

The crowd continued its chatter. Mostly constables. Some political allies of Wax's. He'd chosen to do business with the more reputable people in the city, so Aradel's culling of the lords hadn't hit his house. It was considered an enormous political victory.

"See, I got this plan," Wayne said, tapping his head. "People in this town, they got issues. The folks what work in the factories think havin' more time to themselves is gonna fix their woes, but they gotta do something *with* that time. I've got an idea. It'll fix it all."

"Harmony, Wayne," Wax said. "You're not going to poison the city, are you?"

"Nah," Wayne said. "Not their bodies, at least." He grinned. "You watch. This will work. It's gonna be *amazing.*" He rose, and stumbled, almost falling. He looked at his leg in surprise, as if he'd forgotten about the wound. Then he shook his head, grabbing his crutch and getting to his feet.

Once standing he hesitated, then leaned down. "It'll pass, mate," he said. "My pa once said to me, 'Son, keep a stiff upper lip.' So if things get bad, you bash your face against a wall till your lip bleeds, and you'll feel better. Works for me. Least I think it does. Can't right remember, on account of too many head wounds."

He grinned. Wax kept staring into the flames. Wayne's face fell.

"She'd have wanted you to stop her, you know," Wayne said softly. "If she'd been able to talk to you, been able to think straight, she'd have demanded you kill her. Just like I'd have wanted it. Just like you'd want the same, if you'd lost your copper. You did what you hadda do, mate. And you did it well."

He made a fist at Wax and nodded, then hobbled off, approaching a short young woman with long golden hair. A teenage girl? Wax didn't recognize her.

"I know you, don't I?" Wayne said. "Daughter of Remmingtel Tarcsel? The guy what invented the incandescent lightbulb?"

The girl's jaw dropped. "You know him?" She seized Wayne by the arms. "You know about my father?"

"Sure do!" Wayne said. "He was robbed, I gotta say. Genius. Word is, you're just as smart. That device you whipped up for making speeches sure is nice."

She regarded Wayne, then leaned in. "That's only the start. They've brought it into their houses. Don't you see? It's all around."

"What?" Wayne said.

"Electricity," the girl said. "And I'm going to be the first to use it."

"Huh," Wayne said. "Need some money?"

"Do I . . ." She towed Wayne away through the party, aglow, speaking so quickly Wax couldn't pick out the words.

He didn't care to. He just stared at the fire.

The guests were polite enough not to imply that he was ruining the party by his indifference. Clotide passed by, swapping his cold cup of tea out for a warm one. For all Wax cared, this comfortable chair could have been a hard bench. He didn't feel it, or the warmth of the fire, or the joy of the victory.

How could you hear a bee buzzing in the middle of a thunderstorm?

The guests eventually found excuses to leave, their sedate revels accomplished. Some bade farewell to him. Others did not. About halfway through the protracted death of the party, Marasi settled down on his footstool. She wore her constable's uniform. Odd thing to do at a party, though as he thought about it, the men in the constabulary did it all the time.

Marasi took his tea and sipped it, then placed something else onto the table where the cup had been. Wax's eyes flicked toward it. A small spike, long as a finger, made of some silvery metal with dark red spots, like rusted bits.

"That's one of the spikes she was using, Waxillium," Marasi said softly. "MeLaan wanted me to show it to you."

Wax closed his eyes. They thought he wanted to *see* something like that?

"Waxillium," Marasi said. "We can't identify the metal. It's nothing we've ever seen before. It certainly wasn't one of the spikes she started with. That means she removed both, and stuck one like this in instead. Where did she get them? Who gave them to her?"

"I don't care," he whispered, opening his eyes.

Marasi grew quiet. "Wax . . ."

"He sent her to me, Marasi. He sent a *kandra* to *seduce* me."

"No," Marasi said, firm. "He sent a bodyguard to watch over you in the Roughs. I spoke to TenSoon. The seduction was her idea. And yours, presumably."

"Harmony knew," Wax said hoarsely. "He saw what would happen."

"Maybe He didn't."

"Then what kind of God is He? What *good* is a God like Him, Marasi? Tell me that."

Marasi fidgeted, then she sighed and took the strange spike back. She dropped something else onto the table as she rose. A small earring, just a stud with the back bent over. "They sent this for you."

Wax didn't look at it. He left that earring right where it was, as Marasi made her farewells and stepped out of the party. Others came to him, offered bland encouragement, of the type you might write on a card.

He nodded, but didn't listen.

Marasi stopped by the precinct offices on her way home from the party at Ladrian Mansion, intent on retrieving her copy of the Lord Mistborn's Hemalurgy book, which she'd locked in her drawer. The offices were dark and quiet—a direct contrast to the chaos of a few nights back. Though some constables were out on patrol, most had been given time off. Only those with jail watch would be on duty.

So it surprised her when she found lights on at the back of the main chamber. She walked up and leaned against the doorframe, looking in at Aradel, who had a stack of papers out and was working on them by candlelight.

"I find it hard to believe," Marasi noted, "that there's nothing better for the governor to do on his first day in office than equipment-depreciation reports. Not that I mind. You've been ignoring those for . . . how long?"

Aradel's expression soured. "I'm not governor," he said. "Not really."

"The title 'Interim Governor' has the word 'Governor' in it, sir."

"They'll vote someone else into office next month at the proper hearing."

"Frankly, sir, I doubt that."

He slapped one page down on the stack, signed and sealed, then sat there staring at it. Finally he ran a hand through his hair. "Oh, Preservation. What have I done? And why the hell didn't any of you stop me?"

Marasi smiled. "You didn't exactly give us a chance, sir."

"I'll run away," he said. "I'll refuse the appointment. I'll . . ." He looked up at her, and then sighed. "I can't be happy in this position, Colms."

"The ones who are happy in the role, sir, seem to have had their chance. I'm excited to see where it goes from here. You just changed the world."

"Didn't mean to."

"Doesn't matter," Marasi said, glancing to the side as someone else moved through the darkened chamber, approaching. Another constable coming in to catch up on work? "Oh no."

Governor Innate stepped up to the door, holding a belt. "Either of you know how to tie one of these?" the former governor said in MeLaan's voice.

"You don't tie a belt, kandra," Aradel said. "You buckle it."

"No, no," MeLaan said, pulling it tight. "I mean, in making a noose. People always talk about guys hanging themselves in their cells, but I'll be damned if I can figure it out. Hung there for a good ten minutes, and I'm pretty sure it wouldn't have killed even the most frail mortal. I've got it wrong somehow."

She looked up at the two of them, then frowned at their appalled expressions. "What?"

"*Hang* yourself?" Marasi sputtered, finally finding her voice. "You're our linchpin witness!"

"You really think," MeLaan said dryly, "that Harmony would let me sit at trial and testify falsely against people I don't even know? It would make a mockery of justice, kids."

"No," Marasi said. "We have the letters. We know the truth."

"Do you?" MeLaan asked, pulling the belt tight again. "You know for certain Paalm didn't forge those letters, or that Innate himself didn't do it before she took him? You know that those lords and ladies went through with the plans, rather than backing out? You know they weren't just talking about possibilities?"

"We've got good cases, holy immortal," Aradel said. "Lieutenant Colms has done her research. We're pretty sure this is all correct."

"Then convince the judge and jury," MeLaan said with a shrug. "We don't do things like this. People have to be able to trust the law; I'm a lot of things, but I'm *not* going to be the one who sets the precedent that the kandra can lie in order to get someone convicted, even if you're 'pretty sure' you've got the right evidence."

Marasi folded her arms, grinding her teeth. Aradel glanced at her, questioning.

"Without her, they'll wiggle out of it," Marasi said. "We won't be able to keep them in jail. They'll be loose upon the city again." She sighed. "But . . . Blast. She's probably right, sir. I'd have hit on it if I'd thought about it long enough. We can't falsify evidence, however right our cause."

He nodded. "We weren't going to keep them in prison anyway, Colms. They have too much power, even now. They'd find a way to escape conviction, pinning the charges on subordinates." He sat back in his chair. "They'll have the governor's seat again, unless someone does something about it. Damn it. I really have to do this, don't I?"

"Sorry, sir," Marasi said.

"Well, at least I can get my desk clear of paperwork first," he said, leaning forward in determination. "Suggestions for my replacement as constable-general?"

"Reddi," Marasi said.

"He hates you."

"Doesn't make him a bad conner, sir," Marasi said. "So long as someone keeps an eye on him, as you put it. I can do that. I think he'll rise to the challenge."

Aradel nodded, then held up a hand to MeLaan. She tossed him the belt, and he tied it in a loop.

"This part around your neck, holy one," he said. "Make your skin bruise so it looks right, a V shape. You know how to make someone look like they died of strangling?"

"Yeah," MeLaan said. "Unfortunately."

"I'll come cut you down in fifteen minutes," Aradel said. "You'll need to fool the coroner."

"No problem," MeLaan said. "I can breathe through a tracheal system instead of lungs. Arrange to have the body cremated, give me a window, and I'll slip out and leave the bones, which you can burn. Nice and neat."

"Fine," Aradel said, looking sick.

MeLaan bade him farewell, wandering back toward the cells. Marasi joined her after giving Aradel a salute he didn't see.

"How did you get out, anyway?" Marasi asked, catching up to MeLaan.

"Stuck my finger in the lock," MeLaan said, "and melted my skin, shoving a bit in. It's amazing what you can do when you aren't constrained to normal body shapes."

They walked together to the entrance of the jail part of the building. Marasi wasn't going to ask how MeLaan had avoided the guards. Hopefully the two hadn't been hurt.

"Harmony knows, right?" Marasi asked as MeLaan lingered at the door. "If these people are guilty or not?"

"He does."

"So you could simply ask Him if it's just to imprison them. If He says yes, we could go through with it. I'd accept God's word on the matter to satisfy my conscience."

"Still breaks our rules," MeLaan said. "And Harmony probably wouldn't talk."

"Why not?" Marasi said. "You realize what all this has done to Waxillium, right?"

"He'll weather it."

"He shouldn't have to."

"And what would you have Harmony do, *woman*? Give us all the answers? Lead us by the noses, like

Paalm swore that He did? Turn us all into pieces on a board for His amusement?"

Marasi stepped back. She'd never heard such a tone from MeLaan.

"Or maybe you want it the other way?" MeLaan snapped. "Leave us alone completely? Not intervene at all?"

"No, I—"

"Can you imagine what it must be like? Knowing that any action you take is going to help some, but hurt others? Save a man's life now, let him spread a disease that kills a child later in his life. Harmony does the best He can—the best *possible,* by the very definition. Yes, He hurt Wax. He hurt him badly. But He put the pain where He knew it could be borne."

Marasi blushed, then—annoyed at herself—dug in her purse and brought out the strange spike. "And this?"

"It's not a metal we know."

"That's what TenSoon said. But Harmony—"

"It's not a metal *Harmony* knows," MeLaan said.

Marasi felt a chill. "Then . . . it's not His? Not from His form, like the old stories of atium and lerasium?"

"No," MeLaan said. "It's from somewhere else. She used these strange spikes to steal attributes, instead of the ones we're familiar with. Maybe that's why she could use stolen Allomancy and Feruchemy, when other kandra can't. Either way, didn't you wonder why Harmony couldn't see Bleeder? Couldn't track her, couldn't predict her? What could stop a god, Marasi Colms? Any guesses?"

"Another god," Marasi whispered.

"Congratulations," MeLaan said, pulling open the door. "You've found proof of something that terrifies us. Think on that for a while, before you go around accusing Harmony—or the kandra—of anything. Now, if you'll excuse me, I'm going to go try to hang myself properly."

She slipped away, closing the door behind her.

Another god, Marasi thought, standing in the darkness. Not Harmony, not Ruin, not Preservation.

She looked down at the small spike in her hands, and heard a name from a year ago, spoken by Miles Hundredlives as he died. The name of a god from the old days. Marasi had researched the name halfheartedly, far more distracted by her interaction with Ironeyes.

Now, however, she determined to dig back into the records and find the answers.

Who, or what, was *Trell*?

The room had probably grown silent long before Wax noticed he was alone. The fire was dying. He should do something about that.

He didn't.

Steris stepped over and set a new log on, then stirred the embers. So he hadn't been alone. She set the poker beside the fireplace, then regarded him. He awaited her words.

None came. Instead, she scooted the footstool around until it was beside his chair. She sat down, legs crossed neatly, hands in her lap.

The two of them remained there, not saying a word, though she did eventually rest her hand on top of his. The fire had felt cold to him, the air frozen, but that hand was warm.

Finally, he turned to the side, rested his head on her shoulder, and wept.

ARS ARCANUM

METALS QUICK REFERENCE CHART

METAL	ALLOMANTIC POWER	FERUCHEMICAL POWER
☿ Iron	Pulls on Nearby Sources of Metal	Stores Physical Weight
☉ Steel	Pushes on Nearby Sources of Metal	Stores Physical Speed
☿ Tin	Increases Senses	Stores Senses
☿ Pewter	Increases Physical Abilities	Stores Physical Strength
☿ Zinc	Riots (Enflames) Emotions	Stores Mental Speed
☿ Brass	Soothes (Dampens) Emotions	Stores Warmth
☿ Copper	Hides Allomantic Pulses	Stores Memories
☿ Bronze	Allows One to Hear Allomantic Pulses	Stores Wakefulness
☿ Cadmium	Slows Down Time	Stores Breath
☿ Bendalloy	Speeds Up Time	Stores Energy
☿ Gold	Reveals Your Past Self	Stores Health
☿ Electrum	Reveals Your Own Future	Stores Determination
☿ Chromium	Wipes Allomantic Reserves of Target	Stores Fortune

METAL	ALLOMANTIC POWER	FERUCHEMICAL POWER
⊛ Nicrosil	Enhances Allomantic Burn of Target	Stores Investiture
⟐ Aluminum	Wipes Internal Allomantic Reserves	Stores Identity
⟡ Duralumin	Enhances the Next Metal Burned	Stores Connection

LIST OF METALS

ALUMINUM: A Mistborn who burns aluminum instantly metabolizes all of his or her metals without giving any other effect, wiping all Allomantic reserves. Mistings who can burn Aluminum are called Aluminum Gnats due to the ineffectiveness of this ability by itself. Trueself Ferrings can store their spiritual sense of identity in an aluminum metalmind. This is an art rarely spoken of outside of Terris communities, and even among them, it is not yet well understood. Aluminum itself and a few of its alloys are Allomantically inert; they cannot be Pushed or Pulled and can be used to shield an individual from emotional Allomancy.

BENDALLOY: Slider Mistings burn bendalloy to compress time in a bubble around themselves, making it pass more quickly within the bubble. This causes events outside the bubble to move at a glacial pace from the point of view of the Slider. Subsumer Ferrings can store nutrition and calories in a bendalloy metalmind; they can eat large amounts of food during active storage without feeling full or gaining weight, and then can go without the need to eat while tapping the metalmind. A separate bendalloy metalmind can be used to similarly regulate fluids intake.

BRASS: Soother Mistings burn brass to Soothe (dampen) the emotions of nearby individuals. This can be directed at a single individual or directed across a general area, and the Soother can focus on specific emotions. Firesoul Ferrings can store warmth in a brass metalmind, cooling themselves off while actively storing. They can tap the metalmind at a later time to warm themselves.

BRONZE: Seeker Mistings burn bronze to "hear" pulses given off by other Allomancers who are burning metals. Different metals produce different pulses. Sentry Ferrings can store wakefulness in a bronze metalmind, making themselves drowsy while actively storing. They can tap the metalmind at a later time to reduce drowsiness or to heighten their awareness.

CADMIUM: Pulser Mistings burn cadmium to stretch time in a bubble around themselves, making it pass more slowly inside the bubble. This causes events outside the bubble to move at blurring speed from the point of view of the Pulser. Gasper Ferrings can store breath inside a cadmium metalmind; during active storage they must hyperventilate in order for their bodies to get enough air. The breath can be retrieved at a later time, eliminating or reducing the need to breathe using the lungs while tapping the metalmind. They can also highly oxygenate their blood.

CHROMIUM: Leecher Mistings who burn chromium while touching another Allomancer will wipe that Allomancer's metal reserves. Spinner Ferrings can store fortune in a chromium metalmind, making themselves unlucky during active storage, and can tap it at a later time to increase their luck.

COPPER: Coppercloud Mistings (a.k.a. Smokers) burn copper to create an invisible cloud around themselves, which hides nearby Allomancers from being detected by a Seeker and which shields the Smoker from the effects of emotional Allomancy. Archivist Ferrings can store memories in a copper metalmind (coppermind); the memory is gone from their head while in storage, and can be retrieved with perfect recall at a later time.

DURALUMIN: A Mistborn who burns duralumin instantly burns away any other metals being burned at the time, releasing an enormous burst of those metals' power. Mistings who can burn Duralumin are called Duralumin Gnats due to the ineffectiveness of this ability by itself. Connecter Ferrings can store spiritual connection in a duralumin metalmind, reducing other people's awareness and friendship with them during active storage, and can tap it at a later time in order to speedily form trust relationships with others.

ELECTRUM: Oracle Mistings burn electrum to see a vision of possible paths their future could take. This is usually limited to a few seconds. Pinnacle Ferrings can store determination in an electrum metalmind, entering a depressed state during active storage, and can tap it at a later time to enter a manic phase.

GOLD: Augur Mistings burn gold to see a vision of a past self or how they would have turned out having made different choices in the past. Bloodmaker Ferrings can store health in a gold metalmind, reducing their health while actively storing, and can tap it at a later time in order to heal quickly or to heal beyond the body's usual abilities.

IRON: Lurcher Mistings who burn iron can Pull on nearby sources of metal. Pulls must be directly toward the Lurcher's center of gravity. Skimmer Ferrings can store physical weight in an iron metalmind, reducing their effective weight while actively storing, and can tap it at a later time to increase their effective weight.

NICROSIL: Nicroburst Mistings who burn nicrosil while touching another Allomancer will instantly burn away any metals being burned by that Allomancer, releasing an enormous (and perhaps unexpected) burst of those metals' power within that Allomancer. Soulbearer Ferrings can store Investiture in a nicrosil metalmind. This is a power that very few know anything about; indeed, I'm certain the people of Terris don't truly know what they are doing when they use these powers.

PEWTER: Pewterarm Mistings (a.k.a. Thugs) burn pewter to increase their physical strength, speed, and durability, also enhancing their bodies' ability to heal. Brute Ferrings can store physical strength in a pewter metalmind, reducing their strength while actively storing, and can tap it at a later time to increase their strength.

STEEL: Coinshot Mistings who burn steel can Push on nearby sources of metal. Pushes must be directly away from the Coinshot's center of gravity. Steelrunner Ferrings can store physical speed in a steel metalmind, slowing them while actively storing, and can tap it at a later time to increase their speed.

TIN: Tineye Mistings who burn tin increases the sensitivity of their five senses. All are increased at the same time. Windwhisperer Ferrings can store the sensitivity of one of the five senses into a tin metalmind; a different tin metalmind must be used for each sense. While storing, their sensitivity in that sense is reduced, and when the metalmind is tapped that sense is enhanced.

ZINC: Rioter Mistings burn zinc to Riot (enflame) the emotions of nearby individuals. This can be directed at a single individual or directed across a general area, and the Rioter can focus on specific emotions. Sparker Ferrings can store mental speed in a zinc metalmind, dulling their ability to think and reason while actively storing, and can tap it at a later time to think and reason more quickly.

ON THE THREE METALLIC ARTS

On Scadrial, there are three prime manifestations of Investiture. Locally, these are spoken of as the "Metallic Arts," though there are other names for them.

Allomancy is the most common of the three. It is end-positive, according to my terminology—meaning that the practitioner draws in power from an external source. The body then filters it into various forms. (The actual outlet of the power is not chosen by the practitioner, but instead is hardwritten into their Spiritweb.) The key to drawing this power comes in the form of various types of metals, with specific compositions being required. Though the metal is consumed in the process, the power itself doesn't actually come from the metal. The metal is a catalyst, you might say, that begins an Investiture and keeps it running.

In truth, this isn't much different from the form-based Investitures one finds on Sel, where specific shape is the key—here, however, the interactions are more limited. Still, one cannot deny the raw power of Allomancy. It is instinctive and intuitive for the practitioner, as opposed to requiring a great deal of study and exactness, as one finds in the form-based Investitures of Sel.

Allomancy is brutal, raw, and powerful. There are sixteen base metals that work, though two others—named the "God Metals" locally—can be used in alloy to craft an entirely different set of sixteen each. As these God Metals are no longer commonly available, however, the other metals are not in wide use.

Feruchemy is still widely known and used at this point on Scadrial. Indeed, you might say that it is more present today than it has been in many eras past, when it was confined to distant Terris or hidden from sight by the Keepers.

Feruchemy is an end-neutral art, meaning that power is neither gained nor lost. The art also requires metal as a focus, but instead of being consumed, the metal acts as a medium by which abilities within the practitioner are shuttled through time. Invest that metal on one day, withdraw the power on another day. It is a well-rounded art, with some feelers in the Physical, some in the Cognitive, and even some in the Spiritual. The last powers are under heavy experimentation by the Terris community, and aren't spoken of to outsiders.

It should be noted that the inbreeding of the Feruchemists with the general population has diluted the power in some ways. It is now common for people to be born with access to only one of the sixteen Feruchemical abilities. It is hypothesized that if one could make metalminds out of alloys with the God Metals, other abilities could be discovered.

Hemalurgy is widely unknown in the modern world of Scadrial. Its secrets were kept close by those who survived their world's rebirth, and the only known practitioners of it now are the kandra, who (for the most part) serve Harmony.

Hemalurgy is an end-negative art. Some power is lost in the practice of it. Though many through history have maligned it as an "evil" art, none of the Investitures are actually evil. At its core, Hemalurgy deals with removing abilities—or attributes—from one person and bestowing them on another. It is primarily concerned with things of the Spiritual Realm, and is of the greatest interest to me. If one of these three arts is of great interest to the cosmere, it is this one. I think there are great possibilities for its use.

COMBINATIONS

It is possible on Scadrial to be born with ability to access both Allomancy and Feruchemy. This has been of specific interest to me lately, as the mixing of different types of Investiture has curious effects. One needs look only at what has happened on Roshar to find this manifested—two powers, combined, often have an almost chemical reaction. Instead of getting out exactly what you put in, you get something new.

On Scadrial, someone with one Allomantic power and one Feruchemical power is called "Twinborn." The effects here are more subtle than they are when mixing Surges on Roshar, but I am convinced that each unique combination also creates something distinctive. Not just two powers, you could say, but two powers . . . and an effect. This demands further study.

ALL YOUR FAVORITE COSMERE TALES
IN ONE PLACE FOR THE FIRST TIME

. . . .

BRANDON SANDERSON

. . . .

ARCANUM UNBOUNDED

. . . .

Featuring an all-new Stormlight Archive novella,
Edgedancer, and the Hugo Award–winning novella
The Emperor's Soul, the first story collection from
#1 *New York Times* bestselling author Brandon
Sanderson includes a total of nine exciting
adventure tales set in the Shardworlds.

. . . .

"I loved this book.
What else is
there to say?"
—PATRICK
ROTHFUSS
on *The Way of Kings*

"You are not
prepared for how
fantastic it is....
Words of Radiance
is a must-read."
—IO9

TOR

tor-forge.com